The Six Murders of Daphne St Clair

MacKenzie Common was born in Newfoundland, Canada but she spent most of her childhood in North Bay, Ontario before spending her twenties in England. She has a PhD in Law and has worked as an expert on human rights issues in social media content moderation. MacKenzie loves swimming, travelling, paddleboarding, good chocolate, bad TV, Mexican food and comedy. She currently lives in Canada with her partner, two children, and one very spoiled pug.

The Six Murders
of
Daphne St Clair

MacKenzie Common

MLP

First published in 2025 by Mountain Leopard Press
An imprint of Headline Publishing Group Limited

I

Cataloguing in Publication Data is available from the British Library

Hardback ISBN 978 1 0354 2575 4
Trade Paperback ISBN 978 1 0354 2579 2
ebook ISBN 978 1 0354 2578 5

Typeset in Times by CC Book Production

Printed and bound in Great Britain by Clays Ltd, Elcograf S.p.A.

MIX
Paper | Supporting
responsible forestry
FSC
www.fsc.org
FSC® C104740

Headline's policy is to use papers that are natural, renewable and
recyclable products and made from wood grown in sustainable forests.
The logging and manufacturing processes are expected to conform to
the environmental regulations of the country of origin.

Headline Publishing Group Limited
An Hachette UK Company
Carmelite House
50 Victoria Embankment
London EC4Y 0DZ

The authorised representative in the EEA is Hachette Ireland,
8 Castlecourt Centre, Dublin 15, D15 XTP3, Ireland
(email: info@hbgi.ie)

www.headline.co.uk
www.hachette.co.uk

To Henry and Remy. Follow your dreams.
Be kind, be curious, be brave. I love you forever.

Prologue

They found him on Thursday morning, wrapped in his duvet as neatly as the paper around a cigarette. He always slept like that but today his face was gray and still. The attendants at the Coconut Grove senior home phoned the hospital, and even though they had performed this ritual many times, the sadness hung a little heavier in the air. Warren Ackerman had been a favorite resident, a charming gentleman who loved to croon ballads to make the nurses smile. He had entered the home a widow and the other residents, who were predominantly female, had acted like schoolgirls, giving him red lipstick smiles and chocolates from their birthday boxes.

After almost a year, Warren had chosen a girlfriend, and the red lipstick was shelved. Being with Daphne St Clair had only made him happier and his dance steps were even lighter when he twirled next to her wheelchair. And now, all that joy and the promise of one more chance to love, and to be loved, was over.

Daphne stood there, watching them carry the shrouded stretcher away, wrapping her frail arms around herself. She looked so small and alone that the other residents turned away, remembering all the shared histories dissolved in a single moment. Almost all of them had made the painful journey from wives to widows, and seeing Daphne and the stretcher only reminded them that they'd be leaving Coconut Grove the same way someday.

The attendants gave Daphne extra care, easing her back onto her pillows, offering soft blankets and company, but she wanted to be left alone. Her twin daughters lived locally but visited with the same frequency as snow here in Florida. It was a shame, really, because Daphne was a lovely old woman: lively but sophisticated, with the regal bearing of someone who had been beautiful for most of her life. Even though age had faded her looks, the memory of being admired still illuminated her features.

When dinner ended and Daphne still hadn't left her room, Rachel—one of the attendants—decided to call her daughter Diane. Daphne clearly needed a reminder that she wasn't alone, that people loved her, and that was a daughter's job. When Diane answered, Rachel informed her of Warren's death, suggesting that she call and check in on her mother. Diane said she might be able to find the time, but she was *very busy.*

"Hi, Mom, I heard you lost someone today," Diane said.

"Yes, I did—a very nice man named Warren," Daphne replied. She sounded more subdued than usual.

"I didn't even know you had a boyfriend," Diane replied.

"We've been seeing each other for almost a year. He was a great comfort to me during the pandemic," Daphne explained quietly.

"It's very sad, Mom, but it's kind of inevitable in an old folks' home. Anyways, it's a bit embarrassing, isn't it? To have a boyfriend at your age?" Her daughter sounded distracted, as if she was watching TV.

"Well, I wouldn't want to embarrass you," Daphne said woodenly. "Anyways, I'd like to go to bed now."

"Okay . . . well, I'll try to come visit soon. Maybe I'll bring Harper," Diane said, but her mother had already hung up. She felt a twinge of guilt that she hadn't been kinder, but she brushed it off. Her mother was a tough old broad. A good night's sleep and she'd be back to her usual self.

After she hung up the phone, Daphne sat on the edge of her bed, the mattress so plush and thick that the soles of her feet only brushed against the floor. She didn't turn the light on and instead sat in the gray-blue twilight that washed her walls. It was that liminal time, the moment between the daylight and the night, when everything seemed too dark but a lamp too bright. Even as the light faded further, Daphne sat there, staring at the blank space around her.

Finally, she picked up the phone on her nightstand and began to dial, her movements precise and without hesitancy.

"Palm Haven Police Station, how can I help you?"

"Hello," she began, clearing her throat and then continuing. "A man named Warren Ackerman was found dead at Coconut Grove Senior Living Facility today. Everyone is assuming he died of old age, but he was actually murdered. And I killed him. In fact, I've killed a lot of people . . ."

The First Murder

Chapter One

STATEMENT FROM THE PALM HAVEN POLICE DEPARTMENT

"Good morning. Two days ago, a woman named Daphne St Clair contacted the police and confessed to a series of murders that span four states, two countries, and seven decades. These alleged murders involve several men that Ms. St Clair was romantically involved with. One of these murders, the poisoning of Warren Ackerman, occurred three days ago at a local retirement home. Yesterday, an autopsy was conducted on Mr. Ackerman, and we now have enough credible evidence to charge Ms. St Clair with murder in the first degree. At this time, we will not be disclosing any information about the other murders as we have no independent evidence to confirm them. Ms. St Clair also used many aliases over the years, which will need to be investigated. However, we will be liaising with law enforcement in other jurisdictions, who are very interested in what Ms. St Clair has disclosed.

"The murder of Warren Ackerman, which occurred here in Florida, will be the focus of our investigation. We have already been able to preserve a significant amount of relevant evidence, as this murder is so recent. This case is complicated by the fact that Ms. St Clair is ninety years old and in poor health. The District Attorney's office is currently exploring options for facilities that could incarcerate Ms. St Clair in a safe and humane way, but there is a shortage of spaces. We will provide more updates as this case progresses. Thank you."

The day after the police made their statement, my lawyer Arthur Tisdale came out to see me. He stood by the window of my sitting room in his three-piece suit, staring out at the senior center's lawn that was so green, it seemed to glow in the Sunday afternoon sun. Tisdale was apparently a very famous defense attorney, the kind of man who made sure that a real estate tycoon or pro-basketball player in Florida could break every law on heaven and earth and never find out if orange is their color.

"I must say it's very unusual for a serial killer to confess, especially when they're not under any suspicion," he said, studying me as if I was mystery meat.

"I guess when He made me, God broke the mold," I quipped, but Tisdale didn't crack a smile.

"We'll need to have you assessed, to make sure you're mentally sound. Both to have made the confession but also to enter a plea. And we've got a good shot of keeping you out of prison until we enter a guilty plea, because your age and health concerns will make it very difficult for prison authorities to accommodate you, and the staff tell me you don't have the mobility to flee."

"Okay," I said, faintly disappointed that nothing was really going to change yet. I was already imprisoned in my room, no longer allowed to visit common areas or spend time with the other residents. Jeez, you kill one old man and suddenly no one wants to sit at your lunch table. I knew the residents hated me and even the staff who delivered my meals and bathed me did so with stony faces. I don't know if you've ever had someone who thinks you're scum wash your back, but I wouldn't recommend it.

"It's also important you don't leave the home, because this will be a high-profile case, with multiple investigations and many victims, and someone might want to hurt you. I've already had a few people contact our office, trying to get in touch with you. Some will be journalists, but others could be more malicious."

"Well, I guess I'm like the full moon; I bring all the crazies out," I said with a laugh.

"But I do want to make clear that a guilty plea will result in prison time eventually. There are people in their eighties and nineties in prison in this state."

"I know," I said. "This is Florida. Tough on crime. And I suppose killing old people is bad for business in the retirement state." I also knew they didn't take kindly to serial killers. Aileen Wuornos had been executed here and so had Ted Bundy. The local yokels had even thrown 'Bundy Burn' parties on his execution day.

"Finally, other states may seek to extradite you for crimes committed in their jurisdictions. In the coming months, you will likely be getting visits from these investigators from other states, to assist with their inquiries. I, of course, will be present. But I don't think you need to be too concerned about extradition. These processes are—" he cleared his throat, looking embarrassed "—lengthy, and to put it delicately . . ."

"I'll probably die first," I interrupted him.

"Who's dying now?" a voice demanded. I looked up and saw my sixty-year-old twin daughters Rose and Diane and my granddaughter Harper being ushered through the door.

"Ah. I see you have visitors. That's fine, we were essentially finished," Tisdale said, waving formally and slipping out. Diane's eyes followed him on the way out. She always was a sucker for a good suit.

"Well, what brings you two out?" I asked. Even though they only lived an hour's drive away, it had been months since I'd seen them last. People don't like visiting their elderly parents. I get it; most old people only have one topic of conversation: the many exciting ways their bodies are packing it in. I've always been interesting, even if people didn't fully grasp that until now.

Here's a fun fact about life: when your children are young, you can't imagine the assholes they're capable of becoming. But give it enough time and you'll see for yourself. My son went from being a good child to a clever, decent man but unfortunately my twins flopped like soufflés. I gave them everything but instead of making them satisfied, they just wanted more, more, more. When I was pregnant with the twins, my nails started cracking and I lost two teeth. They were leeching the minerals from my bones, literally devouring me alive. And that's how they've always been: four grasping hands and two mean little mouths demanding more.

My girls were both engaged in a furious fight against time, injecting their faces with so much Botox and filler that their skin seemed tight and shiny, like overfilled balloons. From a block away, they did look attractive; they both dyed their hair a honey blonde and they had golden tans and flashing white teeth. But all I saw when I looked at them were price tags. Even their teeth were veneers. Their real teeth, the ones I had watched poke through their gums and taught them how to brush, had been whittled down to spikes and covered in porcelain.

"Okay, your little cry for help has worked; we're visiting you. Now will you tell the police you made this up to get attention?" Diane said as she paced in front of my chair, her voice dripping with condescension, as if I were a child who told her class she rode a dinosaur to school.

"Diane—" I began but was interrupted by a groan and a flap of a manicured hand.

"Mother, I've told you a million times, call me Dian-*ah*. Diane sounds like the name of a waitress."

"Oh, so a woman with a job? Yes, much better to sound unemployed," I said with a sniff. "I birthed you. I think I earned the right to name you." I knew I was being hypocritical. Diane wanted to change one syllable of her name, whereas I changed my name as often as I did phone providers. But Diane's insistence on a classier name emphasized the greedy streak that dominated the twins' characters. They would trade every scrap of happiness they possessed for a swimming pool, a black American Express card, and a desirable zip code. In fact, they already had.

"Diana's name isn't the point," Rose interjected. Darling Rose, always the second to speak and the last to think. "Mother, what is going on? You told the police you killed an old man?"

"Well, among others," I said mildly. "I've killed *a lot* of men actually. I might need to sit down with pencil and paper to work out how many."

"Is this a dementia thing?" Rose asked Diane in low tones.

Diane shrugged. "Her doctors say no. And I don't know about the . . . others, but the police think she's telling the truth about Warren." Diane glanced at me and raised her voice, just on the off-chance I'd turned senile in the last ten seconds.

"MOTHER, ARE YOU GETTING CONFUSED? MAYBE YOU JUST THINK YOU KILLED THOSE PEOPLE . . . OR FANTASIZED ABOUT IT?"

"No, sweetheart. If I actually killed every person I fantasized about killing then I would be much more prolific than, say, the Green River Killer or the Golden State Killer. Both very famous murderers, you know," I said. I met Harper's eyes and winked. She smiled back and then looked down at her book, pretending to read.

"You're telling the truth?" Diane asked, roughly grabbing my arm and then releasing it when she felt how spindly it was. I used to haul a twin around under each arm and now she could have snapped me like a breadstick. Getting old is the pits.

"Bingo. Hey, parents can surprise you," I said, feeling a surge of energy. I had spent seventy years telling lie after lie and it was exhilarating to stop pretending.

"Oh Jesus Christ! Mother, what have you done? Do you know how *humiliating* it is to be the daughter of a serial killer?" Diane asked, her voice rising to such a shrill pitch that I thought the mirror would crack.

"No, darling, I don't," I said serenely, and gave her my most pleasant smile. "My mother never hurt a fly."

"Everyone is talking about us. I've canceled our membership to the club, because God knows, I can't show my face in there. Harper's heartbroken—she loved the tennis there," Diane said.

"I really don't mind," Harper piped up. She was sitting cross-legged on my bed, reading a Harry Potter book with a stern look on her face. "I hated the club. All the other kids just wanted to take selfies and make TikToks. It's so boring."

I smiled at Harper. She was my favorite grandchild. It had taken a while for me to get one that I loved. I had to wait for Diane's second marriage and a surrogate pregnancy after nature told her no more. To my generation, a baby at forty-eight was unheard of, of course, but late-in-life babies seemed to be a status symbol among my daughters' friends, the Birkin bags of the new millennium. It made me miss the good old days, when rich women embraced old age by swanning around in fur coats and pearls, surviving on a steady diet of cigarettes and Manhattans and passing out at 4 p.m.

Unfortunately, Harper didn't inherit my looks. She had thick glasses and gray-brown hair that hung limply around her face like boiled spaghetti. Her front teeth were also curiously long and rounded, like a rabbit's. But she was smart, and even at her age, she got the joke. And you don't have to be beautiful when you're born rich.

"Don't you understand what this could do to Reid's political career? Why did you have to confess before an election?" Rose demanded. Her husband was a senator, just another boy who was born on third base and thought he'd hit a triple.

"Yes, I suppose you all really are the biggest victims in this," I said gravely.

"Well, at least you understand that," Diane muttered.

"Girls, don't worry. Tomorrow some politician—now I'm not saying it will be your husband, Rose—will be caught with his pecker out and the newspapers will forget about me."

"Are you deluded? Mom, there is nothing Americans love more than murder. Your story is all over the news! People are already trying to dig up information about you and your family! Harper told me she's even heard your name mentioned on a podcast!" Diane snapped.

"Podcasts . . . those are like radio shows, right?" I asked. "A couple of them have already contacted me via my lawyer, asking for interviews."

"What did you say?" Rose asked. I shrugged and turned to Harper.

"What do you think? Should Grandma do the podcasts?"

Harper nodded at me. "Yeah, you should go on *My Favorite Murder*; that's the best one," she said. Diane's eyes bulged.

"And I'll have to pick one, will I? A favorite murder?" I asked.

"No, it's just a name," Harper said. "Why?" she asked, eyes lighting up with curiosity. "Do you have one?"

"Of course," I said. "Isn't that inevitable?"

"Look at what you've done!" Diane cried, collapsing onto

the bed. I frowned at the way the springs squeaked. I am very particular about mattresses. I never let the children jump on them when they were kids. "Harper is going to be permanently scarred by all this!"

"I think it's kind of cool actually. My grandma is a famous murderer!" Harper said brightly. We all frowned at her. Even I felt a bit strange about that one and I loved the little weirdo.

"Harper, go wait in the lobby," Diane ordered, thrusting her lean, gym-toned arm at the door. Harper frowned and skulked off, hunching over her Harry Potter book so that no one could see her preteen body. When she was gone, Rose sat next to Diane on the bed. It always shocked me to realize that they were in their sixties, as if my brain was stuck in the time when they were little girls, and I was in my thirties.

"Why did you do it, Mom?" Diane asked quietly. I was surprised by the question. The twins had always been incurious, willing to accept anything so long as they got their ice creams and sparkly dresses. I could have shot someone right in front of them and all they would have asked was if you could get bloodstains out of silk.

"Well, it's complicated," I began, thinking about how to explain how few options I'd had, how many people had hurt me. But Diane cut me off.

"Why did you have to confess? Fine, you did some terrible things. But nobody knew! You're like a minute from death; you could have taken this to the grave and saved us the embarrassment!"

"Yes, I could have," I said with a nod. "But sometimes you just want to make something *happen.*"

"Well, now I have to ask. Did you kill our father? The police said you confessed to killing people in different states. Was New York one of them?" Rose asked.

"Do you really want to know?" I replied. "Or do you just want to wait for the podcast?"

Chapter Two

It was around that time that I decided to actually do a podcast. Nobody read books anymore. Even when I was born, folks were worrying that the radio would kill reading. Now, people wanted everything in a sentence or less or their minds started wandering. Besides, I was ninety years old; I wanted my story to come out *now*. I could have done a documentary or a TV interview, but podcasts seemed to be the new thing. And Harper loved them, so that sealed the deal.

Choosing the podcast, however, would be a tough decision. I had been contacted by a handful of people through Arthur Tisdale, who had disapprovingly passed on the messages (lawyers never approved of interviews), and so, on Tuesday, I sat down and called each of them back. It had been less than a week since I had killed Warren, less than a week since I'd done the most radical thing I could think of: confess. And already life was getting interesting again.

The first was a woman called Holly Blue, although I suspect that if I checked her birth certificate, I would find something blander.

"I do a podcast called *Badass Women*, and I would love

to do a whole season devoted to you. My last season was on Heidi Fleiss, a woman who ran an upscale prostitution ring in Hollywood. I also did a season on Bonnie Parker, you know from Bonnie and Clyde?"

"Tell me, what exactly is your definition of badass? Is it a good thing? Because you seem to be mostly focusing on whores and killers," I said, squinting in confusion.

"A badass woman is independent. She knows what she wants out of life and isn't afraid to get it. She often goes against what society expects of her, whether that's in how she dresses or who she sleeps with. You may not like her, but you have to respect her," Holly replied. She recited her spiel in a sing-song way, as if she'd memorized it.

"So, it's okay for women to murder people to get what they want?" I asked.

"Well, maybe not murder," Holly backtracked. "But you know . . . if she wants to wear revealing clothes or sleep with a lot of guys, no one should judge her for that. Or if she wants to have adventures, or become an outlaw, that's cool."

I hung up, already bored of this woman's ramblings.

The next people I talked to, a trio named Andy, Tobin, and Greg, immediately turned me off by telling me they did "comedy true crime" and that they were "stand-up comedians" as well as podcasters.

"Yeah, so we tell crime stories, but we improvise and riff along the way. Some people can't handle it, because we're not afraid to get a little offensive, but most of our listeners fucking love us," Andy bragged. He seemed like a boy who communicated mostly through high fives.

"What kind of jokes would you be making about me?" I asked. There was a pause as they considered this. If they had been smart, they would have soft pedaled it, tried to get me on board. But then again, if they had any sense, they would have become stockbrokers, not comedians.

"Well . . . you just killed your elderly boyfriend, so we'd probably make some jokes about your sex life, you know, whether your pussy was full of dust. And you poisoned him, so we'd probably do a bit where we realize that you've put something in our drinks and panic because we think you've roofied us and are going to rape us. And then I guess we'd be relieved when we realized that we were going to die instead." Their raucous laughter echoed down the phone.

"Right. So, the joke is I'm an old lady and no one wants to have sex with me," I said acidly. "Groundbreaking stuff."

Of course, I turned them down. When you're old, you really have to savor the time you have left. And none of that time should be spent listening to man-boys cracking bad jokes.

The fourth person was Gayle MacPherson, an NBC reporter for *Dateline*.

"So, I should say up front that I have my doubts about asking you to participate in this podcast," Gayle began bluntly. "If we did agree on it, you'd have to know that I would be asking you tough questions."

"Well, this is an interesting way to pitch to someone," I said.

"Look, we'll be doing a podcast about you whether you participate or not," Gayle said briskly. "Admittedly, it's not great timing for us, as we just wrapped a podcast about two elderly women who were killing men for insurance money."

"Sorry for the inconvenience. I should have waited and confessed next year," I chipped in, but she kept talking over me.

"But we *have* to do your story. It's perfect for *Dateline*. And we've had a lot of success with our women killer podcasts. I don't know if you've listened to 'The Thing about Pam' or 'Mommy Doomsday' but they've been big hits."

"Congratulations," I said. I felt as if we were in a business meeting, and she was about to start going over the numbers with me. Didn't she understand that I had something valuable? According to Harper, murder podcasts were a dime a dozen. But a *murderer's* podcast? That was new.

"So, are you interested in participating?" Gayle asked.

"No," I said.

"Fine by me," she said flatly and hung up.

The final person I talked to was a woman named Ruth Robinson, a journalist in her early thirties who lived locally. She'd never written for any newspaper I had heard of, and she seemed as new to the podcasting world as I was.

"So, what's your plan for the podcast? Because I've had pitches from *Badass Women*, *Died Laughing*, and *Dateline*," I said. I didn't tell her that I had already rejected all of them. If I didn't go with Ruth, I'd have to buy Harper some recording equipment and tell her to have at it. That might be worth it just for the look on Diane's face.

"*Dateline*? Wow, okay. I don't really have a plan, exactly . . ." Ruth said, her voice quavering. "I thought that we would just sit and talk about your life, and then I could shape that into a story. I'd want to do some background research as well, try to

20

talk to other people in your life or even people who are experts on . . . your situation."

"*I'm* the only expert on my situation," I retorted.

"Oh of course," Ruth stuttered, backing down. I was thankful that we were on the phone so she couldn't see me smile. "I suppose I'd just want to do a podcast from your perspective. There are so many true crime shows out there where a presenter just tells you about a crime. But hearing a show where the perpetrator tells their story? That's so unique." Her earnestness was almost dripping through the phone. She was like a Girl Scout pushing Thin Mints.

"What would you call it?" I asked, enjoying giving Ruth a good grilling.

"Well, I thought *The Murders of Daphne St Clair* could work, as your name is so elegant," Ruth said.

"A bit wishy-washy," I harrumphed, rolling my eyes. "But I'm willing to give this a try. And if you're not a good fit, I'll pull the plug."

"Really? Wow, thank you so much. I promise, you won't regret this!" she squeaked.

"Come by tomorrow afternoon," I said. "But don't tell anyone else where I live. I'm supposed to be keeping that under wraps for safety reasons."

There was nothing special about Ruth, she just seemed much less annoying than the other people who wanted to tell my story to the masses and make a buck off it. In fact, she seemed unsure of herself, which suited me fine. People are like dogs; it's better for everyone when they know who's in charge.

Chapter Three

EPISODE ONE: 1932–1948

RUTH: Hello, my name is Ruth Robinson and I will be interviewing Daphne St Clair. So, what do we know so far? We know that Daphne has been charged with the first-degree murder of Warren Ackerman here in Florida. We also know that Daphne has confessed to killing more people across numerous decades and in different locations. She has given details about these murders to the police, but these details have not been shared publicly yet. And because Daphne has confessed to murdering Warren and will almost certainly plead guilty, she will never have a full criminal trial. So, this podcast is a record of history, a chance to get to the heart of the facts before Daphne is imprisoned, or—realistically, considering her age—dies, taking the stories with her. Keep in mind, however, that Daphne will probably only give you her version of events. So, let's solve a mystery together. Let's find out who Daphne St Clair is. And what, exactly, has she done?

Ruth Robinson was escorted through Coconut Grove by a grim-faced woman. She was very petite and Ruth, who was five foot eleven, towered over her. She walked briskly, ushering Ruth past rooms where wrinkled faces peered out at her. She might be projecting, but the residents looked frightened. The senior center felt hushed and leaden, as if the knowledge that a murder had been committed in their midst, that the killer was just down the hall, had paralyzed them all.

"Wait, do you mind if we stop at the bathroom?" Ruth asked as they passed a washroom. The woman huffed in irritation but stopped walking, glowering outside as Ruth went in.

Ruth stood at the sink, feeling a strange wave of anxiety wash over her. She splashed water on her face and fixed her lank ponytail in the mirror, staring at her reflection. It wasn't exactly awe-inspiring. Sure, she had good eyebrows, thick and dark, with a strong arch. But her skin was sallow, which was rare for a lifelong Floridian, and a recent breakup had left her with sleep-deprived shadows under her eyes as dark as bruises.

She knew she needed to leave this bathroom, to meet Daphne, to launch a groundbreaking podcast and kickstart her career, but she couldn't seem to make her feet move. Lately, she'd felt so frustrated and angry with life. She couldn't seem to get out of this hole she'd been floundering in since her mid-twenties, couldn't seem to break free of the past. This was her big break, an opportunity to change everything. But what if she fucked it up? Ruth wished she could call Jenn. For the last two years, Jenn had been the one talking Ruth down. But that was the whole point of a breakup: you had to figure it out for yourself.

Ruth took a deep breath, yanked the hem of her shirt down,

and stormed out of the bathroom, hoping that momentum would carry her even if willpower wouldn't. The Coconut Grove employee fell into step beside her, not saying a word until she stopped abruptly.

"That's her door," the woman said, pointing around the corner.

"I thought someone might be posted outside her door," Ruth said.

The woman scoffed, her white teeth flashing under the dim overhead lights. "She can barely walk more than a few steps. We keep her door and the patio doors locked and our facility already has excellent security."

"Okay. Well, thanks for bringing me," Ruth replied.

"It's my job. Personally, I think it's disgusting that you're here. We all loved Warren," the woman replied flatly, knocking and then opening Daphne's door with her key.

RUTH (Voiceover): It's a strange situation, interviewing a serial killer in an old folks' home. There were no shackles or armed guards to keep me safe. Instead, I found myself in a spacious apartment with an old woman sitting in a striped armchair, the sunlight glinting off her dyed black perm. Daphne didn't look dangerous; she looked like she was one slippery bathmat away from death. But I knew there was milk in my fridge older than her last kill and I reminded myself not to eat or drink anything in this place. Daphne said hello and offered me a seat, and I was struck by her voice immediately. It was flatter in person, a cut-the-crap tone, as if she only had a minute to talk before she needed to get back to her chores.

RUTH: Hello, thanks so much for having me, Mrs. St Clair.

DAPHNE: You can call me Daphne. We're going to be spending a lot of time together so we might as well dispense with all the Mrs. bullshit.

RUTH: Okay, Daphne, then please call me Ruth.

DAPHNE: Ruth? There are a lot of Ruths in here. Everyone here is named Ruth, Doris, or Phyllis. But young people aren't named Ruth anymore.

RUTH: I guess my mother hates me.

DAPHNE: It's certainly possible. But she'll probably never admit it.

RUTH: Are you normally this blunt or just with journalists?

DAPHNE: Don't get your undies in a twist. This is just how I talk.

RUTH: Well, we are here to talk about you. So, why did you decide to confess to these murders?

DAPHNE: I was bored. In this place, every day feels exactly the same. I just felt like making something happen.

RUTH: You do realize that prison is also a place where every day will feel the same. And that it'll be much less nice than this place?

DAPHNE: Yes, Ruth, I'm not senile. Maybe I also wanted people to know that I'm not your typical fogey. When you get away with something for so long, you want people to know.

RUTH: Okay, so you're not like other girls. It's not common though, for serial killers to just call up and confess to a murder that's being treated as a natural death, is it?

DAPHNE: No. Usually they only confess when the police already have enough to nail 'em. And the Palm Haven Police were never going to catch me; they're a bunch of yokels with sunburns and Segways.

RUTH: I don't disagree. They have a history of bungling murder investigations. They got lucky when you confessed.

DAPHNE: But serial killers do confess, you know, every now and then. Ed Kemper called up the police and confessed. I'm pretty sure the Railroad Killer did too.

RUTH: Do you know a lot about serial killers?

DAPHNE: I read a lot of true crime books. I read a lot in general, though. Not much else to do around here. So don't make a big deal about that.

RUTH: So do I. Books, documentaries, podcasts, ever since I was a kid and found an old copy of Ann Rule's *The Stranger Beside Me* in a motel. After that, it was a bit of an obsession.

DAPHNE: And here you are, finally getting into the mind of a killer. That's why you liked them, right? Because they taught you about monsters?

RUTH: Hmm . . . I suppose that is interesting. But for me, it was the solving of the mystery. My favorite part was always when they'd caught the killer and were trying to make him confess, to reveal all the people he'd killed and all the places he'd dumped the bodies. But I guess your story is different because you confessed when nobody even thought a murder had happened. Was it guilt that made you do that?

DAPHNE: No, I don't think that's the case. I've always had very high self-esteem.

[A knock on the door.]

ATTENDANT: Pills.

DAPHNE: Service with a smile, huh?

[Door slams.]

DAPHNE: Oooeee! Touchy. I'll just take these in the bathroom. Let's take a break.

[Sounds of Daphne getting up, shuffling along, opening doors.]

RUTH (Voiceover): Daphne was gone for a while. I got up and began to roam around her living room. There was a large television and a bookshelf stuffed full of books. Most old people had rooms full of photos of their families, but the only pictures in the living room were paintings. I saw a couple of Edward Hopper prints and a few David Hockneys (one of which I had a feeling might have even been an original). The bedroom door was ajar, so I pushed it open, aware that I was now definitely snooping. There was a large hospital-style bed that could be raised and reclined. The closet was bursting with clothes, shoes, and jewelry, all relatively new. On the far bedside table, I found the only photograph in the apartment: a small framed black and white photo of a woman holding a little boy, maybe around two or three. The woman had dark hair and ivory skin, and a luminous smile. She was stunning, dressed in a tight Fifties pencil dress. But it was the way she had her arms wrapped around the little boy, their cheeks pressed together as they laughed, that stopped me. This was a moment of real happiness.

DAPHNE: What are you doing?

RUTH: I, uh . . . sorry!

[Feet shuffle out of the room, and the door slams.]

DAPHNE: Classic journalist, always digging through people's garbage.

RUTH: I'm really sorry . . . You know, I'm sure this must be tiring for you. I could come back tomorrow.

DAPHNE: Okay, come visit again, just keep your mitts off my stuff.

RUTH (Voiceover): And that was the first interview. It was clear that Daphne was toying with me. She shrugged when I asked her questions, as if to telegraph that she didn't take anything, even murder, too seriously. And I could see that she didn't want me to dig too deep, to reveal herself fully. I knew that the next time I visited, I'd need to have a better plan for controlling the interview.

Ruth drove away from Coconut Grove, trying to shake off her uneasiness. She felt like the sea on a windy day, churned up into a soupy froth, all bubbles and whirlpools. It was humid out, and she grabbed her hair and lifted it off the back of her neck, trying to take deep breaths.

Ruth had pretended to be awed by Daphne to get the job, figuring that Daphne didn't want a journalist who was going to grill her. But now there was a power imbalance as Daphne was steamrolling Ruth, which would make doing a podcast difficult. The listeners needed to know who Daphne was: as a child, as a woman, as a mother, and as a murderer. Anything less wouldn't be the truth. But Daphne didn't seem interested in revealing everything.

She wondered again why Daphne had even confessed.

Daphne had a cushy life; why would she trade it all for a stark prison cell, fluorescent lightbulbs, concrete floors, and a world calling her a monster? Why would anyone go through the hell of a murder investigation if they could avoid it?

Chapter Four

After a pathetic dinner of scrambled eggs on toast, Ruth sat down at her rickety old IKEA desk. When Jenn lived here, Ruth had borrowed her antique rolltop desk whenever she could. Jenn had been a writer as well, a moderately successful indie author who wrote sci-fi/dystopian novels and had a surprisingly rabid online fan base. She was disciplined too, writing and working out every day, filling the apartment with the lemony smells of fresh Mediterranean cooking. But Jenn, her desk, and lovely smells were all gone now, and Ruth's lackluster dinners and uncomfortable work setup were just more evidence that her life was in pieces.

But enough ruminating. Ruth had to get through to Daphne and she couldn't afford to waste time, not when Daphne might go to prison at any moment. Ruth needed a way to cut through Daphne's bullshit.

The hard part would be the lack of Internet resources for a woman born in the 1930s. In fact, there was very little information about Daphne in the public domain at all. To make matters worse, Daphne had changed her name over the years, wrapping herself in noms de plume and married names like onion layers.

But there were people. And Ruth had a hunch that over the years, Daphne would have revealed slivers of her true self to others, even if they were just fragments. Like Daphne's murders, these people would likely be scattered all over the country. But Ruth could find them.

Ruth had always prided herself on her research skills. When she was at university, she'd been nominated for a national student journalism prize for a long-form article she'd written about an infamous New Year's Eve party in Miami in 2002. What had started as a massive, glamorous party of Florida's biggest and brightest had ended in tragedy after eighteen guests were hospitalized with abdominal pain and convulsions and four guests died. Over the years there had been many theories: ergot contamination, tainted cheese, a militant waiter with extremist links, a recently fired employee looking for revenge, but the case remained a mystery. Ruth had found working on that article fascinating. She had spent months interviewing scientists and first responders, and while she couldn't present any clear solution, her prize nomination had made her believe that a career in journalism might actually be possible.

Unfortunately, she now put her skills to use researching the hottest TikTok trends and what had happened to child stars from the Nineties as a freelance journalist for clickbait websites. The work was badly paid and idiotic, but Ruth had tried and failed to find a better job so many times that she'd given up searching.

The obvious place to start was Daphne's daughters. Unlike their mother, Diane Hatton and Rose Prescott were all over the Internet. Their images were splashed across the Florida society pages, a million bland pictures of them smiling at charity events, arm in arm with a bevy of rich people with gleaming suntans and frozen foreheads. Diane was married to a local real estate investor, the kind of man who didn't think twice about draining a wetland to build just one more golf course. (Didn't Florida have enough?) Rose was married to a hardline Republican senator, and Ruth was glad he'd be having some sleepless nights about the reputational damage his mother-in-law's confession was creating.

She didn't expect Rose and her senator husband would be listed, but it was easy to find Diane's home phone number online.

"Hello?" a woman's voice answered. She sounded distracted and Ruth could hear a TV playing in the background.

"Hello, Diane? My name is Ruth Robinson and I'm a journalist. Your mother and I are doing a podcast about her life. I'm hoping to get some background information from you," Ruth said quickly, knowing that Diane might hang up the moment she mentioned her mother.

"You have some nerve calling me! If you mention my sister or me on this show, I'll have my lawyer bankrupt you!" Diane spat into the phone, making Ruth pull it away from her ear.

Diane was clearly someone who was used to getting what she wanted. Ruth had known women like this before—women who used their anger and histrionic reactions to badger everyone into submission. She decided to appeal to Diane's keen sense of self-preservation.

"Diane, I've already got a platform for the podcast, and I intend to start releasing episodes immediately. And I can guarantee you a podcast that features interviews with a serial killer is going to be huge. This is your chance to share your perspective."

"What perspective? I didn't know a thing about this until she confessed."

"See? You need to tell people that. Because if you don't, people will see two daughters who lived a very long time with a serial killer for a mother. And they might start to wonder . . . how could you have *not* known?" Ruth said, surprised at how forceful she sounded, as if the thrill of the chase was awakening some long-dormant impulses in her.

There was a prolonged silence, as Diane considered Ruth's words, and the threat hidden beneath them.

"If I do this, you need to protect our reputations. In hindsight, there might have been some . . . suspicious events over the years. But we really didn't know anything. Children just accept whatever their mother says."

"I won't distort any facts. But I won't try to smear you. You were just kids, after all," Ruth said, trying to phrase her words carefully so that she could keep her options open. If the twins were guilty of anything, it was probably ignorance with a dash of willful blindness. But they might be as criminal as their mother, and she had to be prepared to nail them to the wall if she needed to.

"Will Rose participate as well?" Ruth asked.

"I'll speak for both of us. She has to be very careful with her husband being a senator."

"Okay. So, I'll want to set up some interviews with you in the coming weeks. But what I need right now is some background information. What is your mother's birth name? And where did she grow up?"

"I know her first name, but I don't know her maiden name. Her real name is Loretta. She told me one night after too many wines, said she'd always hated it."

"And her hometown?"

"It's in . . . Canada," she said, as if it was a dirty secret. "It's a place called Lucan in Southern Saskatchewan. I only know that because sometimes she would rant about how she was never going back there, how we were lucky to grow up in a city full of exciting people. I can't say I disagree with her," Diane said with a dry laugh.

"Okay, I can work with that. Just one last question. Would you say she was a good mother?"

There was a long pause on the other end of the line. When Diane spoke again, her voice was lower and thicker, as if she was congested.

"I don't know. Depends on the day." And then she hung up.

Later, Ruth sat watching coverage of Daphne's case on TV. While the police had released very little information, someone (probably a Coconut Grove staff member) had leaked pictures of Daphne to the media, a few shots of her as an old woman and one of her looking glamorous and young in a Fifties bikini. Everybody was dissecting the images and the unconfirmed report that Daphne was a serial poisoner. Body language experts debated whether she had 'evil eyes,' feminists and men's rights activists argued over what this case represented, there was even a comedy sketch where a man dressed up as an old crone pretended to host a cooking show where all the guests ended up dead. Daphne was being discussed in other mediums too. The incels on Reddit were using Daphne to back up all their poorly thought-out theories about women. Ruth had read think pieces in major newspapers that talked about how Daphne represented an era, a problem, a question, even though no one was quite clear on which one.

Everyone was talking about Daphne. Particularly women. This mysterious man-killer seemed to comfort them in a secret, shameful way, this idea that there might be something dangerous lurking within all of them, that they might not be as fragile as men presumed. And of course everyone wanted to know why exactly she had confessed. What kind of self-respecting serial killer turned themselves in?

Ruth was watching a CNN expert discuss incarcerating the elderly when she glanced down at her phone and noticed that she had a missed call from her mom. Louise Robinson worked in a call center near Tampa. It was mind-numbing work, but it was more manageable for Louise than waitressing and delivery gigs since Louise had been diagnosed with early onset Parkinson's disease. After a life of working hard as a young, single mother, now Louise was working even harder to stay afloat in a country that had very little time for people with chronic illness. It was hard watching her mother get sicker, hard watching the doctors play Whac-A-Mole with the million different symptoms that reared up, hard thinking about how much Louise's illness would cost as it progressed, a cost Ruth would have to bear alone.

With a twinge of guilt, Ruth decided not to call her back. She hadn't spoken to her mother in a while, and she worried that if she did speak to Louise, she'd end up telling her about the podcast. She hoped she hadn't heard about it already. It was the worst feeling in the world, worrying her mom, and Ruth had been doing it for years. But this was different. Her mom was going to hate this.

Chapter Five

Ruth returned to Coconut Grove the next day with a renewed commitment to get the story out of Daphne. She was early so she sat in her car, organizing her bag and answering emails. On impulse, Ruth checked Jenn's Instagram, looking for any clues about her new life. She did it almost unconsciously but the pain of seeing Jenn's face surprised her every time, like pressing her thumb into a sore spot on her body. Her most recent post was about a book signing and Ruth scrutinized an image of Jenn standing suspiciously close to an unidentified woman. Was she dating already? Should Ruth start dating again? It was hard dating in your thirties; people had certain expectations about what a person should have achieved by then. Her romantic life was another thing that had been rocky for the last six years, and her sexual fluidity only meant that she'd frustrated and disappointed people of all genders.

It was morning but the day was already hot and humid, as if she was breathing through a pillow clamped over her mouth. Ruth sighed and stared out at a nearby billboard for the Sunshine Development Group, the largest property development company in the city. Those billboards were all over the city, reminding everyone that while they toiled away writing poorly paid articles about celebrity butt implants, wealthy families like the Montgomerys—the owners of Sunshine Development—got rich building slums and McMansions, passing their wealth and their companies down from generation to generation. Ruth's apartment building had been built by Sunshine Development, and every time she passed the sign at the entrance, she fantasized about putting her fist through it.

Once again, an attendant escorted Ruth to Daphne's room. This time, the attendant handed Daphne her pills. Daphne disappeared into the bathroom while Ruth set up her equipment. Once she had emerged and settled into her armchair, Ruth launched into her questions.

"Let's start at the beginning," she said.

"Listen, I'm ninety years old. That's a lot of life to get through. Let's just jump to when things get interesting," Daphne started but Ruth interrupted her.

"No, I think the beginning is important. People love hearing that kind of stuff. Where did you grow up?"

"New York. A little apartment in Midtown," Daphne said quickly, tossing it on the table like pocket change.

"Really? Because your daughter said you're from a small town in Canada," Ruth said, trying not to look triumphant. There was a flash of darkness in Daphne's eyes. Ruth had angered her. Well, too bad.

"Well, why ask if you already knew the answer?" Daphne asked sourly. She crossed her arms over her cherry silk blouse and glowered.

"I wanted to know if you would lie to me," Ruth replied

plainly, settling her unopened notebook on her lap. The recording equipment was doing the heavy lifting, leaving her free to focus on the expressions that flickered across Daphne's face, as quick as a starling passing in front of the sun. She watched Daphne smooth the anger off her face, leaving it as crisp and clean as a freshly ironed sheet.

"Okay, so you got me there. But isn't the whole point of America that a person can be anything they want? I'm a New Yorker at heart; it's only bad luck that I was born in the ass-crack of nowhere."

"What did your parents do for a living?"

"They were farmers. *Obviously*. Everyone in Saskatchewan is a farmer," Daphne snapped, as if Ruth knew anything about Saskatchewan. Or Canada for that matter. It couldn't be that great up there; they always seemed to be coming to Florida for vacation.

"Did you have a happy childhood?" Ruth asked.

Daphne rolled her eyes. "Have you met many serial killers who had happy childhoods? It's hard to go to bed with a full belly and a happy heart and think: 'Shit, the only thing missing is a drawer full of hookers' teeth.'"

She's trying to shock me, Ruth thought, and so she kept her face neutral, not giving Daphne the reaction she wanted. The bluntness, the profanity, it served the same purpose as the superficial charm she probably used with men; it was all to keep people at arm's length. But Ruth needed to push harder, to get beneath the brittle surface.

"What made your childhood unhappy?"

"Ask me what made it happy; it's a much shorter list," Daphne

39

said. Another bumper-sticker quip. Ruth sat there, letting the silence fill the room until Daphne sighed and continued. "My parents were dirt-poor, and they had too many kids. To top it off, I was born in the Thirties, in the Dust Bowl. It was the worst decade to be on a farm. People lost everything."

"How many children did they have?"

"Seven. And I was the oldest, which meant I spent my childhood boiling diapers and chasing after toddlers."

"What about your parents? Did they make you unhappy?"

"Of course they did. My mother never had time to take care of us. She was too busy working, always working, trying to keep the farm above water. That woman was the hardest worker I ever met, and it showed. She looked about sixty by the time she turned thirty, all bony and gray. I can probably count on one hand the times I saw her smile." Her voice was a strange mixture of pride and bitterness.

"What about your father? Did you have a better relationship with him?" Ruth asked, almost certain the answer was no. Daphne had confessed to killing a lot of men. That didn't exactly scream 'Daddy's Girl.' Still, she needed to hear it out loud.

"No, we didn't. He was a bastard," Daphne said.

"How so?"

"If you think I'm going to talk about my father, you've got another thing coming." Daphne flashed with anger, for a moment becoming a different person, a mask slipping out of place before it was thrust back into position. There was truth behind the façade, a sense of frustration Ruth instantly recognized. But Ruth needed to be careful asking about Daphne's father. She knew there were some things that cost too much to share. So she let Daphne take control of the narrative. At least for now.

It's hard to explain to a young person how much can change during one person's life. The way I grew up doesn't exist any- more. The things people take for granted today: exotic fruit, owning more than one set of clothes at a time, traveling to other countries, were impossible things to me as a child. It was a different world, a time before Hitler, the Cold War, television, birth control. Young people don't understand that one day they'll change countries without ever moving their feet, that the world they grew up in will disappear forever.

I'm not one of those grandmothers who constantly narrates her life story to her grandkids, hoping that they'll memorize every detail and love me long after I'm fertilizer. Most of my grandchildren are idiots who either ignore me or try to make me dance in videos with them so that strangers on the Internet will think they're funny.

I was born in 1932 in Lucan, Saskatchewan. It was a flat, hard place. That's all there was to it. By the time I was born, Saskatchewan had been in a drought for two years; people called it the Hard Times. The crops burned under the sun, and everything became so dry that the topsoil was lifted up and carried away. Soon, we were living in the Dust Bowl, where rolling dust storms choked out the sun, blew down houses, and suffocated the cattle. The dust coated me, filling my hair and eyes with grit, collecting on my clothes and in the cracks of my body, drying me out, fossilizing me. Sometimes the dust was the only thing in my stomach, during the lean months. And all that dust got in our lungs, making us cough all day long. I had a doctor in New York once tell me that he could see scars in my lungs from all the dirt I breathed in as a child. He had trained in Oklahoma and said he could spot a Duster from a mile away. I never went back to that doctor. I hated the idea that my body was giving up my secrets.

Then the grasshoppers came to Saskatchewan, like a Biblical plague. They ate the rest of the crops, the vegetables from the garden, even the clothes and bedding hanging on the line. All we could hear was a strange humming sound, as if the air had been electrified. It was unsettling. There were so many grasshoppers that the trains couldn't run because their squashed bodies were gumming up the tracks. And every time you stepped out of your house, you walked on a carpet of grasshoppers, feeling them crush beneath your feet like bones breaking.

Things got so bad that the province set up a Grasshopper Control Committee to try to stop the outbreaks that returned every season. The committee distributed Criddle Mixture (a grasshopper poison) to farmers everywhere. By the time I was born, over one hundred thousand gallons of arsenic were being used in Saskatchewan every year. People would walk through their fields, flinging ladlefuls of poison everywhere. You see, I was born in a cloud of poison. Poison was ours. It was how we fought back against a world that was trying to break us.

And it broke so many of us. There was one year where my uncle was in danger of losing his farm, but he had managed to raise a small crop of wheat. But on the day they went to harvest the wheat, they saw the hailstorm on the horizon. The whole family stood at the edge of the field praying to God, every single one of them from the parents all the way down to their four-year-old son. It was moving eastwards and for a moment it looked like it was going to miss the farm. But then, at the last moment, the storm turned and headed straight for them. In the end, they lost the farm. My uncle ended up in an insane asylum and my aunt and cousins went to a flophouse.

How can you explain to someone born in the Nineties what it was like back then? We were living in hell. Burning in a dirty, ugly world that just overwhelmed you, until you couldn't feel anything at all. Life just happened to you back then, and you were too poor and too tired to do anything about it. You can see why I prefer to tell people I grew up in Manhattan.

Maybe it would have been manageable if I came from a happy family, but I didn't. I was a Cowell, born into a family that everyone thought wasn't worth shit. We lived in a one-room shack, a place so small that a person's anger could fill the room. My father was a drinker and a real son of a bitch. We were out there alone on a patch of dirt and he acted like God, king, and country combined. He'd come in bone-tired from a long day of farming but he still found the energy to beat us black and blue. When he had no money for liquor, he doubled down on the beatings, since they were his only stress reliever.

He did other things as well, but I'd prefer not to talk about that. Let's just say that I learned a lot about love and marriage from my father, none of it good. They say hard places make hard people. Well, hard people also make hard people.

RUTH: Was your family close with other people in Lucan?

DAPHNE: No. People saw us as trash. They didn't like my father because he was a drunk and they didn't like how ratty we all looked. In that town, you could get away with anything as long as you looked respectable.

RUTH: What sort of things did people get away with in Lucan?

DAPHNE: I'll give you an example. There was a preacher, Michael Cole. He had been married but his wife, who was twenty years younger than him, had died of pneumonia when I was six. Most people felt sorry for him, especially the great and good of our little town. But there was this rumor—it probably started with their kitchen girl—that the preacher liked to discipline his nineteen-year-old wife by locking her outside the house in the dead of winter. That she would stand at the door in minus forty degrees Fahrenheit, wearing nothing but a housedress and slippers, begging to be let inside as the skin on her face and hands went white and frozen.

RUTH: Jesus, and she went on to die of pneumonia?

DAPHNE: Well, she'd always been frail. People used to die different back then. It happened all the time.

RUTH: What happened to the preacher? Was he sent to prison?

DAPHNE: Nothing happened to him. He was so refined, and he had the support of the town; this was just a rumor among the poor folks. Besides, the wife was from the city. No one cared much about wives back then anyways, but especially not for ones who weren't local.

RUTH: What do you think this story says about people? What are you trying to explain to the listeners?

DAPHNE: Well, shit, I don't know, Ruth. You wanted me to talk about my childhood, the storms outside the house and the storms inside as well. What does any of it mean? It's just a memory.

Reddit: r/MurdersofDaphneStClairPodcast

u/Automoderator: Hello and welcome to r/MurdersofDaphneStClairPodcast! This subreddit is dedicated to discussing the newest podcast sensation *The Murders of Daphne St Clair*, which is already storming the charts even though it has only published its first episode! This is the place to discuss the podcast, the life of Daphne St Clair, theories about the crimes she committed and the places she lived!

ShockAndBlah:

Okayyy how obsessed are we already with this podcast? One episode and it's made me forget about *Serial*, *Casefile*, and *My Favorite Murder*!!

StopDropAndTroll:

Basic bitch choices. Listen to something less mainstream. Like *Last Podcast on the Left*.

ShockAndBlah:

I didn't ask for your opinion about podcasts. I want to talk about THIS podcast.

BurntheBookBurnerz:

Oh, sweetie, but he's not done mansplaining to you yet. And *Last Podcast* is just as mainstream, but he's an edgelord. He wants to show everyone how hardcore he is.

PreyAllDay:

Was the Dust Bowl really that bad in Canada? Wasn't it in Oklahoma?

BurntheBookBurnerz:

I think it was all over. I did a quick Google and Saskatchewan (fuck that's hard to spell, thank you, autocorrect!) seemed to be the worst bit of it in Canada. And those grasshoppers, man . . . disgusting.

StopDropAndTroll:

But it was a protein source. You'll never starve if you can live off the land. That was the problem with these people—they weren't prepping.

BurntheBookBurnerz:

Stop with the prepper bullshit, seriously.

PreyAllDay:

FFS if I grew up in a hot-ass dust storm full of bugs and poison I'd be a serial killer too!

Chapter Six

Ruth was setting up her equipment for recording episode two when Daphne walked behind her. Ruth's laptop screensaver was a selection of photos from Ruth's life: pictures of her visiting her best friend Chelsea in New York, cuddled on the couch with her mother as a little girl, old pictures of her grandmother, her father, her college graduation, all endlessly shuffling past the screen. There were even some shots of Jenn that made her chest tighten and Ruth made a mental note to remove those from the carousel.

"Are you doing research on me?" Daphne asked suddenly.

"What do you mean?" Ruth asked in surprise.

"That man, he just looks familiar, is all," Daphne replied. She was frowning, as if trying to access a long-buried file from a very full hard drive. Ruth's stomach lurched and she resisted the urge to close the laptop, although she did turn the screen slightly away from Daphne. She didn't want Daphne to look at pictures of her family, didn't want them contaminated with her presence.

"You haven't even told me about your life yet, so how could I have researched you? I'm not a mind reader," Ruth scoffed, trying to sound casual. She was aware that Daphne was watching her, and it made her skin prickle. She'd never really considered what it would feel like to be trapped in a room with a serial killer, elderly or not. She felt as if she was swimming in deep water, so deep there was nothing but blue below her legs, only to be suddenly aware of a long dark shadow circling beneath her.

"Well, he looks a little old for you, more my type than yours," Daphne said with a dry chuckle. Ruth watched the crepey skin on her neck shudder with the movement.

"That's a family member, and this is Florida, not Alabama. But what exactly *is* your type?" Ruth asked. She wondered what Daphne would think if she'd told her that she'd just broken up with a woman.

"Rich," Daphne said. "My type is rich. And I can always spot the ones with money. This guy looks familiar but, I don't know, I've dated a lot of wealthy codgers in Florida; they all blur together."

"The wonders of aging, huh?" Ruth said, pulling out her microphone, trying to keep her voice casual. "Anyways, we've got almost ninety years of life history to cover, so we better get cracking."

"I suppose," Daphne said with a shrug. Her eyes trailed up to Ruth's face again, as if she was trying to work something out, but then the moment passed.

RUTH (Voiceover): The next time I came to the seniors home, I wanted to talk more about Lucan and Daphne's childhood, since people want to know how killers are made. But Daphne seemed to think the subject was exhausted.

*[Daphne's room. She is making a tutting noise
as if Ruth has irritated her.]*

DAPHNE: There's nothing else to say really. My childhood was dirt. Dirt storms, dirt poor, and being treated like dirt. My favorite memory of Lucan was leaving it. What about you? What was your childhood like?

RUTH: Me? Why are we talking about me?

DAPHNE: Because I feel like it.

RUTH: Well, I grew up around here. I was raised by a single mother who worked really hard to keep a roof over our heads.

DAPHNE: Touching stuff.

RUTH: Now, could you tell me how old you were when you left home?

DAPHNE: Sixteen? Around that age. When you've lived as long as I have, some of the details get a bit fuzzy.

RUTH: What about school?

DAPHNE: I quit school at twelve. Things were different then. They couldn't even pay teachers in the Depression. The school board gave them IOUs and families took turns hosting them. Sometimes they had to share beds with their own students! Nobody cared about my education, they wanted me home working. I barely remember those years, every day was the same.

[A faint sigh, barely audible, escapes Daphne's lips.]

RUTH: What about World War Two? What do you remember about that?

DAPHNE: Well, there was that time Hitler came goose-stepping
down Lucan's main street . . . What do you think changed?
There were a few less men around and women knitted socks
for soldiers. It was a total snooze.

RUTH (sounding irritated): Surely *something* happened . . .

DAPHNE: I guess a few things did.

*And then, finally, the drought eased off and the dust began to
settle. The insects were long gone; the government's poison
campaign having worked its gruesome magic. But before
people could really relax, World War Two began.*

*My father didn't go to war. A farmer could contribute to the
war effort by growing food for the country, but many farmers
still went. The ones who stayed behind weren't always treated
well. Everyone knew I was the daughter of a drunk, but now
they saw me as the daughter of a coward. We went to town even
less, preferring to avoid all the muttered slurs and accusing
stares.*

*At fourteen I felt like my whole world was the size of a
penny and it was closing in fast. I hated the farm and I hated
my father. Every day felt like a struggle, one that left me tired
and dirty in a way that I have trouble remembering now. Even
though the drought was long gone, and Saskatchewan was no
longer a dust bowl, I still felt it on my skin, the way your cheek
burns when you remember someone slapping it.*

*I was changing too, from a girl to a woman. I started to walk
with my arms across my chest because I couldn't afford a bra,
and my breasts swayed and clapped together with every step. At
first my features seemed too large, my mouth plump and huge,*

my eyes bulging, and my cheekbones jutting out like blades from my face. But then I grew taller and my face widened and it was as if all my features slotted into place and suddenly I was beautiful. I looked a lot like Ava Gardner; we both had coal-black hair and dark green eyes. Not that this discovery gave me any pleasure. It was safer to be invisible.

By sixteen I was fending off boys, but not in a nice way. They didn't show up in their Sunday best and ask to take me for a picnic. Those gestures were saved for the girls who mattered: the girls with shining hair and dresses freshly sewn by their fat, gossipy mothers; girls who lived in tidy little houses in town and expected kindness because that's all they'd ever been given. Girls like me still got married but never to anyone worth a damn and only because we had nowhere else to go.

One Sunday, after church, the preacher asked me to stay behind. He smiled at me kindly and explained in a lowered voice that he wanted help organizing a dance for the local young people. I was proud that he had chosen me, that he saw me as something other than a dirtbag Cowell. When I think about who I was back then, I feel a strange kind of ache in my chest. I was just a pathetic little girl, hoping someone would like me.

The following Saturday, we met again, this time in his office at the church. I had spent the week rehearsing my ideas and was excited to share them. I was wearing my family's best clothes: my mother's plaid skirt and a thick green sweater.

"So, for the dance, I was thinking we could do a spring theme, with paper flowers. I know how to make them; I just need some colored paper," I said. I was suddenly aware that

I was talking too much and far too quick. I wanted him to be dazzled by my ideas.

I'd never had the opportunity to be good at anything. I had to take turns going to school with some of my sisters because the family didn't have enough clothing and shoes for all of us. At times, I was forced to go to school barefoot and wearing tops made of bleached flour sacks, which was a source of endless shame. No one wanted to be friends with the kids in flour sacks because they were the poorest of the poor. I had actually liked learning but all anyone saw when they looked at me was a stupid girl from a bad family.

"Am I blabbering?" I asked, talking through my curled-up fingers. The preacher smiled and patted my arm.

"Of course not! That's why I chose you, because you have so many ideas!" A warm flush ran through me. I could live for months on a couple of kind words; they were like gasoline for my soul.

"I want to hang the garlands from the ceiling, so they dangle like vines?" I continued, studying his face for any more positive reactions.

"Then that's what we'll do," he said. "Now, should we have a little wine to celebrate?"

"Oh-okay," I said. I'd never drunk alcohol before. I tried to smother the flicker of discomfort I always felt when a man started drinking around me, like I could feel my safety draining away with every sip.

"Let's toast to a new friendship," he said, offering me a small crystal glass full of red wine. I took it, aware that it was the nicest thing I'd ever held, but still nervous about its contents.

"Have a good sip, really taste those flavors," the preacher
said, and I noticed with a queasy realization that his hand
was on my knee.

DAPHNE: You know what happened next. I won't spell it out
for you.

RUTH: Why not?

DAPHNE: Look, I'm fine to describe the men I killed. You want to
hear about how they moaned and vomited while I was downstairs crushing up pills? Sure. But I don't like remembering the
times I was a victim. Besides, you've heard it a million times;
you can picture it already, can't you?

RUTH: Well, I—

DAPHNE (upset): Rough carpet, scrabbling hands, his weight
crushing me. The scared noises I made, how betrayed I
felt . . . you KNOW this story. EVERYONE'S heard THIS story.
What is there to gain from another story about a woman
being victimized?

RUTH: Well, it's the truth . . . There's something to gain from
telling the truth isn't there? Even if there's no happy ending.

DAPHNE: Not in my experience, no. He raped me. And afterwards he showed me out and told me to keep the wine a
secret or else people might think I was a bad girl. He didn't
say anything about the rape because he knew I couldn't tell
anyone about that.

RUTH: What a disgusting person. Do you think he did it to others?

DAPHNE: He probably did. People just didn't talk about it back
then. No one gave girls the words to say it out loud. After
that I walked home. My legs shook and the wind threw me

53

around like I was made of paper. I remember that I shut my eyes against the wind and then I just kept them like that, walking blind into the gusts. That day was the last day I felt whole . . . It killed something in me. I lost my faith.

RUTH: In God?

DAPHNE: Oh no, I never believed in *that*. But in people.

RUTH: Do you think you would have become a murderer if that hadn't happened? Could you have found some way to move on, to put it all behind you, even if the people who hurt you never faced justice?

DAPHNE: Well, that's a heavy question. I'm not sure. It's not exactly a math equation. The preacher wasn't the first and he wasn't the last to hurt me like that. But there was something particularly evil about what he did. That rape killed the old me. And I guess I've been killing the preacher ever since.

That night at home I lay in bed, praying that my dad would stay passed out because I felt like I would lose my mind if another man tried to touch me. I was surrounded by my sleeping siblings, all mashed into bed with me like puppies, and usually their warm, squirming bodies (which smelled faintly of pee) would have lulled me to sleep, but I was wide awake. I stared up at the blackness and tried to breathe deeply, even as the room seemed to fill with sour air.

My whole life I had just accepted what I'd been given, even though it was usually shit in a cereal bowl. Now, though, I lay in bed with my good sweater stuffed between my legs, trying to dull the pain that came from deep inside me and seemed to echo through the room with every throb. Why did I deserve this? I had tried in school, I had helped the scrawny kids when the bigger kids picked on them, I dried my siblings' tears and made them laugh when it didn't seem like anything could make them smile. Why should I let people like my father and the preacher crush me? Why should I wait around for my own no-good husband to give me a shack of battered children?

It all felt so simple and clear. In that moment I knew that I had two choices: kill myself or leave. Because I couldn't watch the sun go down again in Lucan, Saskatchewan.

The next day, Sunday, I got up early, before any of my siblings started stirring, and crept out of the house. I didn't bother taking anything with me because everything I owned was shared among my siblings. I already felt guilty enough leaving them, knowing that so few would ever escape. I felt especially bad for the girls, but I knew there was nothing I could do. They were too small to take with me. Instead, I took one last look at my sisters and brothers, all crammed into bed, their little faces peeking out, and then I left. I wish I could tell you that I felt all kinds of dramatic emotions but, in that moment, I just felt numb. Some part of me wanted to curl up in a ditch and die, but my feet kept walking, and my eyes followed the road to town, and somehow, I made it there.

By the time I arrived, the preacher, along with most of the good townspeople in Lucan, was at church. My family didn't go very often, although sometimes I went by myself because I liked the music. I went to the preacher's house (nobody locked their doors in Lucan) and walked right in. The house was two stories and while it wouldn't be large by today's standards, it seemed incredibly grand to a girl from a one-room shack on the outskirts of town. The living room was cluttered with glass vases, porcelain ornaments, a real piano, and a thick, plush rug that sank beneath my weight. This whole house was like a museum of things that I'd never had.

I moved through the preacher's house, imagining sending his glass vases toppling like dominoes, swinging an axe into his writing desk, taking a crap on his velvet armchair. My whole body shook with the thought of all that carnage, of how it would feel to take all my rage and send it careening through his beautiful home. There was even a dark part of me that fantasized about waiting until he got home and using the same axe to reduce him to kindling. But instead, I clenched my fists and glanced at the grandfather clock. I had less than an hour before I needed to be on the train platform for the 10:15 to Moose Jaw. I could choose revenge, or I could choose freedom, but I could only have one.

I climbed the stairs carefully, having very little experience with staircases. Pictures were hung above the steps, portraits of dour-looking relations of the preacher and a few of a sad-eyed girl with wispy blonde hair.

First, I took all the money I could find in the house. It was enough for my train fare and a few weeks' room and board. I was still upstairs, prowling around, when I noticed an old wardrobe in the guest bedroom. I swung the doors open slowly and found it stuffed with women's things: dresses, coats, even a simple white wedding dress. I knew immediately that it was the dead wife's possessions. How lonely she must have felt, far from home, sharing a house with a monster.

I pulled out her old valise, my fingers fumbling as I hurried, and filled it with her clothes. I even changed out of my dirty dress and boots, stuffing them inside the bag, just in case I needed them someday, and put on a green dress and a pair of leather shoes with a small heel. The dress fit perfectly, and it felt like the dead woman was giving me her blessing. She had died in this house, surrounded by these things, but she wanted me to take them and live.

I walked out of the room with the suitcase and paused in front of the preacher's bedroom as if in a trance. I stuck my fingers inside of myself, aware that I was still bleeding from the attack. Then I reached out and smeared my hand down his bedspread.

Soon, I was on the train, tucked up against a window, seeing Lucan pass by for the last time. I clutched the valise and made a solemn promise to myself that no matter how bad things got, I would never go back.

RUTH (Voiceover): All was quiet for a second, after Daphne talked about running away from home. Her body language was closed off. Daphne was sitting with her arms folded and her lips pressed together, as if she couldn't risk any more words tumbling out. She looked furious and yet, somehow, defiant. I wasn't sure what to say after these revelations. They were terrible experiences, and yet this woman had done monstrous things, likely more than she'd confessed to. I didn't want to like her, didn't want to sympathize with her, but it was hard not to in these circumstances. Finally, I just kept going.

RUTH: Where did you go?

DAPHNE: Well, from Moose Jaw, I got a ticket to Regina, and then from there a ticket to Winnipeg. I wanted to be out of Saskatchewan and Winnipeg was one province over. I didn't want to spend too much money, but I wished I could have gone farther, somewhere I'd never see another farmer.

RUTH: Did you ever see your family again?

DAPHNE: No. I don't think about them.

RUTH: Come on, you must think about your sisters and brothers. Or your mother? Think of all the nieces and nephews, the great-nieces and great-nephews you have now. Some could even be in America. Don't you want to find them?

DAPHNE: No. I'm not a Cowell anymore; I haven't been since 1948.

RUTH: What if I did some research? Started contacting them? It would be great to get some background.

DAPHNE: Why are you so gung-ho to talk to people from my past? You've already landed a whale, what do you care about some small fry? I told you to drop it!

RUTH: Why does it bother you so much? Is it the idea of people talking about you? Or are you worried they might tell me something you don't want people to know?

DAPHNE: Me? Worried? Don't be ridiculous! I'm not hiding anything! I just don't want you going behind my back!

RUTH (Voiceover): Daphne seemed angry and I worried that she was hiding something, keeping a few skeletons tucked away from all of us. But I wondered if she was also scared to find out what happened to her family, how her siblings may have suffered after she left. As long as she didn't know for sure, she could pretend that everyone had just blinked out of existence the moment she walked away. It was an important skill for a budding serial killer, knowing how to erase people. It was a skill I'm sure many of us wished we had as well.

BurntheBookBurnerz:

So that preacher was a piece of shit. Here's his obit. He died back in 1972. I hope he's burning in hell.

StopDropAndTroll:

Well . . . IF you believe her. She could have just made it up for sympathy. 'Oh boohoo, feel sorry for me. I'm a viccctimmmm.'

BurntheBookBurnerz:

You seriously find it that hard to believe that a MAN RAPED SOMEONE?!?! Or what, is it because he's a preacher? Because yeah, NO religious dudes EVER rape anyone!?!

CapoteParty:

I think he's real. I don't think she would have made up a story where she was the victim.

BurntheBookBurnerz:

What did Ruth mean at the beginning of the episode when she said 'let's solve a mystery'? Daphne confessed. What's the mystery?

StopDropAndTroll:

She just said it to make it all dramatic. She's a clickbait writer, what do you expect?

ShockAndBlah:

Maybe the mystery is WHY she confessed. I LITERALLY can't wait for the next podcast!!! This is INSANE!!

TikTok Channel for HauteHistoire: "Hi everyone, my name is Alexis and this is HauteHistoire. What do you do when you have a passion for fashion, and a BA in History and Literature gathering dust? You start the TikTok channel for outfits inspired by the silver screen, your phone screen, and everything in between!

"We've done it all here, from 1930s gangster fashion à la Bonnie and Clyde to Y2K gangsta fashion from the music video for '03 Bonnie and Clyde! Today, I'm excited to announce we'll be doing a deep dive on Daphne St Clair and the new podcast sensation *The Murders of Daphne St Clair.* We'll be serving looks from every decade of Daphne's life! And don't worry, we won't be committing any fashion crimes, even if stripes are having a major moment! So, join us as we follow along with the podcast, exploring how style, like Daphne, can slay all day!

"So, for the first episode I thought we'd start with a cottagecore aesthetic to reflect this glamorous woman's not-so-glamorous beginnings. We're channeling Dorothy in old-timey Kansas, Alexis Bledel in *Tuck Everlasting,* and the girl in your high school who might have been in a cult. I've chosen an O Pioneers floral dress and toughened it up with some lace-up boots just in case I have to do any farmwork. Which would be surprising . . . since I live in Brooklyn. I'm pairing it with a Lack of Colors sunhat to keep out that harsh midwestern sun and, you know, the *dust* . . ."

Chapter Seven

It was a beautiful, breezy morning and Ruth was sitting in The Long Bean, her favorite coffee shop, trying to remedy another sleep-deprived night with caffeine. Ruth had always had problems sleeping. She used to think it was the shitty couches she slept on as a child, but lately it seemed like every time she went to sleep, she remembered the past. Her mom. Her dad. Her time in college. The moments in her life when everything seemed to be on a smooth trajectory, just before it all went wrong again.

Last night she had tossed and turned, running through Daphne's story of the preacher, trying to understand how a victim made the transition to victimizer, whether it was an incremental process or whether it happened all at once. It was just another dark thought that Ruth's antidepressants couldn't quite touch.

But in the light of day, even if glimpsed through bloodshot eyes, Ruth could see that good things were beginning. Within the first two days, Ruth's podcast had over ten thousand listens, which put her in the top 0.05 percent of podcasts. It was at the top of the true crime charts and was being recommended by everyone from *Entertainment Weekly* to your aunt's book club.

Her inbox was already filling with an endless stream of messages from prospective agents, managers, and book publishers. They all knew that Ruth had something unique: the scoop of the decade, and they all wanted a piece.

But interviewing Daphne was *hard work*. She went off-topic a lot, turned the questions back on Ruth, and constantly swerved memories that made her seem vulnerable. And yet there was something so relatable about Daphne. Ruth knew what it was like to be poor, and angry, and frustrated. To feel like the whole world was lined up against you. Sure, she'd never worn a flour sack as a top, but in seventh grade, Katie Weir had asked why Ruth wore the same three shirts to school, over and over and whether she owned any other clothes. Ruth needed to maintain a journalistic distance, but it was difficult to sit there day after day, hearing someone's life story, and not feel a connection.

"Ruth Robinson?" Ruth looked up and there, standing in front of her in a white tennis dress and designer sneakers was a blast from the past. And not a welcome one.

Erin Demarco. Ruth had gone to college with her. For four years they had existed in constant proximity to each other: in the dorm, in journalism classes, at the college paper, without ever enjoying each other's company. They had friends in common, close friends in fact, but Erin and Ruth were just too different. Erin had a dermatologist on speed dial whereas Ruth had bought a case of facewash at a fire sale. After college, Erin had parlayed the generational wealth that she had always flaunted into a string of internships in New York, subsidized by her parents and then onwards to a job at *Vanity Fair*.

It didn't help that Erin was also kind of a bitch.

"That's me," Ruth said, making a little salute (*Why, God, why did she do that?*) and smiling.

"God, it's been so long, but you look the same! Well, same clothes anyways! You probably couldn't pass for twenty-one anymore!" Erin said with a laugh, smoothing her glossy walnut hair.

"Are you living in Florida again?" Ruth asked, determined to move this conversation along.

"Just home for a break. I've been so busy recently. The Hollywood Issue's coming out soon . . ." Erin trailed off. She looked at Ruth expectantly, as if Ruth was going to badger her for some gossipy details.

Ruth refused to take the bait. "Hollywood Issue of what?"

"*Vanity Fair*! And of course, then we need to think about Oscars season and the after-party . . . so much to do! And what are you doing with your life? Still delivering packages for Amazon?" Erin asked.

Ruth rolled her eyes. She hadn't done that in years. The noble profession of writing articles about plastic surgery fails had replaced delivery driving.

"I'm doing a podcast right now. *The Murders of Daphne St Clair*? I'm interviewing Daphne, getting her life story down and sharing detailed confessions about her crimes."

"Oh, I hadn't heard of it," Erin said, but her lack of eye contact told a different story. Erin pasted a sappy, concerned look on her face. "I'm surprised you, of all people, would be doing true crime? Isn't that uncomfortable for you?"

"Is having the number-one true crime podcast in the country uncomfortable for me? Yeah, I think somehow, I'll manage," Ruth scoffed, pointedly ignoring Erin's little digs.

"Yes, well, I suppose it's just a podcast," Erin said, her delicate pout emphasizing the 'just.' Erin seemed to consider saying something more before thinking better of it.

"One of the fastest growing forms of media. But uh, how's the magazine industry doing?" Ruth asked, fully aware that they were swiftly moving out of passive-aggressive territory and into pure aggression.

"Well, I should go but good luck with the whole podcast thing. I think it's a bit crass to romanticize a serial killer but if you don't have a problem with that, kudos!"

"Well, actually—" Ruth began but she was already out the door. She might not have had the last word, but Ruth had seen Erin's flinch of recognition at the name of the podcast. And there was nothing more satisfying than the knowledge that Erin Demarco was jealous of her.

And she hadn't seen anything yet.

Chapter Eight

Ruth's phone rang as she was parking her car at Coconut Grove. It wasn't a number she recognized but she answered, in case it might be someone calling her about Daphne.

"Hi, Ruth, it's Officer Rankin. I don't know if you remember me . . . It's been a while."

"Yes, I remember you," Ruth said, gripping her steering wheel. She had already rolled her windows up and so she sat in the stuffy car, feeling the heat rising around her, as if she were a lobster in water slowly being brought to a boil.

"You're probably surprised to hear from me," he said with a chuckle, as if the idea of Ruth being caught off guard made him smile.

"Uh, yes, I am," Ruth said curtly. In fact, she'd been hoping to never hear from Officer Rankin again. Or any of the Palm Haven police, really.

"Well, the thing is, Ruth, this podcast you're doing . . . it's a problem. It's a problem for the Montgomerys and it's a problem for the police. And well, let's just say I represent both those interests. So, I would suggest you leave this alone. This is an active investigation. We still don't know why she's confessed to all this or even that she's telling the truth about the other murders. You could end up subpoenaed; some might even see you as obstructing justice. We really don't know how a DA or a judge would see it. They might just throw the book at you, make an example to all the other influencers and wannabe journalists making life difficult."

"Making life difficult for the Montgomerys?" Ruth asked.

"For all of us, Ruth," he said softly, a threat held back between his teeth. Ruth had always wondered how close the Montgomerys were to Officer Rankin, how much influence they had on the cases he tried to pursue, the people he wanted to investigate. This conversation made it a lot clearer.

Ruth threw the car door open and took a deep breath, trying to stay calm, even as a million profanities began to form on her lips.

"I'm not interfering with the investigation. And the First Amendment protects the press. Besides, this podcast could be helpful. I've got detailed recordings of Daphne confessing to crimes," Ruth responded.

Rankin grunted. "You're lecturing *me* about the law? I'm a police officer, Ruth. I think I know a bit more about the law than you do. And when motivated enough, we can usually find some kind of infraction . . ."

"Is that a threat?" Ruth asked, feeling a spike of fury travel through her. They thought she was still some naïve girl in her twenties that they could push around. But they didn't understand. It was 2022 and no one trusted cops anymore.

"Of course not, the police don't threaten anyone, especially not journalists. Consider it a suggestion. This podcast . . . well, it could cause a lot of problems for you," he said, his voice smooth and satisfied, as if he understood exactly who held the power here.

"Great, well, thanks for the feedback," Ruth muttered. She hung up and stormed into Coconut Grove, barely waiting for the attendant to escort her. She slammed her feet down with considerable force on the carpeted floor, trying to burn off the lingering dread that phone call had given her.

"Someone kill your cat?" Daphne asked, shuffling over with her walker to sit in her armchair.

"I don't have a cat," Ruth grumbled, throwing herself down on the seat across from her.

"And yet you seem like you should. So, what's wrong?" Daphne asked.

"I just had a phone call from the Palm Haven police, essentially threatening me not to do the podcast. The cops around here are just ignorant, incompetent bullies!" Ruth fumed, clenching and unclenching her fists. She took a deep breath, reminding herself that she was a journalist, a professional, and she wanted Daphne to see her calm and collected.

"Yeah, I can't say I'm a big fan of the thin blue line myself," Daphne said, still studying her. Ruth didn't like being scrutinized by her; Daphne was too good at reading people.

Ruth took a deep breath. The conversation with Officer Rankin had provoked her, but she knew she needed to calm down and focus on the interview. The best way to flip the proverbial bird to thugs like Officer Rankin was to put out a banger of a second episode.

"Obviously we're still doing the podcast. So, tell me about

your first murder," Ruth said. After she'd cracked the whip last time, Daphne seemed to be behaving much better. Her first episode had been a complete success and Ruth had begun to feel hopeful that she might just get what she'd come for, ideally while netting a bit of cash along the way.

"Well, you never forget your first," Daphne responded with a laugh. Ruth resisted the urge to roll her eyes. Instead, she just sat silently until Daphne continued, like a teacher waiting for the class clown to settle down.

"He was a . . . boyfriend. Seems kind of funny to call a man in his thirties a boy, but he was my first boyfriend. I had only been in Winnipeg a few weeks when I met him."

"So, you were sixteen. Do you still think about him?"

"No, he's dead," Daphne said with a shrug. "Once they're dead, you can just . . . forget them." Ruth glanced away so Daphne wouldn't see her grimace. It was such a heartless thing to say, especially as family members of Daphne's victims might be listening. But then again, it was a fantastic quote for the podcast. It was a strange experience, to be sitting here, talking with Daphne while simultaneously editing it all in her head, polishing it for her imaginary audience.

"But people won't forget you after you're dead, not now."

"Yeah, that's the point," Daphne said. "Ninety-nine percent of the people alive today don't want to be forgotten, but almost all of them will be. Let's face it, you wouldn't give a shit about Ted, a guy who died in another country over seventy years ago, if it weren't for me. That's gotta count for something."

Count with who? Ruth wondered.

EPISODE TWO: 1948–1952

RUTH: What were your first impressions of Winnipeg?

DAPHNE: Well, I'd never been in a real city. I knew so little about the world that I couldn't think too much about it or I would have started to panic. Instead, I just had to plunge in, like a cow barreling through an old fence. I *needed* my life to get better.

RUTH: What was better to you?

DAPHNE: Well, at that time, I think I wanted to be safe. I wanted a job, the freedom to make my own choices, and maybe a little excitement. I found a room in a boardinghouse pretty quickly. My room was a single bed crammed into the old larder.

RUTH: What's a larder?

DAPHNE: Christ, I thought you had a college degree! You must have gone to one of those fake colleges they advertise on TV. It's a room where you store food, like a pantry but colder. As I was saying, I liked the house because people were always moving in and out, so I knew no one would pay attention to me. But the problem was, I couldn't find a job. The town was full of former farmers who'd watched their dreams dry up and blow away in the Depression, and former soldiers who watched their squadrons get torn up and blown away in the war, and all of them wanted jobs. And every day I went without work was another day I ate my money. Soon, I only had enough for one more week at the boardinghouse and I was scared.

RUTH: Scared of going home?

DAPHNE: Oh, I knew I'd never go back to Lucan. I would have jumped in front of a train before I did that. But just scared of being on the street, of maybe even having to sell my body for money, when I was already so sick of men. It's funny, all these years later, I can still remember how terrified I was. I'd just lie in bed at night, paralyzed by the weight of it all. And that's when I met Ted, at my lowest point. But that's always when you meet men like Ted—when life has beaten the fight outta you . . .

That last desperate week was one of the worst times of my life. I walked all day, looking for work around the city, my whole body coursing with anxiety. My feet hurt from the dead wife's shoes, but I couldn't wear my old boots because then everyone would know exactly what I was. Most of them guessed anyways. I walked into a bakery and the woman behind the counter took one look at me, sunburnt and nervous, in an outfit that didn't belong to me, and told me they didn't hire trash. I tried every shop and restaurant I could find, but none of them had a job for a teenage girl with no schooling and no work experience other than dirt farming.

A shop owner pointed at the veterans lining up outside, hoping someone would give them a day job as a laborer, and asked me what made me think I was better than them. I hung my head and left, even though I really wanted to ask him what made him think he was better than me, even if all I had was a suitcase full of stolen clothes that I was already starting to sell off to other women in the boardinghouse.

I had moved to Winnipeg with something new—hope—and

having it taken away so quickly hurt worse than never having it. I couldn't eat. My mouth was full of a sour, dry taste, and my stomach churned constantly. I felt like the whole world was about to end. All I could hear was a loud, ticking clock, drowning out the rhythm of my own heartbeat.

"What's a pretty little thing like you crying for?" A voice, low and warm. I was sitting on the back steps again, furiously wiping away loose tears, scraping my face with my red and bony hands. I had two days left at the boardinghouse before my money ran out.

"I'm not crying," I mumbled, glancing up. A man was standing in front of me in a crisp white shirt and sharply creased trousers. He looked like he was in his early thirties but it was hard to tell; his blond hair and rosy cheeks made him look younger. He was smiling at me and that little bit of kindness after my desperate weeks as a stranger in Winnipeg made me want to cry harder.

"Don't lie, I can always tell when a pretty gal is lying," he said, his eyes twinkling. He sat down on the steps next to me, but not so close that our legs touched. He wasn't bad-looking. He was trim and had clear blue eyes like two windows opening out on the sky. But his large ears, which stuck out from his head so far that his fedora seemed to rest on them, stopped him from being truly handsome.

"I can't find a job," I admitted, trying not to let my voice waver. "I moved here by myself and I'm almost out of money, and I've tried everywhere." My voice broke and the tears bubbled up again under my hands.

"Darling, there's no shame in it. Jobs are tough to find in

this town. Look, you seem like a nice girl. Let me guess, you probably grew up in a small town, right? Why don't you just go back? City life ain't for everyone."

"No," I said firmly. "I can't go back." This brought on more tears, and I expected him to get up and leave, filing me away as just another lost cause, blown in from the prairies and destined for the streets.

But he stayed sitting next to me. I felt him press a handker-chief into my palm and I clutched it to my face, my whole body shaking with the effort to hold back the sobs.

"Aw, look, I shouldn't do this, but I can't stand to see a young girl in trouble. I rent out apartments in the North End of town. I've got a place you can stay. It's nothing fancy, just one room with a shared bathroom at the end of the hall, but it's yours. You could do housekeeping in my properties instead of rent."

"Really?" I asked quietly, not quite believing what he was saying.

"Sure," he said, writing an address down on the back of a matchbook. "Come by tomorrow. I'm Ted by the way."

"I'm . . . Rose," I said, giving him the name I'd chosen for myself when I got to Winnipeg. I felt the door to my old life shut behind me, the last shreds of Loretta Cowell falling away. But what lay ahead, I didn't know.

HauteHistoire: "Hi, guys, welcome to my TikTok series inspired by Daphne St Clair and the podcast *The Murders of Daphne St Clair*. I was sort of hoping things would get a bit more glamorous this episode. But well . . . it didn't. But rest assured, I know from the news that Daphne does become wealthy at some point in her life, so we'll have that to look forward to . . . But anyways, here we are. So fashion-wise, the Forties were . . . a bit shit. Everyone was too busy fighting wars and rationing fabric to have any fun. But there were a lot of skirt suits back then, so I've gone for a white Miu Miu one with strong shoulders and paired it with a cropped basketball top to keep it modern. This is kind of an office look. Not that Daphne worked in an office . . . but it's definitely the kind of look that might inspire a young schemer to get to the top, no matter the consequences. Look, guys, I'm just really hoping she gets rich soon."

The next day I went down to the North End, past the train yards and Ted showed me around the apartment. It was one room with a tidy little kitchen and a bed under a window overlooking a street bustling with all the immigrants to the city. I smiled. My own room. I had grown up in a one-room shack I had to share with my whole family, and now I got the luxury of my own room?

I was probably in that apartment twenty minutes before we had sex, barely enough time for my eyes to adjust.

I wasn't an idiot. I knew that I would have to sleep with Ted. The whole city was awash with new arrivals, but Ted had decided to help the young, beautiful girl who was in no position to say no. This apartment—this clean, quiet place—rippled with hidden strings.

But I figured that sleeping with one guy was preferable

to becoming a prostitute, and I was running out of options. I didn't feel good about it, of course. In fact, the thought of sleeping with Ted disgusted me. I had wanted to leave all that shameful stuff back in Lucan, back with Loretta Cowell, the dirty daughter of the town drunk. The kind of girl who needed to be kept away from the other girls so she wouldn't contaminate them with her hard-earned knowledge about the nasty side of life.

But growing up in Lucan in the Depression had taught me something else. I had seen person after person—kind, decent people—lose their farms because they didn't have enough crops to sell. It didn't matter how good you were, how much you had helped other people in the past, if you couldn't pay the bank, your family was homeless and you were ruined. In the Hard Times, we all became what we could sell. All those finer qualities—charity, empathy, chastity—could come later, when we could make choices again.

In the moment when I decided to sleep with Ted, I tried to be optimistic. Maybe this was the beginning of a grand romance. Maybe the sex would be so enticing that I wouldn't even recognize it as the same thing that had only ever been forced on me. I wanted to use sex to erase the past, to leave my slate blank. It was a tall order for something farm animals did.

"I'm so grateful, Ted," I said, leaning against the wall. He stroked my cheek and smiled.

"Don't worry, darling, you're safe now." He leaned over and softly kissed my mouth. It was a warm moment, and I found myself thinking that this really did seem different, that perhaps we were going to make love.

That hope was deflated as soon as Ted launched into a pattern of moves, clearly none of which he'd ever consulted a girl on. He kneaded my breasts like bread dough and stuck a slim finger inside of me and wiggled it around. He treated foreplay like the introduction to a novel, something he could skim through with no real need to pay attention, before bending me over the table and pumping away. For a moment, I felt a flash of fear, as if I was being suffocated and I had to take deep, shuddering breaths and remind myself that I wasn't back in Lucan.

Ted noticed my overwhelmed reaction but assumed I was just overcome by the power of Ted and was encouraged to saw away even faster. I kept breathing until finally, the panic subsided and all that was left was boredom. I stared at the counter and mentally counted numbers—One Mississippi, Two Mississippi—hoping he'd climax soon. It took until 179.

"Thanks for that. You're a great gal," Ted said, after he straightened up his clothes.

"You too," I said, relieved that I had paid my bill.

I moved in that day. Of course, I would take the room and job. In 1948, if the devil himself was offering me a cozy little place in hell, I would have taken it. And I did.

Chapter Nine

DAPHNE: At first everything seemed tolerable. I woke up every morning and went out to clean. I liked walking through the city, liked how my neighborhood in the North End was full of people from around the world. It was working class but there was a real energy there—lots of communists.

RUTH: That's interesting. Would you say you're political? I know you have a politician as a son-in-law.

DAPHNE: No, I'm not political. Hell, coming out as either a Republican or a Democrat might be the only way I could get people to hate me more. And I don't know much about my son-in-law's work, but I will say that I would never vote for a man who likes his socks ironed and his wife silent.

RUTH: Tell me about your work.

DAPHNE: Well, it was cleaning, what's to say? I realized pretty quick that most of the places I cleaned didn't belong to Ted, that he was charging these people for my services. But I was excited to have my own place. If Ted wasn't visiting, I'd spend my evenings curled up in bed with a library book. It had been years since I'd been in school but once I got to Winnipeg I resolved to become well-read. So, at first I was somewhat content.

RUTH: But you were dependent on a man again: first your father and now Ted. You'd been hoping for a paying job and independence.

DAPHNE: Well, we all *hope* for things. What about you? You went to college right? When you graduated, what job were you hoping for?

RUTH: Journalist at *Slate Magazine.* Or *The Huffington Post.*

DAPHNE: Whatever those are. And what did you get?

RUTH: Amazon delivery driver . . . and an unpaid internship at *Florida Horoscope Magazine.* But then the magazine went under a couple weeks after I started.

DAPHNE: They didn't see that one coming, huh? But there you go. Sure, my job was tiring, and I had to give Ted a meal and a feel every few days, but at first everything felt manageable.

I wasn't surprised the first time Ted hit me. He was mad that a tenant had moved out in the dead of night to avoid paying rent. Then he began lecturing me on how I wasn't grateful enough, how I didn't understand how he'd saved me. The similarity between this drunken idiot and my father made me woozy and I made the mistake of turning away from Ted and staring out the window at the cold yellow night, trying to reassure myself that I wasn't back in Saskatchewan. Ted, enraged that I had stopped listening to his sermon on the mount, shoved me against the window, smashing my head against the frame.

In that moment, I had the strangest reaction. It was as if I'd been waiting for this for weeks. My whole body was already tense in anticipation. When he finally hit me, I thought: 'Ah. Yes. There it is.' I felt a kind of grim relief that the universe was what I thought it was, that men didn't just want to fuck me, they also wanted to hurt me.

After he finally stormed out, I crawled into bed and pulled the blanket up to my nose. I felt grateful to be alone. But I knew he would be back.

DAPHNE: If Lucan was the frying pan then Ted was the fire. It was funny. I'd left to find freedom and all I'd found was a new kind of cage.

RUTH: Yeah, it seems like it. Did you marry Ted?

DAPHNE: No, thank God. He was already married, with a wife and kids. So, I wasn't even a battered wife, I was a battered mistress! I'm sure he beat her too, someone that hot on abuse doesn't just do it as a part-time thing.

RUTH: Can I ask how you survived it all? How you coped with so much hardship?

DAPHNE: The words, the beatings, I just tried to block it all out. Over the years, I've had so many men try to convince me that I'm worthless. You either have to believe them completely or not at all. Even at that age, I was starting to realize that none of the men who abused me were prime examples of the human race. Ruth, a girl learns how men should treat her from her daddy. What's your dad like?

RUTH: Oh, I . . . didn't have one growing up.

DAPHNE: Not at all?

RUTH: Not really. My father was older and didn't want anything serious. He already had kids and didn't want any more. When I was a kid, my mom wouldn't even talk about him. He did contact me as an adult though.

DAPHNE: Was he married? You know, when your mom was dating him?

RUTH: I'd prefer not to discuss this.

DAPHNE: Ah, so he was married! Well, these things happen. But a bad father teaches you to look for bad men. And every lesson I got from my dad sent me straight to Ted.

RUTH: But you were working, right?

DAPHNE: Yeah, but I was never paid a dime; it was all for my room and board. Which amounted to a room and the odd bag of groceries when Ted was feeling generous.

RUTH: Did you ever think about getting another job?

DAPHNE: Yeah, I thought about it. I knew I needed money to get out from under Ted. But I was just so bone-tired. I grew up on a farm; I can work. But there's being tired in your body, and then there's being tired in your soul. In Winnipeg, I once saw a plane with a faulty engine, sputtering and stalling, skimming over treetops, struggling to get altitude. And that's what I felt like. There was no freedom, no money. There was just Ted. Ted Today, Ted Tomorrow, Ted Forever. At that time, all I could feel was tired and bitter.

RUTH: Bitter is an interesting word. Would you say you're a bitter person?

DAPHNE: Sure, isn't it obvious? And I would say, Ruth, it takes one to know one. My whole life, I've had a sour taste in my mouth. It started when I was a kid and I lived through all those hungry nights and violent mornings. I've never really been happy, even when things were going my way.

RUTH: But you're rich now. You're sitting in a luxury retirement home, decked out in designer clothes. What could you be bitter about?

DAPHNE: Getting old. Becoming invisible. Losing my health and mobility.

RUTH: Sure, but you're in your nineties. Some people out there lose their health and mobility much younger, and they don't have attendants and cushy places to take care of them.

DAPHNE: What do you want me to say? Life's a bitch. I've never really been happy, not for very long. Turns out serial killers aren't the most well-adjusted lot . . .

ShockAndBlah:

What other crimes do we think Daphne committed? I have a theory that she might have committed the Black Dahlia Murder. Because when you look at old pictures of Daphne, she had a really similar look to Elizabeth Short. And maybe Daphne didn't like that.

BurntheBookBurnerz:

WTF? The Black Dahlia was killed in 1947 when Daphne was fifteen!!! You really think some dirt-poor farmer's daughter traveled across the country to play Jack the Ripper? Besides Daphne kills men. I don't get it. No matter the killer, someone always brings up the Black Dahlia. It's like true crime's answer to Godwin's law.

ShockAndBlah:

That's what a Nazi would say lollll.

CapoteParty:

What about Gabrielle Hanks? That one seems like a possible match.

StopDropAndTroll:

Wrong gender again, you noob.

PreyAllDay:

THE TYLENOL MURDERS! That's the one we should be looking into!! We know Daphne has poisoned people—that's how she killed Warren Ackerman! They happened in 1982 so she was fifty years old. And it got a ton of publicity and it's obvious that Daphne likes attention! And honestly, old people LOVE Tylenol. My meemaw treats it like a food group!

CapoteParty:

Do we even know if Daphne was in Chicago in 1982?

PreyAllDay:

We DON'T know that she WASN'T there!!

ShockAndBlah:

Ok well if that's all the proof you need then I'm putting Black Dahlia back on the table!

StopDropAndTroll:

[This comment has been removed by a moderator.]

BurntheBookBurnerz:

What about that Miami New Year's Party in the 2000s? The one where all those people died? I think *True Crime Cantina* did an episode on it?

ShockAndBlah:

Now THAT I could get behind. Although we don't really know for sure if they were poisoned, right? Weren't some of the theories things like expired food and faulty air conditioners? My grandma ended up unconscious in a hospital after eating dairy in Mexico. Stuff like that can happen . . .

CapoteParty:

It does seem out of character, doesn't it? Daphne was successful for so long because no one even knew any crimes had been committed. Something big and splashy like this doesn't really fit.

StopDropAndTroll:

I heard it was illegal immigrants. That's why they never figured it out. They didn't know who was really at the party.

BurntheBookBurnerz:

Oh yeah, because Americans couldn't possibly kill anyone?? RIGHT??

ShockAndBlah:

I still think it was dairy.

Chapter Ten

One night, Ted came over. He was plastered, drunker than I'd ever seen him. His eyes were rolling around inside his face like he was on a carnival ride. But he was happy because he had won big gambling, bigger than he'd ever won before.

"Maybe, if you ask me real nice, I'll take you to dinner tomorrow," Ted said, trying to light a cigarette. It took him four tries to find his mouth.

"That'd be nice," I said woodenly, not caring if we went to dinner. My treats were the nights he didn't come over. When he was here, he blotted out my entire existence, like a shadow over the sun.

"Ah, to hell with you," he slurred, flicking his cigarette at me. "Why would I take such an ungrateful bitch out to dinner?"

"I'm not ungrateful," I muttered, stooping down to pick up the cigarette that lay smoldering on the floor. My floor.

"You are! Nothing I do for you is ever good enough!" he snapped, slamming his hand down on the table.

I grew still. I realized that he was in a dangerous mood, that everything was balanced on a knife point. If I did the wrong thing, then it all would come crashing down. So, I did nothing.

84

Sometimes I wished I had that kind of power, a man's power, to change the weather in the house just with my mood.

"Oh? Now you're too good to even answer me?" Before I knew it, he was out of his seat. He wrapped his fist in my hair and pulled hard. "Don't forget, I saved your ass. If it weren't for me, you'd be dead in a gutter by now!"

"I know, thank you so much, Ted," I said in a soothing voice, even though it felt like my scalp was lifting off my skull. "Look, it's been a big day for you. Why don't you go home, sleep it off, and tomorrow we'll celebrate properly!" I opened the door gently, hoping that he'd stagger home, that I'd make it through another night.

But instead, Ted made a noise of pure, wordless rage and lunged at me, wrapping his hands around my neck. He was squeezing with all of his strength, collapsing my throat as easily as if he were crumpling paper. My eyes fluttered. I was going to die in this apartment, having wasted my short, shitty life. Just another girl that a man decided to kill.

In a final act of desperation, I raised one leg and kneed him in the balls. By that point I was seeing white holes in my vision, like snow covering up a cabin's window. But my knee connected, there was a moan, and I felt his hands fall from my neck.

I took rapid breaths, trying to clear my vision. Ted had staggered onto the landing, just outside my open door. He was doubled up, clutching himself. For a second, I thought the moment had passed, that we could call it a night, shocked at how far this whole thing had gotten.

"You fucking bitch!" he snarled, straightening up. Ted's hands were already raised, set on throttling me, when I kicked

him in the stomach. He tilted backwards, his arms swinging like a dancer in a music hall, and then he fell down the stairs, going head over heels until I couldn't see him anymore.

I stood at the top, trying to hear anything over the sound of my own wheezing breath. Silence. I waited longer, my hand hovering on the doorknob in case he came running up the stairs and I needed to barricade myself in the apartment. But then, finally, I got up the courage to descend into the darkness.

He was lying on the ground, his neck bent at an unnatural angle. I barely recognized him. His face was minced meat from the trip down the stairs and there was a big gash on the side of his head.

I knew he was dead the moment I saw him. I stood there, amazed at how a whole life could be snuffed out in a flash. My body was tingling and I felt strangely excited, like I was sitting front row at a magic show and had been dazzled by a trick.

I leaned down and pulled his wallet out, carefully extracting his gambling winnings, leaving a little cash behind so he didn't look like he'd been robbed. The places where Ted gambled were seedy, back-alley spots, the kinds of places that didn't exist by day. No one would ever know that he'd won big.

I hurried upstairs and grabbed the few things I owned, hiding my bag under my coat. I needed to get out of there as quickly as possible, just in case the neighbors had heard us fighting. People kept their heads down in this neighborhood and I doubted anyone would alert the police, but if the cops came knocking, someone might tell them about Ted's girl upstairs.

I paused for one last, tender glance at Ted's body. Seeing him lying there made me feel brave. And then I stepped over his body and out into the night. I needed to get to the station and get a ticket on the next train going anywhere big. It didn't really matter where I started, I already knew where I was going.

Theft had gotten me to Winnipeg. Murder was going to take me to New York City.

"And that was my first murder," Daphne said. "That was when I learned I was capable of killing someone."

"But it was self-defense. So, how can you really say that's murder?" Ruth asked, trying to keep the irritation out of her voice. This death didn't tell her anything about Daphne, about what she was capable of. This wasn't the kind of murder she was hoping to find.

Daphne was quiet for a moment. She was scrutinizing Ruth's face with cold, flat eyes. *She's trying to decide how much truth to give me*, Ruth thought.

"It was murder because of how I felt after I did it. I didn't feel regret. I felt . . . calm. Like I had finally taken control."

There was a long silence, punctuated finally by Daphne laughing, an angry little snort of a laugh.

"These early episodes are making for grim listening. I wish we didn't have to go through this laundry list of men who treated me like shit. If I could, I'd just forget the first twenty years or so of my life." She sighed. "I almost feel embarrassed about how much crap I took."

"You shouldn't be," Ruth said. "You didn't have a choice." She wondered if that was what murder represented for Daphne: a choice.

"Well, there you go, now you know how I went from pastoral

farm girl to cosmopolitan murderer," Daphne said, slapping her bony hands against her knees to punctuate her sentence. Ruth nodded. She'd already noticed that Daphne spoke in a strange mixture of colloquialisms, profanity, and five-dollar vocabulary words (occasionally mispronounced as if she'd only seen them in text), the voice of a very well-read person with little formal education.

"Almost a rags-to-riches story," Ruth said, smiling so Daphne knew it was a joke. Should she be joking with Daphne? It might get Daphne to trust her, to believe that she was on her side.

Daphne snorted. "More like hick to homicide."

ShockAndBlah:

That's not murder. He was going to kill her if she didn't kill him!

PreyAllDay:

When are the real murders gonna start? I hate those podcasts that take twelve episodes to cover one freaking murder!!! You can do a murder in thirty minutes and move on!

ShockAndBlah:

Tough day?

StopDropAndTroll:

This is only if you BELIEVE her! SHE's the one saying he was abusive. SHE's the one saying they were fighting that night! Maybe she just pushed him down the stairs to steal his money!!!

PreyAllDay:

But if you think she's lying about everything why bother listening???

StopDropAndTroll:

Becuz I wanna see her get nailed to the wall.

BurntheBookBurnerz:

Fucking incel.

PreyAllDay:

Do we think Daphne confessed just to become famous?

ShockAndBlah:

Well if she did . . . it's working!

StopDropAndTroll:

Only idiots want to become famous.

BurntheBookBurnerz:

Honestly, this isn't the kind of fame I would ever want. But then again, I didn't spend my life murdering people either so I don't really know what's going on inside her head. I'm sure Ruth will figure it out eventually.

It was early evening and Ruth was home, picking at her girl dinner of crackers and grapes while she stared at Jenn's Instagram, salivating over the sight of her pomegranate stew and almond rice. They were the same age, but Jenn had been a real adult, a 'freezing her eggs for future babies, going to the farmer's market, writing a schedule' person, whereas the only thing Ruth ever froze was burritos.

After dinner, Ruth popped down to the apartment mailboxes. Some part of her was hoping she might find a letter for Jenn that would give her an excuse to contact her, even though she knew that was pathetic.

Instead, she found a manila envelope with her name on it. Ruth frowned and began tearing it open as she walked up the steps to the apartment. The letter read:

```
Dear Ruth Robinson,
    I have become aware of a new project you've
undertaken, a true crime podcast about a local
crime story, and have shared this information
with the rest of the family and our lawyers.
I would urge you to think carefully about
continuing such a harmful podcast that paints
our community in a bad light. Palm Haven is a
warm, friendly place and we want investors and
tourists to focus on its positive aspects.
    I would also warn you that this podcast
should contain no reference to the Montgomery
family, the Sunshine Development Group or any of
its trustees. Any comments that bring us into
```

```
disrepute will be treated as slander and pursued
at the highest legal level. Please remember
that as a tenant of a Sunshine Development
Group property, you should also refrain from any
activities that damage our business interests.
    Best,
    Lucy Montgomery
```

Ruth wadded up the letter and threw it in the trash in a fit of anger. Lucy Montgomery was chief realtor for the Sunshine buildings and personally handled the luxury sales for the company. Ruth always had the sense that she had a lot of influence in the family as well as the company (although at forty-seven, Lucy wasn't exactly a girlboss). When Ruth had spent time with the Montgomerys, she had noticed that everyone kowtowed to Lucy, even her aunts and uncles. Only her father seemed capable of keeping Lucy in line, as if he'd developed an immunity to her power games. And now Lucy had set her sights on Ruth and her exciting new podcast.

Lucy had gotten everything in life. It was time Ruth claimed her share.

Chapter Eleven

RUTH (Voiceover): Lisa Diaz runs an Etsy shop dedicated to female serial killer merchandise.

RUTH: So, Lisa, I see you're wearing a Daphne T-shirt today. For the listeners, there's a sketch of Daphne smiling with 'Homewrecker' written under it.

LISA: Yeah, you like it?

RUTH: It's . . . interesting. Have you had a lot of sales in your Etsy shop?

LISA: Sure, Daphne merch is way outselling Aileen Wuornos products, my usual top earner. Gotta love those Florida gals!

RUTH: What's been your biggest seller?

LISA: Probably the Daphne wine glasses. It's a range of big wine glasses with slogans and pictures of her. There seems to be a huge overlap between people who love true crime and people who love wine. I've never quite figured out why . . . But we also have these great aprons that say: 'Daphne's Killer Cooking!'

RUTH: How do you respond to critics who might say you're glorifying these murderers?

LISA: Well, go home and look at the 'serial killer merch' section of Etsy. This is big business. People want to buy these things and who are we to tell them it's wrong? It's not illegal and it's not hurting anybody.

RUTH: Why do you think the public is so fascinated with Daphne?

LISA: I think everyone's wondering the same thing. Why would a woman who'd gotten away with murder for decades call up one day and confess? She could have taken it to her grave, which, let's be honest, isn't far away! Has she told you why yet?

RUTH: She says she wanted to make something happen, that she was bored. And that she wanted everyone to know that she'd got away with murder so many times.

LISA: That's all she said? I don't know, I bet there's more to the story. But whatever the reason, Daphne St Clair is good for business! And to top it off, she was a hottie when she was younger, so the merch is a bit more photogenic. Nobody *really* wants a T-shirt with Nannie Doss or Rose West on it. I learned that the hard way after losing big on a line of Rose West crop tops.

RUTH: Is it mostly women buying your merch?

LISA: I think so. Maybe, in a funny way, they find it empowering. We focus so much on female victims that it's refreshing to hear a story of a female serial killer. And maybe this is a way for women to say: don't assume you can take advantage of me. If you look at the Etsy shops that sell male-serial-killer-themed stuff, they're far more popular. I'm just saying, before you buy a Ted Bundy T-shirt or a John Wayne Gacy poster, think about a Myra Hindley sweatshirt or a Belle Gunness coaster. I'll send you a Daphne wine glass. You'll love it.

RUTH: Might be an interesting choice for a party but I could pass it on to Daphne. She'd love a big wine glass with her face on it.

LISA: Bit of a narcissist?

RUTH: You said it, not me.

After quite a lot of badgering, Daphne's daughter Diane finally set a date for Ruth to interview her. Ruth drove down the gleaming streets of Diane's gated community, squinting at the massive McMansions, looking for the right address.

The houses were a confusing mix of styles. She'd driven by a black and white Tudor home with ivy that sat next to a plantation-style home with great columns stretching up to the sky and then by a home that seemed to have no recognizable architectural style at all unless "Big" counted. Being rich felt like another country to her. Ruth slumped in her seat. She wondered if any of the Montgomerys lived in this gated community. Not Lucy, of course—Ruth knew exactly which luxury building Lucy lived in.

Ruth was still reeling from the letter the Montgomerys had sent her, and she'd been up past midnight reading law blogs about journalistic rights. Not that it would be much use if the Montgomerys decided to go after her. She didn't have the money to fight them in court and she suspected that real estate developers might have some shady people on speed dial, people who found extrajudicial ways to get their point across.

The threat of eviction also weighed heavily on her mind. When Ruth was seven years old, they had been kicked out of a rental and ended up at a pay-by-the-week motel, where she could always hear the cars driving by and smell their exhaust fumes. Ruth would walk to school, terrified that one of her classmates would find out where she was living. Her situation had felt so alien and embarrassing even though every motel room housed a different family crammed in with their worldly possessions.

They'd been there for weeks, until finally her mom had broken down and called Ruth's father for help, something she did only twice in Ruth's childhood. Louise never talked about her father, never even told her daughter his name. Ruth had only found out who he was in her late twenties, when he'd reached out to her. But she still remembered seeing him for the first time. He pulled up in a Lexus and handed her mom an envelope of cash. She remembered seeing the suntanned arm, the Sunshine Development parking tag, the shiny gold Rolex on his wrist. He had barely glanced at little Ruth, sitting on a curb nearby, alone and afraid, before driving away. Ruth had learned from a very young age that she had very little control in life; the constant threat of eviction and poverty had taught her that.

Daphne had grown up in a similar way but seemed to have come to a very different conclusion. It was wrong, of course, but Ruth couldn't help thinking that maybe anything was better than a perpetual sense of powerlessness.

"Hello," Diane said stiffly, as she opened the door. "Please come inside." She was wearing a fuchsia silk dress and was covered in gold jewelry. Ruth was surprised she could still stand upright with that much metal strapped to her.

Her heels echoed on the marble floor as Ruth shuffled behind her, her cheap loafers already beginning to chafe her heels as she moved through Diane's palatial home. She wondered what kind of person she would have been if she'd grown up in her father's home and not her mother's, if this was what normal looked like for her. She felt disloyal just for thinking it, but maybe a tough childhood didn't sting so much when you had your own horse. It would have at least taken the edge off.

"If any of the neighbors see you and ask why you're here, tell them you're my dog's masseuse. I've been meaning to hire one anyways, to help with her anxiety."

"How do you know she's anxious?" Ruth asked.

"She pees on our laptops," Diane said, rolling her eyes as if Ruth should have known that a keyboard dripping in dog urine was the telltale sign of a canine mental health crisis.

Diane showed Ruth into a lounge whose décor could only be described as 'expensive hideous.' The couches were a mix of animal prints, and the walls were patterned in gold Versace wallpaper.

A housekeeper bustled into the room with a pitcher of cucumber water and Gucci branded glasses. Ruth took a deep sip before glancing in her glass.

"Are those—" she began.

"Yes, Gucci ice cubes," Diane said, tapping the pitcher, which was full of floating G's.

"Nice," Ruth said. She thought it was fucking stupid, but she was also dying to know how much rich idiots would pay for a branded ice cube tray. She wondered if they sold Gucci water to match.

"So, I only have a limited amount of time," Diane said

96

frostily. "And I would like this done before my daughter comes home from school, to protect her from this."

"Sure," Ruth said, pulling out her recording equipment. She had heard Daphne talking on the phone to Harper before and been surprised at their relaxed, friendly conversation. Ruth had been close to her grandmother, but her grandmother watched game shows and complained about her care workers, all very harmless activities for an old woman. Was it healthy for Harper to be so close to a woman who had confessed to murder? Then again, everyone lost their grandmother eventually—for Ruth it was an aneurysm, for Harper it would be a jail cell.

"So, I'll start recording now," she began hesitantly, pressing the button. "Just as a preliminary, have you been listening to the podcast?"

"No," Diane scoffed. "Why would I want to give my mother more attention? Especially now? But Harper is listening so I'm sure she'll tell me if I miss anything important."

"Oh okay," Ruth said, momentarily taken aback. "So, how are you coping with your mother's confession?" Ruth asked.

Diane exhaled a rush of air. "It's been a nightmare. I still don't understand why she confessed, when she must have known how hard it would be for her children. My social life has been decimated. Nobody wants me on their charity boards or at their fundraisers. I've even been kicked off the Peony Foundation's Board, and I was MC'ing the gala this year!" Diane said, slapping a hand on the table.

"What's the Peony Foundation?"

"It's a charity that helps victims of crime move on with their lives. Apparently, they don't like the optics," Diane said bitterly, making air quotations. "They don't understand that I am a victim of my mother's crimes!"

"Well, that's unfortunate," Ruth said. She meant Diane calling herself a victim, but Diane assumed she was being sympathetic.

"Yes, I just want to help people, you know? And I already bought the most *beautiful* Dolce & Gabbana dress for the gala."

"I'm sorry," Ruth said insincerely.

"Thank you. We've been disinvited from every party from here to Miami. And we always spend the holidays in Miami, so that one is particularly painful," Diane said. "And of course, I worry how this will affect my husband's real estate business." She sighed and gestured at her Versace walls. "You have to understand, Brad built this from the ground up. Sure, he had some family loans and there was always the trust fund, but really, that gave him just a couple years, five tops, to become successful. And the thought of all that hard work being destroyed is tragic."

"I bet," Ruth said.

"Speaking of my husband's business," Diane said carefully. "Someone at Sunshine Development reached out to me, Lucy Montgomery? She asked me not to participate in the podcast, said you were a risk to the company," Diane explained. She smiled but her eyes were examining Ruth, as if still trying to decide for herself. "I told her that we wouldn't be discussing the Montgomerys, that this was just an opportunity to set the record straight about my relationship with my mother, but it was a strange call. My husband does a lot of work with Sunshine. I wouldn't want there to be any fallout."

Ruth snorted. So, Diane's husband was in bed with Sunshine

Development. As if she needed a reason to like these people even less.

"Don't worry about it. It's a family thing. I won't get you in any trouble with Lucy, I promise. Let's just move on. How did it feel to find out that your mother was a killer, that she's confessed to killing a lot of people?" Ruth asked, before Diane could push for any more details about why the Montgomerys would care about a true crime podcast. Diane blinked slowly, as if trying to get her bearings.

"Well, I feel bad for them of course. But you have to understand, some of the men she married, well . . . some were more innocent than others," Diane said, her voice soaked with an implication that only she understood.

"How did your father die?" Ruth asked.

"He was terminally ill when they got married. I was very young when he died so I don't remember him. But I've certainly read about his family, which was a very old and prominent one in New York," Diane said. A silence fell in the room, one so full of meaning that Ruth felt surprised that she even had to ask the next question.

"Do you think your mother killed your father?" Ruth asked.

"No. My mother always told Rose and I that he had cancer. You know, people were very unhealthy back then. My father smoked a pack a day, drank at every lunch and dinner, and ate nothing but steak and potatoes. He never gave one thought to antioxidants or the importance of self-care," Diane said stiffly. "Thirty-seven for a man in that time is like sixty-seven now."

"Okay," Ruth said, ignoring the big, homicidal elephant in the room.

"I'm sure she would have warned us now if she killed our dad. What's the point of hiding anything?" Diane asked, a hint of doubt in her voice.

Ruth looked down, studying her Gucci tumbler. Daphne was using the podcast to tell her story, unspooling her murders for her avid listeners, but there was no telling how many she'd admit to and how many she might try to keep hidden forever. But Diane didn't seem to care about the truth, she just wanted to live in the lie.

"That's a good point," Ruth said, deciding to change the subject. "What was Daphne like as a mother when you were growing up?"

"Well, it was always her show. She was the star, and we were the supporting characters. You know, Rose and I got a lot of attention because we were twins, and we were cute kids. And I think that made Mom jealous. She always liked our older brother more. James was her favorite," Diane said, casting a sullen eye over her designer ice.

"I know that your brother and mother are estranged. Are you still in contact with him?" Ruth asked, thinking of the photo she saw of Daphne cuddling her son. As hard it might be to believe, the love in that photo was obvious.

"No, not since he finished college, back in the Eighties," Diane said sharply.

"Do you know why they fell out?"

"I don't think she told us they *had* fallen out. She just said he was going traveling overseas and wouldn't be in contact. And then the years went by, and we just never heard from him," Diane said.

Another long, refined pause. Even more awkward than the last. Ruth shifted in her seat, resisting the urge to adjust her bra, which was biting painfully into her ribs.

"Do you think your mother could . . ."

"Never," Diane said firmly. "He's the one person she would never have hurt. She loves him more than anything."

More than herself? Ruth thought. What if James had found out the truth about Daphne and threatened to turn her in? How could someone like Daphne truly love another person? How deep could the well be when it was poisoned with so much violence?

Ruth wondered if James was really out there traveling the world or if he was buried in a ravine in some wet, shadowy place that the sun never touched.

"Are you sure? You didn't know she'd killed anyone until recently. How well do you really know her?"

"Well, that's the million-dollar question, isn't it?" Diane replied. "My mom has ruined her children's lives, probably her grandchildren's as well. And you have to think, what kind of woman would hurt her own family like that?"

Ruth stayed silent, not sure if Diane was expecting an answer or not. In a strange way, knowing that Diane's mother was a murderer cast her in a different light, made her seem stronger, or more interesting than she really was. This was just a banal woman who had been transformed by events outside her control.

"A monster, that's who," Diane said finally.

BurntheBookBurnerz:

Diane is such a Karen. Rich, entitled, totally oblivious of other people.

ShockAndBlah:

But it can't have been easy to have Daphne as a mother . . . even before you found out she was a killer.

CapoteParty:

She was probably nervous. She knows everyone is listening to this podcast, including people she knows. What's the right way to react to finding out your mother is a murderer?

PreyAllDay:

Remorse. Concern for the victims, some of whom she would have known.

ShockAndBlah:

Maybe she didn't like a lot of them. And why should she be remorseful? She didn't do anything.

HauteHistoire: "Hi, guys, today's TikTok episode is devoted to Daphne's twin daughters, who are an aesthetic all on their own! Now, in the media, twins get a bad rap. Think *The Shining*. Think *Dead Ringers*. Think Patty and Selma from *The Simpsons*. And there is something a little creepy about the St Clair twins. They're often photographed together at events, they dress so similarly that they always seem to be matching even if they're in different colors, and you just *know* they're getting plastic surgery together because that's the only way they'd stay so identical! So yes, they are the kind of twins that might haunt your dreams . . . and they've got Freddy Krueger for a mother! But let's not forget that twins can be chic, and fashion owes a debt to the iconic Mary-Kate and Ashley.

"So, we know the twins love labels. One quick Google and you'll be blinded by the Versace, Gucci, Pucci. If it's got a soft c and a big price tag, they're wearing it. I've opted for a vintage Gucci silk shirt, a Prada headband and some tight, patterned Versace shorts. Finish with heels and you've got the perfect look for shopping, chilling at the club bar in Palm Beach or visiting your mother in a federal prison."

Things were finally changing for Ruth. The podcast was a hit, and money was starting to trickle in. It was on this newfound high that she agreed to go to a party with her best friend Chelsea, who was home for a visit from New York. Usually, Ruth would have refused to attend a party full of their old college friends, painfully aware that she was a cautionary tale of the successful student who had failed to launch. And of course they would have heard the rumors about her. Everyone did. But this time she had the podcast and half a bottle of prosecco in her stomach, so why not? As they got ready, Ruth thought of Daphne and chose a clingy miniskirt and plum lipstick. It was a far cry from her usual slogan tees and outdated skinny jeans (*was her favorite pair really from Costco? Christ*) but she couldn't deny that the look suited her tall frame.

Chelsea was still doing her makeup (when had everyone but Ruth learned to contour?) so Ruth sat on the couch and pulled out her phone.

Two more missed calls from her mom. Fuck. But this time she'd left a voicemail. There was her mother's voice, but much more strained and anxious than usual, as if she only had a moment to talk and she desperately wanted Ruth to hear her.

"Ruth, you have to stop this podcast. The things you're saying . . . this is *dangerous*. Stop this now, before something happens."

Ruth put the phone down and took a gulp of prosecco. Her mother sounded so anxious and afraid, and that made Ruth's mood sink. Ruth knew that Parkinson's could make people paranoid, that it could also intensify personality traits and stop them filtering themselves. But Ruth also knew that her mother had some very good reasons to warn her off this podcast, even if she was determined to continue.

Besides, Louise might not want to admit it, but they needed money. In a few years, Louise might need healthcare attendants and specialist treatment, stairlifts and walk-in baths, and Ruth would need a way to help pay for it. It occurred to Ruth that she could see why someone might kill for money. Why *she* might kill for money.

Ruth drained the glass of prosecco and deleted the phone message. Hopefully Louise would understand once the podcast was finished. Besides, this wasn't a good time to think about dark things. She had a party to go to.

As soon as Ruth walked in, she felt the full force of the party's attention find her.

"Ruth, I love the podcast! I thought to myself: yes, finally, this is the Ruth we've all been waiting for!"

"Ruth, how did we lose touch? It's been too long! What's Daphne really like? And why did she call the cops up and confess? Was someone on to her?"

"Have you interviewed the police? I remember you got into some trouble with them a while back. Is this triggering for you?"

It hadn't really hit her yet how many people listened to the podcast. But here were the people she knew from college, all suddenly fascinated by her work. It was a bit disarming because while she did count some of these people as genuine friends, many of the others hadn't bothered to keep in touch once Ruth's life became a depressing vortex of money problems, anxiety, and personal tragedies. But against all odds, Ruth, the grade grind from college with generic sneakers and a whopping student debt, had pulled it off.

Ruth downed a couple of tequila sodas and tried to channel Daphne, the confident femme fatale on the prowl for a victim. She felt a new kind of power surge through her as she talked to people, aware that everyone now saw her as different and exciting. A few of them even saw her as something more: enticing.

The thought made her body ache as she considered how long it had been since she'd had fun with someone, shorn from the complexities of a long-term relationship. How long had it been since she'd gone out into the night, ready to make some deliciously bad decisions?

She didn't go home alone that night.

The Second Murder

Chapter Twelve

EPISODE THREE: 1952

DAPHNE: The story will really pick up now that I've gone to New York. Have you been there?

RUTH: Yeah, a few times.

DAPHNE: Don't you love it? Wouldn't you just *kill* to be a New Yorker?

RUTH: I don't know. It just seems so expensive there. And cold. Honestly, I think some people use living in New York as a substitute for a personality.

DAPHNE (annoyed): Well, what would you know? You're from *Florida*.

RUTH: And you're from *Canada*.

DAPHNE: Oh, I see, Miss Liberal PC thinks I should go back to my own country! I'm from New York. If you live in the city for more than ten years you can call yourself a New Yorker. Well, I lived there for fifty years. If that was a marriage, we'd have celebrated our golden wedding anniversary.

RUTH: So, a lot longer than your real marriages . . .

DAPHNE: That's because New York never disappointed me. It never got boring. I always knew I'd end up there. When I was growing up, people used it to mean the opposite of Lucan. They would criticize the new music playing at a dance or a teacher's fashion sense by complaining that this wasn't New York City. They were saying New York had no morals but all I heard was that it was nothing like Lucan. Then I got to Winnipeg and discovered that cities, like men, aren't equally good. I wanted somewhere bigger, better, a place that really *mattered*. I wanted somewhere I could become myself.

RUTH: God, you could write the tourism ads for New York.

DAPHNE: They couldn't afford me.

RUTH: So, what did you do when you got to the city?

DAPHNE: I found work in a factory and a place to live. Both were terrible but I was relieved to be able to take care of myself. I wasn't planning on finding another Ted ever again . . .

[Daphne chuckles, a dry laugh like a smoker's cough.]

RUTH: What's funny?

DAPHNE: Well, I *did* find another Ted, in a way. My first apartment in New York was a shithole in Brooklyn, the kind of place even rats would consider rock bottom. There was a family that lived next door, the Flanagans, although the walls were so thin, we might as well have been shacking up. Every dinner conversation, every ad on their radio, I could hear it all. And well, what I heard sounded awful familiar . . .

RUTH: The Flanagans, huh, so tell me more about them. It was an abusive home?

DAPHNE: The dad, Frankie Flanagan, was a real piece of shit.

He had three kids, all under eight, and he hit everyone he could get his hands on: the wife, the kids, and if he could have punched through a wall I'm sure he would have got me too. From the moment he came home from work, all you would hear was the screaming, the crying, and the hittin'. He was meaner than a rattlesnake, as awful sober as he was drunk.

RUTH: That must have been disturbing.

DAPHNE: Well, it certainly made sleep hard. I'd lie in bed at night and just grind my teeth, having to listen to all that misery. I'd come to New York to escape my problems and now I was getting a daily reminder from a two-bit thug who couldn't keep his shit together long enough to listen to *Gunsmoke*.

RUTH: Did you ever talk to the wife?

DAPHNE: No, I don't know what I would have said anyways. Sylvia Flanagan was just this scrawny little thing. Always scurrying around, scared half to death. And the kids were miserable. I never saw one of them smile. But I knew she wasn't going to leave him. He was always yelling at her: 'If you try to leave, I'll kill the kids and then I'll kill you.' And Frankie Flanagan was crazier than a shithouse rat so I believed him.

RUTH: How did it end? Do you know?

DAPHNE: How do you think? There's a reason I'm tellin' you this story, and it's not for my health!

RUTH: You killed him? You killed Frankie Flanagan?

DAPHNE: You know, Bible-thumpers say that everyone has to atone for their sins on Judgment Day so I decided to get Mr. Flanagan in front of God a little faster, before he killed one of those kids.

RUTH: You have a thing about bad fathers, don't you? You

always seem to mention if you think a man was a bad husband or a bad father. But is that enough to justify killing them?
People are complicated; most people do some good things
and some bad things.

DAPHNE: I'm sorry, are we talking about Frankie Flanagan still?
Because from what I saw, he didn't do a lick of good for
anyone.

RUTH: I just meant more generally. Is that something that moti-
vates you? Do you see yourself as some kind of avenger?

DAPHNE: This is a little left-field. I've never thought about it like
that.

RUTH: Well it's a simple question: do you see yourself as using
murder as a way to achieve some kind of justice?

DAPHNE: Maybe I'm just a fan of the underdog. And sometimes
that underdog is a battered wife and kids. And sometimes
it's me.

RUTH: Okay, so you heard a man abusing his wife and kids
daily, even threatening to kill them. Why didn't you just call
the police? No one would even have to know it was you.

DAPHNE: Yeah right. Like the cops gave two shits what a man
got up to in his own home in the Fifties. I don't know that it's
much different now. Did you see that article in the paper this
morning about the guy who murdered his ex-wife? She did
everything right: wrote down license plates, logged phone
calls, got a restraining order, and yet when she called the
cops to tell them he was hanging around the neighborhood,
did they go out right away? Nope. And by the time they did,
he'd already stabbed her to death in front of her son.

RUTH: Welcome to Florida. The cops cause more murders than they solve.

DAPHNE: You sure don't like the boys in blue! What's the story? You get busted for something? Jaywalking or streetwalking?

RUTH: No, I have a problem with a police force with a history of racism, police brutality, and corruption. Unlike you, I don't make everything about my own experiences.

DAPHNE: All right, all right, I was just joking. Jesus, I didn't know you could find a snowflake in Florida!

RUTH: Look, let's just move on. I wanted to ask you about the podcast title. I was thinking I could change the title to reflect the number of murders the podcast features. So, we'd be on *The Two Murders of Daphne St Clair* now and I'd just keep revising it as we go. Unless you'd be willing to give me the full number of people you killed now? Maybe a little preview of their names and locations?

DAPHNE: Now where's the fun in that? Don't rush the story. But I like your idea for the title. Go with that.

RUTH (sighs): So, what happened to Frankie Flanagan?

One day, I was up at 6 a.m. to go to work. I was working in a textile factory in the Garment District then, a hot, noisy place that gave me a sore back and buzzing ears. I was walking down the steps of my local subway station when I saw him, just ahead of me. Frankie Flanagan, probably off to unload deliveries at the bar where he worked. He had thinning blond hair the same color as his grayish skin and the muscular body of a brawler. His oldest son was with him and even though he was around eight, I was certain his dad would be forcing him to haul heavy kegs for a little cash in hand, child safety be damned.

I'd never met Frankie. I'd only ever seen him from afar, but I already hated him. Night after night, hearing the violence he meted out set my heart racing and had me smoking cigarette after cigarette to soothe my nerves.

I walked behind them as they entered the station and continued down to the same platform I used. He wasn't even talking to his son. The only time he acknowledged his existence was when the boy wasn't walking fast enough, and he grabbed him by the collar of his coat and shoved him forward. The boy barely reacted, as if this was a normal way to treat someone.

The platform was busy with the usual morning crush and the air was murky with cigarette smoke. Frankie pushed his way to the front of the crowd, throwing elbows and forcing himself past old women and young families. He was pushing his son in front of him while I followed behind, moving through the spaces his large body left. I was mesmerized by his hands, so thick and meaty, with red-raw knuckles. Being hit by one of those must have felt like being hit by a train.

Frankie and his son ended up at the very front, although I noticed his son drift a few feet away from his dad, just out of reach of those balled-up fists. I stood behind Frankie, staring hard at the back of his thick neck. It was so crowded that my face was just inches from him. A train was coming, one that didn't stop here. I could hear that unmistakable rumbling and screeching from inside the tunnel like a great beast stirring in its den.

Frankie saw me looking at him, turned to face me, and

curled his lip in disgust. "What the fuck—" But it was too late. My hand shot out and pushed him, so quickly that no one even noticed. His eyes widened as he fell backwards, still staring at my face as the train hit him, pulverizing him. The train tried to brake. The people around us screamed and shouted, so I did as well.

Then I looked over at the boy. He was standing with his mouth gaping and his eyes pinned on me. I could see a bruise above his left eyebrow that had faded to a yellow-green. He looked small and alone as the station platform erupted in noise and chaos.

And then I smiled at him.

A week later I saw Sylvia Flanagan and her children putting their meagre collection of boxes in the hall. I watched as she carried her possessions down the stairs, her children trailing after her like ducklings. When she came up for the final load, I slid out into the hall and said hello. She wiped her brow and smiled tiredly.

"Funny to properly meet on the day we move out," she said. I nodded, studying her carefully. There was no indication that her son had told her what he saw me do.

"So, where are you off to?" I asked.

"Back to Virginia. My parents own a horse farm and riding school there. We'll stay with them. They've always wanted to see the kids, but Frankie wouldn't allow it. I think the kids will love it there. I always did," she replied. There was a strange expression on her face, both wistful and positive. She knew she was getting a second chance at her life.

"Well, best of luck," I said, stepping inside my door. I

wanted to add 'and you're welcome' but knew that killers who gloated ended up behind bars.

Sylvia locked up the apartment and headed downstairs with the kids trailing behind. The last to leave was the oldest son, the boy who saw me on the train platform. He paused at the top of the stairs and glanced back at me, our eyes meeting.

And then he smiled.

RUTH (Voiceover): I had a phone call with Brendan Flanagan, the eldest son of Frankie Flanagan. Brendan was the boy who saw Daphne push his father in front of the train. Brendan is now seventy-eight and lives in rural Virginia. He was surprised to hear from me and shocked to find out that not only had Daphne confessed to killing his father but also that she was actually a serial killer.

BRENDAN: I can't believe it. Of course, I've seen the news but she obviously looked very different when I saw her seventy years ago and she had a different name.

RUTH: So, what do you remember about that day?

BRENDAN: You don't forget the day you see your father die. He was taking me along to work with him. He did that a lot, even on school days, because they'd usually throw him a couple extra bucks for my work. I hated it. So, there we were in the station. I'd caught a glimpse of the woman who lived next to us. She had black hair, pale skin, and these dark green eyes. And she always had red lipstick on. You noticed her because she looked a little more glamorous than the other women in our building, even though she would have been poor like the rest of us. Liz Taylor!

RUTH: I'm sorry, what?

BRENDAN: I always thought she looked like Liz Taylor. Every time I saw Liz Taylor in a movie, for years after, I'd think about her.

RUTH: So, what happened next?

BRENDAN: Well, I'd stepped away from my dad on the platform, because he was real angry that day. I saw him turn around and say something to her, and then she just shoved him. The train hit him, and that was the last time I ever saw him. The police took me home before they got the body out.

RUTH: How did you feel?

BRENDAN: Well, shocked, obviously, but also . . . glad. We were trapped in that place. My mother had no job, no money of her own, and I really believe he would have killed us if we tried to leave. If it wasn't Liz—Daphne—it probably would have been me someday, it was that bad. My mother was Frankie's second wife. The first had killed herself, likely to escape all the abuse. Their kids ended up in an orphanage because he didn't want 'em. It bothers me, knowing I've got a brother and sister out there that I never met. But they were probably better off in that orphanage than with my dad.

RUTH: It's certainly possible. Why do you think Daphne did it?

BRENDAN: Well, I always assumed she did it to save us. She would have heard everything through those walls, I'm sure.

RUTH: So, after your father died, you left New York for Virginia?

BRENDAN: Yep, we moved in with my grandparents. They were really good to us, my grandfather became like a real dad to me. He taught me everything about horses. And that's where I am right now. When they retired, I took over the farm and riding school. My mother remarried when I was in my twenties and moved a mile away so we saw her every day. Now my daughter and granddaughter run the business and I'm free to sit back on the porch with a sweet tea and watch it all happen.

RUTH: Sounds like a nice life.

BRENDAN: There's no place I'd rather be. I had eight bad years followed by seventy great ones. Hey, did she say why she confessed? She killed my dad so long ago, why not take it to her grave?

RUTH: That's what everyone's wondering. I really couldn't tell you why Daphne St Clair did the things she did. But if I figure it out, I'll let you know.

BurntheBookBurnerz:

I see this as female solidarity. Daphne saved this woman and her children.

ShockAndBlah:

Yeah but at the same time, Daphne isn't GOD. She doesn't get to decide who lives and dies. Like, maybe that guy was shitty but maybe he was going to change his life at some point, be a better person. Daphne doesn't get to decide who gets that chance.

BurntheBookBurnerz:

So, we should all sit around and let bad people hurt as many people as they like just on the off-chance that someday they'll reform? Because like Daphne said, the cops weren't gonna help you in 1952. The term 'domestic violence' didn't even appear in official law until 1973.

StopDropAndTroll:

Oh boo fucking hoo. Stop defending a serial killer.

PreyAllDay:

I think the vigilante shit is cool. Pushing a guy in front of a train and just smiling while he gets pulverized? That could be a plot on *Dexter.* I like it.

BurntheBookBurnerz:

So . . . what is it? Parental divorce? Childhood bullying? Anxiety issues? What broke you?

PreyAllDay:

I think you'd be more disturbed by how normal I am.

Chapter Thirteen

EPISODE FOUR: 1953–1957

DAPHNE: So, I stayed in New York, in the same apartment building where the Flanagans had lived. At the beginning, it was enough just to be alone. But after a few years I met Carl, my son's father, the first man I ever really loved.

RUTH: Did you marry him?

DAPHNE: No, you know I didn't marry every man I slept with. It was the 1950s not the 1500s. Besides, Carl left me within the year. I never had time to fall out of love with him.

RUTH: Were you a good couple before that?

DAPHNE: Of course not. I had a friend who used to say 'if you see shit, don't touch it' and Carl was shit. But I couldn't help picking it up and putting it in my purse.

RUTH (muttering): That's uh, very descriptive . . .

DAPHNE: There's no need to be snide. I'm telling you my life story, so I'm going to describe anything I please. I deserve some respect from you.

RUTH (resentfully): Look, I'm just trying to get this done before you get packed off to the slammer, and lately everyone seems to have a problem with this podcast.

DAPHNE: Oh boohoo, it's called a *job*, Ruth. If you can't handle a bit of criticism, just throw in the towel.

RUTH: Is that what you want? You want me to end this here and now? Make this the big finale?

[A tense silence fills the air. It lasts for an uncomfortably long time. An attendant knocks on the door.]

ATTENDANT: Here are your pills.

DAPHNE: Give 'em here. I'll take them after my interview.

[The door closes. There's a cough and the sound of a body shifting in a chair.]

DAPHNE (formally): Would you like to hear about Carl?

RUTH: Yes.

Carl was the most handsome man I'd ever seen. He had that black Irish look: hair as dark as coal, milky skin, and the most beautiful dark blue eyes, like denim drying in the sun. And he could dance. While other men hung on the sidelines, tapping their feet, Carl would slide across the floor, as cool and casual as if he was taking a stroll in the park. And he was always the life of the party, a whiskey in each hand and two cigarettes in his mouth.

He was the first man I was ever attracted to, the first man I enjoyed sleeping with. I usually don't like sex, I've always found it easier to kill a man than have sex with him, but sex with Carl was different. We would come home late from a party and just crash through the room, aroused in that numb, pounding way you get when you're drunk. We would roll around in bed, rough and wild like animals. I've lived a long life but it's those memories that I often think about when I lie awake at night, those moments when everything seemed normal but also extraordinary. I was going by Jacqueline then, my new American name for my new American life.

We were young and good-looking and full of energy, and somehow that made it okay that we were broke and forced to take whatever tiresome jobs we could find. We fought constantly but we made up even more passionately, so I thought it would be okay. Besides I was alone in a new country and just glad to have found someone.

For one year, it felt like my life was finally (finally) beginning to turn right. I could almost feel hopeful about the future because I was happy in the present. Carl talked about traveling and making his fortune somewhere, maybe out to California, or even to South America, and I believed that I would be by his side.

Carl was wild and free and full of adventure. So, of course I got pregnant.

After I missed my period a couple of months in a row, I felt a strange mixture of fear and relief. Fear because I was finally happy and didn't want anything to change, and relief because of all the terrible men who could have knocked me up, I was glad that it was a man I loved who had gotten me in trouble.

Carl left me on a gray Sunday morning in October. He

packed his bag while I was sleeping and then shook me awake to tell me the bad news. Bastard couldn't even let a pregnant woman sleep.

"Jacqueline, I'm leaving. We had fun but this is getting too heavy. I need to make a life for myself, not get tied down by you," he muttered.

I sat on the edge of the bed and stared blankly at the wall. I didn't beg. I was too proud for that, even in that situation. I had suspected this would happen. He had been uneasy since he had found out the news and a coldness had appeared between us.

"Fine," I spat, letting the anger choke out the fear. "Just go then." The luxury of being a man where fatherhood was something you could opt out of, like canceling a magazine subscription!

Carl paused at the door, lighting a cigarette. He wasn't even looking at me anymore, as if I'd already stopped existing.

"For God's sake, go get that taken care of and move on," he snapped, gesturing vaguely at my stomach. "The world has enough unwanted babies." He slammed the door, and I heard his feet dance down the stairs, his footsteps growing lighter and picking up speed as he left me behind.

DAPHNE: Look, I know it's strange. He treats me like shit and gets to live. Other guys treat me far better and get offed. But that's life. Now, Ruth, why don't you get out your phone and find him for me? His name is Carl Fitzroy and he was from Rochester, New York.

RUTH: Okay sure. [Pause] Here's his obituary. Carl died ten years ago. In Orlando, Florida. He had three children and eight grandchildren.

DAPHNE: How 'bout that? He was in Florida. We could have run into each other. But there you go, every bastard who tells you they don't want kids really means they don't want kids with *you*. Well, at least I outlived him. That's something.

RUTH: It's sad though, to think that he just walked away from you and your son. I just don't understand how someone could ever abandon their child, how they could keep on living knowing that their family is out there, struggling without them.

DAPHNE: Well. You said that your father came back into your life as an adult, so he did try to make it right.

RUTH: Yes, but I was talking about James, not me.

DAPHNE: Sure you were. And hey, maybe your dear old dad's listening to this podcast and is proud as punch?

RUTH: He's not.

Chapter Fourteen

After Carl left, I never felt lonelier in my life. The whole city seemed to raise its hackles and bare its teeth at me, and every-thing seemed so much harder than it had a couple of months earlier, when I was in love and every street was lit with star-light. But the one thing that I was certain of was that I wanted this baby. They would be family and my chance to start over. Every night I would come home and lie in bed with my hands wrapped around my stomach, my mind full of half-dreams and wishes I couldn't put into words.

I did my best to take care of myself and my unborn baby. I ate as much red meat as I could afford and only smoked a few cigarettes a day. There was nothing I could do about the city air though, which seemed to shimmer with filth outside my windows. And I still had to work, spending long hours on my feet in laundries and textile factories, because only the shittiest jobs would take an uneducated pregnant woman.

I gave birth in a dingy city hospital, alone except for a dis-approving nurse who kept glancing at my hands, as if expecting a wedding ring to magically appear. It took hours and the pain was unbelievable. My whole being left my body with every contraction and then came crashing down as the baby slowly, painfully inched down through my torso. My body shook with every surge and I felt like I was being torn apart from the inside out. I grew so quiet that the nurse began to feel my pulse, certain that I was dying. But I put my chin into my chest and pushed as hard as I could, feeling a bony carcass come heaving out of my body in a clatter of angles and folds.

"It's a boy," the nurse said, as she handed him to me. A boy. He was screaming hysterically, a high-pitched squeal that brought tears to my eyes. I held the little bundle, all wrapped in cloth, and sobbed with relief.

That night, after he fell asleep, I watched his eyelashes flutter and listened to the warm, even sound of his breathing. I brushed my hands across his tiny fingers and thought about how I wanted to give him everything. I didn't want to raise him in a cramped apartment, chasing cockroaches away from our bed and pinching pennies to buy him a pair of shoes. I looked at my little masterpiece of a boy and knew that I would do anything to give him the life he deserved.

I suppose some part of me had worried that I was too damaged to respond normally to motherhood, that fruit couldn't grow from a poisoned tree. And yet, the moment my son was born, I loved him in a way I'd never loved anyone before. I bet that surprises you. You probably think that a person like me could never love anyone but herself.

But that love was also coupled with a surge of hatred. I didn't hate my son, I hated everything that wasn't him. People seem to think that when a woman becomes a mother, she becomes a mother to the whole world. That having a child cracks her

heart and her arms open, wide enough to embrace everyone.
But they're wrong. A mother is a dangerous creature. She would
burn the whole world down just to make her child smile.

DAPHNE: Do you have children?

[Ruth coughs and sputters in surprise.]

RUTH: Children? I don't even have a dog. I don't even have a
  plant!
DAPHNE: It's not an installment scheme; you don't start with a
  plant and work your way up.
RUTH: I don't know anything about kids!
DAPHNE: God, you're like a child trapped in a woman's body.
  It doesn't take a rocket scientist to take care of a baby. Kids
  used to do it! Your generation just goes around wringing their
  hands about everything. If you don't have a master's degree
  in changing diapers, you don't feel qualified to do it.
RUTH (coolly): I guess I just want to focus on my career right
  now. You didn't really have a career, I suppose?
DAPHNE: No, I didn't. It's a different world now for girls, even
  for poor ones like you and me. Back then, we didn't really
  have words for gender pay gaps, or domestic violence, or
  sexual harassment because they weren't *bad things*, they were
  just . . . life. So, I didn't have the education or the training,
  but over time I did learn about men. I could have a master's
  degree in men! I learned how I could make opportunities
  through them, for me and for my children.
RUTH: That's . . . nice?

DAPHNE: Well, it was better than nothing. And you know, Ruth, if you do want kids, you've got plenty of time to sort your life out. You're what? twenty-four?

RUTH: I'm thirty-two.

DAPHNE: Oh Christ.

Ruth was sitting at her shitty desk, watching the latest Daphne media coverage on her laptop. She saw a police car turn into her parking lot and she slunk down in her seat, peering around her computer. The light caught the driver's face in profile. Was that Officer Rankin? She couldn't be sure, but she felt a flicker of unease. It had certainly looked like him.

The local news reported that earlier in the day, there had been a protest against Daphne downtown, organized by TikToker and men's rights activist Tucker Winn. From the footage it was clear that the protest wasn't very well attended. Of the thirty or so people, only three were women. People were waving signs that said things like "Fry the Bitch" and "Stop the Male Genocide." Tucker stood up at the top of the courthouse steps and began to speak. He was wearing a ribbon pin and a T-shirt that said: 'Men's Lives Matter.'

"Daphne St Clair is a predator who hunts men. This is the kind of woman who is celebrated in our modern society: a woman who goes after what she wants, a woman who doesn't see men as loving authority figures but as obstacles to be removed! Now, I'm not saying women shouldn't have rights. This is America! But women were happier when they weren't trying to be men!"

Ruth wondered when exactly this mythical time was when

women were happier. She knew that the world, and the Internet especially, were still full of people who saw all women, not just Daphne St Clair, as a threat. She remembered something Daphne had once told her. 'Men are all for women's liberation until it costs them something. A babysitter. A home-cooked meal. Having to learn how to iron. And the problem is everything real costs something.'

Ruth's phone pinged. She glanced down. Another two missed calls from her mom and a text that read: Ruth, you have to stop this podcast. It's too dangerous. Leave it alone. Her heart began to beat faster as she stared at the stark warning from her mother. A strange mix of guilt and anger percolated inside her. Of course her mother was worried. Of course she didn't want Ruth to take this risk. But Ruth couldn't just stop.

Tucker's diatribe had moved on to the podcast, *Ruth*'s podcast. "And when I listen to Daphne St Clair's filthy voice on that ... that podcast, laughing about murdering two hard-working family men, *two fathers*, by pushing them down the stairs and in front of subway trains, laughing about killing an old man whose only mistake was to fall for her, I don't feel shocked. *This* is the world feminists want for us! I guarantee you that leftist radicals convinced Daphne to confess so they could hold her up as a hero for the movement! So the feminists can continue the male genocide!"

Ruth closed the video, already sick of listening to Tucker. The murders of Ted and Frankie didn't concern her. Those men were abusive assholes and the world was better off without them. But Ruth knew that Daphne had killed innocent people, that one specific murder had reverberated down through Ruth's life, a black hole that so many people's lives revolved around. And now Ruth was going to get the truth.

Ruth took a deep, shuddering breath and then furiously typed back. Mom, it's her. I know it is. Daphne killed him. And I'm going to prove it. Then she turned off her phone, not waiting for a response.

There was no way she was going to drop this. Daphne St Clair had taken something from her and now Ruth was going to take everything from Daphne.

Chapter Fifteen

PreyAllDay:

So there's no murder this week? I like my true crime gruesome! Ruth better bring up the body count or I'm going back to *Graphic Detail* and *Last Podcast on the Left*!

BurntheBookBurnerz:

You're mad that no one was murdered? That's twisted.

PreyAllDay:

GTFO, we're all here for the same thing.

ShockAndBlah:

I dunno, I like my true crime funny.

StopDropAndTroll:

KK, we'll go find u some more funny murders then. That's more fucked up than liking the gross stuff btw.

ShockAndBlah:

So where's this son of Daphne's? We know who the daughters are, but where's the son? We don't know his last name so we can't google him.

BurntheBookBurnerz:

It *is* strange that the media has been discussing the twins so much but not him.

CapoteParty:

He's probably dead then.

ShockAndBlah:

But she does seem to really love her son. Is that . . . crazy? Can you be a good parent and a serial killer?

PreyAllDay:

BTK's daughter said he was a good dad.

StopDropAndTroll:

Nah, I bet she's lying.

BurntheBookBurnerz:

Do you just think every woman is lying? Wtf is wrong with you?!?

StopDropAndTroll:

Haven't been wrong yet.

Harper called me on the phone. It was 3:30 p.m. so she must have just gotten home from school. I could tell by her hushed, breathless voice that she was phoning me covertly, likely from her bedroom closet.

"Hi, Grandma," she said. I had tried desperately to get the grandchildren to call me something more glamorous, like GiGi or DeeDee, but Diane and Rose had been insistent that I be called Grandma. I suspected they were signaling that I was old now and no longer desirable, shunted off to the kitchen with a baking tray full of cookies. They were always jealous of the attention I got, particularly from men.

"How nice of you to call," I said. "What's new?" We didn't talk that often on the phone; we were always better in person, where we'd talk for a few minutes and then pick up true crime books and start reading together. She seemed to appreciate the silence, after a lifetime of her mother signing her up for horse-back riding lessons and demanding she go on playdates with children who hated her.

"I wanted to tell you that everyone online is talking about your podcast and well, about you!"

"That's nice, dear," I said. "What are they saying?"

"Oh, you know, that you're a monster."

"Fair enough," I replied.

"They've nicknamed you the Gray Widow," Harper said. "You know, like a black widow but old."

"Really?" I asked. "But that's so boring! That's almost as bad as the Giggling Granny."

"Who's that?"

"Oh, she was this killer who used to laugh every time she talked about killing her husbands. They also called her the Lonely Hearts Killer, which is more dignified, but the Giggling Granny was the one that stuck. Maybe I should come up with my own nickname and get Ruth to use it on the podcast. Something like the 'Toxic Temptress' or the 'Borgia of Florida.'"

"That's a good idea. Although I don't think the 'Borgia of Florida' sounds good; it's kind of hard to say. So, how's it going with the podcast? I'm loving it so far!"

"Should you be listening to that? Well, I'm not your mother. Anyway, Ruth isn't quite what I expected. She's nosy and a bit self-righteous; sometimes I catch her staring at me like I've pissed in her cornflakes or something. And she's a bit sneaky. But it's interesting, anyways," I said, reclining in my armchair.

This was the dream of every geezer at Coconut Grove: their grandchildren calling them unprompted, wanting to know about their lives. And all I had to do was confess to multiple murders. I guess 'how I met Grandpa at the church dance' and 'scrimpin' and savin' to buy a winter coat' weren't the barnstorming stories the old folks thought they were.

"Well, I can't wait for the next episode. Everyone at school wants to talk to me now. Yesterday, Buckley brought his emotional support parrot to school but no one cared; they were too busy asking me questions about you. You know, how many people you killed, why you confessed, if you chopped anyone up, those kinds of things."

THE SIX MURDERS OF DAPHNE ST CLAIR

"That's nice," I said, having no clue what an emotional support parrot was. Harper went to a very expensive private school where kids were fed tofu puddings and did yoga instead of dodgeball in gym class. It hadn't stopped her from being bullied though and I was glad that she'd finally found her ticket to popularity. Sorry, Buckley, the Gray Widow trumps parrots.

We were still talking when my phone began to beep, signaling that I was getting another call. Two calls, it was a big day for my landline!

"Harper, I should go. This might be my lawyer," I said. He had helped change my number and only a handful of people knew the new one: my daughters, my lawyer, and Ruth.

We said goodbye and then I switched to the other call.

"This is the front desk," a cool voice said at the other end. Ah, so just another Coconut Grove employee who hated my guts.

"And?" I prompted.

"We just had a phone call from a private investigator. He wouldn't say who his client is but he's calling around to the senior centers in the area, trying to find you. We've refused to talk to him or confirm if you live here but I must ask you to stay away from your windows and keep your curtains drawn. We don't know who this man is working for, or even if he is an investigator, so we're treating him as a possible threat."

"So, I'm supposed to sit inside with my curtains closed like a prisoner just because someone's looking for me? Isn't that excessive?" I demanded.

A pause and then the voice continued, lower and hoarser, as if she was furious but didn't want anyone else to hear.

"I don't really care what you do. I'd tell you that you're putting other people in danger by being here, but you don't care! And we're stuck with you until the cops cart you away! So yes, someone out there is looking for you, someone who might want to cause you harm. It's not my problem what you do with that information."

And then she hung up. Huh, not exactly the quality of customer service I was used to, back when I was just Warren's girlfriend and everyone liked me. But clearly, they were all still smarting from the whole 'murdering Warren' thing. Jeez, forgive and forget already!

Still, I got up and shuffled across the floor with my walker, raising my arthritic arms slowly to shut the curtains. Beyond the lawn was a thick copse of trees draped in Spanish moss and misty in the blue twilight. I stood there for a second, considering these trees for the first time since I'd moved into the Grove. Anyone could be out there, watching, waiting. What would they see right now? An old, white face peering back at them? The face they recognized from the TV?

I wondered if I was going to wake up one night to find a dark figure at the end of my bed, his hands already creeping up to my throat, ready to fulfil some twisted obsession or perhaps avenge an old grievance from the past.

With a huff, I snapped the curtains shut and then checked that the doors were locked.

Let them come. Just . . . not yet.

The Third Murder

Chapter Sixteen

At twenty-eight years old, I was broke, a single mom, and I was still trying to outrun a pretty traumatic past. But I was young and beautiful, and I lived in New York City. In those kinds of circumstances, you can make miracles happen, especially if you don't let morals get in the way.

After a few more dispiriting sweatshop jobs, I lucked out and got a position at Bergdorf Goodman, a beautiful department store on Fifth Avenue. I had a new glamorous image, and a name to match: Jacqueline Dubois, exactly the right name for a woman who worked in Manhattan. Every morning, I would get dressed, carefully apply my makeup and drop off James with my neighbors before catching the subway uptown. Some women were scared of riding the subways by themselves in the Sixties but I knew that every train I was riding already had a murderer on it. And if anyone did threaten me, I already knew how effective a subway could be as a murder weapon.

The best part about working at Bergdorf's was all the wealthy men I met. I would stand behind the glass counters with all the other shopgirls and just wait for them to make a beeline right for me. I dated a lot at that time. Maybe that makes me a whore, but all I can say is that it's easier to be moral once your bills are paid and you can only get on a high horse if you can afford one. My dates weren't always good-looking or particularly young. But I had already tried handsome. Handsome knocked me up and left me high and dry. And New York is a different town when you've got money. New York is at its finest when you're drunk on champagne, the whole city a blur of sparkles and light outside the cab window.

Dating became my second job, and I became adept at knowing what kind of woman my date wanted, both in and out of the bedroom. The sex didn't bother me although I didn't really enjoy it. I guess I've always seen sex as a transaction, but I was a lot happier when men were buying it as opposed to stealing it. And I was always on the lookout for money, whether it was in the form of gifts, meals, or even rent money if a man really wanted to help a damsel in distress.

But I never forgot that I was doing this for James, so that he didn't grow up dirt poor like I did. After every date, I would come home and pick up my son from the neighbors, and we'd go off to bed. I loved it there, cuddled up with my boy as the cool air washed across my sweaty skin. That was when I could truly relax, when I could be silent and still with my sleeping child. In those moments, I knew that the world was against us, but it was also us against the world.

And then it happened. One day at the store, I met the rarest creature in New York: a rich man without a wife.

Geoffrey Van Rensselaer had the pallid, soft skin of a rich alcoholic, as if he was preserved in fluid. He was the kind of person who never really hit rock bottom because every time he

*busted through a safety net, another appeared, usually held by
an old friend of his father's. He was average height and had a
slim build but there was a softness in his chin, the skin swelling
beneath his jaw and drooping towards his collar. But he was
still attractive. He had the fine-boned face and hearty swagger
of New York's Old Money.*

*As I got to know him, I learned that his life was somewhat
tragic, at least as tragic as it could get with a trust fund and an
apartment on the Upper East Side. Geoffrey was an only child
from a wealthy family. His father was dead and his mother was
locked up in the loony bin after one too many shopping trips in
just a bra and rain boots. But these tragedies had happened in
his early twenties, and he was bolstered by a childhood spent
at elite private schools and Ivy League institutions. Geoffrey
exuded danger without consequences, as if he was protected
by the invisible angels of privilege.*

*I had to be careful with Geoffrey. He was rich and unmar-
ried, just the kind of man who might change mine and my son's
lives. But I knew that there was competition. I could feel these
other women, girls just like me: shopgirls, waitresses, aspiring
actresses circling him like sharks, their shadows passing over
my face. I let him see me out with other guys until one day, I
found him hovering outside my work, twisting a newspaper.
I could see ink stains on his forehead from where he'd wiped
his sweat away.*

*"Jacqueline, baby, I can't stand seeing you out with other
men. Running into you with Terrence Havemeyer last night . . .
it nearly killed me. I'm ready to commit; let's go steady," he
pleaded. I felt disgusted by his self-pity. All his life, Geoffrey*

had been spoiled and I didn't doubt that the fact that he couldn't have me was causing him real pain. But it wasn't because he loved me, I didn't really matter, it was because he expected life to give him everything he wanted. But it didn't matter. I had won.

The next couple of months were the most glorious of my life. Geoffrey whirled me through New York and the whole city rolled out the red carpet for me. There wasn't a musician or comedian I didn't see live, and it was rare when I didn't end up drinking martinis or doing speed afterwards with them. He gave me an exorbitant allowance, one that let me quit the store and spend all my time with James, unless Geoffrey wanted a date. And the hotels ... in those few months, we screwed in every five-star establishment New York had to offer and even a couple in the tri-state area as well.

And that's when I got my second stroke of luck. I've had a lot of bad luck in my life but every now and then, fortune throws you a bone. One day, Geoffrey showed up to a date, rumpled and insisting we talk. We found a grimy bar, with flickering lights and a sticky floor. Geoffrey had wanted to find some-where nicer, but I just wanted to get it over with. Whatever 'it' was: a secret wife and family, a gambling habit that left him without a pot to piss in, a desire to become a Catholic priest and stop all the sex. People never wanted to confess something pleasant to you.

"Look, kid, here's the thing," Geoffrey said. I waited, holding my purse, ready to storm out of there when he gave me a reason.

"I've been to the doctor's, and ... it's not good. They say

I've got cancer," he said hesitantly. I had never seen Geoffrey like this, so shaken and clammy, and scared.

"Can they cure you?" I asked.

"Well, there's some treatments they can try, but I've probably only got a year or two," he choked out, tears welling up in his eyes. The man was thirty-seven years old; he probably thought he'd have another forty years of life. The way he drank, I would have given him twenty but having the zero knocked off must have smarted.

"I'm so sorry," I said, meaning it. Geoffrey was a lush and soft as hell, but this whole 'Geoffrey stays alive and throws money at me' agreement had been a mutually beneficial arrangement.

"Jacqueline, I don't want to be alone. I've got no family left, other than my mother who doesn't recognize me. I'm going to fight like hell to get better but regardless I want to have a wife and kids, a family." He took my hand. I was frozen, trying to figure out what he was talking about. Was this a proposal?

"You're saying that you want to marry me?" I asked.

He nodded. "And I think we should have a baby. I want to be a father, to continue the family name, and to know that I didn't waste my life on parties and booze."

But you did, I thought. And it was such fun.

"But what would I do with a baby, if you know . . . the worst happened?" I asked.

Geoffrey wasn't becoming a better man, he was just scared and selfish. It didn't matter what was right for me or his child; Geoffrey wanted to know that he wouldn't miss out, that he could still have a family and a legacy, that there was still time to have everything.

"I'd make sure you and our children would be comfortable even if I . . . wasn't there," he said. Children? Now he wanted more than one? How long was this dingbat planning to be terminally ill for?

"That's a lot to ask of someone," I said, still reeling.

"I know," he said, his eyes pleading. "And I know most women would never marry a man and have children knowing they'd likely be a widow soon. But, Jacqueline, please, give me something to live for," he begged.

He was right. Most women wouldn't take a second look at him. And that gave me power. I could feel the delicious taste of leverage on my tongue.

"I . . . I want to be your wife and the mother of your children," I began gently, getting a toothache from how syrupy it sounded. "But there's something I have to tell you. My sister, she died in childbirth. And her husband was driven to drink by the grief. So, I adopted her little boy. He's almost four years old."

There was silence as my deceit hung in the air. Geoffrey narrowed his eyes. We both knew I was lying: at that time, every unmarried starlet in Hollywood pulled the same trick, 'adopting' a baby that looked just like them. Any other day he would have dropped me like a hot potato, an unwed, single-mother hot potato. But Geoffrey was desperate. Tomorrow he might feel stronger, but I had him today.

"What a noble thing to do," he said finally, taking my hand. "How about this: you give me a baby, and I'll adopt the boy. I'll provide for him."

"That's very kind of you," I said smoothly, as if we were

negotiating a business arrangement. Which, I suppose, we were.

"I think we'll be happy together, Geoffrey. And who's to say you won't beat this thing?" I said, already hoping he wouldn't.

"I'd like that," Geoffrey said and drained his glass.

It was the best day of my life. A terminally ill rich man wanted to marry me and adopt my son. All I had to do was give him a few happy memories and a baby.

EPISODE FIVE: 1960–1963

RUTH: I don't understand. Before you met Geoffrey, you seemed almost happy, when you were talking about working in the department store, going on dates, and spending time with James.

DAPHNE: Happy might be overstating it. I was working my ass off and schtupping a lot of schlubs on the side. But I did like the independence. It was the first time in my life I was really standing on my own two feet, with no one else controlling me.

RUTH: You could have stayed with that. Maybe you would have even met a real partner eventually. Instead, you just chucked it all away to marry a drunk you didn't even love.

[EDIT: DO NOT INCLUDE IN PODCAST]

DAPHNE: You think I should have done what your mother did? Just keep working my tail off as a single mother?

RUTH: Is that so bad?

DAPHNE: Wouldn't you have preferred to grow up rich, with a mother who was never worried about money? A mother who could give you a future?

RUTH: Maybe. But I wouldn't have wanted her to marry some drunk asshole to make it happen. And I would have liked her to be happy too.

DAPHNE: What can I say? I don't think I ever knew how to make myself happy. Are you happy?

RUTH: Uh, well, not totally . . . things have been kind of tough for me recently.

DAPHNE: And you're telling me a little money wouldn't make you happier?

RUTH: Well, it probably would . . .

DAPHNE: Why don't you ask your dad for help? What does he do for work?

RUTH: Well, he was a plastic surgeon before he retired, and he had a family business. But that's not an option. He . . . he's not in a position to help.

DAPHNE: Plastic surgeons make a lot of dough, especially here. Are you at least in the will?

RUTH: Uh, that's really quite complicated . . . I can't talk about that for legal reasons. But short answer . . . no.

DAPHNE: Christ, you really got the shit end of the stick, didn't you? Maybe you should be the one marrying a terminally ill rich guy. Now, should I tell you about my wedding to Geoffrey?

RUTH: Yeah.

[END OF REMOVED SECTION]

DAPHNE: We eloped quickly, before he had time to start thinking reasonably. It was easy to get married back then, before anyone had computers to check up on your identity. I wore a lace mini dress with bell sleeves. Of all the wedding dresses I've worn, that was my favorite. I really was stunning back when I was young. I don't think I could have gotten away with half the stuff I did if I was unattractive. Ruth, people will forgive a beautiful woman of almost anything. I wish you could experience that just once. It's intoxicating.

RUTH (irritated): Thanks. So, what happened after the wedding?

DAPHNE: I got pregnant almost immediately. Apparently, Geoffrey was extremely fertile despite being an alcoholic with a terminal disease! But I guess God gives with one hand and takes with the other. Geoffrey was excited about the baby, talking about how he wanted to name him Geoffrey Jr. and how he could send his son to his old prep school.

RUTH: He was certain it was a boy?

DAPHNE: He wanted a boy. Mostly so his son could live the exact same life Geoffrey had lived, like he was trying to copy himself. I found it bizarre. Rich people want nothing to change for their children, while poor people want *everything* to be different.

RUTH: Where were you living?

DAPHNE: The apartment Geoffrey grew up in on the Upper East Side. It was huge and full of antiques. I'd never seen an apartment like that in New York; there were whole rooms we never used, full of stuff we never touched, everything from his father's papers to his mother's old medications. James got his bedroom full of toys, although I actually missed sharing a bed with him. I spent my days shopping, taking James to the zoo, and having martinis with the other rich wives.

RUTH: But you were pregnant.

DAPHNE: Pregnancy in the Sixties was more fun. You could smoke and drink still.

RUTH: So you were happy there?

DAPHNE: I should have been, because I was finally rich and had a glamorous life. But I hated being pregnant again. This time, I felt so heavy, so pinned down by the world, like a breed sow. It didn't help that the bigger I got, the more Geoffrey stepped out on me. The cancer diagnosis had made him party even harder, as if he could drink and screw his fear away. I have learned over and over in my life to never expect loyalty from a man. If you want loyalty, buy a dog. If you want something that won't hump every leg in town, buy a plant.

RUTH: That's shitty, to be stepping out on your pregnant wife. Were you mad about the cheating?

DAPHNE: Touched a nerve, huh? Well, I was mad about being left alone. And he barely tolerated my son. He only seemed to like James if he was completely silent in another room. But that's old money for you! They love their dogs and hate their kids! I wouldn't have cared except he still hadn't adopted my son. He kept saying he'd get around to it, but he wasn't budging. It was a concern. I'd married Geoffrey and gotten pregnant so my son could have a better life, and now I was starting to worry that the price had been too high . . .

Chapter Seventeen

I went into labor on a steamy July evening in New York. I had wanted to rent a summer house in the countryside, a place where James could swim and canoe, and where I could sleep under a cool breeze from the lake. But Geoffrey had insisted that the best doctors were in the city and that I didn't want to give birth in some hick doctor's office in the Catskills. Of course, I knew that the real reason was that New York had the highest rate of whores per square mile, and you can't fuck a pretty view.

I had been feeling particularly achy that day, unable to eat anything, and all I wanted to do was lie in bed and watch my soaps. But my son had wanted to play so I took him out, spending the last hour spread out like a picnic on the grass, staring vacantly at the white-hot sky.

We were crossing a busy street when the first wave of pain came rumbling up from my ankles, rolling over me like a tidal wave and making the street dissolve around me. I sent James off to a friend who lived in the building and prayed that I would see him again. I could feel the boundary between life and death starting to thin. It's not like now; back then when you went into labor, you felt death hovering in the doorway, waiting to slip inside. If it has to be one of us, I prayed, take the baby. Geoffrey was totally unreliable. If I died, he would stick my son in an orphanage long before his own end came. But I didn't even know who I was praying to. I didn't believe in God, and even if He did exist, He'd never taken my feedback before.

If Geoffrey had rushed into the hospital at that moment, when I was so scared and alone, he would have won my loyalty forever. Or at least for another year or two, long enough for him to kick the bucket. I had left a message with the doorman, but I doubted Geoffrey would return home in time to collect it. I promised myself that if I survived the night, I would fix my life. I didn't want things to go back to the way they were before, when I was working long hours and never seeing James. I wanted the life Geoffrey owed me; I just didn't want him in it.

I lay in a hospital bed, unsure if hours had passed or only minutes. Sometimes there were other people in the room, doctors and nurses, flickering like shadows across the wall, but in my memories, I am always alone. I was dimly aware that I could see the red flare of a sunset on the horizon. My mind pitched back to the stadium-sized sunsets I'd watched on the Saskatchewan prairie, when I was pausing to wipe the sweat off my face or hurrying to the outhouse as the frozen winds howled across snow as dry as sand. I felt scared again, like a trapped animal all white-eyed and skittering, and it reminded me of being back on that farm, living in fear of the weather and my father. And then, mercifully, another contraction blotted out the memories, and I was staring out at apartment buildings lit up like birthday cakes.

"It's time to push," they said. But I already knew. There are things that the world teaches a woman, and there are things you are born knowing. Something was coming away inside, separating from me. Pain seared through my lower half, leaving my arms scrabbling and clutching the bed. I screamed and pushed and then suddenly, something fell out of me, all crumped and slimy, like an uncooked chicken. I heard a high-pitched squeal and collapsed back on the bed, knowing that the baby was here.

"It's a girl," the doctor announced. I smiled tiredly. There went Geoffrey's plans for Geoffrey Junior. Some part of me was glad that he wouldn't get to name my creation, sloppily stamping his identity all over my baby like the drunken kisses he planted on my face. Somewhere in the city, that asshole was hitting on someone else's daughter, not even knowing that he'd just become a father.

The drama of the moment was draining out of me. Childbirth is indescribable. It's a moment of danger, of insanity, of so many feelings that never get names. Feelings that women look back on periodically in their lives, trying to use their small, ineffectual words to describe things that could never be grasped.

And then another wave of pain gripped me, and I screamed, shocked by my body's betrayal. I had pushed the baby out. What more did it want?

The doctor and the nurse felt my stomach carefully, murmuring medical terms to each other. I lay there, barely aware of the little girl that a nurse had taken away to clean.

"It's twins. We need to deliver that second baby."

I fell back on the bed, writhing in pain and clutching my

stomach. That was the moment I knew I was dying. I was already so exhausted that I was starting to hear voices. I had put everything into the first birth, had torn myself up from the roots, leaving me scraped out and exposed on the bed. I could feel my pathetic life, the dirt, the desperation, the things men did to me, beginning to fade away. My vision was darkening and blurring, and I saw a figure hovering in the corner. Was it Ted? Waiting to finally drag me to hell? Was it my father? Come to take me back home? In that case, I'd take Ted.

I shut my eyes, ready for it all to be over. I had struggled for long enough. But then something occurred to me. Yes, there had been so much ugliness. Years and years of it. But I had survived it all. I could have died in so many different ways if I hadn't saved myself. I could have stayed in Lucan and ended up pregnant at sixteen, hemorrhaging to death in my shack as I tried to birth a child born of incest. I could have hanged myself in the barn to avoid another rape by the preacher because I knew no one would believe me. It could have been me at the bottom of Ted's stairs, a crumpled heap of broken bones and pitiful little dreams.

I had already outlived Ted. I was going to outlive my father, the preacher, Geoffrey, the whole fucking world. I was going to do things they'd never dreamed of. I just needed to save myself.

So, I pushed as hard as I could, the pain blotting out everything, filling my world with white. I pushed and pushed, alone in the noise.

"Twin girls and look how sweet they are!" the nurse said with a smile, placing the wrapped bundles in my arms, like loaves

from the bakery. They didn't inspire the same rush of love I'd felt for James. Maybe it was because they reminded me of Geoffrey, or maybe I couldn't quite forgive them for being twins. But even as I lay in that hospital bed, exhausted and bitter, I didn't forget the promise I had made to myself. Things were going to change.

DAPHNE: From Day One I found taking care of two more babies hard. On a bad day, I'd feel trapped beneath their sleeping bodies, like I was being buried alive. And I knew all these kids made me less attractive to men. They must have thought I was the kind of gal who got pregnant every time she stood downwind of a man! It was the Sixties; everyone wanted to be Jackie Kennedy, not Ethel.

RUTH: Did you love your daughters? When they were babies?

DAPHNE: Look, it's complicated. It was easy to love James; even just watching him was a pleasure. He was the proof that I wasn't a bad person. Diane and Rose were harder to love. They were adorable of course, but they were made for each other, not me.

RUTH: That must be tough to admit, especially as they might listen to this?

DAPHNE: Well, I've already confessed to murder, so I might as well bare all. But mothers don't talk about things like this, especially not back then. It's insane. You have this thing happen that damages your body, threatens your life, and then destroys your freedom, and you can't even say it isn't like waltzing through a candy cane forest every fucking day.

But I tried my best for my daughters because I knew what it was like to grow up feeling unwanted.

RUTH: And you grew to love them?

DAPHNE: I did. And it was fun to shop for the girls. I loved going into Bergdorf Goodman to buy expensive toys and outfits from my old co-workers, loved seeing them go green with envy. To be honest, I probably was spending a little too much back then. And just like men, I always fell out of love with my purchases once I brought them home. But after the twins were born, shopping was my only escape, well, that and dieting.

RUTH: Dieting?

DAPHNE: I decided to lose weight quickly after I had the twins. I wanted to be as beautiful as possible when I became a widow, especially as I'd have three kids in tow. You know, just to keep my options open.

RUTH: Geoffrey wasn't even dead, and you were already thinking of your next husband?

DAPHNE: Look, Ruth, in life you gotta have a plan. Or you'll be at the mercy of someone else with one. Look at you, you're clearly someone without a plan. Someone with brains and a college degree like you should have a lot more money by now. You shouldn't have needed an old lady to help you out.

RUTH: I had a plan. A few plans really. But they all went wrong.

DAPHNE: Ha! Don't I know it! Now let me tell you how I lost the weight. You could probably lose a couple pounds; a woman needs to be at her best when she's single.

RUTH: I'm going to ignore that comment. (Sighs) What was your diet regimen?

DAPHNE: Tomato juice, black coffee, grapefruit halves, and cigarettes, with the odd martini to calm my nerves.

RUTH: God, your stomach must have been pure acid.

DAPHNE: Look, no one was healthy back then. Everyone was just too grateful to have made it through the war to give a shit about carbs and second-hand smoke. And sure, I was hungry and felt like crap, but I also felt this funny kind of sharpness, as if after months of being stuck at home, slowly fading away, I was finally waking up. But once I was awake, I began to notice how hollow it all was.

RUTH: Hollow?

DAPHNE: I had lost the weight. I had bought everything I could think of and then did it again in a different color. But there was nothing left to distract me from my biggest problem: Geoffrey.

HauteHistoire: "Hey everyone, it's time for another TikTok video inspired by Daphne's fashion journey! So, I was so relieved that in this podcast episode, she's finally taking an interest in fashion! I've gone for a real Sixties rich-bitch look. This isn't a look for teenage hippies, it's the look for a gold digger done good, who wants the Upper East Side togs to match! And there's really only one designer that'll give you that Jackie-Kennedy-with-a-twist vibe and that's Chanel. I've chosen a vintage black Chanel suit with heeled booties and a studded necklace to make it more modern. Any color of Chanel suit will work although I suggest staying away from pink Chanel suits because they were iconic in the Sixties for ALL the wrong reasons! After all, no one, not even Jackie herself, has successfully pulled off blood spatter as an accessory, although I do wonder if Daphne's given it a whirl!"

Geoffrey noticed my transformation and it revived his interest in me. That was the only downside to the whole journey, how it increased the number of times I woke up in the middle of the night with him pawing at me, whispering sour, filthy things in my ear. It didn't stop him from sleeping with other women though. When a man starts stepping out on you, it becomes a habit that's hard to break, like when a dog starts pissing on the furniture.

At first Geoffrey was delighted with his 'angels' and would admire their tiny, pink lips and their delicate fingernails. But the truth of parenthood sank in quickly: the wet diapers, the squawking, the nights spent walking up and down the hall getting one to sleep only for the other one to wake up. Not that Geoffrey was doing any of that of course. He never lifted a finger, leaving all the work to me and the help. But even having to share an apartment with the babies irritated him. I guess what he had really wanted was for me to birth a ten-year-old, someone ready to be shipped off to private school and only summoned back for the occasional father-son sailing trip.

Geoffrey thought having a child would be like buying a rug, something beautiful to ornament a house and induce envy in others. But the first time one of his rugs puked on his bespoke suit, the fantasy was broken. Then he began to hate us. I would see him come in and stare at us with bleary eyes, slitted like a snake's, and know that he wished he'd never gotten married or had any children. They hadn't saved him. It turns out that babies can't cure cancer. Which is shocking, I know, as they're so famous for their medicinal properties.

To make matters worse, Geoffrey really wasn't dying fast enough. I had nightmares of him chasing tail for decades while I slowly fossilized on the couch, becoming just another forgotten antique in an Upper East Side apartment.

One night, when I felt particularly lonely, I sat on the bed, watching him get ready for a night on the town. I was wearing a new dress and had been to the salon that day, but he was too busy whistling and fixing his tie to notice. I hated how joyful he seemed, how the thought of leaving us all behind was like a balloon tied to his head, lifting him off the floor.

"Hey, how about you stay in tonight?" I asked. "We could open a bottle of wine? Relax?" I felt pathetic just saying this out loud. I didn't even like Geoffrey. It just irritated me that he was still having all the fun I used to have.

"Hmph? Oh, maybe another night," he replied, too busy preening to even look at me.

"Come on, you said you wanted this family life. You gave me that whole spiel. And don't think I've forgotten about your promises to adopt James. That was a load of shit. You can't even take one night off from ogling waitresses?" I asked bitterly.

"Maybe I just don't like your attitude. I give you everything and you nag me for wanting to grab a drink?" he said, his voice as tight as a guitar string.

"You go out every night! And you and I both know you're

sleeping around!" I was aware of how loud I was becoming. I hated how he'd turned me into this clichéd wife. Where was the gratitude? He'd begged me to marry him, to give him a child. I gave him two babies and went right back to being beautiful and this was the thanks I got? A second-hand pecker that still smelt like another woman's toothpaste?

"You don't know shit. You're just some white-trash whore who thinks she's fancy because she worked in a department store. And now I'm stuck with an ungrateful wife, a brat that isn't even mine, and a couple of screaming babies. So I better see some gratitude when I get back!" He spat, every inch the nasty old snob.

"You're just a pathetic drunk who's scared shitless of dying!" I retorted. He shoved me hard and I fell back on the bed as he stormed out of the room.

I lay sprawled across the bed, frozen in the position he left me. A normal woman would have sobbed, turning the bedcover damp and spongy with her tears until she fell into a numb sleep. But I didn't feel like crying. I felt a searing hatred bleach me from the inside out like bone in the desert.

It gets a lot easier to hate your husband after you have a baby. That's a dirty little secret no one tells you. The same new-lywed who can't stop talking about what a special man she's found transforms into a bitter, resentful person who watches her husband keep himself even as she loses everything. These women spend their days wondering if they're crying because of the sleep deprivation, the hormones, or because their wretched husbands don't understand why their wives don't want to be seductresses in their five minutes of free time a day. And there's no escaping it. No matter the city, no matter the class, you see it all the time: women who lose all their light because they're not allowed to keep it.

Of course, most women just swallow their resentment. It seeps out of their pores as they snap at their children or cry in the night, haunted by the person they used to be. But I reckon there are also a lot of women out there who killed just one teeny-tiny husband and got away with it. Women who sleep easy with neither their spouse nor their conscience to bother them. I bet there are even more women who have daydreamed about it. Women need fantasies, even ugly ones, to survive.

For most women, after they have kids, marriage doesn't feel like a choice anymore. But I knew I would do just fine without Geoffrey. There are benefits to having a useless husband. It makes you brave. Every time I saw him walk out the front door, intent on another night on the town, with steaks and champagne, whores and gambling (the whole Thanksgiving dinner!), I saw him spending my future. Every dollar he threw down on a gleaming bar, every minute I spent married to him, it was all coming out of my future happiness. I needed him dead sooner rather than later. And that was when I decided to help him along.

[EDIT: DO NOT INCLUDE IN PODCAST]

RUTH: But you were killing the father of your daughters.

DAPHNE: Why is it so hard to imagine killing a father? Look at you. You told me your father wasn't in your life, that he had an affair with your mother and preferred his original kids to a baby born out of wedlock.

RUTH: Okay I feel like you're elaborating a lot. And it was just the one kid, a daughter.

DAPHNE: And you told me you're not in his will, that he doesn't give you money. Doesn't that make you angry? Wouldn't you like to see him experience some consequences for his actions?

RUTH: . . . No . . . I really don't think about it . . .

DAPHNE: Come on. You're lying.

RUTH: Just drop it.

DAPHNE: Would it be so bad if someone knocked him off? Really?

RUTH: Are you kidding me? It'd be a fucking tragedy if any of my family members died! These are human beings you're talking about. And fine, my father wasn't around when I was growing up, but we've reconnected as adults. I'm not like you, Daphne! I actually have the capacity to forgive people!

[A chair clatters over. Ruth has stood up and gone to the bathroom. Eventually, she returns.]

DAPHNE: Okay, message received. And don't worry, no one's going to kill your family.

RUTH: Just leave it. I-I'm a journalist, trying to do a job. Just leave my family out of this. Please can we move on.

DAPHNE: I don't even remember what we were talking about before your little hissy fit.

[END OF REMOVED SECTION]

RUTH: This was your first poisoning? The police have said that's your favorite MO. Do you agree?

DAPHNE: Yes. Poison's a girl's best friend. Men are violent; they like knives because they can swing them around like their dicks, then stick 'em in someone. But women just want to get the job done, as calmly and as quietly as possible. People say that's cowardly but there's nothing cowardly about growing up being a woman and knowing the whole world (hell, even your own house!) is full of men who might one day decide to rape and kill you. Living with that knowledge without going insane, that takes bravery. Every man I ever married weighed fifty to one hundred pounds more than me. They didn't *earn* that, it was just nature that gave them that advantage. So, I had to use the other advantages you could find in nature.

RUTH: So you're saying poison's a tool of feminism? A great emancipator of women?

DAPHNE: Well, it levels the playing field. But it takes guts, to smile in someone's face while you serve them a piping-hot cup of mortality, to hold them at night while they suffer, and then wake up every day and kill them a little more. Could you do that?

RUTH: No, I could *never* do that.

DAPHNE: Well, it was easy with Geoffrey. Every morning he would take a fistful of tablets to manage his cancer symptoms. He wasn't much of a details person; he was the kind of man who would drink perfume if you left it too close to the liquor cabinet and never wonder why his breath smelled like roses. It was nothing to dig out an old bottle of his father's heart medicine and some downers that his mother used to take before they put her in the funny farm. And then I just switched his pills for theirs. I knew nobody would be suspicious because everyone was *expecting* Geoffrey to die. I figured he would either be poisoned by the pills or die because he wasn't getting the proper medication. Win-win.

RUTH: Well, win for you, lose for Geoffrey.

DAPHNE: Same thing really.

It took a month and a half. I probably could have done it faster, but I wanted to be careful, to make it look natural. Geoffrey developed stomach complaints and doctors pre-scribed him more pills, which he struggled to keep down. He got weaker and weaker, although he heroically refused to stop drinking. One night, he went to bed with a double whiskey and never woke up. That was my first time waking up next to a dead body but it certainly wasn't my last. It's a bit of an occupational hazard.

On the day of his funeral, I dressed the twins (who were ten months old) in little black dresses and James in his first suit. I wore a black Chanel suit and a large hat with a black veil. I didn't want anyone to see the look of triumph on my face when they lowered his coffin into the ground. I would not be buried with him, this weak and disappointing man. He was given everything in life and pissed it up the wall. I would do better.

HauteHistoire: "I couldn't resist doing another Daphne aesthetic for you guys as this podcast episode is the best yet! So, this is my Funeral Chic look. All black of course but it's important to play with textures, so I've gone for a Saint Laurent latex pencil skirt, a blouse with a lace collar, an oversized blazer and a killer pair of Christian Louboutin spike heels, just to signal to any eligible men in the audience that you might be delivering the eulogy today but you're free for drinks tomorrow! And don't forget your mourning veil, ideally hanging from a fabulous hat. It's Jackie Kennedy again, this time at JFK's funeral, but it's also an excellent way to hide the fact that you might not be as sad about becoming a widow as people expect. So that's the look! My aunt recently died in a golf cart accident so I can't wait to rock this look!"

PreyAllDay:

Okay, we've got another poisoning! So far in the podcast, she poisoned Geoffrey and she's pushed Ted and Frankie to their deaths. But we know that she also poisoned Warren Ackerman, we just haven't gotten to that part in the story yet.

StopDropAndTroll:

It's psycho tho, to share a bed with someone while you poison them more and more.

ShockAndBlah:

OOOOH that gives me CHILLS.

CapoteParty:

Hey, does anyone know if you can actually call Daphne? I heard a rumor that she's in an old folks' home and that you can call her on the phone.

PreyAllDay:

There's no way that's true. Too many guys would be getting their rocks off by calling her.

BurntheBookBurnerz:

Interesting that that's where your brain went automatically. Says a lot about you . . .

StopDropAndTroll:

[This comment has been removed by a moderator.]

Chapter Eighteen

Ruth walked slowly along the beach, clutching a thermos of coffee and inhaling the heady ocean air. The sky was still tinged pink from the sunrise and the sand was bathed in a soft light.

She had woken up early, with a head full of to-do lists, and another missed call from her mother. Ruth had hoped to sleep in because she had stayed up past one, trying to wade through all the emails she was receiving, from places like *The New Yorker* or NPR, asking for interviews or inviting her to write pieces. She tried to defer as many as she could until after the podcast was finished, but it was all so tempting.

Ruth had also spent hours the night before editing the latest podcast episode, which was now called *The Three Murders of Daphne St Clair*. The Geoffrey story had been fascinating and would be a real bombshell for his daughters, Rose and Diane, but Ruth was still waiting to hear about a different murder, and it was getting harder to stay patient. Now it was morning, and she had woken up with a racing heart and a pounding headache and needing to do something other than stare at her laptop.

Even though it was still early, the beach was already full of people exercising and walking their dogs, and Ruth marveled at how anyone could be so vigorous so early in the morning. Many of the people she saw were wearing headphones. Were any of them listening to her podcast? Ruth liked to think about her listeners. She often pictured them, scattered around the country, even the world, walking their dogs on a cloudy day, stuck in traffic on a dreary commute, strolling aimlessly through their neighborhoods with screaming babies strapped to their fronts, listening to her voice. It was a comforting thought.

A cluster of luxury apartment buildings stood like blonde sentinels along the road, all built by Sunshine Development. The Ashburton, the Blue Diamond, the Seacrest, some of the most expensive condos in the area. Ruth's eyes slowly traced a route up the curving lines and shimmering glass walls of the Seacrest Building until they landed on the penthouse. It was magnificent, the prow of a grand ship turning out to sea. Ruth knew the views from inside were even more spectacular. She missed seeing them.

This beach meant a lot to Ruth. The first time she ever met her father was in a café here. She had just turned twenty-six and he was in his mid-seventies. She hadn't even known his name until he emailed her out of the blue and introduced himself. They had met a few days later, and Richard had apologized for his absence, admitting that he'd kept his distance to stop his wife from finding out about the affair. But after she died from cancer the year before, he was now trying to change his life. He had retired from both his medical practice and his family business (Sunshine Development), sold his home in the suburbs, and started dating again. But his biggest wish was the opportunity to get to know Ruth. That was the year their relationship settled into a really good place; he had seemed so proud of her achievements and her ambitions, he'd believed that Ruth could do anything, and he wanted to help her.

Months later, he had made her a promise on this beach that would change her life forever. He had been thinking about his legacy, a pressing issue for a man in his seventies with diabetes and a number of other health issues, a man who had watched his beloved wife wither away from cancer. He told her that he hadn't been there for her as a child but now he wanted to give her some real security as an adult. Ruth thought about that moment often, when she had believed that she finally had a father who loved her and that everything was going to be okay. It had been a happy memory for only a moment. And then, for many years after, it was a source of pain.

Ruth took another sip of coffee and stared out at the rolling waves. It felt good to take a break from her laptop, however brief. But Ruth knew that she could only afford a moment's respite. Daphne could be carted off to prison any day now and, once that happened, Ruth would lose her chance at making a new future for herself, one that looked more like what her father had promised her, back when she still believed in happy endings.

Ruth was running out of time.

"Hey, Grandma, I'm still listening to the podcast." Harper always seemed to call in a hushed voice, likely because she had squirreled herself away in a corner to hide from her mother.

"What do you think?"

"It's interesting, but kinda weird for me. I mean, that guy you killed was technically my grandfather," Harper said.

I nodded. "Well, you never would have met him; he was on his way out no matter what I did. Harper . . . I can't stop you listening but try to remember that I'm more than those murders."

"Are you sure you can trust Ruth?" Harper asked. "She doesn't really seem like she's on your side. The things she asks you . . . it's almost like she's working for the police."

"I don't think she's a cop. She actually seems to hate the local police; I think she's got history with them. But I understand what you're saying. She is sneaky."

"Have you ever googled her? I was looking at this Reddit thread about the podcast and it has all these links to true crime articles she wrote. I read one she did about the Miami New Year's party. She's really into investigating unsolved mysteries."

"Oh . . . well that's good to know," I said, wishing I had asked Harper to google her for me before I hired her. What did I really know about Ruth? You know, other than she had terrible taste in clothes and no money. I didn't want someone to investigate me, I just wanted someone to press record and share my story on the Internet. Maybe I had been hasty, hiring her and trusting her with my secrets.

"Anyways, I saw some old photos of you on Sexy Devils," Harper said.

"What in God's name is that?" I asked. "If it's some kind of skin flick then I don't want to know, and neither should you."

"It's an Instagram page that shares pictures of hot criminals, mostly murderers. It's really popular."

"I'm honored," I replied sarcastically. I've never even been on Instagram although I probably would have loved it when I was in my prime. I could have taken pictures of myself all day long when I was young and beautiful. "So, who else made the cut on this illustrious page?"

"Oh, you know, it's mostly guys. Richard Ramirez and Ted Bundy, people like that."

"I never saw the appeal of Ted Bundy," I said. "People always say how handsome he was but one look at those bugged-out eyes and you can tell he was crazier than a shithouse rat."

Harper laughed. I rolled my eyes.

"I think you should stay off those sites. It'll rot your brain."

"But what if one day I grow up and become a homicide detective and solve a bunch of crimes because of the stuff I'm learning now?" Harper asked. I couldn't tell if she was joking or not. That kid loved to stir the pot.

"Oh, like all the clever detectives who caught me? Don't waste your time. Get a job that makes you a lot of money but gives you weekends off. That's the ticket," I said.

"Like what?"

"Be a dentist. Or, if you really want to work in crime, start a crime-scene cleanup business. I saw a TV show about them once. They make a lot of money cleaning up murder scenes and meth labs."

"Isn't that kind of disgusting?" Harper asked.

"Sure, it is. And so is renting porta-potties to music festivals, but I bet those guys make a lot too. You can become rich and powerful if you're willing to do something that most people won't do. That's the secret, Harper," I said, tapping my forehead even though she couldn't see the gesture.

"Like murder?" she asked slyly.

"Don't be a smartass," I said.

"So, what's with the curtains?" Ruth asked Daphne. "It's a beautiful day, why do you have them closed all the time?"

They usually had a few minutes of small talk before they launched into the interview, a chance to get used to each other before the recording started. Daphne usually used this time to criticize her outfit. Today she'd taken one look at Ruth's T-shirt, which had been washed so many times it was almost transparent, and said that Ruth's clothing reminded her of the drifters who rode the rails in the Depression.

"It's always a sunny day in Florida," Daphne scoffed. "But, well . . . the staff have asked me to keep my curtains shut because someone might be trying to find me."

"Find you? What do you mean?" Ruth asked, feeling her stomach clench. She stared at the blocks of shadow that the curtains made, with the warm sun, as yellow as egg yolk, seeping around the sides.

Were there others like her? Others who wanted justice for their unsolved murders but who didn't have the access she did? Or were they after something far darker? Ruth could understand the impulse. It was hard, sitting here day after day, watching Daphne crow about the men she'd killed, especially as the offenses that earned them a death sentence were getting increasingly hard to justify. Ruth's sleep was getting more fractured and her stomach seemed to be permanently roiling. But she had to keep it together no matter the cost, had to hold on until they got to the right time, the right man, the right murder.

"Some kind of private investigator, or a man pretending to be a PI. I don't know, they think he might be dangerous, so they're keeping me under lock and key."

"Strange how everyone's trying to protect a serial killer from the public," Ruth said wryly, trying to keep her face neutral.

"Yeah, life's a hoot. So . . . do people ever ask *you* what it's like interviewing a killer?" Daphne asked.

"All the time," Ruth said, clenching her hands, feeling them ache from the stress of countless hours at the computer.

"And what do you tell them?" Daphne asked, her eyes pinning Ruth down like a butterfly on a specimen board. Ruth didn't like the predatory gleam in Daphne's eyes, as if Daphne had remembered that at ninety years old, she was still capable of being very dangerous.

"Well, I say that you're interesting to talk to . . . I mean *interview*," Ruth stuttered. "But that it's strange to talk to someone who's committed such terrible crimes. That I'll always wonder if you're telling me the whole story, or whether you're planning to keep some secrets tucked away," she said, examining Daphne's reaction. *Just tell me I'm right about him*, Ruth thought.

"I am telling you everything," Daphne snapped. "I'm the one who confessed, remember?"

"Of course, but it's different sitting here now. Some part of you wonders: would she kill someone I care about? Would she kill me too?" Ruth murmured. These questions were at the core of this story, but Ruth tried to act casually, as if she were just a diligent journalist doing some fact-checking.

A silence fell over the room. An uneasy, stomach-squirming silence, as the two women stared at each other. Ruth knew that Daphne hated being put on the spot, hated 'gotcha' journalists. That maybe, in a strange way, she saw Ruth as just as much of a threat as Ruth considered her one.

It made her afraid, the way Daphne was staring at her, the barely contained rage beneath the surface. But it also made her angry. How dare this woman decide who lived and who died? Ever since Ruth had heard about Daphne, had realized that it was her, the killer she'd been waiting for, she'd felt this anger growing inside her, spooling in her intestines, wrapping itself around her heart, her lungs, her head, crowding out her empathy and her tolerance more and more.

"I wouldn't worry," Daphne finally said, her words careful, but with a hint of warning. "I only kill men."

More silence. Ruth felt a strange impulse to grab Daphne's bony shoulders and shake her, watch that dyed black perm and wrinkly face flop around on her brittle neck.

"Let's keep going," Ruth said finally, letting the moment pass, resuming their usual dance. "What happened after Geoffrey died?"

"My whole world opened up," Daphne said. "I sold his place and bought a great place downtown. I got a live-in to help me with the kids and after they went to bed, I hit the town."

"Were you looking for men?" Ruth asked.

Daphne shook her head. "No! At that time, I was batting men away. I was rich! I was free! Sure, I went on the occasional date, but that was it. At that point I believed this would be life forever." Daphne sounded almost giddy. Ruth noticed that this was one of the rare times she seemed happy talking about her past, this brief moment when she believed that she was finally satisfied.

Ruth sighed, feeling suddenly drained. If the story had ended there, if Daphne had gone straight and spent the rest of her life raising her three children, using Geoffrey's money to give them the opportunities she'd never had, then maybe she could have been salvaged. Yes, she had killed four men (and counting) but two were violent assholes and the other was a terminally ill fuckboy. Okay, and there was Warren, but he was very old. All human life was precious of course, but most people would concede that some of it was a *teensy* bit more precious than others. If the story had ended there, some people would have still been able to forgive Daphne.

"So, what changed?" Ruth asked.

Daphne shrugged, a vacant, heavy-lidded stare settling on her face.

"I got bored."

The Fourth Murder

Chapter Nineteen

EPISODE SIX: 1968–1970

DAPHNE: I want you to know that I'm not a monster. I do have regrets about some of the people I had to kill. David Priestly, my second husband, was one of them. I met David in New York in 1968. I was going by the name Cecilia then. We were living downtown, in a new building and I had an incredible Sixties wardrobe to match. I met Andy Warhol at a party, and he begged me to be in one of his art films but I said no way. He gave me the creeps. I'm not surprised a woman shot him. No normal man should be that interested in soup.

RUTH: You met Andy Warhol? Wow, he's so famous.

DAPHNE: If you lived in New York as long as I did, and spent the kind of money I spent, you met them all: Truman Capote, Mia Farrow, Frank Sinatra. My life story's the history of the twentieth century.

RUTH: A nice little chunk of the twenty-first century as well.

DAPHNE: Ah well, I don't count the part I was in Florida for. Florida's where history goes to die. Anyways, there I was in

1968, single, beautiful, and being invited to a different party every night.

[EDIT: DO NOT INCLUDE IN PODCAST]

RUTH: Sounds expensive though, especially for someone living off an inheritance. I would imagine, anyways . . .

DAPHNE: Yeah, you lost your grandmother right? She didn't leave you any cash?

RUTH: No, she didn't have much. Mostly old newspapers and a lot of stuff from her ex-husband. She was a bit obsessed with him because he left her.

DAPHNE: And you're not in your father's will. So it sounds like you'll never get a big inheritance.

RUTH: Definitely not. There was a time when I thought . . . but no.

DAPHNE: Hmm . . .

[END OF REMOVED SECTION]

RUTH: Anyways, you sound like you were really burning through that inheritance. What were you planning to do when it ran out?

DAPHNE: Find another man before it was too late. It's an unusual form of financial planning, but it works.

RUTH: So . . . David?

DAPHNE: David was in New York for work and from Day One I could tell that he was decent. Let's just say he was that one rich man who was actually going to make it into heaven. We had a swell time, and he extended his visit because he'd fallen hard for me. I would catch him looking at me with a kind of wonder on his face as if he couldn't believe his good luck.

RUTH: Did he know you had three children?

DAPHNE: Yep. Sometimes we brought them on dates. It's hard, isn't it? Finding a man who will accept a woman with a body count?

RUTH: Oh . . . I see, you mean the kids! Yeah, it is. My mom was pretty much single until I grew up.

DAPHNE: Is she married now?

RUTH: She's seeing someone, has been for a few years. It's good; he helps her. Her health's . . . not so good so he does the driving and a lot of housework.

DAPHNE: Sounds like a keeper. David was great with the kids. By that time, James was eleven and the twins were six. One day David took us to Coney Island, and we rode roller coasters and ate ice cream on the beach. At the end of his visit, he popped the question in the oyster bar in Grand Central Station, which no New Yorker would have done because that station was a shithole in the Sixties. He asked me to come home with him to Vermont, said that he'd be a father to the children, and I wouldn't have to worry about money. He really gave me the hard sell, like a vacuum cleaner salesman being shown the door.

RUTH (shocked): And you agreed to the marriage? And the move? Just like that?

DAPHNE: Look, people didn't spend decades hemming and hawing about marriage back in the day, they just slapped a ring on and got on with life. Besides, David must have caught me on a raw day because I was starting to think that maybe my problem was all the high living. Sure, I hated small-town life when I was growing up, but I was *poor*. Being rich out there had to be more fun.

RUTH: Well, it certainly couldn't hurt.

DAPHNE: There's never a bad place to be rich. You grew up here, right?

RUTH: Yeah.

DAPHNE: I gotta tell you, you should get out of Florida. It's holding you back. This is where you retire, not where you find success. You should be somewhere buzzy like—

RUTH: Don't say New York.

DAPHNE: New York!

RUTH: The solution to everything is not New York! I'm not ready to leave Florida; there's still things I'm trying to work out. And my mom lives here. But tell me about you and David.

DAPHNE: Well, we got married in New York and then we moved north to Leosville, Vermont. I loved New York, but David would have never lived there. And I wanted to give my kids the best childhood, all the happiness denied to me. I guess I was swept up by the Norman Rockwell picture he'd painted me of the children playing in the apple orchard as I sat in the sunshine with a gin rickey and a *Vogue*.

RUTH: To be fair, that does sound nice. Although I will have to google what a gin rickey is. So, how did the kids react?

DAPHNE: Well, they were shocked at first, but David promised the twins horseback riding lessons and James a dog, and they came around. Besides, they already loved David. The twins had never known their father and Geoffrey had been more like a shitty roommate to my son. David was so grateful for a family too. He was infertile because of a teenage case of the mumps, and he'd always wanted kids. I'd pulled off the triple crown: finding an unmarried man with a good job, great house, and who was excited to be a stepdad.

RUTH: Yeah, that does seem like a rare find.

DAPHNE: And I've only made them more endangered.

[EDIT: DO NOT INCLUDE IN PODCAST]

RUTH: Have you ever broken up a marriage?

DAPHNE: Why? Is that where you draw the line? Killing my husbands is fine but they better have been single when I met them?

RUTH: I'm just wondering . . .

DAPHNE: Just wondering if I'm like your mom?

RUTH (irritated): My mom didn't break up a marriage. She was just a young woman and he was her boss. And she wasn't a homewrecker; he never left his wife.

DAPHNE: Okay, okay, calm down. So, your mom was an unsuccessful homewrecker, big deal. And I wouldn't call you *nothing*. And yes, I dated a few married men but I preferred men with fewer financial commitments. I didn't want to hold someone's hand through a legal battle.

[END OF REMOVED SECTION]

"This is the house," David said, opening the car door for me. I stepped out and craned my neck up. The house was blue with

white trim, three stories with a sharply angled roof. It was freshly painted and gleamed as if someone had spit-polished it. Everything was pristine, from the matching red tartan curtains in every window to the manicured flower gardens beyond the little white gate.

"It's quite the house," I murmured. He smiled as he began to pull suitcases out of the trunk. My children got out and stood next to me, staring up at the house in awe.

"Are we the only ones who live here?" James asked.

I smiled. "Yes, darling, it's not like New York. People don't have apartments here. Although to be fair, most people don't have houses like this," I said.

"This house has been in my family for over a hundred years," David said. "Or should I say, our family," he said tentatively, squeezing James's shoulder. My son smiled up at him and David beamed back. I could see why he was glad to have a family now, a single man would have rattled through a place like this, unable to make enough movement and noise to bring the house to life.

"Welcome home," David whispered in my ear, taking my hand and leading me up the stairs. I couldn't help smiling. Not bad for a farmgirl born in a shack.

The next day, I decided to take the kids to the playground. I was walking hand in hand with James. The twins were following sullenly behind, intentionally kicking the sidewalk with every step to scuff their shoes. We walked in the long shadows of the houses, the street silent around us. It was unsettling, as if everyone lay dead behind their doors, sprawled out on freshly vacuumed carpets and soap-scented bedspreads. I was used to a dogpile of car horns, angry voices slipping out of window cracks, the metallic grinding of a city constantly erecting itself. The playground was livelier and James breathed a sigh of relief to see other children running around and shouting.

A group of Stepford wives had congregated by the benches. They were dressed like Easter eggs, all soft pastels and gentle patterns, with wasp waists that meant they must have girdles surgically attached. I was wearing a black miniskirt and a striped top with a pair of very expensive boots. I looked like a brunette Brigitte Bardot, all boobs and legs, but with a better face. Unfortunately, Doris Day still reigned supreme here.

I lit a cigarette and watched, idly, as three women detached themselves from the flock and cruised over to me. They looked me up and down and smiled, but I could see in their eyes the grudging acknowledgment that I was beautiful and they were merely decorated. I've never had a problem admitting I was attractive. In life, you have to be honest about your strengths and weaknesses or you'll waste your time trying to be a brain surgeon when you're as dumb as a bag of hammers.

"Hello, we've been waiting to meet you!" one of the women exclaimed, as if I had made some mistake by failing to find them.

"You're the new Mrs. Priestly aren't you?" another asked, her eyes fixed on my wedding ring.

"I am!" I said brightly, trying to convey that special new-lywed excitement at hearing my married name. I'd already had so many names at that point that I felt like replying: 'I don't know. Am I?'

I gestured at the children to go and play. Diane and Rose

ran off, hand in hand, and were instantly surrounded by other children who were fascinated by them being identical. It was always the same. Whether it was kids or adults, everyone went crazy for the twins. They accepted this adoration, like they accepted everything they were given.

James hesitated, scanning the playground as he dug his foot into the dirt. My heart began to break at his little face, peeking out shyly from under his bangs. But then he spotted another boy sitting by himself, constructing an elaborate mountain complete with twig trees and stick bridges. Soon they were happily playing, their heads bent together as they earnestly discussed their project. I felt a wave of relief. You can never explain to someone who isn't a mother how your every mood depends on your child, how even everyday disappointments become tragedies when you see your child experience them.

"Welcome to town. I'm Belinda Vaughn. This is Patsy Beauteen and Carol Davidson," the head witch said, gesturing to the rest of the coven. I couldn't help noticing how her hair never moved, not even a quiver, no matter how much the wind tried. She must have put half a can of Aqua Net into that do. Bullets would have bounced off it.

"Pleasure," Patsy said, laying her dainty hand in my palm like it was a gift. I understood their roles instantly. Belinda was the leader, the boss who kept everyone in line. She wasn't pretty but she was thin and knew how to do her makeup and a lot of people mistake that for beauty. Carol actually was good-looking, with thick golden hair and sky-blue eyes but when you met her gaze, you could tell she was a dim bulb. She caught me looking and smiled dreamily, as if she'd had *a lobotomy for lunch. And Patsy was the horsey one, the less attractive friend that the other two kept around in the hope that her life would be crappier than theirs. Bonus points if she had a drunk husband, a shrew of a mother-in-law, and some juvenile delinquents for children.*

"Yes, hello. My name is Cecilia," I said, squeezing Carol's hand and making sure the ruby in my ring jabbed her.

"We hear David met you in New York? And that he proposed after a week?" Belinda said. She was smiling but her eyes were as beady as a city pigeon's.

"It was a few weeks," I said, turning to check on James, who was still happily playing with the other boy. I wondered which children belonged to these women. Knowing my luck, they would all become my children's best friends.

"Why the hurry?" Patsy asked.

I smiled at her and popped a hand on my hip. "Well, I just couldn't wait to get up here and meet you all," I said, my voice dripping with sweetness. They frowned, unable to tell if I was joking or not.

"We're glad he's married though. We all thought David might end up a lifelong bachelor. People were starting to worry about him . . ." Patsy said. The implication was clear. In 1968, 'lifelong bachelor' was the small-town euphemism for a man being light in his loafers. In New York City, you just called them gay.

"And are those your children from a . . . previous marriage?" Belinda asked delicately. Her eyes were fixed on me like a boxer looking for an opening.

"I'm a widow," I said flatly.

*The women visibly relaxed. "Oh good. Well, not good . . ."
Patsy fumbled. I stood there smoking, watching her sputter.*

*"This is a small town, we were just worried you'd be
one of those big-city divorcees. They're a little . . . fast for
Leosville," Belinda explained, as if divorcees were an inva-
sive species, blowing through town like tent caterpillars,
seducing the locals and perverting the children. It seemed
like in Leosville, you could swear off someone for serving an
unfashionable dessert whereas in New York a person would
have to sacrifice a shoeshine boy to the Devil before anyone
raised an eyebrow.*

*"Nope, when I get married, it's 'til death do us part," I said,
smiling. The women smiled back uncertainly.*

*"We do hope you'll get involved with the PTA, the Women's
League, and some of our other local groups. It's women like
us who keep this town from becoming, oh, say . . . New York
City," Belinda said smugly. She was clearly the president of all
of those groups. You probably couldn't run a lemonade stand
in Leosville without Belinda taking over.*

*"I'll pass," I said, already bored with the conversation. "I
think this town could do with a little New York."*

*I used my first cigarette to light my second one before
throwing it on the ground just a little too close to their feet.
They seemed shocked that I wasn't willing to pay tribute to their
dime-store queen. But I don't play nice with other women, especially not a bunch of housewives re-enacting* Lord of the Flies.

*And yes, James's new best friend did turn out to be Belinda's
son.*

ShockAndBlah:

She's not really a girl's girl is she?

BurntheBookBurnerz:

No, she lives for the male gaze. She thinks all women are competition. Although it is interesting she chose a female journalist for the podcast.

ShockAndBlah:

How do you know she chose her?

PreyAllDay:

She could have had anyone. Why choose some random writer no one's ever heard of?

BurntheBookBurnerz:

Maybe she doesn't really respect men, doesn't trust them to tell her story. They're either aggressors or playthings to her.

CapoteParty:

I don't think she respects anyone, really.

DAPHNE: At first, it was kind of fun, like pretending to be a housewife on TV. I'd wear heels to the grocery store. I bought a cookbook. There'd been so much pain in my life, I believed that I could scrub it clean, fill my soul with gleaming surfaces and fresh-cut flowers. I even tried to enjoy the fresh air between cigarettes.

RUTH: Okay, so you were in your tradwife era. What did your children think of Leosville?

DAPHNE: They loved it. They spent all their time playing outside in the orchard with their friends. I even bought them a dog named Ruffles. Seeing my son sitting on the back porch, whispering secrets with his arm around Ruffles almost made up for the occasional shoe full of piss. Almost.

RUTH: That's cute. I would have liked to grow up somewhere like that. Big house in a small town. I would have liked to have a lot of friends living nearby too.

DAPHNE: Did you switch schools a lot?

RUTH: Yeah. I think I went to six or seven schools in twelve years. After a while, I just stopped trying to make friends. I just read a lot of books and kept my head down, waiting for college.

DAPHNE: You remind me of my granddaughter. Although I hope she does a bit better than you have! And just a tip, once you're too old for Girl Scouts, you're too old for a backpack!

RUTH: Wow, okay, rude. But I hope she does better too, even if now you've made her a little infamous.

DAPHNE: I think that could only help her, really. She can write a memoir about me someday, once I'm pushing daisies, a sensitive weepy one about our relationship.

RUTH: To be fair, I could do that too.

DAPHNE: Ah but you'd need a hook. You'd have to give them something the podcast doesn't have.

RUTH: Well, maybe I'll write something really explosive. I could dig up some more skeletons in your closet or prove you fed me a crock of lies.

[There is a pause where nobody speaks.]

DAPHNE: You're not smart enough for that.

RUTH: I guess we'll see . . . I'm sure people have underestimated you too, maybe even some of your victims. But enough distractions. The listeners will want to know about your life in Leosville. Did you make any friends in town?

DAPHNE: Not really. I tried to fit in. That's all I ever seemed to do in Leosville. Try. But I just couldn't do it. Every day was just like the one before, and not because it was non-stop fun. My errands were boring and the TV we watched was boring and the conversations I had with David were boring because really, what was there to talk about when I was wasting my best shoes on the fucking grocery store! You'd find that hard too, Ruth, if you owned any nice shoes.

RUTH: I . . .

DAPHNE: Please don't interrupt my flow. Anyways, in Leosville, time seemed to just drag on, doubling and folding in on itself. I didn't recognize myself anymore. In New York I had been a mom, sure, but that was only part of my fabulous life. In Leosville I could *only* be a wife and mother. And at night I'd lie in bed and try to convince myself that I was happy. When I was poor, I would have killed for a life like this, to have a beautiful home and a kind husband with a fat wallet. But this little voice inside of me was whispering, *Don't waste your life* *here. If you had his money and your freedom, why you could do anything . . .*

[EDIT: DO NOT INCLUDE IN PODCAST]

RUTH: In a strange way, I can relate. I've spent the last decade writing silly articles on the Internet, just so I could pay the rent. I would have killed to have enough money to really be able to pursue journalism.

DAPHNE: *Killed?*

RUTH: Okay, well no . . . Bad choice of words. I would have *loved* to have—

DAPHNE: You seem a little flustered.

RUTH: No, I'm fine. Sorry, I just didn't sleep well . . . I think as the podcast is becoming so high-profile, I'm a little worried about our safety. Yours and mine both. The last time I drove home from here, I could have sworn that a car was following me. But I couldn't be sure . . .

DAPHNE: Well, I can't imagine anyone would go after *you*. I'm the murderer. You're just someone helping me.

RUTH: Well, I don't know that I'm helping you. I'm a journalist trying to establish the truth . . .

DAPHNE: Okay, great, whatever you need to tell yourself when you start making cash off my story.

[END OF REMOVED SECTION]

RUTH: So you weren't happy in Leosville?

DAPHNE: I really felt like I'd lost myself. I was just another faceless woman at the kitchen sink, wishing every girl would make the same choices as her because she couldn't bear knowing other people still had freedom.

RUTH: Sounds challenging.

DAPHNE: You probably don't feel that bad for me. I understand. When I was younger, I would have killed for this kind of rich person problem. In fact, I did! But I just want you to know that I did try. Killing David was never more than my Plan B.

HauteHistoire: "Hello my TikTok fashion junkies, it's time to take a trip back to mid-century America. Think *Stepford Wives*, think Florence Pugh in *Don't Worry Darling*, think Betty Draper before she realized Don Draper was the original fuckboy! Back to the era of vacuuming in heels, getting your hair set, and secret pill addictions! So we've got a red floral Dolce & Gabbana sundress here to help us live out our Tomato Girl fantasies. Then add a pair of chunky plastic heart sunglasses to show that you can still be fun even if you're dying on the inside! And of course, a pair of Roger Vivier heels because in mid-century America, women always wore heels, even on their slippers! If you feel like dressing up as Murder Barbie while you plot your darling hubby's eventual demise, then I've got you covered!"

A year passed and I was even more unhappy. I couldn't even commiserate with anyone because everyone in town seemed so content that they had a nice house and a full TV schedule to occupy them until death came. One evening, as I was washing dishes and David was idling in the kitchen, picking at his second piece of pie, I tried to explain how I was feeling.

"Do you ever feel really frustrated with your life? Like you want to tear it all up and start over?" I asked, glancing at him. He was sitting on the counter, looking like a little boy in a high chair.

"Not anymore. I used to want a family badly. But now I have you and the kids and I'm so happy," David said. His brow was completely smooth, as if he'd never had a serious worry in his life. And maybe he hadn't; he'd grown up wealthy in a quiet little town where everyone knew and liked him. Yes, it had taken him a little while longer to get married but it's universally acknowledged that if you have enough money, someone will marry you eventually. Especially if you're a man. You could have a second nose growing out of your forehead and some busty twenty-five-year-old would still wax poetic about your gentle soul and sly sense of humor.

"I just don't like Leosville," I muttered. "It grates on my nerves. I thought my life was going to be . . . special."

"My darling, things will get easier," David said, slipping his arms around my waist. "Your life has changed, and you just need time to adjust."

"I don't want to adjust," I muttered, stepping out of his grip. He looked hurt and I resisted the urge to slap his face. David was just too nice. I should have liked that after all the bad men I'd dated, but it doesn't matter how much a woman's been through, if she describes a man as 'safe' then he's destined for the scrap heap.

"Give it time; you just have to settle in," David said, ambling out of the room. I rested my forehead on the cupboard door in front of me, staring down at the potato peels floating in the soapy sink. The phrase 'settle in' echoed in my head and I had a sudden image of a rock sinking down to the bottom of a pond.

That night I lay in bed next to my husband. He was sleeping peacefully and that made me resent him. Didn't he care that I was unhappy? Why wasn't he tossing and turning, his mind racing with ideas for how he could help? David was just so grateful to have me but all that gratitude, well it annoyed me. I was used to having something to push against, a hatred that would fill me with drive and energy. I was like a mangy dog who bit the hand that fed it because I only knew how to fight.

It's wrong to kill. I know that. Sure, I didn't go to church anymore (that tends to happen once you've been attacked by a preacher) but 'Thou Shalt Not Kill' is pretty much Christianity 101. But killing never made me feel bad; living did. Living in a world that didn't give a shit about me and what I wanted. Killing was a release from all that. It was my declaration of independence (after all, I was American now!) and it was always a thrill, the feeling that you were the master of the world. I didn't feel ashamed of what I did, only what was done to me.

I stared at the black ceiling and watched the starbursts tingle in the darkness. My heart was pounding in my chest and I felt as if I was going to explode out of my skin if something didn't change. I could just leave David, but I only had enough money in savings to cover six months of expenses in New York. I could live differently of course, but the only place I really felt like me was in the city. Without the money, I was just the same old farmgirl with shit on her shoes. A shadowy certainty crept over me, propelled by my racing thoughts and his gentle snores. I had done it before and, now, I was going to do it again.

David was going to have to lose his life so I didn't lose myself.

Chapter Twenty

BurntheBookBurnerz:

THIS is what the tradwives don't tell you. That behind all the pretty dresses and clean kitchens, women are LOSING IT. Everyone who's got a hard-on for homeschooling and baking bread needs to remember how much women struggled with this stuff. Ring Ring Ring, Betty Friedan, looks like we got a case of 'the problem that has no name'!

PreyAllDay:

Jesus, it feels like you had that one teed up. How long have you been waiting to hit Paste?

StopDropAndTroll:

I don't get ur fucking problem. She meets a nice man who pays for her and gives her a nice life. David was a fucking saint! He's even raising kids that weren't his! She's lucky to find a man like that. What's her issue?? This is why we need MGTOW!

PreyAllDay:

Yahhh, what's the serial killer's issue? I thought she'd be totally sane /s.

ShockAndBlah:

Okay . . . hot take but . . . is anyone else getting beige flag vibes from David? Like I wouldn't want to be married to him . . .

BurntheBookBurnerz:

Well, he wasn't listening to her. She was saying she was unhappy and he ignored that.

CapoteParty:

None of this justifies killing him though.

StopDropAndTroll:

No shit, Sherlock.

DAPHNE: And so, the process began again. It was easier this time because David wasn't the suspicious type. He was the kind of person who never read his receipt or checked his change because his world was full of kind people, and he always had enough to share.

RUTH (regretfully): What a lovely person.

DAPHNE: Yeah, well, don't get too attached.

RUTH: How did you do it? Without being seen?

DAPHNE: I'd sneak out of bed before dawn. That's a woman's time, really, when she can do what she wants in a sleeping house. I'd crush up the pills and put them in the cottage cheese because it was the one breakfast item my kids would never touch. By the time David woke up there was a beautiful breakfast in his sunny kitchen.

RUTH: What did you poison him with?

DAPHNE: Dexylchromate, which is really the most loving way you can poison someone. It doesn't burn the stomach or make you vomit over and over. Instead it goes straight for the brain, making you exhausted and weak. It's really the same as getting old, just on a much faster schedule. David didn't know it, but he was on my timeline now.

RUTH: Poor David.

DAPHNE: All right, you've made your feelings clear about David. And look, I tried to be the sweetest wife possible once the poisoning started. It wasn't hard because from the moment I had my plan, I felt like my old self. The danger of being caught, the knowledge that I had a secret, the power I felt over my husband, it electrified me. And on the first day he complained about exhaustion, I helped him up the stairs before tenderly tucking him into his death bed.

On the fourth day we called the doctor. David was insistent and I knew that people would eventually ask questions if we didn't have him examined. But I still felt a surge of adrenaline when the doorbell rang, and I tried to breathe deeply. I needed to look concerned about David but not like I had something to hide. I needed to control this situation, to keep the doctor unworried while reassuring David that he was getting the help he needed. But my mind was full of nasty visions: the doctor, standing up from examining David and pointing a single accusing finger at me. David turning and scowling at me, his eyes dark with hatred. My children watching me being handcuffed and thrown in the back of a police car.

This was the gamble. It was my riskiest murder yet, because this time there was no life-threatening situation and no termi-nally ill husband. I was killing a perfectly healthy man who posed no real threat to me (unless you can be bored to death). But when I opened the door, my shoulders sagged with relief. Dr. Penney was tall and gangly, and his Adam's apple seemed to bob uncontrollably. His ears stuck out and he had the cow-licked hair of a little boy. He seemed terrified to have been called out and was clutching his doctor's bag with the same fervor as a kid with a teddy bear.

"Hello," he coughed out.

"Please come inside." I gestured and he followed me in, stumbling on the doorframe. He apologized and I had to stop myself from smiling, my confidence growing by the second.

"Are you from here?" I asked as we began the long climb to the bedroom.

"Ye-yes," he said hesitantly. "Of course I went away for school. But I've just finished." Just finished. It was music to my ears. A green doctor with no self-confidence.

"Who was the doctor before?" I asked.

"My father," he admitted. "But he died a few months ago

and the people, they need a doctor . . . so I guess that's me."
Even he didn't sound convinced by the prospect.

"Well, we're glad you could come see us," I said, making
sure my voice sounded grave and low, even though I felt like
skipping down the hall. I pushed the door open and gestured
the doctor into our bedroom. My husband was lying in bed,
his head pressed against the pillows as if a great weight was
pushing him down, leaving him unable to move.

"So, what seems to be the problem, Mr. Priestly?" Dr.
Penney asked.

"David, please," he mumbled. "I've just felt so run down
recently. Every day, I hope I'll wake up having turned the
corner but then I spend the day in bed, barely able to keep
my eyes open." His voice had a pleading, frantic quality. My
husband was begging this man to understand, to fix him.

"Do you have any other symptoms?" the doctor asked as
he fumbled with a blood pressure cuff. He was like a magician
struggling to pull off a new trick.

"My brain feels foggy, like I can't concentrate," David said,
watching the doctor take his blood pressure with all the detach-
ment of someone watching TV.

"Well, your blood pressure is fine. You do look pale though.
I'm wondering if it's an iron deficiency?" Dr. Penney said
with a frown. He looked lost, as if he'd shown up for an exam
without attending the class. I suspected the plan had been for
his father to train up his son before retiring but his untimely
death had launched Penney Jr. into the deep end.

"It could be?" David said, although a question hung in his

voice. He didn't want guesses; he wanted a rock-solid diagnosis and a plan back to normal.

"I'll be sure to cook him lots of red meat," I said smoothly, patting his arm and smiling. "Even if you don't have an iron problem, a steak dinner should lift your spirits."

"Just last week I was out in that yard, chopping wood," he murmured, rolling on his side to stare out the window. "Now I'm stuck in bed."

"You'll be back outside soon," I said, kissing his forehead. "I'll show the doctor out and then make you a steak dinner."

But he was lost in his own world, the dappled light from the window throwing patterns on his haggard face.

"I think it's time for him to be admitted to hospital," Dr. Penney said to me in the kitchen, a week later. It was a warm autumn afternoon, the kind of weather that makes you feel incredibly happy to be outside. The sun was getting lower and the air was full of buttery golden light. I stared out the window, aching to walk away but knowing that this was the moment when I had to be the most cautious, a devoted wife above even the start of suspicion.

"Of course, doctor. He's not getting any better. I just want my David well."

"It's a couple hours' drive to Glendale, the closest hospital with the specialists he might need. I'll call them today but let's take him tomorrow. He's already asleep and the trip will be exhausting for him. We'll set out at eight tomorrow."

"I'll ask the neighbors to take the kids," I said. "I'll see if they can spend the night, so I don't have to sort them out in the morning."

"Okay," Dr. Penney said. He shook his head and tried to speak a couple of times before he finally got the words out. "I'm starting to suspect David has an aggressive form of cancer. I think you should prepare for the worst."

"I don't know what to say," I said. I sighed and rubbed my eyes, bleary from the exhaustion of being David's nurse day and night. He nodded sympathetically.

"Well, we should get some answers soon. I'll see you tomorrow."

"Thank you," I said, showing him out. After he left, I pursed my lips and began making David's soup. I pulled the dexyl-chromate out of my hiding place in the cupboard.

That evening, as the sun faded behind the curtains, I sat with David in the bedroom, all tucked up in bed like a little boy. Strangely, he seemed to know that he was dying. I helped him drink more soup, knowing that it was so full of poison he'd never live to see the bottom of the bowl, not in his weakened state. He seemed so comforted by me, the secret source of all his troubles.

He slipped away peacefully, a smile on his face that made me feel almost good about killing him. He died knowing what it was to be a husband and father and believing that he was loved. Meanwhile I felt a strange thrill at his death, the same feeling I'd had when I stared at Ted's body or contemplated the way I'd changed the Flanagan family's life on a subway platform. Except this time, I felt it even more intensely, as if I was injecting it straight into my veins. It was power. Pure *unadulterated power. I decided who lived and died. Everyone existed at my mercy. And once you've felt that, well, it's hard to go back to tuna casseroles and* I Dream of Jeannie.

David did love me. I still feel a little bad about him. He thought he was going to spend the rest of his life with me. And I suppose he was right.

Chapter Twenty-One

DAPHNE: After David died, Dr. Penney became certain that it had been cancer. I guess it made it easier for him to cope with the fact that one of his first patients died undiagnosed and untreated. So, by the time the obituary ran in the paper, 'cancer' had become 'late-stage leukemia.' Just one of the many sad, ordinary deaths that made up a season in a small town.

RUTH: How long did you stay in Leosville after his death?

DAPHNE: Two months. I hated every minute of it, but I needed to lie low, make sure no one was questioning the death. Then I sold the house to some out-of-towners and pocketed my inheritance. David was richer than I could have imagined, the kind of guy who always earned and never spent a penny on himself, socking it all away for me, his rainy day. He really was the best kind of man. Then I loaded the kids and the dog into the back of the car and left town.

RUTH: The dog came too?

DAPHNE: Oh yeah. Ruffles came too. That damned dog outlived my next two relationships. In the end, he died of old age, a rare occurrence in my house.

RUTH: How did the kids take leaving?

DAPHNE: Oh, they cried and cried, but I knew they'd also been happy in New York. And I felt so excited; the whole world seemed to shine with possibility. Leosville was a dump. Had David lived somewhere with decent shopping and a nightlife, he might have gotten another two years with me.

RUTH: I-I . . . just can't believe you did that! You killed a man who loved your kids, who *loved* you, just because you were bored? Because you hated small-town living and wanted to get back to New York?

DAPHNE: It really was the best thing.

RUTH: According to who? Certainly not David! I would have loved to have a parent like him! Doesn't it bother you? You killed the only proper dad your children ever had! Don't you think about the fact that the men you're killing had mothers, sisters, children?

DAPHNE: Who, exactly, are you talking about? David was alone.

RUTH: I'm talking just generally! The people you killed, it *affects* things.

DAPHNE: Well, it's certainly affected you.

RUTH (flustered): What do you mean by that? I'm just here to tell your story.

DAPHNE: But this podcast has made your career. You should be glad I killed David, it gives the public what they really want: a villain, someone to make them feel better about all their gross little secrets. 'Oh at least I'm not as bad as *her*!'

RUTH: I'm not trying to make you into a villain. Or an angel. I'm just trying to tell the truth about you.

DAPHNE: Yes, well, here it is. David was nice and I *killed* him.

I killed him and I took his money, and I hightailed it back to the big city. And by then, I knew I really had a taste for murder. That I wasn't just using it as a last resort, I was doing it because it was *fun*.

When Daphne finished talking, Ruth sat in silence, her throat seized up with emotion.

For the first time, the reality of the situation was truly striking home. *I'm sitting across from a killer.* She had known it intellectually, but now she truly felt the implications of what Daphne had done. She had robbed people of the only time they would get to spend on earth.

Ruth gazed into Daphne's eyes, which despite being draped in sagging skin were as cunning as a crow's. Before David, the three men Daphne had killed seemed so unlikable that the murders felt almost justified. But it was David's death that transformed the story, severing the link between Daphne as a victim and Daphne as a predator. It proved to her that Daphne was the killer she was looking for, the missing puzzle piece that had eluded her for so long. Because if Daphne could kill David, then she could kill *anyone*.

Ruth pulled her water bottle out of her bag and took a gulp, forcing it down into her roiling stomach. She was stalling for time, trying to quell the panic and horror blotting out her thoughts, telling her to *run, run, run*. Ruth finally understood that if the situation was right, Daphne would have no hesitation in killing her. It didn't matter that she was a good person, or that Ruth's mother would miss her, or that Ruth had never done anything to hurt Daphne, she would kill her just the same.

Because her life didn't matter to Daphne. It was terrifying. It was infuriating.

"Anyway, that's the whole Leosville story," Daphne said, leaning back in her chair and clacking her bony hands against her brittle legs with gusto. It sickened Ruth, the way she did everything but smack her lips at the thought of murdering an innocent person.

"What did you do next?" Ruth asked, trying to move the story along until she could find firmer ground, hoping that they might come to a natural stopping point so she could wrap up the interview and leave. So that she didn't have to look at the woman who'd ruined her life any longer.

"Moved back to New York, of course. I had realized that a normal life, even a comfortable one, wasn't good enough for me. I wanted a fabulous life, full of glamour, excitement, and luxury, and I knew New York was where I could get it. I also decided to use the name Daphne. I knew my kids were getting older and I couldn't keep changing my name, so I decided to pick one I really liked."

"Where did the name come from?" Ruth choked out, trying to keep her water down.

"A TV show," Daphne said with a shrug.

"Was it . . . *Scooby-Doo*?" Ruth asked.

Daphne chuckled. She had a strange laugh, almost as if her throat was cracking and the sound was spilling out.

"No, but it wasn't much better. It was a soap opera called *Confessions* that I got hooked on when I was killing time in Leosville. Daphne was this rich bitch with a string of husbands, so I guess sometimes life imitates art."

"And you've been Daphne ever since?"

"Till the day I die," Daphne said, her voice steady and her face untroubled. It was obvious that death had been a constant companion to this woman for a long time, an old friend that she never tired of seeing.

I'm going to show the world who you are, Ruth thought, as she ended the recording and began to pack up her things. She knew that the first thing she'd do when she got home was start editing these files, to get the next episode out.

But not before she changed the title of her podcast yet again. *The Four Murders of Daphne St Clair.*

Ruth hit terrible traffic on the drive back and by the time she pulled into the parking lot next to her apartment, the sun had already set, although the air was still warm and velvety against her skin. The sky was a royal blue, and the parking lot lamps were few and far between, amber pools of light in a dark land-scape.

The staircase was an internal spiral up the building, and it was dank and dark. As she walked up the stairs, the light above her flickering frantically, Ruth became aware of a presence behind her. She could sense it was a man, a large one at that, who had emerged from the second-floor landing and was now uncomfortably close. Her neck prickled and she felt exposed, not liking the feeling of turning her back on a stranger. Their footsteps echoed in the landing. She was wearing sandals, which slapped against the floor, but she could hear the squeak of his sneakers, and she knew that he was right behind her.

Just pass me, she thought. *Just fucking pass me; you're creeping me out.* Maybe it was innocuous. Men didn't realize how often they inadvertently made women feel unsafe. But a lot did it intentionally too.

His body seemed to grow closer, his feet striking the step just as her foot lifted off from it. They passed the third-floor landing, the stairs looping up above their head into the darkness, like the rafters of an old bell tower.

Should she turn back and glare at him? But what if she saw something dangerous in his face? An expression that told her he'd been waiting for her to look, to understand what was about to happen? What if she just started running? But maybe he was waiting for that too? Besides he was so close that he could easily grab her. She wondered if someone had sent him. Maybe the Montgomerys had hired a thug to throw her down the stairs and make it look like an accident. It would certainly make things convenient for Lucy.

As they neared her landing, she moved as quickly as she could. She pulled the door to the fourth floor open, her heart beating so hard that it felt as if it was bruising her ribs with every thump. She slipped in and went to push the door shut behind her, but he was already there, his solid body blocking the swinging door.

"Oh, Ruth! What a surprise!"

Officer Rankin. In his police uniform and bulletproof vest, smiling at her. There was a triumphant glint in his eye as if he'd known that he'd spooked her.

"I'm just here on some police business. I forgot that you lived here. Apartment 407, right?" he asked.

She nodded warily, her head spinning. Was she safe? She didn't *feel* safe.

"So, I see you're still doing that podcast huh?" he asked, sounding like a disappointed father. Again she nodded, not meeting his eyes. She was scared to walk to her apartment in case he tried to follow her inside. He shook his head ruefully.

"How about that, you interviewing Daphne St Clair. But I suppose it makes sense—you two have *a lot* in common," Officer Rankin said with a laugh tinged with menace. "Although I sure wish you'd take a leaf out of her book and confess. The boys down at the station are still scratching their heads, wondering why she came forward, but I'm just glad some criminals have a little backbone."

Ruth stood frozen to the spot.

"Well goodbye, Ruth. The Montgomerys send their regards. See you again soon," he said, before turning back into the stairwell.

Ruth watched him go down the stairs and then ran to her apartment. From her window she saw him get into a police car and drive away. Officer Rankin had no reason to come to the fourth floor; he *had* been following her. He was probably being paid a handsome salary by the Montgomerys to do it too. But to what end? To frighten her off the podcast or to get her thrown behind bars? There was no way to know.

Ruth had always felt safe when Jenn was living here, the apartment filled with the comforting noises of *MasterChef* reruns and Jenn shuffling around in her slippers. But now the apartment was silent, and every noise reverberated through her body like a gunshot. At night she would lie in bed, adrenaline coursing through her veins, certain that this time, someone had really found her.

It happened. People got murdered in their apartments every day. Ruth knew that better than anyone.

That night, once she had finished packing, Ruth saw a call from her mom light up her phone. She couldn't avoid talking to her any longer.

"Ruth? I've been calling for ages!"

"I know, Mom. I listened to your messages and read the texts. But like I said, I know Daphne killed him, I'm just trying to find proof."

"Ruth, it doesn't matter what you think this woman did. She is dangerous. This whole thing is dangerous! Just take any evidence you've found and—"

"And what? Turn it over to the cops? The only murder they've managed to solve in ages is one where the killer literally had to call them up! They won't give us any justice."

"Ruth, to hell with justice. To hell with the truth and solving mysteries. You think I give a rat's ass?" Louise shouted. "I just want you safe."

"Mom, it's not going to happen," Ruth snapped. "I'm doing this, whether you like it or not. But look, I'm going out of town, on a research trip to Vermont. So, stop worrying about me. Nobody gets hurt in Vermont!" Well, except for David, but Ruth didn't need to mention that right now.

"I'm not giving up, Ruth. I'm not giving up on you," her mom replied.

"It might be better if you did," Ruth responded, but her mom had already hung up.

Ruth sighed and pressed her phone against her cheek, feeling the warm screen stick on her skin. She took a deep breath and stared at the shadows beyond the streetlamp outside. Was that a flicker of movement? It was hard to tell. One thing was certain. No matter what her mom wanted, Ruth knew that she wasn't safe, not anymore.

BurntheBookBurnerz:

Okay, that last episode was fucking hard. I need some self-care after that.

StopDropAndTroll:

Snowflake. Crying those widdle baby tears.

CapoteParty:

Imagine having to live through that. Poor David. Poor kids. I hope people leave Diane and Rose alone now that Daphne's confessed; they've already been through so much.

StopDropAndTroll:

Those twins are total Karens. Fuck 'em. And I doubt the kids even remember David.

ShockAndBlah:

Don't be ridiculous, of course they would. He was their only real father figure.

StopDropAndTroll:

Ruth has some real daddy issues doesn't she? But then again, all the best girls do . . .

BurntheBookBurnerz:

U r gross.

CapoteParty:

Hey, has anyone looked into murders in Abrams, New York? Any Daphne connections there?

StopDropAndTroll:

[This comment has been removed by a moderator.]

PreyAllDay:

I'm too focused on the Tylenol murders right now. I think there's a good chance Daphne did them.

StopDropAndTroll:

Daphne commits murders for MONEY. Nobody made any money off the Tylenol murders so fucking drop it.

ShockAndBlah:

Stop trying to make fetch happen.

Chapter Twenty-Two

Ruth stood in front of the big blue house, awed at the size. It was the kind of house she had dreamed of as a kid, when she was stuck inside a succession of cramped, humid apartments reading *Little Women*. A thought crossed her mind—*I would be happy if I lived here*—before she quickly rejected it. A house couldn't make someone happy. Although, she thought, as she stared up at this gorgeous behemoth and imagined fireplaces and bookshelves, it couldn't hurt.

She had felt something similar the first time she'd visited her father's penthouse apartment in the Seacrest Building. He had moved there after his wife died, because the family home contained too many memories, and Ruth had been amazed at the expansive views across the ocean and Richard's book collections and photos from his life.

The photos dotted around the place were primarily of his wife and daughter, but he had proudly pointed out to Ruth a new photo of the two of them on his desk—a selfie he'd had framed. It had made her smile at the time, had made her feel part of the family, until later, at his birthday party, when Ruth had noticed how everyone had avoided looking at the picture just as much as they had avoided having to make awkward small talk with her.

But that was seven years ago. A different lifetime.

And Ruth had left all of that back in Florida, if only briefly. It was like the credit card she had used to pay for this trip. Today, she could spend freely, but she knew that at some point in the future, her bill would arrive.

The Leosville saga was what true crime fans loved: murderous housewives, picturesque settings, and the secret underbelly of small-town America. Ruth knew that she had to balance out Daphne's interviews about David's murder with local color about the town, her impressions and, most importantly, interviews with people who remembered David and Daphne. Give the listeners a bit of a palate cleanser.

She felt safe here, far from Officer Rankin, the Montgomerys, and Daphne's stalkers. It was also a relief to take a break from Daphne herself, even though she was the focus of this entire trip. It was getting harder to be in the same room with Daphne, to set aside Ruth's own personal grievances and act like an impartial journalist. Especially as Daphne seemed to have a sixth sense for the topics Ruth was trying to avoid, the painful details she didn't want to reveal to a cold-blooded killer. And that was the problem. She had traveled almost fifteen hundred miles, the entire length of America's east coast, but the one thing she couldn't escape were the memories.

EPISODE SEVEN: 2022

RUTH (Voiceover): I walked up the steps, anxious to see if I could talk to the people who lived in this gorgeous house. I also got out my recording equipment because I knew that from a legal standpoint, it was better if they knew that I was a journalist and was recording them right from the start. I hoped they might show me around. I imagined how strange it must be for them to stand in the bedroom where David Priestly died, completely unaware that in sixty years someone would finally be telling his story, his real story. I rang the doorbell and a woman around my age answered. I noticed immediately that she was wearing heels. In the daytime. In her own home!

FEMALE HOMEOWNER (warily): Can I help you?

RUTH: Hello, my name is Ruth Robinson. I'm a journalist and I'm making a podcast called *The Four Murders of Daphne St Clair*. Maybe you've heard of it?

FEMALE HOMEOWNER: No, I haven't heard of it.

RUTH: Well, uh, Daphne St Clair is a ninety-year-old woman who just confessed to killing a number of men throughout her life.

FEMALE HOMEOWNER (sounding distasteful): Oh, that *does* sound familiar. But why are you here at my house?

RUTH: Well, one of the husbands she killed lived . . . here.

FEMALE HOMEOWNER: Here? You're telling me she murdered someone in my house?

RUTH: Yes, sixty years ago. A man named David Priestly.

FEMALE HOMEOWNER: They did say the home had been in the same family for over a hundred years, I think the name *was* Priestly. So, you're visiting town to interview people for your . . . podcast?

RUTH: Yes. And I don't suppose, you could show me around the house? Or I could maybe interview you about the house?

FEMALE HOMEOWNER (coldly): Now, why would I want everyone knowing a murder happened in my house? I don't even want to know that. I think you had better leave now, before I call the police.

[Sound of a door shutting firmly.]

Ruth got back in her car and drove away, feeling the woman's eyes watching her until the house disappeared around the corner. That conversation had been a failure, but Ruth was hopeful that tomorrow's interview with Belinda Vaughn would go better.

Every time she interviewed Daphne, she made sure to pump her for as much verifiable information as possible: addresses, people's names, timelines. The podcast needed additional interviews, of course, but Ruth also knew that she needed to be able to corner Daphne, to box her in with as much truth as possible so she'd have less room to lie.

After interviewing Daphne about Leosville, Ruth had taken the list of names and tried to find people who still remembered her. She was looking for people in their eighties and nineties who still lived in the area and would agree to talk to her. One by one, the names withered and dropped from her list until one remained: *Belinda. The Queen Bee.*

Ruth drove down Main Street, following the directions to her hotel. Looking around, she had the feeling that not much had changed since Daphne had lived there six decades before. The lawns were manicured, the red brick gleamed, and Ruth couldn't see a single panhandler or vacant shopfront. Somehow the opioid epidemic that raged through every other small town in America seemed to have skipped this place, the land fentanyl forgot. In every shop window and crowded corner Ruth felt as if she could see Daphne, young and gorgeous, a crow in a pack of canaries, just out of the corner of her eye, slipping away whenever Ruth tried to get a better look.

The next day, Ruth woke up to a text from her mother wishing her a safe trip but also requesting that she spend this time away really thinking about whether this podcast was worth it. Ruth ignored it.

She checked Jenn's Instagram, noting that Jenn had a new book out and was signing copies in a Palm Haven bookstore. Clearly their breakup hadn't sent Jenn into a doom spiral like her. Ruth's life had always been messy, but Jenn had met Ruth at a particularly low moment, when Ruth's whole life had been knocked off course and Ruth was trying to figure out if it was healthier for her to completely ignore the past or try to solve the mystery that was slowly consuming her. She had swung between repression and obsession until finally, the relationship had ended, ironically just before Ruth had gotten the sign she'd been waiting for: Daphne's confession.

Ruth found Belinda sitting in the lounge of Willowdale Seniors Home. Ruth noticed immediately that the older woman had put a lot of effort into her appearance, coating her sparse eyelashes with mascara and draping her rounded body in a beaded jacket and slacks that made her look like a guest at a wedding. Belinda looked disappointed when she saw Ruth was wearing jeans and hoodie, but perked up when Ruth complimented her.

"I love the jacket. You look so glamorous."

"Oh well, I like to dress up. My generation always took pride in their appearance, unlike people today," she said with a smile. Ruth couldn't tell if that was a jab at her but even if it was, what would she have done? Belinda was the only important interview she had for the weekend, the rest was just getting local color and flipping through old newspapers at the town library.

"I agree. It was so much nicer when men wore suits and hats, and women went out with their hair done," Ruth said, mimicking the boring old shit her grandmother's friends used to say.

"I couldn't agree more," Belinda replied, pleasantly surprised. "Well, I'm glad I could help you with your research. I have to say, I'm surprised Daphne turned out to be a murderer and even more surprised that she'd turn herself in when no one suspected her. I thought she was just your garden-variety gold digger."

"So, what was your first impression of Daphne?" Ruth asked, hurriedly pulling out her recording equipment before she missed any more insults. Belinda laced her hands together and leaned back, obviously ready to hold court.

"Can I swear? Because Daphne, or Cecilia as I knew her, was a real . . . bitch—" Belinda bit off the word and slid it through her teeth, as if it was a particularly chewy piece of toffee. "Daphne would go on and on about how exciting it was in Manhattan, all the fabulous stores and how many celebrities she had met. But I always knew she was just trash wrapped up in a bow. I didn't have time to worry about her though, I was focused on being the best wife and mother I could be," she finished, staring down her nose at her guest. Ruth had assumed all the petty stuff would be washed away when you were staring death in the face but clearly, she was wrong. People were people, no matter their age. And people were usually awful.

"Is your husband . . . around?" Ruth asked, not sure how to ask someone if their husband was asleep by the fireplace or in an urn on the mantel.

"We're not together anymore," Belinda said sourly. "Not for thirty years now." She deflated when she said it, as if talking about a treasured career that ended in redundancy.

"So, do you remember anything strange about Daphne?" Ruth asked.

"Well, she was very attached to her son. Which is funny because I think most women would have made a real fuss over identical twin girls. This was before everyone went to a scientist to have six babies put in them at once. But no, it was the boy she favored. He was a sweetheart. How's he doing?" Belinda asked. "I imagine it's been strange finding out mommie dearest is a killer," she said with barely disguised satisfaction.

Ruth wondered what it was about women that they took such pleasure in everyone else's misfortune? A woman could dine out on infidelity or divorce, making a messy meal out of it, sucking out the marrow and licking her fingers at the end. Maybe you couldn't be lofty and noble when the world denied you so much power. You had to live down in the dirt, scrabbling for crumbs and cataloguing other people's faults and failures.

"They've been estranged for decades, so we don't even know if he's heard about his mother's confession," Ruth said. Belinda nodded, flattening her lips and tucking them inside her mouth.

"Well, I guess we have that in common. My son William is

not in touch either. We had a falling-out about his . . . lifestyle," Belinda said.

Ruth sighed. She never understood how someone could lose a child over something as intrinsic as sexuality. Ruth had never even bothered explaining her sexuality to her mother. Louise was just informed of any new romantic developments in her life and whether the person coming to dinner was vegan, paleo, or just a boring old vegetarian.

"You know, that was the best time in my life, when the kids were young. I felt like I really had a purpose," Belinda said wistfully. It always made Ruth sad when old women talked about how happy they'd been when their husbands were alive and their children were young. It reminded her what was coming for them and what would come for her someday. Even Daphne could get a little nostalgic about her younger days, although she was usually reminiscing about killing men and spending all their money, which was less sweet.

RUTH: What happened after David died? Not to get all Angela Lansbury on you, but no one suspected foul play?

BELINDA (indignantly): Who? And why would anyone think it was foul play, when his own doctor was going around saying it was cancer? I wish that damned fool was still alive—he'd have some explaining to do!

RUTH: And then Daphne sold the house and moved away?

BELINDA: I can't say any of us were surprised. Of course it was sad that the house was no longer in the Priestly family but it was probably for the best. I would have hated it if that horrible woman had stayed in that beautiful house, lording it over the rest of us.

RUTH: Fair enough. Is there anything else you want to say about Daphne or that time?

[Belinda hums and shifts in her chair.]

BELINDA: Only . . . to find out all this now, it makes you wonder what other things you don't know about your own life. How many other lies did I believe?

Ruth (Voiceover): I drove away from Leosville wondering if I'd gained any new insights into Daphne. I had hoped I could use Daphne's past to crack her open and make sense of what I saw inside. And maybe that was why she hated me talking to anyone but her. But all I was learning was that no matter the name, the town, or the husband, Daphne had been the same inscrutable, malevolent force for decades. The people I've talked to have all said the same thing: she was beautiful, clever, and a bit mean, the kind of woman who flirted with the men in the room and ignored their wives. But those descriptions told me nothing. The only ones who might have had a true insight, who had actually seen the real Daphne, weren't around to answer.

Ruth was driving home from the airport, feeling her hair return to its usual humidity-induced frizz (thank you, Florida) when her phone rang. Ruth pulled into the parking lot next to her apartment and glanced at the number. It wasn't one she recognized but she answered anyways, hoping that it might be a nice surprise, like an Amazon deliveryman or a media outlet offering her a permanent job (hey, a girl could dream).

"Hello?" Ruth asked. She glanced down at her gas gauge and then turned the car off and rolled down the window. Even though it was evening, the heat outside gusted in, as if she'd just opened an oven.

"Hello, Ruth? It's Lucy."

"Oh . . . okay. Hello," Ruth sputtered in shock, jerking forward in her seat. Fuck. She always felt like a child around Lucy. It wasn't just that Lucy was fifteen years older than her and from a different generation, it was the way Lucy always seemed perfectly polished and exquisitely tailored, Palm Haven's own Ivanka Trump. It was only a matter of time before she ended up on a reality show about hotshot luxury realtors and Ruth would be forced to write clickbait articles about her.

"I gather you received my letter?" Lucy asked.

"I have, yeah," Ruth said warily, rubbing her tired eyes. "It was so nice to hear from you. Although the tone of the letter left something to be desired . . ."

"And yet you're still making this podcast," Lucy responded coolly. "I'm confused. Don't you realize how much you're risking?"

Ruth's head felt fuzzy, and she wondered if this conversation was as menacing as it felt or whether her exhaustion was making her paranoid. Both seemed entirely possible.

"I don't have anything to lose. You people have blocked every career opportunity I've had for years. But I've finally found someone you can't pressure into blackballing me. I guess serial killers don't scare easy," Ruth responded.

"If it's been so bad then why don't you just leave? You're

not even going to have a home soon; we could evict you at any time. Move to the West Coast and do your little articles there. It would be better for everyone that way, we'd leave you alone," Lucy replied.

Ruth swallowed, aware that this was the first time her suspicions had been confirmed. The Montgomerys really were the reason she'd had so many jobs fall through, so many promising contacts ghost her.

"I'm good. There's a lot I'm still trying to figure out. Besides, I've got this podcast now, so I'm really glad I stuck around," Ruth replied.

"Ruth, this isn't your story to tell. It's my story. My family. My money," Lucy said, her voice wavering. "Just leave us in peace. You're disrespecting his memory."

Ruth swallowed, trying to work out if Lucy was genuinely emotional or if this was a ploy to manipulate her.

"It's my family too," Ruth whispered. "And I'm not trying to hurt you; I really am just trying to find the truth. This podcast . . . it will be a good thing, I promise."

"Ruth, you really think losing a couple of jobs is the worst it could get if you keep this podcast going? There's not a powerful person in this state that we're not friends with. Whatever you think we can do . . . it's worse. Besides this podcast is just disgusting. No one wants to hear from a killer," Lucy said, before hanging up.

Ruth sighed and rested her forehead on the steering wheel, a thousand retorts swirling around her head, already feeling her stomach begin to churn with anxiety.

Lucy was rich, well connected, and—most importantly—angry

with her. Ruth had made a powerful enemy. But Lucy was also wrong.

Everyone wanted to hear from a killer.

PreyAllDay:

Okay, guys, this is weird but I JUST SAW RUTH! She must have just come back from her recording trip! I live in Palm Haven (no doxing pls), in this neighborhood by the beach. There was some coverage saying that Daphne had lived in a luxury condo building down here (the Blue Diamond) before she went into a seniors home but I don't know if it was ever confirmed. But I was coming home tonight and Ruth was parked in a shitty little car, staring out the window. I did a quick Google image search and it was definitely her. She even had a sticker on the back of the car for the college Ruth graduated from!

ShockAndBlah:

Ooh wow! Maybe she lives in the neighborhood too?

PreyAllDay:

Nah, the way she complains about money, she definitely doesn't live around here. I think she's probably doing something for the podcast.

BurntheBookBurnerz:

What was she doing?

PreyAllDay:

Just sitting and watching. I could have said hi but she actually looked really intense!

BurntheBookBurnerz:

So she was watching the Blue Diamond?

PreyAllDay:

No, she was staring at a different one, the Seacrest Building. It's the nicest one around here, super exclusive. Although I seem to remember a story about it. It happened way before I moved in. A suspicious death. I'll have to do some research.

BurntheBookBurnerz:

So you're rich huh? Makes sense.

PreyAllDay:

FFS.

The Fifth Murder

Chapter Twenty-Three

I found out my son-in-law Senator Reid Prescott was running for governor of Florida from the news. No one had bothered to tell me. Reid stood at a podium, all lantern jaw and thick hair, looking like a frat boy whose father just made a rape allegation disappear.

My daughters both married men like their twin sister. Diane had always been the dominant twin, the one who made the decisions and protected Rose. Diane had married Jonathan and then Brad both of whom rolled over and showed Diane their bellies every time she barked. Meanwhile Rose married an alpha like her twin, the kind of man who thought it was romantic to order in restaurants for you without ever asking what you like. Yes, it's Psychology 101 but maybe like history, if you ignore it, you're doomed to repeat it. Diane certainly had with hubby number two.

"I have been planning to run for governor for a number of years, but recent events have only confirmed to me that decent people need to push back against the decay we see all around us," Reid announced, shaking his head dramatically at all the societal rot he could see in the conference room of a four-star hotel. I rolled my eyes. He always gave pompous little speeches like this, even before he became a senator. It was probably why Rose drank so much.

"Recent events being your mother-in-law's confession to murder?" a reporter asked. Reid placed a hand on Rose's shoulder, who stared into her lap, the picture of demure, ladylike shame. Yes, how very selfish of her to have me as a mother. She should have considered the political implications for her future husband when she chose to come sliding down my birth canal.

"Yes. Daphne St Clair represents the way our modern society has eroded the Christian ideals and family values our nation was built on," Reid replied.

Modern society? I was ninety for Christ's sakes! I started murdering back in the Fifties, the decade all these idiots had such a hard-on for! They seemed to think it was all *Leave it to Beaver*, when in reality, people fucked their neighbors and beat their wives; they just didn't show it on TV. And all this tripe about family values and Christianity. Who was more family-oriented than me? Everything I did, I did for my kids. And where were those Christian values when I was getting raped by a preacher?

"Are either of you in contact with her now?" another reporter asked.

"Absolutely not," Reid said vehemently. "I need to protect my family from monsters like her."

"Why do you think she confessed? Do you think this election had anything to do with her timing?"

"It's certainly possible," Reid agreed. "My wife's mother certainly does not share my political convictions."

I snorted. What a joke. As if I needed to blow my life up to stop Reid from becoming governor. Reid didn't need anyone's help to lose the election, he could do it all by himself.

"What do you think should be done with her?" the same reporter asked.

"I believe that anyone who commits a heinous act like murder should receive the death penalty, regardless of their age," Reid replied. Rose's face remained neutral as her husband talked about sending her mother to the electric chair.

Guess I was off the Christmas card list.

The press conference went on, with reporters asking questions about me and the revelations in the podcast while Reid tried to steer the conversation back to his platform and his usual spiel about God, America, and the family. I always found it suspicious how much conservative men liked to talk about families. It always seemed to be the ones who were later found face-down in a pile of cocaine.

It was strange though, to see my own daughter disowning me on television, even if she wasn't the one talking. I knew my confession might cause some hurt feelings in the family, but I didn't think it was really worth cutting me off. I had given my girls so much. Didn't I deserve a little loyalty in return? I had never put a man before myself or my children and I'd always hoped they'd do the same.

At some point Reid gave up on outlining his political views and switched to finding a million different ways of calling me evil. I guess he wanted to differentiate himself from any candidates who were running on a pro-serial killer platform.

"If that's not bad enough, she wasn't even born in this

country. I don't even know if she immigrated legally," Reid said gravely, pausing in case anyone gasped. No one did. "Daphne St Clair is . . . Canadian." Rose covered her face in humiliation.

Another day, another visit with Arthur Tisdale, my lawyer. He wasn't that exciting a guest but at least it broke up the monotony of the day.

"So, what's new?" I asked. "I feel like I've been cooling my heels for almost six weeks and nothing's happening."

Tisdale smiled, a wry little grin as if he found me amusing. I wanted to slap him.

"I've never met someone so eager to go to prison! Before too long we'll have a date for you to enter your guilty plea. But about this podcast . . ."

"We've discussed this before," I snapped. "You don't want me to do it and I'm doing it anyways. What's the worst that could happen? I'm ninety years old; any prison sentence they give me will be for the rest of my life."

"Well, yes," Tisdale muttered. "I understand you don't have much to lose, but what about the journalist? Ruth Robinson? She could end up subpoenaed to testify in any court proceedings. Someone might even try to charge her with something, like obstruction of justice."

"Why? I confessed. And because of her, the lawyers will have gotten hours of information. Obstructing justice, she's done their job for them! This is America. The only right anyone gives a damn about is free speech," I said. "You can be shot in a high school by a lunatic with an AK-47, but you're allowed to have a protest afterward. And she can always use some of that money she's making off me to hire a fancy lawyer like you."

"Well, perhaps. But if you're so insistent about this podcast, be mindful of your safety. A man has been calling our office every day. I've also seen someone suspicious lurking around my car at work. I think a car even tried to follow me home yesterday, but I managed to lose them. I've had to tell my wife to go stay with family in Savannah because I'm concerned about our safety. Daphne, someone is *looking* for you. Maybe more than one person."

"Well they're not gonna find me," I muttered, trying to sound brave even though a knot of dread was forming in my chest. "That's the whole point, isn't it? No one ever caught Daphne St Clair."

Chapter Twenty-Four

Ruth was in Long Bean drinking an iced raspberry matcha and trying to wade through her endless emails when a petite woman with a blonde pixie cut and a cross-fit tank strolled in. Ruth froze.

Jenn.

Their eyes locked. Ruth clung to her matcha cup for comfort. Jenn hesitated, a cloud crossing her sky-blue eyes, before she came over, carefully picking her way between the crowded tables and chairs.

"Hi, Ruth," she said. Ruth sucked on the matcha, inhaling half the cup in one expensive gulp.

"Hi, Jenn, wow, it's you!"

There was a long pause, where they both seemed to be replaying that last awful day. Both of them crying as Jenn packed her things, Ruth raging as Jenn tearfully explained that she couldn't be with someone who seemed determined to be unhappy, who couldn't move on from the life she felt had been denied to her to make a new life worth living. The worst part was that Ruth knew Jenn was right.

"So, you have a podcast now!" Jenn exclaimed.

"Yeah, I do. Have you listened to it?" Ruth asked, almost afraid of Jenn's answer.

"I have," Jenn said sheepishly. "I tried to avoid it at first just because I thought it might be too upsetting."

"Because of the violence?" Ruth asked.

"No," Jenn said, her mouth twisting. "Because of you."

The sentence hung in the air, making Ruth feel nervous but also somewhat exhilarated.

"But you listen to it now?" Ruth asked finally.

Jenn nodded. "Yes. And well, it's fantastic. *This* is your answer, isn't it? You think Daphne killed him?"

"I do, yes," Ruth murmured in shock. "You figured that out from listening to the podcast?"

"Sure, you told me so much about the murder. It was kind of your obsession," Jenn said, and there was an edge in her voice. Because maybe that obsession had starved their relationship of oxygen, had left Ruth a more bitter and paranoid person. "And some of the questions you've been asking her . . . I can see what you're getting at."

"Well, I think we're getting close now. And once that's done, I'll be able to start a new chapter," Ruth said, her eyes lingering on Jenn's face. It hadn't been that long since they were together, all tucked away in her little apartment. But so much had happened in Ruth's life since then that it felt like a very long time ago. She wondered if she'd still be in her apartment by the end of the podcast, or if the Montgomerys would have evicted her by then. Maybe it would be a blessing, not having to be reminded of Jenn so often.

"In the meantime, I'll be listening," Jenn said, giving Ruth a wave goodbye. Ruth waved back, promptly knocking her matcha over. By the time she finished mopping up the spill, Jenn was gone.

A few blocks from Ruth's apartment was a cemetery, with a mosaic memorial wall and a small garden of remembrance. There was a park bench in the garden where Ruth liked to sit at twilight and smell the fragrant musk of the night-blooming jasmine. When she came here, she often thought about him. She didn't know where he was really buried, or even if he was buried at all, so this was her substitute memorial.

She walked over one evening after spending the afternoon with Daphne. Ruth still had a lot of editing to do but she needed a break, an outlet for all the churned-up emotions rolling through her. It was getting harder to be with Daphne, harder to keep a straight face as Daphne joked about murdering people. When she did, Ruth always imagined Daphne looming over him with an insulin needle, a cruel smile playing over her face.

When Ruth was in college, she had once attended a murder trial of a fellow student who had gotten into a drunken brawl at a party and pushed a nineteen-year-old guy off a six-story balcony. Ruth had been covering the case for her college paper. The judge had looked at him there, surrounded by weeping relatives (both his own and his victim's) and told him: "It is a monstrous thing to deprive a person of the natural course of their days." It was a strangely poetic way to describe murder, especially in a criminal trial, but it had stuck with Ruth. This was what Daphne had done to so many people. She had robbed them of the most precious thing: time. That was what she took from Ruth as well: a future with him in it, a million conversations and questions answered, of sunlit brunches and evening strolls, a life that wasn't riven with tragedy and generational trauma.

Ruth took a deep breath, feeling the metal bench slats, still warm from the day's heat, melting her coiled muscles. She was surprised to find that tears were running down her face, flowing as quickly and as easily as a tap. The tears continued down her chin, dripping into her lap and Ruth didn't bother to wipe them away; she just let them come.

She had been running in place for so long, trying to get past something that had never been fully resolved. And now, finally, she had her answer. She just needed Daphne to say it out loud. Say it out loud and free Ruth from years of regret, confusion, and mistrust. Daphne had put her in this hell and now Daphne had the power to free her, if only she would *tell the truth*.

She stayed in the garden until the final traces of sunset had been wiped from the sky and the groundskeeper had gently ushered her out, closing the gates behind her.

Ruth was standing in front of the cemetery gates when she saw the flash of a camera phone pointed in her direction. The light momentarily startled her, and she crouched down, as if she was in danger. By the time she'd regained her senses, the photographer was gone.

Why had they taken her picture? She wondered if they recognized her, or if they just liked the image of a woman leaving a cemetery at dusk. She hoped they wouldn't post it online, even as some sort of aesthetic Instagram post. Because even if they didn't recognize her, someone online might.

And she didn't want anyone to put the pieces together before she did.

There was a police car parked in the Coconut Grove parking lot when Ruth arrived the next day. She could hear her sneakers crunch against the gravel as she walked, and she tried to step lighter, to not draw any more attention than she had to. She found herself holding her breath as she drew level with the car, praying that she wouldn't recognize the police officers inside and that they would ignore her. Ruth would happily go the rest of her life without ever talking to a police officer again, ever seeing a fluorescent bulb and a two-way mirror.

And then Officer Rankin's blond head popped out of the driver's side window. Ruth was so close to him that she could see the reddish skin on his scalp from a recent sunburn. Her heart began to pound and she felt her legs wobble. But she resisted the urge to stop. He gave her a little smirk and slapped his hand against the car door, the whack resounding through the empty parking lot.

"You look tired, Ruth! I know you like to work at night, but come on, one a.m.? That's too late," he said casually. His partner, a redheaded man she didn't recognize, laughed.

Ruth nodded curtly and kept walking, her back and neck feeling vulnerable and unprotected. She didn't look back to see if they were watching her. She knew they were. She hated these little power plays, the many ways that the police could hassle you without fully crossing the line, not that it had ever stopped them before.

It was only when she went inside that the full meaning of

Officer Rankin's words sunk in. Ruth crashed down onto a chair in the lobby, clutching her backpack to her chest. She *had* stayed up late working last night, sitting at her desk in the living room. And she *had* turned the living room lights off and went to bed around 1 a.m. Which meant that the entire time she had been sitting at her desk, combing through audio, stitching an episode together, Officer Rankin had been outside, in a dark corner of the parking lot, watching her every move. Was he also the one who had taken her picture at the cemetery? There was no way to know for sure. Tears rose in her eyes but she blinked them away furiously, scared that someone, anyone might see her crying and post about it online.

After all, people were watching her now. And there was nothing she could do about it.

Ruth found Daphne asleep in her armchair. The chair dwarfed her fragile body and made her look as small as a child. Ruth sat down in the armchair across from her and watched her sleep. Daphne's brow was smooth and untroubled, the wrinkles around her eyes lying slack as her thin lips vibrated with silent murmurs. She slept like an innocent person, when all over the country good people, people who'd lost family members to Daphne, were tossing and turning, anguished and unsettled by her revelations.

Ruth ambled around the apartment thinking of all the ways she could kill Daphne. In her state, it would be easy. A pillow to the face now when she was sleeping would finish her off. Or maybe a hard shove in the bathroom. No one would really care if Daphne died, the authorities would probably be relieved that they wouldn't have to spend any more time and money on their investigation of her. And Ruth too would be free. No more investigations, no more maddening conversations with an elderly sociopath, no more sleepless nights wondering what it all meant.

Daphne St Clair seemed to think it took a certain kind of courage to murder another person. Ruth clutched a tasseled throw pillow and then slowly lifted it up, extending her arm forwards. It would be an unforgettable ending to the podcast. How long would Daphne struggle for? Would she understand why Ruth was doing it?

The pillow brushed against Daphne's cheek, and she jerked her head, muttering something in her sleep. Ruth sighed and dropped the pillow, the cushion landing on the carpet with a soft whump. Ruth wasn't a killer. She knew it, and soon, everyone else would know it too. All she could do was get the story down, to unpack Daphne's life: the good, the bad, and the ugly, to bring it all out into the light.

Ruth slid out of her chair and gently shook Daphne's arm to wake her. It was time to start recording.

[EDIT: DO NOT INCLUDE IN PODCAST]

[Ruth adjusts her microphone and types something into her laptop.]

RUTH: I've been meaning to ask, what exactly happened between you and your son? How did you become estranged?

DAPHNE: I don't want to discuss that. I haven't seen him since he was in his early twenties.

RUTH: That must be hard.

DAPHNE: It's the hardest thing in my life.

RUTH: But you know where he is, right? Or do the twins keep in touch with him?

DAPHNE (angrily): Jesus you're like a dog with a bone. I don't want to talk about this! And you better not put this in the podcast or I'll stop this whole damn thing!

[A knock on the door.]

ATTENDANT: Here's your medication.

DAPHNE: Give it here; I'll take it later! We're busy!

[Door slams.]

Chapter Twenty-Five

I will never tell Ruth what happened to James. I've never told anyone.

On a good morning when I wake up, before I'm really conscious, I find myself reliving my favorite memories as if they were happening for the first time. They always feature James. Sometimes I'm back in our tiny apartment, feeling his toddler body sleeping peacefully next to me in the dark, his soft skin pressed against my cheek. Sometimes I'm driving down the street in a flashy convertible, with my best boy riding beside me. And sometimes I'm back at his graduation, watching him get his degree from Yale.

This morning, I was graced with the dream of his graduation. Watching James cross that stage, so tall and dignified in his black robes, was the proudest moment of my life. All the struggle and pain was worth it to see this man, such a wonderful man, succeed, knowing that I had loved him as hard as I could. And James was graduating from an Ivy League school with not a cent of debt. I had paid for it all. Not bad for a girl who never went to high school. The thought of watching him move through his twenties, finding success and happiness, filled me with indescribable joy. He was my triumph.

It was a shame my husband Roy felt too ill to attend the ceremony. Or the reception. Not even the celebratory dinner. I had been married to Roy for two years at that point. He was long and lean, like a cowboy, with a thick moustache and eyebrows that needed trimming so that they didn't droop in his eyes. He'd made a fortune in industrial agricultural machines, but he seemed more like an old ranch hand than a millionaire. Usually he loved being outside, fixing things in the garage and carting junk off to the dump in his truck. Lately, however, he'd been sick and spent most of his time in bed. The twins were off doing a semester at sea (a cruise ship masquerading as a college) and I was secretly glad that it was just my son and I out on the town that night. We ordered martinis and clinked our glasses together and I stared at my beautiful boy and felt proud that I had pulled it off: I had raised a good man.

"Congratulations, James," I said, as we sipped our drinks. "I'm so proud of you."

"Thanks, Mom, I'm glad you came. I know it must not have been easy, raising all of us . . . I hope someday I can take care of you," he said earnestly, his face shining.

"Oh, honey, don't worry about that," I said, secretly thrilled. "I can take care of myself."

"And Roy of course," my son said, arching his eyebrow. And suddenly, my sick husband was hanging around the table, an invisible mood-killer.

"Yes, I can take care of Roy."

*　　　*　　　*

A few weeks later, James came out to our Montana ranch to sort through his things and plan his next move. We stayed up late talking most nights, sitting out on the porch where we wouldn't disturb Roy's sleep. James was so good to my husband: delivering his trays upstairs and reading him the newspaper when he felt too weak to do it himself.

One morning, I slipped out of bed at 5 a.m. and stole into the kitchen. The house was quiet, and the sky was tinged with the first pink rays of light. My mood matched the sunrise, and I felt buoyant, as if life was easier than usual.

I heated up water and added porridge oats, leaving them to cook on the stove. Then I pulled out my secret stash of pills and began to grind them up. I was so lost in my own happy thoughts that I never heard him walk in.

"Mom, don't," James said, putting his hand on my wrist. I jumped, my nerves jangling.

"James! Don't what?" I asked. He looked so solemn even though he was wearing an old high school T-shirt and some plaid boxers.

"Don't put those pills in Roy's food," he said.

I froze. "I wasn't . . ." I began unconvincingly. But one look at his face confirmed that he was certain, that there was no room for me to make him believe.

"I suppose I've suspected it for a long time. The different names, the constant moves, the fact that I went to more funerals as a kid than some people do in their lifetime," James said slowly. He wouldn't meet my eyes.

"Come on, two husbands got cancer and one killed himself!

*That's just horrible luck—" I began but he ignored me and
kept talking.*

*"But it all seemed impossible. And I never saw anything that
proved it, that even let me name it. Until now," James said. I
didn't say anything, and he stepped forwards, taking my hands.
For a moment his face softened, and I could feel my bones
melting like butter. What could I say to my boy?*

*"Please, Mom. Don't make me feel crazy. Tell me the truth,"
he pleaded.*

*If it had been anyone else, I would have lied. But this was
James. I didn't want him to suffer.*

*"Yes. It's true," I whispered, saying it for the first time.
"But I did it for you and the girls." He frowned and dropped
my hands.*

*"No, you didn't. Geoffrey was rich. We could have lived a
nice, normal life off what he left us. And David? He was like
a father to me! But you just kept thrashing around, looking for
something else. I used to feel sorry for you, for all the people
you lost. But you caused this," he said disdainfully.*

*When someone who loves you looks at you with disgust, a
part of your soul dies.*

*"I wanted to give you everything—" I began, but he kept
talking over me.*

*"And I can't turn you in. You're my mom. And all you've
ever done is love me." His voice broke, and I could see tears
rolling down his cheeks.*

*"Yes, exactly." I reached for him, wanting to comfort him,
but he stepped back, a look of revulsion flashing across his*

face. My hands hung in the air, muscles straining to lift what had suddenly become so heavy.

"But that makes me hate myself. That I know you're a murderer. And I can't stop you!" he cried, jabbing at the ceiling, where Roy lay prone and helpless.

"Oh sweetheart, don't think—" But he cut me off.

"And that makes me hate you as well. Because you did this to us. You ruined us," he said. I didn't try to say anything more. My chest felt like it was caving in on itself. "I never want to see you again."

"No! Please! James!" I burst out but he kept talking, his body as straight as if he was iron-plated.

"I'm going to move far away and I'm going to change my name. And then I'll try to forget all about you," he finished, turning away.

"Please . . ." I moaned, clutching my stomach as if I'd been shot. But he never looked back. He picked up his backpack from the hallway and he walked out the door.

I never saw him again.

I didn't kill Roy. I stopped dosing him and slowly, hesitantly, he regained his strength. It was tiresome as Roy was a whiny patient, taking his recovery as morosely as he'd taken his illness. I waited until he was well and then I left him. It felt anti-climactic, packing a suitcase and calling a lawyer as opposed to watching him die and then calling the undertaker. But every time I imagined killing him, I saw James's pained face. I hoped he would come back to me when he realized that Roy was still alive. But he didn't.

I've experienced some terrible times in my life. But losing my

son was the worst punishment I could ever receive. My daugh-
ters knew not to mention James around me, that I couldn't talk
about him. Maybe I should have just confessed then.

That night, Ruth sat at her computer, her hands poised on the
keyboard, waiting for a flash of inspiration. She had always
prided herself on her investigation skills. It was one of the
things that set her apart from other journalists and gave her an
edge in the dog-eat-dog world of freelancing. Whether it was
helping a woman find her World War Two boyfriend for a sentimental piece or locating a pair of cufflinks that had belonged
to a convicted mobster for a crime website, Ruth had done it all.

That was why, ever since Daphne had told her she hadn't seen
her son in decades, Ruth had wondered if she could find James.
It would be great for the podcast. Ruth could do a whole story
arc about searching for James and if she found him, she might
be the one to break it to him that his mother had confessed to
murder. That was compelling stuff. Besides she could relate to
James. She had also grown up with a single mother in a world
that often felt chaotic and beyond her control. And Daphne's
actions had affected them both, in surprisingly similar ways.

But how could she find someone when she had almost no
information? Ruth sat at the computer for ages and tried to
frame a question, *any question*, to begin her search. She was
looking for a white guy in his late sixties who lived somewhere
in the world and *might* be using the name James. There was
just no way.

Ruth imagined James, a pleasant family man, running
errands and then coming home, flicking the TV on and seeing

his mother and sisters splashed across the news. Would he tell his family? Probably not. Who wanted to share that shame? Instead, he would just sit there, alone and afraid that someone would find him.

Later, Ruth sat at her computer, still squinting at the screen. It was past midnight but the flood of press inquiries and article proposals had only increased with every episode, and it was hard for Ruth to wade through them. She was scared that she would miss a life-changing opportunity, that a single misstep might derail her, and this anxiety was making it hard for her to step away from the inbox. She was smoking a joint as she mindlessly worked her way through her emails, hoping that she might actually be able to get some sleep tonight once the weed kicked in.

Ruth sat back in her chair, studying her apartment for a moment. She didn't like the idea of being forced out of this place, had always disliked moving after having no permanent home as a child. But maybe it would be a blessing to start over in a place free of the memories of Jenn and her run-ins with the Montgomerys.

Ashing the joint in an old Diet Coke can, Ruth opened a file on her computer and flicked through some old pictures, pausing at one with her father's family. Ruth remembered the first time her father had introduced her to his family: his sister and brother, his daughter, his cousins. It was in a palatial home with tall gates and a driveway crammed with luxury cars. Ruth had felt intimidated by the house itself, much less the rich, discerning people inside who would be suspicious of an illegitimate child born of an affair with a secretary. But Richard had patted her hand and reminded her that his actions had nothing to do with her and that he was proud of her.

"This is your family too. And if you give them time, they'll appreciate you just as much as I do. Ruth, today is the first step of your life as a Montgomery."

"Thank you," Ruth had murmured. A father. A family. It was everything she had ever wanted.

At the time, she had felt like Cinderella, plucked from the ashes and transported to the castle. But if it was a fairy tale, it was definitely the Brothers Grimm version. And nobody got a happy ending.

Chapter Twenty-Six

EPISODE EIGHT: 1981–2018

DAPHNE: And then the twins moved out. They did a year of fashion merchandising at college, dropped out, opened a boutique funded by me and then ran it into the ground. Then they got rich husbands from Florida and started having babies. And suddenly I was alone, just at the moment I was really aging. Sure, I was attractive, but not as beautiful as I used to be. But you don't care about that, do you? No one wants to hear about how aging can be traumatic for a woman. Or how you go from being the most important thing in your children's lives to a bit player. No. All you want to know was whether there were more murders.

RUTH: Well, were there?

DAPHNE: Yes. Honestly, I'm like a drunk who falls off the wagon. I had the money, I had the freedom, but I just kept doing it.

RUTH: Okay. So, who was it? Let's get going.

DAPHNE: So impatient! How many murders do you people need? I guess you and your ghoulish listeners would say the more the merrier. There was one murder, just one, and then I retired until

Warren Ackerman's death. His name was Donald St Clair. I was in my mid-fifties, and he was a decade older. You could learn a little something from Donald, Ruth. All he cared about was his career and by the time I met him, he'd had three divorces, a heart attack that forced him into retirement, and children who never called because he'd never really been around. Careers are great and all, but if that's all that matters to you, you'll end up alone and afraid of getting stuck on the toilet.

RUTH: Okay, I'll keep trying to live a happy, fulfilling life with mountains of student debt, rent I can barely afford, and a parent who will need home healthcare before too long. Thanks for the life advice.

DAPHNE: No need to be snippy, I'm just saying life isn't all about money. Although it is a really nice distraction! But Donald St Clair was at the point where all he really wanted was a wife. We met in Hawaii in 1990, which is a great place to find rich old buzzards. Soon I was living in his Colorado mansion, which looked like that place in *The Shining*.

[EDIT: DO NOT INCLUDE IN PODCAST]

RUTH: Where exactly in Colorado were you?

DAPHNE: Near Aspen.

RUTH: Oh, I have family in Colorado. My mom grew up there. They moved to Florida after my grandfather left the family for another woman.

DAPHNE: Jesus, the women in your family sure can't keep a man.

RUTH: Men or women, we can't seem to keep anyone . . . so how long did the marriage last?

[END OF REMOVED SECTION]

DAPHNE: The marriage lasted two years. Maybe less. At first, I thought there'd be enough luxury to keep me occupied. I'd seen *Dynasty*; I knew Colorado was full of rich people. But eventually I got bored of snowed-out roads and stories about how Donald used to be a big shot. So, I had to kill him to save myself from another winter in the mountains. I was back in New York with neon in my eyes before Christmas '91! And that's all I can really say about Donald. Our marriage was short, but one thing lived on. His last name. I liked Daphne St Clair so much that I decided to keep it.

RUTH: So that's it? You talked for ages about some of your other murders, but this poor man barely gets a paragraph? You know how insulting that is for his family?

DAPHNE: Well, how much more offended are they gonna get? I already killed the guy!

RUTH: At first, you seemed to have been murdering guys who mistreated you, but it seems like now no one was good enough for you. That these men didn't *matter* to you at all.

DAPHNE: Ooh fascinating insight into the criminal psyche. I don't know what you're getting so worked up about, this guy was nothing special.

[Ruth takes a deep breath and doesn't say anything for a minute.]

RUTH: What about his children? Do you know their names? I'd like to interview one. Their father deserved better.

DAPHNE: God, why waste your time?

RUTH: We've discussed this before. You might as well tell me what you remember. Whether you help me or not, I'll find out.

DAPHNE: Is that a threat?

RUTH: More of a promise. Of course, that's only if you're taking me for a ride.

DAPHNE: Christ you're paranoid! I've told you nothing but the truth!

RUTH: The whole truth?

DAPHNE: So help me God.

RUTH: Because you should know, a lot of people are discussing this case online, trying to connect you to famous unsolved murders. I've read the threads: the Tylenol Murders, the Black Dahlia, some small-town murders in New York State, even the Miami New Year's poisonings . . . I just want to confirm that you didn't kill *anyone* else.

DAPHNE: Ruth, what are you trying to say?

RUTH: I'm wondering if you've confessed to all the murders you've committed.

DAPHNE: That's ridiculous. Why would I lie? The only reason people know that I'm a killer, that any of these people were even murdered, is because of me!

RUTH: Well . . . lots of killers lie, even after they're caught. Sometimes it's a control thing, like how a lot of people believe Charles Manson ordered more murders but he liked keeping that secret from the public. And for others, it's a bargaining chip. Ted Bundy used to say he'd committed more murders than people knew, and that he would help the police if they delayed his execution.

DAPHNE: Yes, but those killers all didn't want to be caught. I *confessed*. So again, why would I lie?

RUTH: That's a very good question . . . Maybe you've killed quite a few more people than you're letting on . . . Or maybe you've done things that might make people think worse of you. Or maybe you're doing this to taunt me. The thing is, no one really gets *why* you confessed. People ask me about it all the time. I don't know what your motivations are with this, so for all I know you could be lying about lots of things.

DAPHNE: Honestly, you're getting tiresome! I don't know if you need a stiff drink or a roll in the sheets, but something has to change! Get out!

ShockAndBlah:

Wow Donald got short shrift didn't he?

PreyAllDay:

I guess when you've killed so many times, they all start to blur together.

ShockAndBlah:

It is a good last name though. Daphne St Clair is very Sasha Fierce.

StopDropAndTroll:

Da fuck? It's a hooker name.

ShockAndBlah:

Wow, so Ruth is reading our comments!! What does Ruth think Daphne's hiding?

PreyAllDay:

Maybe nothing? But she does seem to be challenging her, as if she knows something specific.

StopDropAndTroll:

That's a weird way to say thank you for giving her some clout and a payday. Daphne's her freaking meal ticket!

ShockAndBlah:

I dunno, maybe it's personal . . .

CapoteParty:

Don't you feel like we jumped over some years though? One moment it's 1970 and now it's 1991? What happened in between? Maybe that's what Ruth is getting at.

ShockAndBlah:

Probably nothing. Maybe she told Ruth, and it didn't make for a good podcast.

PreyAllDay:

Yes, all killer, no filler please!

INTERVIEW WITH LEAH SIMMONDS, DONALD ST CLAIR'S DAUGHTER

RUTH: So, now you know. Did you ever meet Daphne?

LEAH: No . . . I hadn't seen my father for over a decade by that point. Still, I can't believe he was murdered. I was shocked when the police reached out.

RUTH: How do you feel?

LEAH: My dad deserved better than this. All people do. I'm the product of marriage number two, which only lasted four years. But he was still my father. Some part of me always hoped that later, when he retired, we might actually get to know each other, that he might actually take an interest in me, but Daphne took that chance away.

RUTH: I'm sorry for your loss. I know that your mother has passed away, but I don't suppose you could give me any information about Donald's third wife. I understand that he had a daughter with her?

LEAH: Honestly, I couldn't tell you. My dad just really didn't feature in my life. He worked constantly and seemed to hop from woman to woman, marriage to marriage. Children were just a byproduct to him.

RUTH: I'm sorry you had to grow up like that. Father-daughter relationships can be so complicated.

LEAH: Yeah. Hey, now that we know he was murdered, is there any way to recoup the inheritance? Should I maybe talk to a lawyer?

RUTH: You can certainly try but I have a feeling she spent it all. She's not much of a saver.

LEAH: That monster.

The rest of my fifties passed in a bitter blur. I spent money. I went to tropical places. I started having cocktails at lunch just to make the day go quicker. Life, which had seemed to shimmer with opportunities when I was in my twenties and working at Bergdorf's, now seemed so dull. I had all the money I needed for the rest of my life. I had an apartment on the Upper West Side and a home in the Hamptons. I was still attractive and now that my children were adults, I was free to do whatever I felt like. But somehow that freedom made it impossible to dream. When I was a teenager, I had wanted so many things: three square meals, new clothes, and for my father to keep his hands to himself. Now though, I couldn't think of a single thing I wanted.

At the time, I felt so unbelievably old, which of course is funny now that I'm old as dust. Back then I was living independently, never having to worry if I was one folded rug away from a body bag. And yet, at the time, I really felt like I was waiting to die.

I began to drink more and more. I liked to spend my evenings lying on the couch in my dark living room in front of the flickering TV. I would tip back rum and Cokes, knowing that I'd hit my sweet spot when I'd start talking to the TV characters and laughing at my own jokes.

Why was I drinking? Just to stop the boredom really. And maybe because I'd been trying to outrun so many things in my life and they were finally catching up. I had played so many parts over the years that I felt like I had fragments of identities floating around my body like shrapnel. After all the drama and the glamour, somehow it had ended with me becoming just another middle-aged woman, alone and invisible, lost to her son.

Everything was coming undone. I stopped telling my daughters if I was dating anyone, stopped telling people I dated that I had adult children. Sometimes I'd tell so many stories that I'd get them twisted and contradict myself. I wasn't living a consistent life anymore, not even a consistent lie.

That was also the decade when I first started learning about serial killers. In a funny way, I never saw myself as a serial murderer. It was more like I fell into crazy situations where I had to kill myself back to single. But when I started to read more about serial killers, I realized that my terrible childhood probably played a part. But people feel bad for Oliver Twist; they don't feel bad for Ted Bundy. Not that I really identified with all those sacks of shit who raped and killed women. It's monsters like them who make monsters like me. And I was never caught. Seventy years of murder and they never caught me. It makes you wonder how many other people got away with it.

And then, in my late sixties, I left New York for the last time. It was December 2001, and I didn't even recognize New York anymore, the heart had gone out of the city. But I was still sad to leave. New York had been my North Star, always guiding me home from my detours around the country. Diane had invited me to move into her home in Florida. She had just gotten divorced and was feeling sentimental. I agreed, mostly because I assumed I'd die soon anyways and thought it'd be nice to die with a suntan. If I had known I had over twenty years left in me, I might have given it more thought.

Diane thought we'd get closer and that I'd share my stock of folksy wisdom and stories about good ol'-fashioned decent people with my grandchildren. Unfortunately, my grandkids were selfish teenagers and Meemaw had spent her life offing rich guys for money. To make matters worse, Diane and I began to argue. I was frustrated with my daughter. I did terrible things to give her a good life and she wasted it. Sure, she was rich, but she had the same life I had: living off men and her looks. I had given her so many opportunities and she had squandered them all.

After a few years, I moved out. Diane didn't care by that point because she had a new husband. I was alone in Florida, cut adrift from my life before. And that can be a dangerous way to live.

HauteHistoire: "Okay, we've got two very different aesthetics for this TikTok video. First, we've got Colorado millionaire's wife, an aesthetic for those who like SUVs, roaring fires, and doing cocaine in an outdoor hot tub! Think suede boots, a pleated wool skirt and a chunky concho belt, think cozy turtlenecks and turquoise jewelry. The perfect look for a mountain murder!

"Now we're moving on to our Coastal Grandma look, an old favorite of yours, but I'm updating it to be more of a Coastal Killer look. So, we've got our linen shirt, our fisherman's pants, but we're adding a net bag for all that wine Daphne's drinking and a pair of Tory Burch woven slides because no matter how much Daphne's struggling, I don't think she'd be caught dead in a pair of Birkenstocks. Especially as Daphne doesn't need any reminders of her time in the great state of Vermont. This is a look for riding your bicycle next to the beach, contemplating your own mortality and all the men you helped on their merry way!"

Chapter Twenty-Seven

After I left Diane's house, I bought a condo on Sweetwater Beach in a luxurious building called the Blue Diamond. My apartment was an airy palace with gauzy curtains and a balcony that overlooked the ocean. I sat out there in the evenings, drinking coffee and thinking about death. I had seen it happen so many times, had watched that indefinable spark fade from someone's eyes, rendering them dull and clouded, and yet I still didn't understand the whys and hows of it all. It was the same feeling I had the first time I held my son James, unable to believe that I had created life, that I could be so close to the mysteries of the universe and still not understand any of it.

After a couple months on the balcony, I realized that I needed to put down my coffee and do what I do best. Meet some men. I didn't think it would make me happy but at least it was a good distraction. And who doesn't love a dinner on someone else's dime?

If you're looking for old rich men who are tired of drinking alone, Florida is your El Dorado. There were plenty of fish in the sea so long as you didn't mind a fish with wrinkles. I might have been in my seventies but I had a trim body, an ass like a peach, and a face that didn't look like it had melted. Of course, dating at my age meant you had to hear about the wars they fought in (my dating pool spanned World War Two, Korea, and the start of Vietnam) but as long as you were willing to listen to the same old story about how they held poor Shorty's hand as his guts fell out, then they'd do whatever you liked.

I had all kinds of fun. I spent countless afternoons on yachts and sailboats. I ate the best seafood in Florida and developed a taste for top-shelf rums and tequilas. Men bought me a whole new wardrobe of designer resort wear and gave me brown Louis Vuitton bags that matched their leathery skin. And the best part was that they barely wanted to screw you. If you tired them out a couple times at the start of dating, then they were satisfied that they were still virile. And everyone could conserve their energy for salsa dancing and trips to the Caribbean.

HauteHistoire: "Hello TikTokers, I've got a bonus aesthetic for this episode! So this is our yacht girl ensemble, slightly updated for the older lady living her best life down in tropical climes. We've got our wide-legged white jeans, our ribbed Breton-striped tank, and the chunky brown Louis Vuitton bag that just screams 'A new money man bought this for me!' Like the Burberry bag in *Succession*, it's sure to rub WASPs the wrong way but that's the fun of Florida; it doesn't matter. We've got the gold Versace sunglasses and some heeled sandals because Daphne doesn't seem like the kind of woman to favor a sensible shoe even on a boat. This is a sunny look for a shady person and just perfect for a woman getting on the apps in her seventies while trying to leave her murderous past behind!"

One evening I was out with a new guy called Joseph McLaughlin. He was in his late seventies and was originally from Chicago (the Winnipeg of America), where he'd made a fortune in property development before retiring to Florida.

Joe was nice enough although he was tired and seemed to be struggling to hold up his end of the conversation, which annoyed me. Dating was different in your seventies, but that didn't mean I wanted to be romanced by a stroke victim. Still, we sat on the restaurant patio watching the ocean shimmer in the pink evening light and drank chilled white wine. It was pleasant but forgettable and I was already filing Joe under B for 'Backup' in my mental rolodex when he asked if I wouldn't mind escorting him back to his place.

"I just feel so light-headed. I think the wine might be interacting with my medication," he murmured, wiping his forehead. I wondered if this was a seduction ploy (if so, it was a poor one) but he really did look weak and clammy so I agreed.

Joe lived alone in one of those modern glass houses that look like nothing. I walked him into the house, my arm hooked in his as he hunched against me. I could feel his body shaking with the effort of standing. It was clear that Joe had lived alone for a long time. Despite being an expensive house, it was barely furnished. The furniture was all nondescript and beige, as if he'd bought it directly from a hotel.

I walked Joe into the living room, a large room that only

contained one La-Z-Boy, a giant TV and a bulb dangling from a tilted plastic lampshade. I was just about to ease him down into the chair, already looking forward to leaving this museum of sad old men, when Joe stiffened and made a grunting noise.

Before I could grab him, Joe fell to the floor and started wheezing and clutching his chest. I'm no doctor but you don't get to seventy-five without being able to recognize a heart attack. His panicked eyes found me, and I could see how afraid he was, how much he wanted to live. I turned around, searching for a telephone to call an ambulance. And then I . . . just stopped. Slowly, carefully, I sat down in the La-Z-Boy and watched him convulse on the floor. He could barely speak but he was moaning, trying to ask why I was doing this. But I couldn't explain. I hoped he knew it wasn't personal though. The date wasn't perfect, but it wasn't that bad.

I didn't poison him, and I doubt an ambulance would have saved him, but it sure was fun sitting there, knowing I had the power to call for help or not. I felt like a person who had strayed from their faith and suddenly found themselves back in church, experiencing a revelation. I sat there with him, as his wild white eyes began to shut, knowing I was witnessing his final moments in this world. It was thrilling, a dark kind of power that very few people ever discover or feel able to enjoy. I loved it.

Afterwards, I left his house, shutting the door behind me but leaving it unlocked. His cleaner or a neighbor would find him eventually. I walked away, confident that if anyone did see me, they'd forgot me almost instantly. That's the best and worst part of growing old: becoming invisible.

After Joe died, I found myself wishing more old men would die in front of me. But no matter how much I tried to get their blood pressure up, it never happened again. I didn't take it any further though. After all, I had come to Florida for the same reason as everyone else: to retire.

ShockAndBlah:

Literal chills. That is so messed up. I feel like I need to listen to five episodes of *My Dad Wrote a Porno* just to detox from that.

PreyAllDay:

Here's his obituary. I found it online.

ShockAndBlah:

Aww it says that for decades he helped refugees get affordable housing in Chicago. Is what Daphne did a crime? Not getting help?

BurntheBookBurnerz:

I don't really know about the law; I went to art school. It FEELS like it should be? Maybe it's manslaughter?

StopDropAndTroll:

Of course YOU went to art school. Who gives a fuck at this point about counting her crimes? She's going to die in prison anyways.

ShockAndBlah:

She's living this dream life in Florida and she's still pulling shit like this. I just don't get it.

CapoteParty:

She probably doesn't either.

BurntheBookBurnerz:

It almost feels like she's devolving. You see that happen with some killers—they just become more depraved and reckless. It's not about the money or revenge anymore; she gets a kick out of seeing men die. That's probably why she killed Warren.

PreyAllDay:

Yeah, like Ted Bundy. He starts out luring college girls into his car, but by the end he's breaking into sororities to slaughter groups of them. His last murder was a twelve-year-old girl, by far his youngest victim.

ShockAndBlah:

Funny, isn't that when Ted Bundy moved to Florida? Maybe it's Florida that makes these killers devolve.

PreyAllDay:

Well, that's the Florida Man phenomenon for you . . . even serial killers aren't immune.

CapoteParty:

Out of curiosity, does anyone know what senior center she ended up in? I'm visiting Florida soon and thought it would be cool to see where this is all happening. I know the town but there's so many old folks' homes . . .

StopDropAndTroll:

Really? In Florida? Surprising.

PreyAllDay:

Hey I'm local. I think they're trying to keep it quiet, you know to stop someone from offing her. But . . . my cousin used to work at Coconut Grove Seniors Center, and she remembers Daphne and Warren Ackerman . . . so there you go.

The day's interview did not get off to a good start. Ruth had tossed and turned all night, getting up to check and recheck that every curtain and blind in her house was firmly shut and that both locks on her door were in place. At one point, a garbage can had fallen over outside and Ruth had been startled awake, certain that someone was breaking down the door. To make matters worse, Ruth kept running through the Joe McLaughlin story Daphne had told her.

This murder-by-omission was so close in fact to the murder Ruth was trying to solve that for a moment she wondered if Daphne had changed the names and fiddled the details, so she wouldn't catch another murder charge in Florida. Daphne had described the scene so well that Ruth could envision her sitting in a different living room, watching a different man get increasingly disoriented, fall to the floor and start seizing, limbs jerking sporadically before, finally, going still with death. All that was missing was the vial of insulin. Then she could see Daphne, absorbing it all with a satisfied look on her face before walking next door to her own apartment building. It was a repulsive image, but it played incessantly in Ruth's mind, looping over and over as she tried to drift off.

Ruth slept through her alarm and was over an hour late to Coconut Grove, finding Daphne grumpy and unsettled. They had only been recording for a few minutes when Daphne began to shift uncomfortably, clutching her stomach.

"I need a break," Daphne said, wiping her forehead. She was uncharacteristically disheveled, her skin clammy and pale.

"Are you okay? Should I call someone?" Ruth asked, pausing the recording. Was Daphne about to drop dead in front of her?

"No," Daphne said, dragging herself up with the walker. "I'm just a bit sick. My guts are bothering me." She limped across the floor, wilting over her walker. Ruth could tell by the way she closed the door that she would be in there a while.

In one smooth motion, Ruth leapt up and scurried over to Daphne's bedroom, trying to move as quietly as possible.

Back at the beginning of the podcast, Daphne had been incensed to find Ruth looking around her bedroom and so Ruth had given it a wide berth ever since. But something had been niggling at Ruth ever since that day, a little incongruity that bothered her. Most of the things in Daphne's closet were new, the bags and boxes gleaming and fresh. But tucked away in the back there had been a battered brown shoebox from

Roger Vivier, so old that it must have been from the Sixties or Seventies. Daphne wasn't the kind to keep old shoes, no matter how fabulous, and Ruth had found herself thinking about that shoebox ever since, wondering what it contained.

She pulled down the box, glancing behind her to make sure that Daphne was still in the bathroom. The box was light and clearly didn't contain shoes. Ruth knelt down on the plush carpet and pulled the lid off. Sitting on top was a small mesh bag containing five rings: a glistening emerald, two diamonds that sparkled like snowflakes (one in a gold band and one in platinum), a canary yellow diamond, and an antique sapphire. Were these Daphne's engagement rings? It certainly seemed possible.

Under the rings were a stack of pictures. Many of them with the faded, pastel colors of 1960s photography. Ruth recognized Daphne, as tall and glamorous as a model, with slender curves and a wardrobe to rival a movie star's. Here was Daphne in a leopard-print coat and hat, holding the hand of a dark-haired boy in a peacoat. Here was Daphne sitting on a velvet couch, swathed in black tulle, smoking a cigarette, while her twin toddlers played with dolls in front of her. Ruth smiled. Daphne really had been stunning. A consolation prize for all the other disadvantages she'd been born with and a tremendous asset when combined with her ruthless ambition.

There were pictures of men too. A slim, balding man with jug-ears and a big smile sprawled on the floor wrestling with the kids. Based on their ages in the picture, Ruth assumed this was David. A younger man in a slim, stylish suit with a cigarette hanging from his lip. Possibly Geoffrey. Another photo of a handsome, black-haired man with his arm around an impossibly young Daphne, all black hair and red lipstick smiles. That had to be Carl, James's father. Countless pictures of the kids, from early childhood all the way up to the twins' weddings and even a few baby photos of her grandchildren. She didn't see a picture of Warren. There were other men in the photos, although none she recognized or could conclusively identify. *Where was he?*

And that was when she spotted it. A formal family picture, everyone dressed in their good clothes, posing stiffly for a photographer. Daphne was standing, resplendent in a silk shirt and tuxedo pants, dripping in jewelry. Diane and Rose wore sequined dresses, two beautiful blonde preteen girls. They weren't smiling but stared straight into the camera, looking serious. James sat next to them, a young teenager with dark hair shielding his eyes and a suit with a flared collar. He had a small smile, but it didn't quite reach his eyes. This was not a happy family picture.

But it was the other two people in the photo that gave Ruth pause. There was a man standing next to Daphne, his wedding band glinting in the photo as he flashed a big toothy grin. He was tall and middle-aged, his dark hair speckled with gray, and was wearing a three-piece suit. Ruth frowned. She didn't recognize this man. Ruth had thought that Daphne had been single after David for quite a while. No one had ever mentioned another marriage.

And then there was the girl. She was sitting between James and one of the twins. Dressed in a navy sweater and pearls, she was smiling at the camera, a velvet hairband tucked into her shining hair. She was younger than James but only looked slightly older than the twins.

Who was this third girl? She had dark hair and fair skin like Daphne, so it was possible they were related. Ruth felt a flicker of unease. Had Daphne covered up the existence of a fourth child? One born just before the twins? Ruth could think of only one reason someone like Daphne might do that. But surely that was too big a secret to keep. Diane and Rose would have remembered a sister. Of course, James would have remembered too. Was that why he went away?

The toilet flushed.

Ruth clapped the lid down on the box and hurriedly shoved it back into the closet, almost slipping on the slick carpet. While she could hear the tap running, Ruth hurried into the living room and sat down as quickly as possible, trying to steady her breathing. She was petrified that, later, Daphne might notice that the pictures were in a different order in the box, but it was too late to go back. Besides, she had bigger concerns than Daphne getting suspicious of her. That picture of the unknown girl haunted her, made her question everything she'd learned so far in this podcast.

Who was Daphne St Clair?

DAPHNE: I was seventy-five when I left Diane's house and moved into a luxury apartment building on the beach. I lived in that apartment for eleven years and every day I felt surprised to still be alive. I'd killed my first man over half a century ago and I suppose I've been waiting for the other shoe to drop ever since.

RUTH: But here you were, in a luxury apartment—

DAPHNE: Paid for by a string of dead husbands, I know. It turns out the Bible-thumpers were wrong, the wages of sin are premium coastal real estate.

RUTH: And during those eleven years, did you commit any more murders?

DAPHNE: Nope.

RUTH (sounding frustrated): Why would you stop after all these years? Especially when you'd just gotten a rush from watching an old man die?

DAPHNE: Sorry, I guess I should have killed more people for your entertainment. What can I say? I'm an enigma, even to myself. I was just . . . tired of it all.

RUTH: Daphne, this is important. Tell the truth.

DAPHNE: I am! Nothing really happened in those years. Well, Diane remarried and in 2010 had an absurdly late-in-life daughter. I couldn't help but feel bad for that poor sucker: forged in a premenopausal oven, carried by a surrogate, and spat out into a marriage on its last legs.

RUTH: You really love her, don't you? Your granddaughter?

DAPHNE: I suppose I have a soft spot for her.

RUTH: This is probably going to reverberate through her life forever: what you did. How will she be able to trust anyone? Knowing that her grandmother is a lying murderer? How can she have a normal life after what you did?

DAPHNE: Whooee, someone's suddenly very concerned about the children! Look, my granddaughter grew up rich, in no small part because of the opportunities I gave her mother. So, when she's sitting in a house with an Ivy League degree and a trust fund, I'm sure she'll find a way to muddle through.

RUTH: Fine. But what finally made you leave that apartment? Were you trying to escape something you did?

DAPHNE (sounding confused): No? I was eighty-six years old. And aging is *hard*. You're exhausted and frail. And the whole time you're haunted by the person you used to be, who could dance the night away and never had to worry about places to sit and walk-in showers. The final straw was when I fell in the bathroom. I lay there for hours, thinking about my life. I really believed that I would die there, which was frustrating because I'd always hoped the end would come without me noticing. But finally, the doorman found me and that's when I moved into a retirement home.

The Sixth Murder

Chapter Twenty-Eight

EPISODE NINE: 2018–2022

DAPHNE: The seniors home felt like the final chapter of my life. Although now I suppose I've added a few more! At first, I tried to keep myself busy. I read my serial killer books, I swam in the pool, I went to the center's dances and did chair fitness. But soon I was too frail to salsa, too nervous to swim. I stopped being able to walk more than a few steps on my own, started needing a walker and then a wheelchair when I left my room.

RUTH: I have a parent who is starting to experience mobility issues and it's hard to watch ... You still remember how healthy and vibrant they used to be.

DAPHNE: Yeah, great, I feel so bad for all the people who have to watch me get sick.

RUTH: (Tuts) What was it like here when the pandemic started?

DAPHNE: Oh, it was grim. I would just sit in this apartment, day in and day out, watching the world die on TV.

RUTH: When did you start dating Warren Ackerman?

DAPHNE: A year ago. I was eighty-nine, we were in the middle of the pandemic, and I couldn't watch another episode of

NCIS without hanging myself. Of all the men in my age group, he was the most charming. But there was competition. At my age there are three women for every man. It reminded me of my twenties in New York when I had to compete with the other Bergdorf Goodman girls for dates. And I've always been Best in Show.

RUTH (sadly): And when did you decide to . . . kill him?

DAPHNE: Just after I turned ninety. It had been ages since I had killed anyone, but the pandemic had made me feel like I needed to take some risks and I wanted to know if I still had it in me. He was an easy target; no one blinks an eye when an old fart kicks the bucket.

RUTH: So, how did you do it? You can barely get to the bathroom by yourself.

DAPHNE: All right, Ruth, no need to rub my nose in it. But yes, it was difficult. I have arthritis and so even slipping the crushed-up pills into his coffee was hard. But on the plus side Warren was not the sharpest tool in the shed so he didn't notice how bad his coffee tasted. That's what decades of smoking can do to you, so there's a good lesson for all the smokers listening.

RUTH: So he died. And people assumed it was natural causes.

DAPHNE: Exactly.

RUTH: And that bothered you? Isn't that your usual method? To make it look like a health problem? To make it look like their cancer, their hearts, even their diabetes finished them off?

DAPHNE: Diabetes? Where did that come from? Well, yes, I was a tiny bit disappointed that I'd pulled it off. Maybe this time I wanted to get caught; I don't know. I didn't do this one for money; we were never married. I did it for a thrill, to capture that buzz again, but I just felt lost afterwards. This was my last adventure, and it was over. That is . . . until I decided it wasn't.

RUTH (irritated): I just don't buy it, that there wasn't more to your confession. Surely there are other ways to get a thrill. And I suppose I should remind you that this was a human being you killed, that the sad part of this story was not that you found this murder anticlimactic.

DAPHNE: Yeah, yeah, you can just patch a lecture in later when you're editing this thing. Save us all from hearing the sermon on the mount again.

RUTH (Voiceover): It was hard listening to Daphne crow about murdering an elderly man. But I knew that she didn't care that her comments made me uncomfortable, that I worried about what Warren Ackerman's friends and family might think when they heard this podcast. She didn't care about Warren and she didn't care about me and she thought we were all fools for caring so much. I wondered what it would be like to live like that, whether the freedom it offered was worth the pain it caused.

ShockAndBlah:

I still don't understand why she did it. Why she killed all those people. Or even why she confessed to it all when no one suspected a thing. Was it a control thing? Only she got to write the ending to her story? I don't know.

PreyAllDay:

Come on, what did you expect? 'Oh it turns out that I'm allergic to gluten. THAT'S why I was killing everyone!!' Why do any of us do the things we do?

BurntheBookBurnerz:

Because of patriarchy, capitalism, colonialism. It all really boils down to that. She's the dark side of the American dream, or the byproduct of it anyways.

StopDropAndTroll:

[This comment has been removed by a moderator.]

PreyAllDay:

But Ruth will do more episodes right? I think even a second season. I want to hear about prison. And if she finds any connections to the Tylenol Murders.

StopDropAndTroll:

SHUT UP ABOUT THE TYLENOL MURDERS.

By Ruth's count, her podcast was now called *The Six Murders of Daphne St Clair.* Joe's death did pose a challenge for her podcast title. Was it murder to watch someone have a heart attack and refuse to call 911? Morally, it was obviously wrong, but did it actually count the same as her other sins? Should Ruth call it *The Six and a Half Murders of Daphne St Clair* just to be sure? Somehow it didn't have the same ring.

"So, you're really not leaving anything out?" Ruth probed

again. "Because the gap between the murders of Donald St Clair and Warren Ackerman is quite big." Ruth swallowed, trying to control the rising desperation she was feeling. This couldn't be the end. Daphne was robbing her of the chance to explain why this all mattered to her, how Daphne had changed her life without ever knowing she existed.

"I'm not an addict, you know! Lots of killers stop. Sometimes they start again, like BTK, sometimes they don't, like the Golden State Killer—"

"Yes, we all know you know fun facts about serial killers," Ruth snapped before she could stop herself.

She glanced down at her hands, which were wrapped around the microphone so tightly that her fingers ached. She had a vision of knocking the old woman to the floor and kicking her with the shoes Daphne mocked so frequently. "I don't want to know about them. I'm asking why *you* stopped? What could possibly account for such a long period between murders?"

"I think you need a break. You're sweating like a whore in church," Daphne said slowly. She was sitting very still, watching Ruth out of the corner of her eye, like a bird of prey. Ruth brought her hand up to her face and realized that her face was slick with sweat.

"Okay," Ruth said, her legs shaking as she stood up. "I might go splash some water on my face."

Ruth tottered to the bathroom and shut the door firmly, feeling her chest rattle with every breath. All the coffee she'd consumed to counteract her bad sleep was making her feel hot and queasy.

In all the hours she had spent in Daphne's place, Ruth had never actually used Daphne's bathroom before. It had always felt too awkward and intimate. How could you keep some psychological distance from your subject once you sat on their still-warm toilet seat? And this was definitely an old woman's bathroom. There were handles on both sides of the toilet and a large shower with a porous, plastic shower seat. Ruth tried not to imagine Daphne sitting on that seat, naked and sagging, as a glowering attendant scrubbed her with a washcloth.

Ruth doused her face with water and washed her hands with a soap that smelled heady and floral. There was a small assortment of lipsticks and face creams on the countertop, all designer brands. In an effort to calm down, Ruth read the names of the Chanel lipsticks, each of which probably cost as much as her last grocery bill. Antoinette, Marie, Gabrielle, Etienne, and Adrienne. The kind of glamorous names Daphne had chosen and changed throughout her life, with as little care as changing lipsticks. After all, Chanel wasn't going to make a fifty-dollar lipstick named Loretta.

After a few minutes Ruth felt moderately calmer, even though her head ached and her hands were still shaky. She took a final breath, staring at herself in the mirror.

It's almost over, she told herself. *Make her confess and you're done.*

As she was leaving the bathroom, almost as an afterthought, Ruth slipped one of the lipsticks, a red-gold one named Gabrielle, into her pocket, her small act of rebellion against Daphne.

Ruth noticed instantly that Daphne was sitting on the edge of her seat and seemed to be panting slightly, as if she had just exerted herself. Slowly, Ruth's eyes tracked over to her water bottle, which was sitting on the coffee table. While Ruth had never accepted any food or drink from Daphne, she had gotten into the habit of bringing her reusable metal bottle with her, to keep her voice smooth for interviews. But this was the first time she had ever left Daphne unattended with her drink.

Had the bottle been moved? Maybe. Ruth thought she remembered it being closer to the center of the table, but she wasn't certain. She sat down, painfully aware of her own pounding heart. Daphne was watching her, a small smile playing on her lips. Had she put something in her bottle? Cleaning fluid? Medication? Or had she moved the bottle to make Ruth think she'd tampered with it? Or was this all paranoia fueled from sleep deprivation and the knowledge she was in a room with a fucking murderer?

Daphne was watching her, and then slowly, unmistakably, her eyes traveled over to the bottle. But what did that mean? Should she unscrew the top and look inside? See if the surface was frothing or there was a pill still dissolving? Daphne didn't move very quickly. Would she have even had enough time to tamper with the bottle while Ruth was in the bathroom?

Ruth's mouth suddenly felt dry and her hand twitched, as if reaching for the bottle. Daphne was still watching her as Ruth desperately tried to work out what to do. Examine the bottle's contents? Storm out of here? Demand an explanation?

Finally, Daphne spoke. "So, what was it you were badgering me about?"

"Why you stopped killing. Why there was such a large gap between Donald and Warren . . ." Ruth croaked, tearing her eyes from the bottle.

"I was old, I suppose, and tired. It takes a lot of effort, pretending to be the person someone wants, hooking them, marrying them, waiting a decent amount of time before you start poisoning them. I was just tired of other people. Tired of pretending," Daphne murmured, her bony shoulders rising in a shrug. She was staring at the table—at the bottle?—with a detached, vacant gaze.

"Okay well, that's probably enough for the day. If you say you didn't kill anyone else, then you didn't," Ruth said, the words tumbling out her dry, cracked lips. All her plans to confront Daphne that day, to corner her into a confession, had dried up with the terror that Daphne might have tried to poison her. Why hadn't it occurred to her earlier that it could be dangerous, trying to get Daphne to reveal something she was hiding? That a cornered killer was particularly deadly?

"Exactly. I didn't," Daphne said. She was still staring at the table, but her eyes were stormy. Ruth frowned. Daphne's answer sounded sincere. She was a damn good liar.

Somebody knocked on the door. Ruth glanced at her watch. It would be an attendant with Daphne's pills.

The moment Daphne closed the bathroom door to take them, Ruth tore the lid off her bottle and examined its contents. It looked like water, the same tap water she'd filled it with in her apartment. Ruth sniffed the rim gingerly, but there was no chemical scent. She considered touching the liquid to her lips but she couldn't force herself to do it.

As she exited the building, she threw the bottle in the trash.

Was Daphne just playing games with her? Or was it a warning? *Ruth was close. Too close.*

That evening, Ruth was standing on the sidewalk in front of the Seacrest Building, recording some background noise. She could hear the ocean, the seagulls, and the passing cars, many of which cost more than her college degree. It was times like this, when Ruth was working on the mechanics of the podcast, setting up her equipment, structuring episodes in her head, that she felt at peace.

"Why are you here?" a voice demanded, jolting her out of her reverie. Ruth whirled around and there she was. Lucy.

Lucy cut an intimidating figure. She was even taller than Ruth and was dressed in cream exercise gear and carrying a Chanel yoga mat. Lucy's platinum ponytail was polished and she looked better coming back from yoga than most people did on their wedding day, but there was a look of icy rage on her face.

"I've seen you parked nearby but now you're actually loitering in front of my home?" Lucy asked, her voice imperious as she glared down her nose at Ruth.

"I'm on public property. I'm not doing anything wrong," Ruth replied.

Lucy rolled her eyes. "Not doing anything wrong? Everyone knows what you're up to with this podcast. It's pretty transparent and, honestly, a bit pathetic," Lucy said. Her haughty tone took Ruth right back to grade school, when Ruth's bookishness and cheap, second-hand clothing made her a target for all the good-looking rich girls.

"I'm just trying to find the truth," Ruth replied.

Lucy issued an abrupt laugh, almost a bark.

"The truth? We all know the truth. You killed him," Lucy said quietly. "You killed him, and you got away with it, and you don't even have the decency to leave us in peace."

"No, I didn't. I would never hurt anyone," Ruth protested, her voice wobbling. She had heard it all before, but it stung every time.

"I asked you to stop; I warned you of the risks. Don't act like a victim, Ruth. You make your own consequences."

"It's my family too," Ruth retorted. "You might not like it, but it's true. That's my family and you're my half-sister."

"Oh please," Lucy snorted. "My parents were married for over forty years. He had one little fling with your mother, and you think that's the same? It's not. You're not a Montgomery. We all dropped you as soon as you showed your true colors."

As Lucy talked, she backed Ruth against a column, her words slicing into Ruth like a knife. Ruth swallowed, trying to keep hold of her rising anxiety.

"You know, he *begged* your mother to get an abortion. If he'd had his way, you would have never been born. That would have been better for everyone," Lucy continued, a cruel smile playing on her lips. "Even you must see that. Then again, I'd settle for seeing you locked up in jail. And there's still time, Ruth, there's still time."

"That's how you people deal with everything isn't it? You just bully everyone into obeying you," Ruth snapped. It felt good to say it, after so many years of resentment and frustration, of sensing but never knowing for sure if the Montgomerys were the source of all her bad luck.

"Yes, and if I were you, I'd fall in line," Lucy replied, before turning and gliding through the front door, as confident of her place in the world as Ruth was unsure of hers. Ruth could see her talking to the doorman, pointing at Ruth and then at the phone. Knowing that Lucy was likely telling him to call the police, Ruth grabbed her equipment and hurried away. She peeled off in her car and only when she was a few blocks away, stuck at a red light, did Ruth lean over and throw up in an old coffee cup, her body shaking with stress.

Lucy had *scared* her. She seemed cold and calm, but she felt almost combustible, as tightly coiled as a snake waiting to strike. Ruth needed to finish the podcast as quickly as possible, to get Daphne's full confession out into the world before the Montgomerys stopped her. It was the only way she might be safe.

PreyAllDay:

Another Ruth sighting! This one was kind of strange. So, I'm near my building when I see Ruth with her filming equipment outside the Seacrest. Suddenly, this other woman comes up to her and they get into a heated conversation. Then the woman goes inside the lobby and Ruth runs off. I guess she was worried the cops were going to turn up.

BurntheBookBurnerz:

Okay that IS a good sighting! Was the woman mad that Ruth was recording there?

PreyAllDay:

No, the way they were talking, it felt like they knew each other. But it wasn't friendly. I think she even called Ruth a murderer? But maybe she was just mad that Ruth was giving Daphne a platform?

ShockAndBlah:

Did you recognize the other woman?

PreyAllDay:

No, she looked like a lot of women around here: plastic faces and designer bags.

BurntheBookBurnerz:

Didn't you say Daphne lived in that building? Maybe the woman knew her and didn't want to be interviewed.

PreyAllDay:

That was the Blue Diamond, which is on the same block. But this is the second time I've seen Ruth by the Seacrest. I dunno, I seem to remember hearing that *something* happened there a few years back, but just rumors. I didn't live there at the time. I think whatever happened, the people were rich enough that they kept it out of the papers.

ShockAndBlah:

Maybe Ruth is already researching season two!!!!

BurntheBookBurnerz:

God I hope so. Although I don't know how she'll ever top this season. But hey, sounds like you got a preview! Lucky!

PreyAllDay:

I just wish I could remember what happened at the Seacrest . . .

Chapter Twenty-Nine

Lucan. Ruth always knew that she would have to come here. This was where it all began, the bitter soil where Daphne had been planted, then cultivated by other people's cruelty.

She had been planning this trip for ages but had to wait for her first passport to arrive in the mail. It was a demanding itinerary; it had taken a number of flights and a long drive to reach Lucan. And now she stood on the edge of town, surrounded by an unfamiliar landscape. In Florida, the sky was a watery backdrop, pinned up and sagging. Here it was like a bowl turned over on the land, a vast dome that seemed as deep as eternity. The sunlight was uncompromising, flat and harsh, the horizon humming across the landscape, with only the odd tree or house to break up the noise.

It seemed like a strange time to leave Florida, to take a hiatus from her regularly scheduled life, but this trip was essential for the podcast. She just hoped she could keep it together on such a demanding journey. Ruth's insomnia was getting out of control. She moved through her waking hours as if she were underwater, fuzzy-headed and irritated from all the coffee she drank to compensate. But at night it was as if her body was seized with an incredible fear, her nerves so jangled that every time the wind blew or the pipes gurgled, she shot straight up in bed.

She had felt so scared recently: a nameless fear that she couldn't quite put into words. Death and fear were at the heart of it all and Ruth knew that she couldn't keep doing this forever, that she needed to finish this story and move on. Ruth hoped that by going back to where it all started, she might find a way for it to end.

EPISODE TEN: 2022

RUTH: Hello, and welcome to *The Six Murders of Daphne St Clair*. I'm your host, Ruth Robinson. Today, I'm in Lucan, Saskatchewan, population nine hundred. This town has almost no information online, with no famous events or notable people to distinguish it. Or so they thought. Because as you know, this is the birthplace of Loretta Cowell, the girl who would become Daphne St Clair. I'm hoping by coming here that we can find someone who might remember Daphne, even though it was a long time ago.

[Sounds of a diner. People chatting and laughing, cutlery clinking.]

WAITRESS: Do you want anything else to eat?

RUTH: Just the bill please. And I'm working on a research project about a woman named Loretta Cowell who grew up here in the Thirties and Forties. I don't suppose you remember her?

WAITRESS: It was before my time but I remember hearing about the Cowell family. But it was a big family, so I don't know if

I've ever heard the name Loretta. People left in droves back then, looking for work.

RUTH: The other Cowell children, do you know what happened to them?

[The waitress laughs.]

WAITRESS: Why don't you just ask Buzzy? He's still here.

RUTH: Buzzy?

WAITRESS: Russell Cowell. One of the youngest Cowell children. Don't know why everyone calls him Buzzy.

RUTH: Loretta's brother?

WAITRESS: Yeah. I don't know why you're surprised. Some people leave here first chance they get; some people stay forever. But he's the only Cowell in Lucan on this side of the ground so he'd be the one to talk to.

RUTH: Thanks.

There was only one old folks' home in town, which consisted of a set of apartments and rooms attached to the local hospital, so it was easy to find Buzzy.

Ruth approached a woman in a wheelchair smoking in front of the center and she pointed to an old man sitting outside. He had leathery skin, a plain cotton jacket, and a baseball hat planted firmly on his thinning hair. He was sitting on a patio chair, hands lying flat on each thigh, staring at the horizon as if an important decision depended on the weather.

"Hi, Buzzy?" Ruth asked, approaching him. She fumbled in her backpack for her microphone.

"Yeah, that's me," Buzzy said, examining Ruth warily.

"My name is Ruth Robinson. I'm a journalist. The reason I'm here, Mr. Cowell, is to talk to you about your sister Loretta," Ruth said.

His eyebrows shot up over his square, tinted glasses. "Loretta? It's been a long time since I heard that name! I haven't seen her in over seventy years! Why the heck are you interested in Loretta?" he asked, his whole demeanor changing. He gestured at the other lawn chair and Ruth sat down, holding her microphone out in front of her.

"I'll explain everything. But first, I just wanted to confirm that you remember her?"

"Of course! She was my older sister. She took care of us kids, always the first to pick us up when we were crying or distract us when Dad was mad. But she left when I was seven," Buzzy said.

"Do you know why she left?" Ruth asked, wondering if her connection to the preacher, or the fact that she'd stolen from him, had ever become public knowledge.

"No," he said bluntly. "But I never wondered. My dad was a son of a bitch. Especially to the girls," he said ominously. Ruth knew she'd have to get him to spell it out. Implications didn't make for good podcast interviews. But it wasn't her happiest moment as a journalist.

"What did he do to the girls?" she asked. He glared at her and for a moment she thought he was going to ask her to leave. But he clearly wanted to know about his sister and maybe he was even just pleased to be talking to someone new. If Ruth had learned anything in the last few months, it was that seniors' centers tended to be the same, day in and day out, and most people struggled with a frustrated sense of boredom.

"He . . . abused them. But I don't want to talk about that," Buzzy said, swatting the air away. "There's not a lot of secrets in a one-room cabin but that don't mean I need to go dredging it all up."

"What was it like after she left?" Ruth asked.

Buzzy frowned. "Well, us young kids cried a lot. And my mom got quieter and quieter, almost as if she was invisible. But my dad acted like nothing happened. One time he backhanded my brother Ray for talking about her. After that, we didn't speak about Loretta anymore."

He sighed and went quiet, as if saying all those words had tired him out. Ruth and Buzzy sat, squinting at the dry horizon for a few minutes, baking in the heat.

"That house could make you mean. It taught you not to care about anyone but yourself," he said finally, breaking the silence. "So, you going to tell me why you're asking about Loretta?"

"Loretta . . . changed her name. She goes by Daphne St Clair now," Ruth began. She wondered if she would see a flicker of recognition but there was nothing. Maybe American news wasn't shown much up here, or maybe Buzzy just stuck to the sports channel. "Daphne lives in Florida, and recently she confessed to multiple murders. She would marry men for their money and then poison them." It was an oversimplification of Daphne's life, but it was a lot of life to cover in one explanation.

Silence. Buzzy's face remained frozen for a long time, until finally he raised his gnarled hands to his face and emitted a wet cough.

"That's a shock," he said. "You'd never expect it to be someone you know, even if you haven't seen them for a long time."

Ruth recognized that he was speaking in generalities as a kind of mental protection. They were discussing what it was like to have a murderer for a sister in the abstract, nothing to do with him. Ruth could understand, sometimes she used the same technique when she was talking to Daphne, so she could momentarily forget that Daphne was the reason her life was ruined, so that she could stand to be in the same room with her.

Buzzy whistled, his dry lips contorting into a pucker.

"I feel like I'm about to fall off my chair," he said. "Well at least she didn't keep her name."

Ruth stayed silent, waiting for him to react further.

But he just kept shaking his head, looking shell-shocked.

"And the police caught her?" Buzzy asked finally.

"No, she just confessed out of the blue after they treated her most recent murder as a natural death."

"Why would she do that?" he asked. "Out of guilt?"

Ruth remembered Daphne's smug smile as she recounted Warren's death.

"Definitely not guilt. It's a mystery, really," Ruth said with a shrug.

"Have you told people in town about her?" Buzzy asked slowly.

"No," Ruth said. "I only just got here. And the waitress didn't ask why."

"Good, keep it to yourself. When my dad died, and my older brother, who was a bit wild and moved out west, people stopped talking about those no-good Cowells. I built a nice life here, raised a good family. I don't want the town talking about us again."

"But . . . people will find out," Ruth said. "It's a huge news story, and this podcast is getting bigger by the day."

Buzzy smiled and said confidently, "You'd be surprised how much gets overlooked here. Unless it's baseball or hockey, people don't care."

"Okay," Ruth said, knowing that Buzzy was stuck in the past.

"She was so kind," Buzzy said, almost to himself. Ruth felt a wave of surprise. She had interviewed a lot of people who had known Daphne and Buzzy was the only one who had called her kind. "Why would she do those things?"

"I don't know," Ruth said. "Daphne usually says she had a hard life, that she did what she had to do. But that's clearly not the full story."

They sat and talked for a long time. Ruth told Buzzy about Daphne, her life story, and what she was like now. He kept nodding impassively but always asking more questions. When there was a lull in the conversation, Ruth decided to get a couple of her own questions in.

"What happened to the rest of your siblings?" Ruth asked.

"Well, most of the girls married men as shitty as my father, probably because it was what they knew. They were good mothers, but I don't know how much use that is when you're saddled with a bad husband. And some of the boys struggled; one went to jail for burglary. Others had broken marriages and problems with drinking and gambling. But a couple of the kids did okay, me included."

Buzzy picked up the cup of coffee on the table and drank

deeply, even though it must be cold and stale. Then he resumed talking.

"You know, Loretta was pretty close to my next oldest sister, Irene."

"Is she still . . . with us?" Ruth asked, trying to find a polite way to ask if Irene was six doors down or six feet under.

"No, she died in '86," Buzzy said. "Car crash. Hard to say what happened but I think she did herself in. Or at least drank so much that she didn't care either way."

"She was troubled?"

"Oh yeah. She was married three times, each man drunker and meaner than the last. She drank too, but she was depressed. Honestly, it's a relief when I lose touch with one of my siblings. I don't like to hear their stories," Buzzy said quietly. He suddenly looked even frailer, almost like a child again.

Ruth nodded. Irene's story was an object lesson in what would have happened if Daphne had stayed.

She'd hoped Lucan would give her clarity but she only felt more confused. Here was a family of neglected, abused children who had all grown into wildly different people. Some had made happy, healthy lives for themselves while others had fallen into bad marriages, addiction, and crime. And one had become a monster. Why had they all taken different paths? And how much control did Daphne really have over her journey into darkness? For the last six years, Ruth had watched her life spiral downwards, a tailspin into failed relationships, a stalled career, and an obsession with the mystery at the heart of it. She had become a different person, and none of it had felt like a choice. She and Daphne were both stuck on dark paths, both unable to break free of their own natures, even when it would be better for everyone if they did.

Buzzy waited until she shut down her recording equipment, his red-rimmed eyes watching her zip up her bag.

"Will you let her know I said hey?" he asked, his voice round and vulnerable.

"Sure, but I can also give you her phone number. You could give her a call," Ruth suggested, slinging the bag across her shoulder blades. Buzzy shook his head, letting the brim of his Saskatchewan Roughriders cap cover his face.

"No, it'd be like talking to a stranger. Just tell her hello from me," he muttered.

Ruth nodded. "I understand. Thank you for your time. I really appreciate it."

She was already walking away when she heard him croak: "Okay! Give me the number, just in case."

HauteHistoire: "Okay well, not a lot to work with this episode for a fashion TikTok. I've gone for kind of a farmer look . . . Levi's jeans . . . and a Carhartt jacket with a baseball hat. Honestly . . . this isn't my best work."

PreyAllDay:

Hey, guys, just wanted to share something creepy. My cousin, who used to work at Coconut Grove, is friends with someone who still works there. Anyways, she said the staff have seen someone lurking around the center. A man with a backpack and a baseball hat who disappears in the woods whenever he's spotted. The staff are really freaked out and walking to their cars in groups.

ShockAndBlah:

Okay, I know this is left field but what if it's a GHOST? Daphne killed so many men, surely one of their spirits is restless!?!

StopDropAndTroll:

Were you dropped on the head? Best-case scenario for Daphne it's a reporter; worst-case scenario it's one of her victim's family members, out for a revenge. Or a deranged fan who wants to wear her skin like a coat.

PreyAllDay:

Lololol . . . It's gonna take A LOT of lotion to get those wrinkles out!

BTW, CapoteParty, did you get to Florida yet?

The Seventh Murder?

Chapter Thirty

"New York state authorities have now tentatively connected Daphne St Clair to an unsolved hit-and-run involving a twelve-year-old girl in 1974. The police have reason to believe that Gabrielle Hanks was the stepdaughter of Daphne St Clair, who was going by Daphne Hanks at the time. Shortly after Gabrielle's death, her father Robert Hanks also died in an apparent suicide."

Ruth was welded to the spot, watching the stream on her laptop. The story had broken after someone in Abrams had recognized Daphne on the news and contacted the police. She didn't know what evidence the police had, but finding out that a victim of an unsolved crime was the stepchild of a serial killer certainly merited the police investigating further.

Her stomach rose up and she ran to the bathroom, gagging. When she was done throwing up, she curled up next to the toilet, feeling the cold porcelain press against her feverish forehead.

Daphne was a murderer. *A child murderer.*

It all made sense. Daphne had skillfully glossed over

the years when her kids had been in high school as being uneventful, carefully maneuvering Ruth away from Robert and Gabrielle Hanks. She thought back to the picture she had found in Daphne's things, the dark-haired girl in the photo. *Gabrielle.* Ruth realized once again that she was navigating unfamiliar terrain with an unreliable navigator, someone who might actually want to do her harm. She was putting a podcast out that could be full of lies, no matter how many background interviews she did and how much research she put into it. Ruth could end up more hated than Daphne herself.

Why did she think she could outsmart Daphne? There would always be another lie, another murder hidden away. Daphne had taken everything from her once before. And now she was doing it again.

StopDropAndTroll:

Scum. Fucking scum.

BurntheBookBurnerz:

This is completely different. I thought she killed MEN. I don't understand . . .

StopDropAndTroll:

AWW did the serial killer disappoint u?

ShockAndBlah:

She's lost me. I can't like her anymore.

StopDropAndTroll:

Ur not supposed to like her, u psychopath.

ShockAndBlah:

Hey, didn't someone mention that town before? In a discussion about unsolved murders Daphne may have committed?

BurntheBookBurnerz:

Oh yeah . . . you're right!

PreyAllDay:

It was CapoteParty . . . u/CapoteParty, why did you ask that? What do you know?

ShockAndBlah:

CapoteParty?

After that, people really started to hate me. When everyone thought I had only killed men, I was interesting to them. Maybe in their heart of hearts, other people understood why you might like to smile to someone's face as you slipped poison into their coffee. Maybe everyone just loved a murder story full of love, sex, and lotsa money.

But a child killer? That was no fun.

I had never felt so alone. And somehow that made me even more worried about stalkers. I'd already given them so much ammunition, but this would push someone over the edge. I was right to worry.

"The front desk wanted me to inform you that there was an incident tonight," the Coconut Grove attendant said coolly, almost robotically. She handed me my medication, thrusting it into my hand with so much force that my arm ached.

"Is this you informing me? Because you haven't told me jack shit," I protested, clutching the pills tightly in my hand. My arthritic fingers ached with the effort. The girl sighed, as if to say: *Oh dear, Difficult Daphne is at it again.*

"They had a man approach the front desk and ask to leave you a letter. The staff said we didn't have anyone by that name living here and refused to take the letter. He became irate, insisting that he knew you were here and that they were lying. It was only when they threatened to call the police that he left."

"Hmmm . . . wonder what was in the letter?" I mused.

"They just wanted to make you aware of this event and caution you again to stay out of sight—"

"Yeah, yeah," I interrupted, gesturing behind me with the hand that wasn't holding my medication. "The doors are locked, the curtains are shut. It's darker than a witch's asshole in here, don't worry."

The attendant's face hardened and she stepped close, uncomfortably close. I stepped back, my free hand leaning on my walker as my knees wobbled.

"I wouldn't push us. You know, we're all getting sick of protecting you, especially now that we've heard you killed a child!

It would be a real shame if we made a mistake," she hissed, before walking off. Now I wish I'd gotten her name.

Trusting these attendants was a real concern. One of the staff could be incentivized (either by money or just pure hatred) to leave a side door unlocked, to point out my window to a person who wanted to harm me. Or they could slip something in my pills. After all, they all wanted me gone from here; that was abundantly clear. I couldn't trust anyone, and certainly not *them*. It was a shame because they loved me before the whole Warren thing, probably because I was one of the least incontinent people in my age range.

I left the pills in my bathroom and sat in my armchair with my hand on the phone for a moment. The apartment was completely silent except for the sound of the ticking clock, relentlessly reminding me that I was alone, and my days were numbered. I stared at the thick swathes of fabric covering the windows. Curtains should make you feel safer, as if you were shielded from the world. But there was something about not being able to see outside that made it scarier.

Anyone could be out there.

BurntheBookBurnerz:

Kind of disgusting to be giving a platform to a child-killer.

ShockAndBlah:

Should Ruth even be doing this podcast? Honestly, I'm starting to wonder about her . . .

HauteHistoire: "Hi, guys, I won't be doing any more Daphne aesthetic videos on my TikTok. I understand now that my videos glorified and glamorized a senseless murderer and that I was contributing to a culture of violence in our country. Discovering that she may have killed a child only further confirms this decision, although I'd actually been thinking about this for a long, long time. These videos have hugely increased my followers, so I hope you'll all go on a journey with me as we reflect on how it's wrong to monetize other people's pain. I'm still learning every day so thank you all for teaching me. I'm trying to better myself on this crazy experience called life. Anyways, stay tuned for tomorrow's video where I dive into the Nineties heroin-chic craze and how you too can look like a heroin addict, just one with a platinum card! Okay, thanks, peace and love, byeeee."

Ruth tried to call Daphne, but she wouldn't pick up, which was incredibly frustrating since Ruth knew that she was confined to her apartment, always in earshot of her phone. She spent hours watching coverage of the allegations, mainlining sour Skittles and waiting for someone to dig up some concrete evidence that either proved or disproved that Daphne had killed a child.

Should Ruth even continue with the podcast? It could destroy her career if people were outraged enough. People might believe she was on Daphne's side or that she had *known* that Daphne was a child-killer and did this anyway. Ruth didn't do well in high-pressure scenarios. She felt as if she was back in the Palm Haven police station, staring at a two-way mirror, trying desperately to explain how an innocent person could look so damn guilty.

The Reddit comments online were demanding that she put out an episode, that Ruth provide a full explanation of what she had known and what she might have suspected, that she give them a damn good reason to absolve herself. Ruth stopped leaving her apartment, stopped opening her curtains, stopped leaving her bed.

All the media wanted to talk about was Daphne and her dead stepdaughter. The coverage was news releases and rants from outrage magnets. Gone were all the activists, academics, and rebels who'd previously argued that Daphne deserved under-standing, if not a little sympathy. No one wanted to appear on TV defending a woman who might have killed a young girl. The public stopped wearing Daphne shirts and *SNL* stopped doing sketches about her. Everyone agreed that Daphne St Clair was no longer fun. It was just so *hard* to find a truly ethical serial killer, a sympathetic murderer who aligned perfectly with larger societal issues about class, gender, violence, and power.

Ruth had always thought that the central story of Daphne (the Black Widow who had been repeatedly victimized by men and decided to start victimizing men right back) was true. Now she understood that Daphne would kill anyone who stood in the way of what she wanted. Just because that had typically been men, the people who held the money and the power, didn't mean it *had* to be men.

After all, Robin Hood was just a legend. The true story looked a lot more like Daphne St Clair.

*   *   *

In desperation, Ruth called her mom. When Louise picked up, Ruth explained about the allegations, and how she didn't know if they were true or not, but that it was giving her second thoughts about doing the podcast. She expected her mom to crow about being right and tell her to abandon it immediately, but her mother surprised her.

"Ruth, at this point, what's done is done. Quitting the podcast now will only hurt your career. Maybe you'll be able to get a good job out of this and can move far away. Florida's not safe for you anymore, so now you just need some money and a reason to go."

"I shouldn't have to leave home. I'm innocent," Ruth protested. Louise sighed. Ruth could hear that she was exhausted, that a long day of work and managing her symptoms had left her depleted and irritable.

"Forget about the past and focus on your future. This podcast won't bring him back and you'll never see a cent of that inheritance. So just use it as a springboard to something else."

"But I worry that it sends the wrong message. Giving her this platform," Ruth explained, trying to make sense of all the mixed-up emotions inside of her.

"Ruth, you can't pay the rent on a moral high ground. So, hold your nose and do it for the money because you sure as shit know there's nothing noble about being poor," Louise said, her voice frosty. Her mother had always worked minimum-wage jobs, bouncing from offices, restaurants, factories, anything she could get her hands on. There was no time for academic debates in Louise Robinson's world; there was no time for anything really. She was sick, and she was tired, and her daughter was being a coward.

"But—" Ruth began.

"Ruth, I'm exhausted. This whole thing has been hard for me too. You made your bed, so now, you're just going to have to lie in it," Louise said. "Finish this."

Ruth woke in the middle of the night to the sound of a gentle rapping on her front door. It was so quiet that Ruth wasn't sure that it was real. Was it a dream? A tree tapping on the wall of her building? No. There it was again.

Ruth sat frozen in bed, unsure of what she should do. It was past midnight, and her apartment was pitch-black since the curtains were all shut. Ruth turned the flashlight of her phone on and sat there, listening to the knocking, frozen, unsure what to do.

"Ruth . . . Ruth . . ." a voice called from the door. Ruth slowly, quietly, slipped out of bed, carefully skirting the creaky spot on the floor. She crept along the little hallway, past her kitchen, where her appliances seemed to gurgle and groan in their slumber.

"Ruth . . . Ruth . . ." The voice again. A man's voice. Quiet. Cajoling. Ruth edged over to the door and carefully checked that both locks were in place. She clutched her phone, ready to call 911 if he came crashing through the door. Slowly, painfully slowly, she raised her eye to the peephole. She held her breath, aware that there was a man just inches away from her, a man who seemed determined to find her.

The hallway was shadowy, and the figure was wearing a dark green sweatshirt with the hood up. But then he turned, and the dim overhead light caught his face.

It was Officer Rankin. But he wasn't wearing his uniform, and he was alone. Ruth eyed the loose sweatshirt. There was no way to tell if he was armed.

"I can hear you through the door. I know you're there ..." he murmured.

Ruth stepped back from the peephole, covering her mouth in terror. She glanced down at her phone, suddenly aware that she had no one to call—certainly not the police. She was alone in an apartment where the only exit was being blocked by a strange man.

She couldn't go back to bed, not when he was still out there. Instead, she slowly slid down the wall, taking hot, shallow breaths through her clasped hands. How long would he stay out there?

"You've had a good run. But it's time to end this," he said with a smirk in his voice.

Ruth didn't say anything, so he tried another tack.

"You've drawn too much attention to yourself. You want to plaster yourself all over the Internet? Well, I'm listening, Ruth. And it's time you told us the truth."

She tried to keep breathing, even though her chest was getting tighter and tighter.

"You can't keep doing this, Ruth. We won't allow it. Nobody gets away with murder. You should know that by now, you stupid bitch."

He hasn't come here as a cop, not tonight. This wasn't the kind of thing an officer on duty would do, and there was no partner in sight. Ruth knew that Officer Rankin was working for the Montgomerys and it was obvious that he was here on their business. *Was he going to kill her?* Anything seemed possible in the middle of the night.

"*Ruth . . . Ruth . . .*" he whispered, his voice barely passing through the door. She shivered and held herself even tighter.

Ruth sat there for ages; her body paralyzed with fear. At some point he stopped talking, stopped threatening and cajoling. She sat there longer, afraid that he was only lulling her into a false sense of security, so that she might do something stupid like unlock the door to check if the coast was clear. Finally, she worked up the courage to look out the peephole. The hallway was empty, still bathed in shadows.

It was only the next morning, when Ruth finally ventured out that she found the picture taped to her door. It was an old picture of her with the Montgomerys, arm in arm with all the people who now wanted her gone.

Standing next to the man Daphne had murdered.

Chapter Thirty-One

Ruth decided to continue the podcast.

She was now in the public eye, and she had to make sure that the story of Daphne St Clair and Ruth Robinson was the right one. How she handled this Gabrielle wrinkle would either make or break her in public life.

When Daphne finally answered the phone and agreed to an interview, Ruth drove to Coconut Grove, hoping to get this episode out as soon as possible, before people abandoned the show. Her listeners needed to know that she was going to give them the truth, the whole truth. About Daphne, yes, but also about Ruth. And she had to do it fast, before they started drawing their own conclusions.

The car was silent as Ruth drove to Coconut Grove. The only sounds were the hum of the engine and the wind buffeting her ears. Ruth wiped her face at a red light and was surprised to see that she was covered in a slick, cold sweat. Her face looked bloodshot and lined in the mirror. This investigation had taken so much out of her, had brought so much to the surface, and Ruth knew that she wouldn't last much longer. Whether it was Daphne or Ruth, something had to give.

There was a police car parked outside the seniors' center but Ruth strode past it, refusing to look inside. There was nothing they could say, nothing they could do, that could stop her. She knew the stakes, knew what would happen if she failed and how many people were hoping she would do exactly that. Today was the day.

As soon as Ruth walked into Daphne's room, she could tell that Daphne knew that today would be different too. The air felt like it did before a major tropical storm, when it seemed hazy and charged with electricity. She felt Daphne watching her set up her recording equipment and when their eyes met, Ruth saw that cold, predatory gaze that Daphne's face lapsed into when she wasn't consciously trying to obscure it. Daphne didn't know how Ruth would handle these new allegations, what story the podcast would endorse. Ruth didn't know yet herself.

So, she took a deep breath and began recording, praying that she wouldn't fail.

EPISODE ELEVEN: 1972–1974

RUTH: Daphne, a news story broke this week, a very controversial one. Let's talk about your time in Abrams, New York.

DAPHNE: Sure, that's essentially where I was at in the story anyways.

RUTH: Well, no we were actually up to 2022 the last time we talked, so this would be oh . . . fifty years earlier.

DAPHNE: Maybe if you didn't yap so much, I wouldn't have forgotten about the Seventies! Let's see, after Leosville, I went back to New York. The kids went to the best schools in the city, they did every kind of extracurricular, and we had summers in the Hamptons. Anything they wanted I bought them.

RUTH: All with David's money.

DAPHNE: Yes, obviously. Anyways, when I was forty, I married my next husband, Robert Hanks. I had been feeling so bored and I really thought it would be different this time.

RUTH: Tell me about Robert.

DAPHNE: Robert was my white whale. A rich, childless man who didn't mind a few stepchildren. He was never much for babies but he wasn't fazed by a few preteens in the house. It's hard to find a man over forty who hasn't moved to the suburbs and isn't saddled with a nest of brats.

RUTH: How long were you together before you got engaged?

DAPHNE: A year. We were taking it slow, keeping our own separate lives. There's something about marriage; too often, in a man's eyes, it transforms you from an alluring seductress into the nag in the bathrobe blocking the TV. Even the best men let themselves slide when you get married and suddenly Friday evenings at the champagne bar become TV dinners and ball-scratching.

RUTH: But he did propose.

DAPHNE: Boy, you're really hurrying me along today! Yes, I guess he was less jaded about marriage than me. He took me to Lutèce, one of the best restaurants in New York in the early Seventies. He gave me a huge emerald ring in a champagne glass. There was a bit of awkwardness as he tried to fish it out with his stubby fingers but then he gave me his Big Speech, about how we would live in New York, travel the world, and have fun. My first husband had been a cheat, the second a bore, maybe Robert would be Just Right. So, I said yes and slapped that ring on my trotter.

That night we lay in bed, heads still buzzing from the bubbly and the excitement.

"I want this to work out," Robert whispered. "I just can't go through another divorce."

"Was it hard?" I asked. At that point the only man who'd ever gotten away from me alive was Carl, my son's father, so I didn't have much experience with breakups.

"It was terrible. We were only married for two years and after the first six months we just . . . fell out of love with each other. We spent the next year and a half making each other miserable. Then she started cheating on me."

"How did it end?" I asked, wishing he'd wrap this story up and focus on me.

"She waited until I was on a business trip and then she stripped the apartment of everything valuable and moved to the West Coast. A week later she wrote to me, asking for a divorce. We got a quickie divorce in Nevada and I never saw her again."

"That's tough," I said absent-mindedly. I was enjoying how my ring glistened in the lamplight. He rolled over on his side and stroked my hair.

"Of course, I can't imagine how hard it must have been for you, losing the father of your children, becoming a widow . . ." Okay, so I had taken a little artistic license and cleaned up my backstory; giving the kids one dead father instead of a string of bad dads and suspicious deaths.

"But at least you know your husband didn't want to leave you. He didn't want to die," Robert said.

"No," I agreed. "He really didn't want to die."

The next year passed in a flood of happiness. We got married in a small civil ceremony because—and this might surprise you—I've never been much for weddings. Wedding announcements, hundreds of guests, pictures in the paper, it's all just a recipe for getting caught. Then we moved into a gorgeous penthouse apartment, the kind of place that makes you feel right in the center of the city even when you're just standing in your living room.

Robert and I got along great. He seemed to enjoy being a husband again after so many years of bachelorhood and I was happy to play the little wife since he didn't expect me to cook, clean, or have babies. We'd often meet up for lunch in the middle of the day to break up his workday and then in the evening it was dinner parties, restaurants, and theater shows. Robert let me do what I wanted while he footed the bill. He was the perfect husband.

My kids, however, seemed somewhat detached from Robert. One time I asked James about it. I was sitting on his bed, the wind howling outside on a cold November evening, watching him glue a model airplane in the dim light of his desk lamp. We had just come back from a movie theater trip. I had dragged James to the new Audrey Hepburn movie and he had agreed, knowing that I'd loved her ever since I saw Breakfast at Tiffany's.

"James, do you like Robert?"

A shrug rippled through his bony, adolescent shoulders. I could see his shoulder blades shift beneath his shirt and I *suddenly wished that I could kiss them, that I could cover him with kisses the way I had when he was a baby, when his body had belonged to me. But of course, I didn't kiss him now. The mother of a teenage boy is only permitted a couple of grudging hugs on a semi-annual basis, usually after a large gift. It made me sad, watching him grow up and grow away from me.*

"He's okay," James said. His voice was completely neutral, as if I'd asked him whether he liked bread.

"Maybe you could be warmer to him. He's giving us a good life," I said. It was the closest I'd ever come to lecturing James, my perfect boy. But I didn't think it was too much to ask him to smile in exchange for the private school tuition, the museum tickets, the trips abroad. In my life, I'd had to do much more for far less.

James spun in his chair and looked at me, clasping his hands. His dark hair flopped in his eyes and I resisted the urge to brush it off his shiny forehead.

"Mom, there's been a lot of guys over the years. I just don't want to get attached."

"But, darling, Robert's different. This one is going to last."

"That's what you said about David," he said quietly.

"Well, how was I to know he was going to get cancer?" I asked.

James didn't say anything for a moment. He just stared hard at me and rolled his hands together. I shifted uncomfortably, not sure what he was thinking.

"All I'm saying is, it's just easier not to get attached," he muttered. I sighed and got up to leave, patting his shoulder as I brushed past. I wished that my son, the person who knew me best in the world, had a little more faith in my marriage, in me. Then again, he did know me pretty well . . .

It could have ended there. I could have stayed happily married to Robert in Manhattan. I really believe that we could have made it work, if it hadn't been for Gabrielle.

It's funny, you expect the girl who ruins your marriage to be a twenty-something cocktail waitress with zero-gravity boobs. But in my case, it was a twelve-year-old girl.

It all started one day when I came home from a productive afternoon shopping to find my husband sitting on the floor by the phone, his face the same shade of gray as his wool suit.

"Are you all right?" I asked, carefully depositing my shopping bags on a table as gently as you'd lay down a baby, then crouching down next to him.

"I got some news," Robert murmured. "I don't even know where to start."

"Just tell me," I said firmly, helping him up onto the couch. He didn't say anything for a moment, and I resisted the urge to tap my toe like a schoolmarm waiting for an answer.

"Today I was contacted by a lawyer in California. My ex-wife has died," he said quietly. I shrugged. Who cared? If I fell apart every time a spouse died, I'd never get anything done!

"Maybe that's a bit sad but you haven't seen her for over a decade," I replied. Robert took a rattling breath and then wiped his mouth. His face seemed slack and rubbery, as if it was numb from visiting the dentist.

"The lawyer . . . he told me that Sheila was pregnant when we got divorced, that I have a twelve-year-old daughter."

"What?"

"I'm named on the birth certificate. I just can't believe she kept this from me," he said bitterly. "That was Sheila all right."

"Are you going to meet this girl?" I asked, already wondering if I might be able to spin this in a way that would benefit me. I had never been to California before.

"Meet her? She's coming to live with us," Robert snapped.

"What?" I said again, dumbfounded.

"Sheila's will said that she wants Gabrielle to come live with me," Robert said, his voice still angry. He never snapped at me. I hadn't even met this kid and she was already affecting my marriage.

"You can't though," I said faintly. "You don't even know this girl!"

"I'm aware!" Robert growled. "But what do you expect me to do? Besides, this house is full of kids anyways, we might as well throw another one on the pile!" He leapt up and stalked away.

"She might not even be yours!" I called after him.

My hope that Sheila was a lying whore disappeared the moment I met Gabrielle. She was the spitting image of Robert; the same dark hair, lean face, and gray-blue eyes. Sheila had been telling the truth. I hated the dead bitch.

Gabrielle didn't look like a Californian. More of a Bostonian really, with her milky skin and expensive features. She stood in the hall, wrapped in the red designer coat I'd chosen for her and sent out with Robert, since we assumed she wouldn't have clothes fit for a New York winter.

"Hello," I said, reaching out to pat her shoulder.

"Hello," she responded woodenly. I had thought she might be intimidated meeting me but her half-lidded eyes barely flickered. She reminded me of an iguana I had once seen

319

perched on a branch at the zoo, not moving a muscle even as schoolchildren hammered on the glass.

"My name is Daphne Hanks. I'm not sure what you'd like to call me. You can call me Mrs. Hanks or Auntie, whatever feels right," I said. I hoped she got the hint that "Mommy" was off the table. I waited for her to speak but she said nothing, just stared at me imperiously, so I continued.

"My kids and I are looking forward to getting to know you and show you around the city." Not true but I felt saintly for saying it. All those other rich wives were out there, throwing benefits to help children, but how many of them were doing the truly charitable thing of bringing an unknown child into their home?

Still no response from Gabrielle. Tough crowd. The last time I heard crickets like that was at the twins' violin recital, but they earned those, dammit. I was just trying to be nice.

"Would you like to see your bedroom? I'm sure you could use a rest."

She nodded and I led her down the hall.

Her bedroom had been my vanity room until recently. I had sullenly packed away my makeup and jewelry, already feeling like this girl was crowding me out of Robert's life. But I had thrown myself into shopping, creating a dream bedroom for a preteen girl: white wicker furniture, a canopy bed with blue silk hangings, floral wallpaper sprigged with forget-me-nots. I opened the door with a sense of ceremony, as if I was unveiling it, and glanced at her for a reaction, maybe a smile or a gasp. But her expression didn't change. She shrugged off her new coat, letting it flop to the floor and flung herself on the bed without taking off her shoes. Finally, she spoke.

*"Can you shut the door, Daphne?" Gabrielle asked inso-
lently, her eyes challenging me. I nodded and resisted the urge
to slam the door on my way out.*

We weren't off to a great start.

*Things didn't improve in the following days. I'd always had a
favorite child but now, at last, I had a least favorite one as well.*

*Gabrielle was sullen and had a habit of not responding to
things I said, even when it was a direct question, which is a
simple but incredibly effective way to infuriate someone. She'd
glare at me as if to signal 'I don't want a new mother' even
though I had no interest in applying for the job.*

*Even worse was the way she would glom onto Robert, like
a barnacle on a ship, or a flesh-eating disease. There was
something unsettling about the way she'd climb into his lap on
the couch, wrapping her lanky adolescent arms around him
like a much younger child. Her eyes would glint acquisitively
as she cooed at him in a babyish voice. One time, I remember
the twins studying her intently while we watched TV, as she
whispered into Robert's ear, and then averting their eyes in
disgust. Even my ten-year-olds thought she was laying it on
a bit thick.*

*My children tried to be welcoming. James took on the role
of the benevolent older brother, asking her about school and
offering her trips to the movies, but she largely ignored him. The
twins, who were only two years younger than her, should have
been the perfect friends for Gabrielle. But it was clear Gabrielle
saw them as competition. She'd come to her long-lost father's
home only to find two attractive blonde girls already living there.
There were problems between the girls almost immediately.*

"Mom, our riding ribbons are missing," Diane reported to me on Day Two.

I found them crammed into the cistern of the guest toilet.

"Mom, my school skirt has been cut into two."

I spotted the scissors from the sewing box in Gabrielle's room.

"Mom, our pillows are wet."

I didn't even want to solve that mystery.

It could have been bearable if I could have laughed it off with Robert, but he was totally besotted with Gabrielle. Typical man. They spend decades declaring they don't want children, wasting a lot of women's time and ovarian reserves, only to announce later in life that fatherhood was the most fulfilling thing they've ever done.

In Robert's eyes, Gabrielle could do no wrong. It didn't matter how much she tortured the twins or disobeyed me, the kid with his face was perfect. And people say parenting isn't about narcissism.

And then one day Robert announced that he wanted us to move upstate to the country.

"Absolutely not," I said flatly. It was nighttime and we were in bed. Robert folded his hands over his blue cotton pajamas, doing his best Father Knows Best impression.

"Daphne, it would be much better for the kids. They don't have enough space in this apartment and Gabrielle is used to a more rural life."

"You thought the city was perfectly fine when it was just my kids living here," I retorted. Robert was born and raised in New York. People like him always had a hard-on for country life, *which was something I found incredibly irritating. What did they think happened out there? Birds brought you your morning coffee while a milkmaid gave you a hand job?*

"*I realize now that I was being selfish. Having Gabrielle here has taught me that the kids' needs must come first,*" *Robert said.*

I rolled my eyes. The man had been a parent for a second and suddenly he was Father Teresa. He had managed to skip the years of sleepless nights and stinking diapers and was now patting himself on the back for spending a couple of hours with a grateful twelve-year-old after work.

"*But why? They're only going to move out in a couple of years!*" *I burst out, as flashbacks to Leosville danced through my head. "Besides, it's the Seventies, they need to know how to live in a city! What do you think they're going to do for jobs someday? Goat herding?*" *And that was when Robert, my lovely, pliant Robert, decided to grow a backbone and pull rank.*

"*I make the money and if you want to keep enjoying the lifestyle I've given you then you'll be moving to the country,*" *Robert snapped.*

I sighed.

Men will claim you're equal partners but at the end of the day, he who holds the checkbook has the power. I wanted to shout 'enjoy the smell of cow shit' and storm out, but I wasn't quite ready to quit on Robert. He was just so very rich. Maybe I needed to bide my time and hope that he would hate rural life and realize that we didn't belong in a place where you couldn't get Chinese food at 2 a.m. Or at any time for that matter.

Chapter Thirty-Two

DAPHNE: When the school year ended, we packed up and moved to Abrams, a wealthy commuter town in the middle of nowhere. It was just close enough to the city that it was possible to commute but far enough away that only men going in for work ever bothered. On weekdays, the town was eerily empty of men, the streets filled only with mothers and children.

RUTH: You seem to dislike everywhere that isn't New York City.

DAPHNE: Well, only because people keep dragging me to the back-ass of nowhere. I would have been open to Los Angeles, London or Paris. But Abrams? I'd spent my childhood busting my ass on a farm, what did I care about nature? And don't even get me started on small-town values!

RUTH: Were the kids happy?

DAPHNE: The twins were happy because we lived near a famous stable. They'd been riding for years but only once a week; now they could go all the time. It was a bit tedious, listening to them yammer away about dressage and quarter horses all day, but I liked seeing them compete in their fancy velvet coats and tall boots. Geoffrey had loved reminding me that I was trash, but no one would ever do that to my girls.

RUTH: And James?

DAPHNE: He was a city boy like me. We'd put them all in the local private school, Abrams Country Day, and it was full of jocks. It was hard for him to make friends there because my son didn't want to play lacrosse; he wanted to be at a museum or taking pictures. I was worried about James and I was worried about my marriage with Robert. I was starting to hear that little voice again, that little whisper that reminded me how much easier it was to keep the money but not the man. But I was trying to ignore it.

RUTH: You haven't mentioned Gabrielle yet.

DAPHNE: Well, it turns out fresh air isn't a cure for being an asshole. She was rude, and she'd steal stuff that belonged to the twins and me. In Abrams, she made friends with kids who were older than her and would be out at parties, smoking and drinking. She was so defiant of me. And the worst part was that Robert never noticed.

One night, when we were in the bedroom, I tried to talk to Robert again.

"Robert, Gabrielle has been so rude lately. And she's always out. During the week when you're not around, she never makes her curfew," I said, curling up against him in bed.

"You keep telling me this but I see a sweet little girl," he replied, shifting as if he was trying to get out from under my body.

"She's manipulating you. Trust me, she's not that sweet. I know she smokes and drinks, and those sleepovers are just house parties," I snapped.

325

"Maybe you can't stand the fact that I have a daughter. Maybe you're just jealous. She's a little girl who lost her mother and all you do is antagonize her," Robert said coldly, turning over in bed so he was facing away from me.

"She antagonizes me! And she's making the twins' lives hell," I protested. Slowly, stiffly, he climbed out of bed, clutching his pillow.

"I don't believe a word you're saying. And I think it's disgusting that you're trying to poison me against my own child." Robert stomped to the doorway in his pajamas, still clutching his pillow. "I'm going to move to the guest bedroom. I'll come back when your attitude improves."

"Fine," I hissed. "Then just leave!"

He shut the door but not before glancing back at me one last time in bewilderment. I balled up my hands and punched a pillow, my ring cutting into my finger with every hit.

That night I didn't sleep, too consumed by all the old feelings.

DAPHNE: Almost a year passed. It was October 1974 and I was still living in Abrams. I had no friends, no hobbies, and so much hired help that I couldn't even distract myself with housework, not that I was ever *that* tempted. Robert would get up early and leave for work in the city and I would drive the kids to school. And then I would just . . . sit around until it was time to pick them up.

RUTH: That's it? You'd just sit around?

DAPHNE: Pretty much. I watched a lot of TV. I made cocktails. Sometimes I took a Valium, just to forget about it all. But that's it, really.

RUTH: This seems out of character for you. Did you think about the past?

DAPHNE: All the time. Sometimes it would just hit me. I'd be driving back from the grocery store or watching the twins compete in dressage and I'd think: I killed four men. And when I was poisoning David and Geoffrey, I'd felt like I had so much power over my own life. Remembering that impressed me but it also made me sad. I used to make things happen. Now life was just happening to me.

RUTH: How was your marriage to Robert?

DAPHNE: Terrible. After he moved into the other bedroom, he never moved back. He claimed it was insomnia, but I knew he couldn't forgive me for not loving his daughter. And I couldn't forgive him for ruining our happy life.

RUTH: This might sound callous to ask, but why hadn't you already killed him?

DAPHNE: Now, I've always been a big believer in murder as a way to fix my problems, but killing Robert wouldn't solve anything as there was still the problem of Gabrielle.

RUTH: Then what about divorce?

DAPHNE: Well that's expensive, and if I planned on going back to the city, I wanted to afford a good life for my kids. Robert was also very clever with money and he had a lot of lawyer friends. I didn't want to leave him and end up penniless.

RUTH: What did you fight about?

DAPHNE: Gabrielle mostly, and the way we argued. It infuriated me; I couldn't control anything in my life, not even a kid. Robert blamed me for it, saying that I was cold to her and treated her worse than my own children. Everything was my fault.

RUTH: Seems like you were definitely out of the honeymoon phase.

DAPHNE: Yes, the margaritas had melted and we were all sunburnt. Honestly by that point it was pretty obvious that Robert didn't even like me anymore, much less love me. And that feeling was sure as shit mutual.

My kids were still struggling with Gabrielle as well. James, reacting to all the conflict in the house, seemed to retreat further into himself, spending more and more time at the library. He was at the top of his class and never caused me any trouble, but I missed my best friend and hated that he didn't feel comfortable at home anymore. The twins had it worst though. They seemed particularly vulnerable to her torture because they were only two years younger than Gabrielle. One night, I found Rose sobbing in her bathroom, long after everyone else had gone to sleep. She was huddled up by the toilet, crushing a towel into her face to muffle the noise.

"Please don't make me go to school tomorrow," Rose begged plaintively.

"Why? Are you sick?" I asked, sitting on the toilet and rubbing her hard little back.

"No . . . Gabrielle . . . she told everyone lies about us!" Rose squeaked out, tears streaming down her face.

"What did she say?" I asked, feeling a strange predatory cold come over me.

"She-she-she told people that Diane and I are freaks! That we take b-b-baths together and kiss each other!" Rose whispered through her tears, looking ashamed. "And now no one wants to be friends with us."

"Oh, Rose," I sighed, shaking my head and pulling her into me. "You two can stay home tomorrow. And don't worry, we can figure something out," I murmured into her hair.

I could feel Rose trembling against me. "Please don't tell Robert," she whispered. "He'll just get mad and take her side."

"I won't."

Two days later Rose and Diane were still staying home from school. I had ordered brochures for new private schools for the girls but I resented Gabrielle for running my girls out of their school, when they'd already had to start over so many times.

That night, a Thursday, Robert came home earlier than usual and noticed that Gabrielle hadn't returned for her curfew, yet again.

"Did you call around to her friends?" Robert asked.

"The ones I know," I replied. "She's very secretive."

"She could be lying in a ditch somewhere," Robert retorted. I had been sitting in the living room with the twins watching TV when he confronted me, and they shuffled off to bed, casting worried looks back at me.

"She does this all the time!" I protested. "And if I tell her she's grounded, she just ignores me! I've told you time and time again! What do you expect me to do?"

Robert stood there, cold and seething. He was unrecognizable from the man he'd been when we'd first married, back when his commute was a fifteen-minute cab ride and his biggest concern was where we could get dinner reservations. Now he was permanently exhausted from the long days, brittle from our fights, and obsessed with his new daughter. He didn't care about me anymore.

"I work hard all day and the only thing you're expected to do is take care of the kids," Robert said, throwing my purse at me. "Now, go out there and look for her. And don't come back until you find her!"

RUTH: Did you find her?

DAPHNE: No. I did look but I figured she was probably at a party, smoking grass and drinking beer. Robert was furious when I got home, and he went out to look too but he was back within twenty minutes. I knew he wasn't really prepared to drive around all night; he just wanted to prove that he cared more than me. A couple hours later, there was a cop on our front step. He had tears in his eyes and his hat in his hands. Gabrielle had been killed in a hit-and-run on a country road out the other side of town. The driver hadn't stopped, and it had taken over an hour for anyone to find her. As soon as he heard, Robert fell to the floor and lay there, howling. I hugged him for ages, tried to give what comfort I could.

RUTH: How did you feel about her dying?

DAPHNE: Obviously, a child dying is horrible but she made life so hard for me and the kids. And she was always flouting my rules. If she'd actually respected her curfew, she wouldn't have been biking so late at night.

RUTH: But I'm sure Robert was devastated.

DAPHNE: Oh yes. He was a wreck, a bloodless, sleepless wreck. He'd only been a father for eighteen months, but he was very upset about it ending. You see, I didn't kill Gabrielle but her death did make things awfully convenient. Even more so when, a few weeks later, Robert killed himself out of grief. And the thoughtful way he did it, jumping off his office building, left no question that it was suicide. He was my freebie.

ShockAndBlah:

Is anyone buying this?

BurntheBookBurnerz:

No. It just . . . sounds like a lie. Like a lie she didn't have time to really practice.

ShockAndBlah:

Do you think that Gabrielle was as terrible as Daphne says?

PreyAllDay:

No.

BurntheBookBurnerz:

Maybe? But she was also just a kid who'd lost the only parent she'd ever known. So that probably wasn't her being an asshole, that was grief.

StopDropAndTroll:

My mom died when I was a kid.

PreyAllDay:

That tracks.

ShockAndBlah:

I'm shocked no one's tried to off Daphne yet, especially now that we know she kills children. I feel like enough people know where she lives. I'm surprised no one's snuck in and finished her off.

PreyAllDay:

If they want to, they better hurry. She'll be going to prison any day now.

CapoteParty:

How do you know?

PreyAllDay:

Friend of a friend. I can't say more without implicating them. But it'll be this week for sure.

ShockAndBlah:

Wait, CapoteParty?? You're back!! We've been wondering about you!?!?

ShockAndBlah:

. . . CapoteParty?

ShockAndBlah:

Ah fuck. They're gone again.

Chapter Thirty-Three

At least, that's what I told Ruth.

Everything was true, except for that last little bit. A woman has to have some secrets, and why wouldn't you want to hide the 'worst' thing you ever did? Especially when you don't feel any regret over it? You see, I did find Gabrielle that night but the whole story actually started a few weeks earlier when I came home from grocery shopping and found her smoking in her bedroom when she should have been at school.

Gabrielle sat in a white wicker chair, her bare feet up on the matching desk, yellow-painted toenails wiggling, looking as smug and sinister as a Bond villain. She'd been brushing her hair and the walnut color shone in the sunlight like a piece of expensive antique furniture. A lit cigarette was in her mouth, the curls of smoke insouciantly crowning her hair. She met my eyes and coolly tapped the cigarette in Diane's sterling silver Tiffany's christening cup.

"Are you serious? You think you're allowed to smoke? And don't think I don't recognize my brand, you little thief," I hissed. She just smiled and took another drag. A flicker of unease struck me. This was bold, even for Gabrielle.

"You know, Rose did something interesting yesterday. She was working on a family tree for school and I saw that she wrote down your name as Cecilia Dubois and then erased it and wrote down Daphne Hanks. Which I thought was kind of funny. What kind of idiot doesn't know her own mom's name?" Gabrielle mused.

Oh, Rose. She wasn't the brightest bulb. Thank God she was pretty and had a sister to stop her from joining the first cult who told her about their groovy little pad in Guyana.

"Well, that's my middle name—" I began but Gabrielle cut me off.

"So, I took Rose off for a little talk. She didn't want to give anything away, but I told her that I'd spread another rumor about her and Diane. Something real disgusting. So, she told me that you used to go by the name Cecilia Dubois when you were married to a man named David. I asked if that was her dad, but she said no. That her dad died when she was a baby. That was important, but I knew I needed more."

I frowned. More for what?

"So, then I went through the suitcase you keep in the attic. I always knew it was up there; I just didn't think you had any interesting secrets. And there were some pictures in there, you with different men, quite a lot of men really. And there were papers. Important ones."

My heart sank. I kept very little incriminating evidence from my past but there were certain things that were necessary to keep around. Especially if I ever needed to run. Gabrielle continued, still watching me as she smoked my cigarette with glee.

"I found the bank account documents. And each account

had a different name: Jacqueline, Cecilia, Daphne . . . so many names, all with different last names too. Why would you have those? That's the kind of thing criminals do. And I found an adoption certificate for James to a man named Geoffrey Van Rensselaer. That was from around the time the twins were born so I guess that was their dad. But he certainly wasn't James's."

She smiled in that self-satisfied way teenagers have, like they truly understand the adult world and see through it all. My fists clenched and I could feel my painted nails dig into my palms.

"So, either you were married three times, or you never married James's dad. Either way, that doesn't look good. You lied to my daddy. You told him you were married once. But you were married twice. Maybe even three times. Or you had a baby without being married. And you've used different names and lied about your past. I don't think he'd like that. I don't think he'd like that at all."

"Oh please, he knows all about it," I bluffed. "Just because no one bothered to tell you doesn't make it some big dark secret." I hoped that I was a good enough actor to pull it off, but she just smiled and shook her head.

"No, I think it is a secret. A big one. I think you've done something very bad and you're on the run. That's why you keep changing your name. And I don't think my daddy knows a thing about it."

"He wouldn't tell anyone though. A scandal would hurt his career," I said carefully. Would Robert keep my secrets? There was already so much distance in our marriage, so much resentment. Even if he did cover this up, he would hate me for it. He might even demand a quickie divorce in exchange for his

silence, a divorce that would leave me penniless. He might even be able to get an annulment because of all the lies I'd told him.

"Hmm, maybe you're right. Maybe I should just go straight to the police," Gabrielle offered, pointing at the telephone on her desk. She reached forward, her hand hovering over it, watching me for a reaction. I stood there stone-faced, holding her gaze without blinking. Was this really how it ended? Decades of secrets exposed by a teenage girl with an Electra complex?

"And if you didn't?" I asked flatly. I felt as if we were playing high-stakes poker, but it was becoming increasingly clear that I didn't have the winning hand.

Gabrielle sat back in her chair and laced her fingers together, a smile creeping across her face.

"Then I own you. From now on, there's no curfew, no rules, no school unless I feel like it. If I want candy for lunch, you get it. If I want you to buy me beer, you do it. If I want to stay out all night at a party, you don't say a thing. Any attitude, and I'll tell Daddy and the police everything."

The little shit was loving this. Although who wouldn't love being a teenager giving that lecture to a hated stepmother? I'm sure Cinderella had a similar expression when she flipped her stepmom the bird and headed off with the prince.

"Fine," I managed to say through gritted teeth. I turned and stiffly walked out of the room, shocked that I'd been outmaneuvered by a teenage girl. My stomach began to bubble with anxiety. Someone was finally on to my secret. And it was the worst possible person.

The next two weeks were agony. Gabrielle did whatever she wanted. When my husband wasn't around, she would sit down *at the breakfast table, pull a cigarette out of my pack and motion me to light it. She would sashay out the house with full bottles of wine, telling me next time not to buy the cheap stuff. My kids watched it all in shocked dismay and total confusion. Only Rose had an inkling and avoided making eye contact with me. I didn't talk to her about it though. I didn't want my children to know how precarious our situation was, how our lives now depended on the charitable impulses of a teenage sociopath.*

Gabrielle would catch my eye and slowly smile, as if to remind me that I was now living on her charity and that she might choose to turn me in at any moment. And I knew that eventually, no matter what I did, she would call the police. Because Gabrielle didn't want to live with me and my three kids; she only wanted her father. And once the novelty of controlling me wore off, I was going to prison.

I needed a plan. I had managed to escape sticky situations before: my hellish life in Lucan, my abusive relationship in Winnipeg, a life as a struggling single mother in New York. That was my secret power: I was a survivor.

But no matter how I thought about this one, I didn't see a way out. I could let Gabrielle call the police and just try to brazen it out, act like she was a silly little schoolgirl who'd been reading too many Nancy Drew novels. But I'd only gotten away with it for so long because no one really paid much attention to me, and I'd never given them a reason to. Once you really started making a chronology of my life, it would be obvious that something was wrong. The police would notice that any man who got too close to me seemed to have a suspiciously early expiration date.

I could take my kids and run away, changing my name and starting over. But Gabrielle would still know. And sooner or later (probably sooner) she would tell everyone and then people would come after me, hunting me down like a dog. Because Gabrielle hated me. It wasn't enough to get rid of me, I had to be punished.

If I went to prison, Robert wouldn't take care of my kids, not now that he had his precious daughter. My kids would end up in foster care so fast it would make their heads spin. My babies didn't deserve that. Why should they be punished because of my actions?

I stopped sleeping. After everyone went to bed, I would wander the house for hours in my silk robe, a ghostly trail of cigarette smoke following me up the stairs. I would wonder if this was my last night before everything changed, if by this time tomorrow I would be in a jail cell, no longer a mother, no longer rich, no longer free or anything that mattered at all. I was so exhausted that sometimes I felt as if I was halluci- nating, as if the house and the trees outside were whispering to me, telling me that there really was only one way out. If I was willing to take that final step down to hell . . .

You see, Gabrielle didn't realize what she'd done. She thought I had something to hide but she didn't know the scope of my secrets. Gabrielle had cornered a killer and that's when we're at our most deadly. More than that, she was coming between a mother and her children, and that might be the most dangerous position of all.

The night Gabrielle stayed out and Robert told me to go find her, I was in a real bind. Robert expected me to enforce rules and keep Gabrielle in line, but I couldn't, not with my vicious little stepdaughter calling the shots. And my nerves were shot from walking on eggshells for weeks, waiting for Gabrielle to make a move, endlessly running through scenarios in my head. I was stuck between a blackmailing stepdaughter and a husband who seemed to have lost all respect for me. The fact that both of them were controlling me, a grown woman who usually didn't take crap from anyone, enraged me.

I drove for a few miles, running through every scenario of how I could escape this family with finances and freedom intact. Half-formed thoughts drifted through my head, each clever plan full of holes.

The road was dark. There were very few streetlights on these country lanes, and the trees and hedges crowded the edge of the asphalt, pressing my car into the center of the narrow road. Rickety tree branches appeared in my headlights, and I scanned the road intently through a cloud of cigarette smoke, nervous that I would slam into a deer leaping out of the hedges.

And then suddenly she was there. She was like a mirage in front of me, her skinny legs pedaling furiously, her bony back rising and falling with every exertion. I rolled my eyes. It was almost midnight and here she was, biking home from a big rager. I knew that later she would come sauntering through the door, carrying a swagger and insouciance that were completely at odds with her young age. It infuriated me. This little princess had never been scared in her life.

But here she was: the source of my problems, biking alone on a dark road. You have to admit, if you were in the same situation, you would be tempted. She was biking so fast that

339

it was almost as if she was prey trying to outrun a predator. I hesitated for a minute. Killing a kid, even one as horrible as her, had never been the plan. Those were the kind of crimes that upset people, that cops made a priority, that communities never forgot. I worked best when no one even knew a crime had occurred. But I had gone through every alternative in my head, and I couldn't see a way out of this where Gabrielle got to live. She had started this awful business and now I had to end it.

And then I was accelerating, my foot pressed against the floor of the car. There was a brief glimpse of her terrified, white face and then a very satisfying Whump! It was the opposite of poison, a brief explosion of sound and movement instead of the slow, shadowy process of gently leading someone to death.

The road was so empty, the world quiet, that I hazarded a quick stop just to confirm she was dead. I'd have had a hard time explaining myself to Robert if she had dragged her broken body through the front door, ready to point the finger. There are some problems too big for marriage counselling.

I stopped the car and hopped out, careful not to get my heels bloody. She was lying in a crumpled mess, her eyes white with pain. She took one last, jagged breath and then she died, her body coming to a great, shuddering halt. But in that last glance, I saw her recognize me and realize what I had done to her. In that moment, I saw fear in her face, the knowledge that her safe little world hadn't been so reliable after all. Did I enjoy that moment? After eighteen months of disrespect and weeks of threats to my family? Not particularly. As a mother, the thought of killing a child disgusted me. And I do regret that things came to that.

The funny thing is, in the weeks between Gabrielle's death and his own, I caught Robert looking at me; just little, sideways glances when he thought I was preoccupied. And these little glances showed me that he had some doubts. And then those doubts started to crystallize into suspicions. And as the days went on, his gaze grew harder, and I knew that he was certain. In the end, both the father and daughter died knowing the truth about me.

You know, when Robert and I got married, he promised me that this would be our last marriage.

He was half-right.

Chapter Thirty-Four

Did Daphne really think Ruth would buy this bullshit? After hours and hours of interviews spent together, did she really think so little of Ruth? Daphne had definitely killed Gabrielle. It wasn't just that Daphne had hated her. It was the way she told the story, slowly unwinding her case against her stepdaughter before dropping the thread abruptly at the end, a long line of truths finished off with a lie. An ice cream sundae garnished with a cigarette. Fucking Daphne St Clair. She had confessed to a set of murders, sure, but how many others had she detoured around when leading Ruth through her life?

"You said it was convenient that Gabrielle died, but a lot of people would say it's a little too convenient to be accidental," Ruth began.

"Life's funny huh?" Daphne responded smoothly. Ruth glanced away, repulsed by Daphne's satisfied smile.

"Come on. Gabrielle would have inherited her father's money if he died. She was making your daughters' lives miserable. You *killed* her," Ruth urged.

"A boy was hit by lightning when I was living in Leosville. Maybe you think I'm responsible for that too?" Daphne said, raising her eyebrows so high that her wrinkles advanced into her thinning hair line. "I admit that I poisoned my husbands, and that I pushed a couple of abusive men to their deaths. But I never killed a kid." She seemed so adamant that doubt began to creep into Ruth's brain but she shook it off.

"You're already spending the rest of your life in prison, you might as well be honest now," Ruth said, surprised at how resentful she sounded.

Something had changed between them. The air crackled with electricity as a new tension emerged. It was clear that Daphne was surprised that Ruth wasn't entirely on her side. Maybe she felt that she was giving Ruth the story of a lifetime and that Ruth should sit down and shut up. But Ruth was done being quiet.

"I've always been honest. Do remember, the only reason anyone knows about these crimes at all, is because I confessed to them. It takes a lot of courage to do that," Daphne said, her voice stiff and haughty.

"Do you really think listeners will be applauding you for your courage?" Ruth asked skeptically.

"Sure, why not? At least I took some action. Most women just sit around and take whatever's given to 'em. Look at you! You grew up in the best time in America to be a woman and what have you done? What's so special about *you*? You're too afraid to leave goddamned Florida! If you were me, you'd never have gotten out of Lucan." Daphne's voice was dripping with disdain. She looked so proud of herself, a frail old woman with bile on her lips, that all Ruth felt was disgust.

"So, what? People are supposed to find your story

inspirational? You got ahead by lying and killing! You cheated your way into everything!"

"I'm sorry, I missed the part of life where people are fair. They rig the system against you and then they expect you to play by the rules? That's just stupid," Daphne said, her voice prickly with sarcasm.

Ruth could certainly relate to feeling cheated out of what was rightfully hers, but Daphne had never stopped at what belonged to her, or even what she deserved; Daphne always wanted more.

"I suppose I'll never understand it," Ruth said.

"What?" Daphne snapped.

"How you could do those things, how you could hurt those people."

"And yet you don't wonder how those men could hurt *me*. Everyone seems to just rush through that part of the story, like it explains everything but means nothing," Daphne replied, her shrewd eyes glittering like a crow's in the lamplight. "At least I gave my husbands some happy memories. The men who hurt me never gave me that."

"Yes, but you didn't just kill violent men, you killed innocent people. You fixate on the people who hurt you but you're also a victimizer," Ruth said coolly, staring directly at Daphne.

"What's your point? That I'm a bad person? I'm a serial killer! What did you expect?" Daphne scoffed.

I expected to understand, Ruth thought. *I really believed that if I stared at this long enough it would make sense in my head. But the violence you did, and the violence that was done to you, none of it makes sense. My life was completely derailed by a passing impulse.*

"Why did you confess then? You say you're a bad person, but doesn't that show some sort of remorse?" Ruth asked. It was one of the many unanswered questions about Daphne but it seemed like one of the most essential.

"No, that's not it," Daphne said. "I liked the idea of showing everyone what I'd gotten away with."

Ruth narrowed her eyes. She'd heard that answer already. Daphne had said it multiple times, the words tumbling out of her mouth as smooth and polished as river pebbles. Whatever her reason for confessing, it wasn't that.

"You just wanted people to know how smart you are?" Ruth asked, incredulous.

"Sure," Daphne said. "People only pay attention to women when they want to fuck them or murder them. And no one pays attention to old women at all. I was proud of getting away with it, but it's no fun if no one knows that you've won."

"People will hate you for that," Ruth said. "If there really is no larger reason, no way for them to understand."

Daphne huffed, her mouth flattened into a thin line.

"Well, let's talk turkey, Ruth. You're not interviewing me because you think I'm Mother Teresa. You're here because you know that people can't get enough of murder. They want all the gory details, and they want it straight from the monster's mouth."

"People care about true crime because it's gripping and they learn about investigations and . . . society," Ruth finished lamely.

"They like it for the same reason people rubberneck at car accidents. Because misery *excites* people. And you know that every terrible thing I tell you is going to get you more listeners, more fame, and more money. But it will never be enough. People out there are listening to this podcast, wishing I'd killed more people in worse ways. Because even murder bores them now. You're here to make a buck off of people's worst impulses, just like I made a buck off my own."

Ruth felt a searing fury, an anger so deep and elemental that she had to stop herself from slamming her fist through Daphne's glass coffee table. She couldn't take this a second longer.

"Actually, Daphne, I'm here because you killed my father."

The Eighth Murder?

Chapter Thirty-Five

DRAFT: DO NOT USE IN PODCAST

RUTH: If you're listening to this then I've gotten Daphne to confess to my father's murder. That was my main motivation for this podcast. Find the truth, solve the mystery, get justice for my father, and prove to everyone that I had nothing to do with it.

DRAFT: DO NOT USE IN PODCAST

RUTH: When my father died, the police hauled me in for questioning. His family, the Montgomery family, told the cops that I had recently come back into his life the year before and he planned to change his will, to give me half. They made me out to be some sort of grifter who had pressured him for money, as if the relationship Richard and I were developing wasn't real.

The police told me that someone had shot Richard with insulin, that he would have experienced seizures before going into a coma and stopping breathing. That this person had wiped the insulin bottles and the needle clean. They told me how my father died, and then they watched how I reacted. It was terrifying, sitting across from two police officers, knowing if I said the wrong thing, I might start a chain of events that could destroy my life and send me to prison. The way the cops acted . . . it was clear that they were just looking for something to *prove* I was guilty.

The last thing they told me was that Richard had made an appointment with his lawyer to change his will and had informed his family that he would be splitting his wealth equally between his two daughters. But that appointment was for Monday, and he had died on the Sunday, so I wouldn't be getting a cent. I know the money shouldn't matter, the sad part was losing my father, just at the moment we were finally building a relationship. But I didn't know that when Richard died, he'd take my whole future with him.

[There is a muffled sob.]

DRAFT: DO NOT USE IN PODCAST

I worried for months that the police would find something to connect me to the murder, or that a police officer, perhaps motivated by a connection to my father's family, would plant some incriminating evidence. I was afraid that I'd be made to pay for his death, and I suppose I have. Richard's family made sure that everyone knew they suspected me of murdering him and job opportunities had a nasty habit of drying up under their influence. I saw police officers everywhere and knew they were just waiting for me to slip up. I obsessed constantly about the life I would have had if Richard had lived, of how much easier everything would be. My relationship failed and I struggled to get close to people because I was terrified of being hurt again. Five years passed and it felt like Richard's death would never be solved.

DRAFT: DO NOT USE IN PODCAST

RUTH: The first time I saw a news broadcast about Daphne, they showed the building she used to live in, the Blue Diamond, before going into the retirement home. I recognized it immediately. It was the building next to the Seacrest, the building where my father had lived and died, an unsolved mystery of a wealthy, older man who had just started dating again. Everything fit, slotting together, so smoothly and cleanly, that I knew immediately Daphne was the answer I was looking for. She had killed him.

"Actually, Daphne, I'm here because you killed my father."

"What?" Daphne sputtered. For the first time, she looked truly surprised. Her wrinkled mouth flapped open and shut with a dry sound, like a trout gasping for breath in a fisherman's boat.

"My father, Richard Montgomery, died on the tenth of April 2016. Not only was he a wealthy surgeon, but he was also on the board of the Sunshine Development Group, his family's real estate empire. Richard died in his condo, which was one building over from where you were living at the time and he'd recently told me he had started dating again. He was in his late seventies, and a diabetic, but he died of an insulin overdose that the police treated as suspicious because he had a needle mark on the back of his neck. You even saw a picture of him I had on my computer and said that he looked familiar. I knew as soon as I saw the news, I *felt* it. It's over, Daphne. You killed him."

Daphne was still staring at her as if she was completely unrecognizable. Ruth knew that Daphne prided herself on her ability to read people; it was how she'd always been so good at ensnaring men. She would have never expected that someone like Ruth could fool her.

"So, this whole thing was about you trying to catch me out? Are you even a journalist?" Daphne demanded.

Ruth felt triumphant. For the first time, Daphne was on the back foot, and she had the upper hand.

"Yes, I am a journalist, and yes, I also needed the money. But I started this podcast to record your confession of his murder or to find something that tied you to his death. And to show everyone what it's like for your victims' families, how you've derailed their lives. I lost everything when he died. His family suspected that I did it and cut me out of their lives and sabotaged my career. The police hounded me, trying to pressure me into cracking and confessing. My relationship ended because I was so obsessed with his death and what happened to me. I spent years on antidepressants—"

"Well, that's just America for you. Everyone these days—" Daphne tried to interrupt, to steer the conversation, but Ruth wasn't letting go.

"And that case cost me my inheritance. He told me the day before he died that he was planning to change his will, so that I would get half and my half-sister, Lucy, the daughter he raised, would get half. It was a lot of money, the kind of money that would have bought me a home, paid off my student debt, and allowed me to really launch my career. I think it was his way of saying sorry for not being in my life, but it also showed how much he believed in me, so it meant a lot. But the appointment with his lawyer was set for Monday and he died on the Sunday. So, I lost my father and I got nothing."

"Bad luck," Daphne said, wincing amiably, but Ruth barreled on, ignoring her, trying to say what she needed to say without Daphne interjecting again.

"I *know* it was you, so why not admit it? It's not going to change anything for you; it's just one more murder to add to your list of confessions, but it would give me some peace of mind. This case . . . it ruined my life. Your life is almost over; you could help!" Ruth stopped talking, uncomfortably aware of the pleading note in her voice. Daphne was the only person who could give her this closure, who could finally prove that Ruth wasn't a murderer, and she wasn't delusional. Daphne could absolve her of all of this.

"Well, you got me," Daphne said, and Ruth held her breath. "We lived on the same block, and he certainly sounds like my type. Rich and handsome. And I sure do love watching old men die," Daphne said, a mocking smile on her face. "It must have pissed you off. You finally thought your ship had come in and your father pops his clogs. It sure puts the dead in deadbeat dad!"

"So, you're confessing?" Ruth asked wildly, unable to believe that this hell was finally coming to an end.

"Am I?" Daphne mused. "I don't know that I am. Warren's the

only death I confessed to in Florida; adding another might . . . complicate things." There was a sparkle in her eyes. She thrived on this: misery and trauma. Everyone else struggled in these moments but Daphne clearly loved it.

"Are you fucking kidding?" Ruth snapped, slamming her hand on the table, knocking her laptop on the floor. White-hot rage surged through her, blotting out everything but the monster sitting across from her. Should she just strangle Daphne? It wouldn't be hard to crush that bony neck, her death would be its own kind of closure. "It doesn't matter now. The game is over. Just tell the truth!"

"Whooee! I've never seen you get this riled up. I'm glad we've got that on tape for posterity! You're right, it doesn't matter. Maybe I killed him, maybe it was someone else. The world is full of people who got away with murder. They're just walking around, enjoying life, while the rest of you tie yourself into little knots trying to follow the rules." Daphne hooted with laughter, her face ablaze with triumph.

Ruth turned away, feeling her body shake with the strain of this moment, of all the years she'd spent agonizing over this case. Why wouldn't Daphne confess to this murder? It wasn't like the Gabrielle murder; it wouldn't fundamentally change what people thought of her. In Daphne-land, killing Richard Montgomery was just par for the course. Was she refusing to confess to have power over Ruth? So that she could dangle hints and watch Ruth try desperately to catch her? Or did she just like the feeling of being in control? Of finding one more person to hurt even now when murder was off the table? That thought made Ruth sick.

"You're disgusting," Ruth hissed.

"That's not exactly a minority opinion," Daphne said with a shrug. "Why don't you sit down, settle your kettle, and lay out your case against me. Who knows? I might be compelled to confess."

Daphne was smiling but there was a flinty glint in her eye.

Is she enjoying this? Ruth slowly felt her rage cool down into revulsion. Here was this funny, intelligent, unique woman who spent the first part of her life being preyed upon only to spend the rest of her life as a predator. What a waste of a person. Ruth couldn't stand to be here any longer, especially now that she'd shared something so important from her life. Ruth looked at Daphne with fresh eyes and all she saw was frustration and disappointment. This woman couldn't free Ruth. She couldn't even free herself. Ruth was going to have to find her own way to move on.

"No, we're done here. It's obvious that you're going to keep lying to me, about Gabrielle and about my father. I don't need this," Ruth said abruptly, shoving her laptop into her bag.

Daphne seemed surprised. She probably thought this would go on as long as she wanted. That Ruth was going to sit here and say thank you for all the shit she shoveled.

"Now you're just being ungrateful! I've given you the story of a lifetime," Daphne said, her pride obviously wounded. But Ruth didn't care. She couldn't sit here any longer, listening to Daphne twist the truth and find a million justifications for cold-blooded murder. It was like poison seeping into her blood, blurring her vision and leaving her nauseous. She would never get the truth out of her and maybe, at the end of the day, it didn't matter. The dead were dead, and the living would just have to find a way to muddle through.

"Yes, but every story has an ending," Ruth retorted.

She left Daphne sitting there alone, too frail to follow her. By the time she left the building and walked into the light, Ruth felt like she could breathe again.

PreyAllDay:

So is that it? Ruth confronts her about Gabrielle Hanks's death, they argue, and then it just ends with Daphne comparing true crime fans to people who stare at car accidents. And then the podcast just stops?!? Was that an artistic choice or do you think Ruth had a technical problem?

> **ShockAndBlah:**
>
> Is the podcast over?? Or maybe Ruth's just waiting for the sentencing to pick up the story?

>> **BurntheBookBurnerz:**
>>
>> You guys . . . what am I supposed to listen to now?

ShockAndBlah:

Okay weird theory, but does anyone think CapoteParty might be . . . Ruth? Think about it, they always seem to know more about the case than everyone else. And they went from posting every day, all day, to almost never being around?

> **PreyAllDay:**
>
> But why ask what senior home Daphne is in? Ruth obviously knows that.

ShockAndBlah:

To throw us off her scent.

BurntheBookBurnerz:

Or . . . maybe it's Diane? Or one of her grandchildren?

StopDropAndTroll:

Or . . . just a total nobody with no link to the case. FFS y'all sound more paranoid than me and I think the government invented Sandy Hook and Covid!!!

BurntheBookBurnerz:

[This post has been removed by moderators.]

PreyAllDay:

[This post has been removed by moderators.]

Chapter Thirty-Six

It was late evening, and I had fallen asleep in my chair, an open copy of *The Monster of Florence* resting on my chest. It had been an upsetting day, and I was exhausted.

It had been a shock to find out that Ruth, the person I had trusted with my story, had been lying to my face. It was an intense betrayal, and one that I hadn't seen coming even after years of being let down by people. I knew it hadn't been kind to taunt her and that she might never speak to me again, but I was caught off guard, and so furious that I'd just wanted to punish her.

Suddenly, I heard shouting outside, a lot of it. This was unheard of at the Grove, where residents might get a little testy over a substandard tiramisu or a canceled Zumba Gold class, but never truly heated. I hauled myself up using my walker and shuffled over to the window, hooking my fingers around the curtain and peeling it back to see what was happening.

It was dark but the lights spilling out from the other windows illuminated a figure, a man standing outside my apartment. His back was to me, but I could see he was wearing a baseball hat and a hooded sweatshirt.

My hands trembled. There really was a lurker. The staff hadn't just been trying to scare me. I felt a sudden bolt of fear that I had forgotten to lock the door, that he would turn around and deftly slide it open, his eyes never leaving my own, knowing that he would have seconds, maybe minutes, to do whatever he pleased with me. I fumbled for the door handle, my arthritic hands shaking with effort, and found that it was locked.

Another shout and my eyes were blinded by a dazzling light, the silhouette of the man briefly outlined against my door. Was there something familiar about him? The man broke into a run as flashlight beams bounced wildly around him. It was clear that he was heading for the trees to evade the security guards, who were trying to hunt him down.

I stood frozen with fear. I felt certain that at any moment, the man would be back, hammering at my door, wild-eyed and desperate to get at me. The lock would be no match for someone so determined, and eventually the guards would go home, while this man would stay and wait for however long it took. These fears were confirmed when I saw that one by one, after an hour of searching the forest, the guards all emerged empty-handed.

Well, whoever he was, he knew where I was now. I let the curtain drop and checked once more that the doors were securely fastened. I didn't know who would come for me first, the state of Florida or him.

The next morning, my phone rang. It was my lawyer on the line. I answered, feeling leaden and tense after a night spent sat up in my armchair, too afraid to go to bed, too afraid to look behind the curtains again, in case I saw the man standing there.

"Yes?" I grumbled, taking a sip from a stale cup of water on my coffee table.

"I have some news. You know that I've pushed hard to keep you out of prison during the preliminaries; how I've argued that you're in too fragile a condition," he said.

"Yes."

"And you know that once you plead guilty, you will go to prison to await sentencing?"

"Obviously," I said. "And then I'll be sentenced to jail for the rest of my life." I was trying to stay rational, to focus on the words and not the meaning of what I was saying.

"Well, it's time. They want you in court tomorrow. It's a . . . scheduling thing."

I felt cold. A long, slow shiver spread across my skin. I always knew it would end like this, from the first moment I picked up that phone and confessed. All the things that had happened along the way—the podcast with Ruth, my moment in the public eye, the chance to show my family the truth of who I was—those were all diversions on the road to *here*. Something that had been set into motion ninety years ago, on a dust-scarred patch of prairie, was finally coming to an end.

"So, this is my last night of freedom?" I asked, although being on house arrest in a seniors' home wasn't my exact definition of freedom.

"Yes. If you have any nice bottles of wine, I'd recommend opening them. And tomorrow, I'll be right by your side, supporting you in any way that I can."

"Right, smoke 'em if you got 'em. Okay, well I've got some

calls to make. Bye," I said woodenly, before hanging up, the phone wobbling in my hand.

I sat in the chair for a few minutes, suddenly aware that the moment that had been out there waiting for me for decades had finally arrived. It was the end. It felt sad and frustrating, but inevitable. I wondered if that was how the people I'd poisoned felt. I'd never really considered it, what they thought about when they knew it was almost over. Things just always felt more real when they happened to me.

Slowly, numbly, I picked up the phone and dialed Ruth. I felt like I needed to talk to her; our last meeting had been so terrible. She answered after a few rings. I could tell that she had been sleeping.

"Hello?" she asked, her voice as husky as a teenage boy's.

"I just wanted to tell you that I'll be pleading guilty tomorrow and then I'll be going to prison afterwards. So, you can put that information in your podcast."

There was a long silence. People really don't know how to respond to 'I'm going to prison for the rest of my life tomorrow.' No Hallmark card for that one.

"Okay, I'll record an update," Ruth said hesitantly.

"Please can you play this podcast for my daughters? They haven't listened so far but maybe you can make them understand."

"Sure. And well, I know things are complicated but I do appreciate you letting me interview you," she said through gritted teeth.

"Well, I probably wouldn't have agreed if I'd known you were investigating me."

"Please, Daphne, just tell me. Did you do it? I need to know," Ruth asked. I wasn't sure if she was talking about Richard or Gabrielle but my answer was the same regardless.

"Maybe we'll save that for season two. By the way, what title did you go with?"

"*The Six Murders of Daphne St Clair*," Ruth said, irritation creeping into her voice. It was clear she hadn't forgiven me yet, that she wasn't going to let this go. I nodded resolutely.

"Good, I'm glad you're not buying into this Gabrielle story."

"I just . . . well . . . I'd already ordered the merch. So now I don't really know how to count them. The first killing wasn't strictly murder, a good lawyer might have even got you off the next two charges, so I guess the numbers don't matter."

The Six Murders of Daphne St Clair. It was a title that meant so much and so little at the same time. My entire story stripped away, made catchy and clickable for the Internet, in the hopes that it would attract all the people who wanted to hear a story about murder. No need for social commentary, or humor, or any attempt at originality, just the murder please, as many as you've got.

"Yes, that's probably right," I said and hung up. I clapped the phone down faster than I meant to. Sometimes I found it hard to talk to Ruth. She reminded me of everything I had wanted when I was younger, everything I never got.

"Can I come visit you in prison?" Harper asked after I phoned her with the news.

"I don't think that's a good idea," I replied. "You're a little young to be visiting convicts."

"Maybe we can talk on the phone?" she asked sadly.

"We'll see. Let me get settled in and then maybe," I said, not wanting to get the girl's hopes up. She was a good kid, and I wanted to protect her now, even if I couldn't later.

I should have hung up but I lingered, feeling an unfamiliar urge to impart some grandmotherly life advice.

"You know, Harper, you need to figure out what makes you happy. I never knew what would make me happy, even now."

"That's sad, Grandma," Harper said, her voice solemn. I nodded even though she couldn't see me. All these years, I had been thrashing around in the darkness, trying to figure out what would fill up all the emptiness inside of me and I never found it.

"What if I can't figure it out?" Harper asked.

"You will. A girl like you, you can do anything. Just don't become a little shit when you grow up," I said, hanging up before she responded. I reached for another drink, trying to dislodge the lump in my throat.

It was midnight but I couldn't sleep, not when I knew that everything was about to change. I was sitting in my chair with my curtains open and the door cracked a smidge, just to let the breeze in. I wasn't giving up my last chance to get some fresh air and see the stars.

That was when he appeared, a dark figure melting out of the woods behind him, loping across the grass directly at me. His steps were silent on the soft lawn, his body low and lean against the horizon.

I grabbed my walker and pulled myself up, trying to move quickly to the door but knowing I would never get there before

him. He was like a terrifying specter from my past, an amal-
gamation of all the horrible men I'd bested over the years,
come back to drag me to hell. My body trembled as I shuffled
forward, moving so damned slow, even now when I was in the
greatest danger.

And then suddenly he spoke: "Mom?"

I stood there, frozen. "James?"

"Yes." He sounded almost the same, although his voice was
lower, more gravelly. I made a tortured sound as if my organs
were crumpling inside of me and I had to cling on to the walker
to keep myself upright.

"Come in, come in," I managed to croak, slumping back into
my chair. He shut the door and pulled off the cap, and there he
was. My James. My eyes filled with tears and I sat there sobbing, grateful but also indescribably tired. I had been waiting
for this for decades.

James sat in the chair across from me, the chair I'd started
to think of as Ruth's chair. My eyes raked over him, trying to
soak up every detail. He had been a young man the last time
I saw him and now he was in his sixties. His dark hair had
turned light gray and he had a full beard that hid the dimple in
his chin, but he still had the same warm eyes and closed-mouth
smile. Just looking at him made me happier than anything I'd
experienced in the last forty years. I felt as if I was traveling
back in time to when he was a toddler, to that little apartment
in Brooklyn where we would lie in bed and I would touch his
soft face and smell his freshly washed hair. Back when it was
us against the world.

"You're here," I whispered, reaching over and clutching his

hand like it was an exquisite gift. He nodded, although I noticed that he slowly withdrew his hand.

"Yes. I heard that you're going to prison soon. I thought this would probably be my last chance."

"Why all the subterfuge though?" I asked. "Skulking around at night?"

"Do you know how much media attention your case is getting? I was worried that if I called up your lawyer or the senior center and told them who I was that it would get leaked to the press. I don't want people to find me, to know who I really am," James said.

"How *did* you find me?" I asked.

"Well, I've been listening to the podcast of course, so I knew you were in Florida. Then I hired a private detective, but he didn't get me anything concrete. But I also joined some online groups that discussed the case, to see if I could get any information while remaining anonymous. Somebody on there told me about Coconut Grove." He smiled. "You'd like the name I used; it was kind of an homage to you."

"What was it?" I asked, hoping it wasn't something heinous like 'OldBitch' or 'WrinklySatan.'

"CapoteParty."

"Oh, because he wrote *In Cold Blood*? The best murder book out there?" I asked.

James laughed and shook his head.

"No, because he wrote *Breakfast at Tiffany's*! You always said that was your favorite movie. You dragged me to see it whenever it was playing." The things he knew about me, the memories we shared, it warmed my heart. James was the best part of me, and he'd been lost to me for so long.

"It's still my favorite movie," I said. "She was everything I ever wanted to be."

"She *was* you," he said, looking at me like I was crazy. We sat in silence for a moment.

"What do you think about the podcast?" I asked, for something to say.

"It can be hard to listen to . . . especially when you're talking about things I remember. But in a way I'm glad that it's finally all out there. I was surprised you agreed to it. Although I was also surprised you confessed when you'd gotten away with it," James said.

I shook my head. I knew now that I hadn't gotten away with it, not really, not when I'd lost the person I loved most in the process.

"I hoped . . . I hoped that if it all came out that you might find me again."

"Is that why you confessed?" he asked, surprise in his voice. I smiled, feeling modest and noble even though I didn't deserve to.

"Yes. You didn't want to keep my secrets. So now you don't have to." His eyes filled with tears and he hunched over.

I saw his shoulders shake as if he was trying to bite back the sobs, to tamp it all down inside. He used to do that when he was younger too. It started not long after he lost David. My eyes began to tingle, and I felt as if I might cry too. I hated seeing my boy upset. This whole thing had been about finding him and setting him free. I wanted him to be happy.

THE SIX MURDERS OF DAPHNE ST CLAIR

"But Mom . . ." he started, after he collected himself, drying his face and sitting straighter in his chair. "I also wanted you to stop killing." There was a deep sadness in his voice, a crushing disappointment. So, he knew about Donald. And Warren. I could have tried to tell him that it was all in the past, but Warren was barely in the ground. I really shouldn't have killed him, but I suppose it was a bit of Dutch courage, a little reminder of what I could do before I finally came out into the open. Besides, I needed proof, a verifiable murder for the cops to take me seriously.

"Well, baby, sometimes you just have to accept people for who they are. Can you . . . tell me about yourself?" I asked hesitantly, scared that if I said the wrong thing then the door would slam shut again. He took a deep breath and I thought he might cry some more, but finally he began to speak.

"Well, I live in New Zealand now. Originally, I moved to Australia, but New Zealand suits me better. It's the most beautiful place I've ever seen. I'm a science teacher at the local high school but I'll retire soon. I've been married twice. The first was a short marriage. I think I had some issues that I needed help with, but now I've been married twenty-five years."

"Any kids?" I asked.

"Yes. I've got a seventeen-year-old son and a nineteen-year-old daughter. I'm an old dad! But I'm having the time of my life."

"I'm sure you're a great father," I said, remembering the kindness I'd seen ever since he was a child. "Finding out what happened to you . . . I couldn't ask for anything more. You're all I think about."

He didn't say anything back. This conversation was difficult, like navigating a treacherous mountain path, so different from the smooth, easy way we used to talk.

"Are you scared of prison?" James asked.

"No. I've seen so much in my life, it's hard to be afraid," I said awkwardly. "But maybe, once I go, would you consider phoning your sisters? I know they miss you too."

James didn't say anything for a moment, likely considering what it would mean to re-establish contact with them, how his life might be permanently changed. Finally, he nodded. I sighed with relief. I didn't want him out there, disconnected from us any longer.

"Have you told your wife and kids . . . about me?" I asked.

He didn't reply immediately, just took a deep breath, gathering his thoughts. I imagined kissing him, just as I'd done when he was a little boy, when I'd kiss him a million times a day but never feel like it was enough. I settled for grabbing his hand again, feeling his bones against mine.

"I told them that you were a good mother, the kind of mother who read me stories at night and threw me birthday parties. That you were loving, and kind, and very glamorous. But that you died a long time ago," James said quietly.

"Yes," I said. "I think that's about right."

Let's be honest, I never intended to go to prison, to leave this comfortable room with its memory foam mattress and plush cream carpets for a prison cell with a thin bed and an open toilet in the corner. It was my decision to confess, as a last-ditch effort to find my son and to set him free from the burden of keeping my secrets. I had never lost control, and I didn't plan on relinquishing it now. I just wanted one final adventure before my curtain call, one chance to change things.

I've said things out loud that I had thought would die with me and it was liberating. All of the people who'd hurt me were dead, forgotten by history and unremarked upon. But I had outlived the bastards and now no one would ever forget me. It was a good ending.

Once James left, I picked up the prescription pills I'd been hoarding ever since I confessed, pills I always assured the attendants I would take in the privacy of my bathroom. Now, I began to take handfuls of them, forcing them down with gulps of water. Then I climbed into bed. It was time to go.

Ruth had asked me once if I believed in God and I said no and that there was probably no afterlife either. "But doesn't that make your crimes worse?" she had asked. "If you believe you're sending people into nothingness?" I had shrugged and said that I wasn't in charge of what happened to people after death, just how they got there.

I'd always wondered when I died if I would see the people I killed. I figured that instead of my life flashing before my eyes, maybe I would just see the lives I'd ended, the people whose last sight had been my face hovering above them. The thought didn't scare me. It'd be nice to see them one last time.

And there they were.

They were clustered around my bed, looming over me like a canopy. Most of them looked angry, their faces accusing as they scowled down at me. David, however, just looked sad: his eyebrows furrowed as if he could finally see who I was and it pained him. Robert and Gabrielle stood at the foot of my bed, having been given pride of place by the other apparitions. Gabrielle was wearing the clothes she'd been in the night I hit her with my car, and I could see gravel glinting in her hair. Robert had his arm around her and was crying. His mouth was moving and even though I heard no words, I knew he was asking me *why*. They wanted to know why; why instead of hurting the people who had actually harmed me, I had turned on people who had only wanted the things all people want: love, companionship, the chance to be appreciated.

But I had no answers for them. We never do. I smiled. And then everything went black.

Chapter Thirty-Seven

The next morning, the care attendants found Daphne St Clair dead in her bed. She had taken an overdose of pills in the night and passed away in her sleep. The attendants who found her had seen many dead bodies, even a few possible suicides among the elderly. But this one unsettled them. It might have been the way the shadows fell on her face, but it almost looked like she was smiling.

And life repeated itself, the story coming full circle. Once again, a body was carried out of the Coconut Grove care home. But instead of a lone girlfriend, the parking lot was packed with TV journalists breathlessly reporting the breaking news, tipped off by someone who worked there.

When news about Daphne's death was broadcast on the nightly news, most people shrugged and scoffed, making throwaway comments about saving the taxpayers' money and how only the good die young. But throughout the country, women found themselves standing there, rhythmically drying the same dish, or staring unseeing at their dusky backyards, feeling a strange mix of sadness, guilt, excitement, and regret.

Only women could understand the anger Daphne felt, the

rage that gets jammed down and compacted like an overfull garbage bag. Only women could recognize how a single crack widens into a fissure that splits you in two. In men, anger is an explosion. In women, it's an abscess.

They understood that Daphne had lived her life in frustration. And maybe that was what these women could relate to. The submerging of your own dreams and desires, whether that was out of fear or simply because it was expected of you and so you expected it of yourself. There had been so many times when a woman had sat in a chair with a baby asleep on her, wishing she could move, to shake out her limbs and run through the streets as carefree as she'd done as a child. There had been so many times when a woman had stood in a brightly lit kitchen, alone in a sleeping house, her eyes filling with tears and feeling unbearably sad, yet knowing that this sadness would change nothing. And then there were the darker parts of womanhood, hidden below the surface like murky forms in a flooded quarry. The violence, the threats the first moment you feared being raped, a terror that bloomed into consciousness at some point in girlhood and never left until you were dying, when it was too late for the fuckers to get you or get you again.

To all these women, Daphne felt both familiar and also like a revelation. She had existed in constant agitation, trying to dodge all the predatory men of her childhood, trying to find a place where a girl who grew up poor on a Dust Bowl farm could be celebrated. Until finally she had absorbed all that pain and fear that women ate like bread and butter, and she had *become* it.

And none of these normal, good women would admit it, but learning how Daphne had torn through life, ravaging everyone, a force as violent and terrifying as a tornado, made it easier for them to breathe. It awakened something that had lain dormant inside of them for so long, made them hungry again. Not for murder necessarily, but to be the kind of woman who could do *anything*, the kind of woman who could walk down a dark alley at night with no fear because she knew that the shadows shrank away from her.

And maybe, if the world was a little less demanding of women, didn't spend all its time keeping them in line with a carousel of violence, and judgment, and cognitive distortions, then there wouldn't need to be women like Daphne St Clair. But knowing that she had lived, and that she had found the darkest kind of freedom, made the long evenings at home just a little easier to bear.

Chapter Thirty-Eight

Ruth woke up to a text from her mother telling her that Daphne was dead. She grabbed her laptop and began streaming the coverage, her mouth dry from sleep and her head hot and clouded.

Ruth sat there, unsure of what she was feeling, or even what was appropriate to feel. She had felt so many different things about Daphne: rage, resentment, protectiveness, it all swirled together in an emotional quagmire. Daphne had done a lot of cruel things in her life. She knew what it was like to look in the eyes of someone who loved her and make them die. She had also likely killed Ruth's father. But she wasn't born that way, Buzzy's memories made that clear, and Ruth would always wonder who she would have been if she had grown up in a different time and a different place.

Still, Ruth had to admire the dramatic flair. Daphne had taken her final victim. In doing so, she had guaranteed that Ruth's exclusive really was just that. She had changed Ruth's life, both for the better and the worse, and Ruth knew that someday, if she ended up as an old woman in a nursing home, reporters might still occasionally visit to ask her what it had been like to interview the Gray Widow. She suspected that Daphne would continue to define Ruth's days, long after her death.

"Don't record me today," Diane said as soon as she opened her door. She looked more muted than the last time they'd spoken, dressed in navy chinos and a striped top, with very little jewelry. It was as if she'd turned the volume down on everything, from her clothes to her makeup.

"I wasn't planning on it," Ruth replied.

Ruth had set up this meeting with Diane to play her some of the podcast episodes and answer any questions she had. Ruth had arrived shortly after Harper had left for school so that Diane would have time to listen to the episodes in peace.

"How are you doing?" Ruth asked, acutely aware that she was visiting someone who had just lost her mother, the only parent she'd ever known. Diane's face turned frosty and she gestured to a stiff armchair for Ruth to sit in.

The same water pitcher full of Gucci ice cubes sat on the table, the condensation shimmering in the morning light.

"Let's just play the episodes, since it meant so much to my mother," she replied formally. Ruth nodded and got out her phone. Diane clearly had as much tolerance for emotional discussions as Daphne had.

Ruth played her the first five episodes: the ones covering her life in Lucan, Winnipeg, and, most explosively, the murder of Geoffrey, Diane's father. Diane sat unmoving on the couch throughout the episodes, pausing only for bathroom breaks and the occasional water refill. Ruth studied her out of the corner of her eye, trying not to make her feel watched. She looked nothing like her mother but there was something in her stillness, in the way Diane sat with every muscle tensed, that reminded her of Daphne. The only sign that she was stressed were her fingers twitching, and Ruth wondered if she was a former smoker experiencing a long-dormant craving.

It was early afternoon when the fourth episode ended and the two sat in silence, the only sound coming from an antique carriage clock in the hall.

"So, she really did kill my father," Diane muttered in a strange, detached voice. "Harper warned me but it's different hearing her confess to it. She always told us he had cancer."

"Well, he did have cancer," Ruth said and then immediately regretted it. She had spent so long with Daphne that sometimes she felt as if she had absorbed her voice, that she would spend the rest of her life seeing the world through two sets of lenses.

"And I find out when it's too late to confront her," Diane said with a bitter laugh. "That is classic. My mother was a master at dodging consequences."

"Yes."

"I don't know if this changes anything," Diane said finally. Ruth wasn't quite sure what she meant by 'this': the podcast? Daphne's death? How she felt about her mother? She waited but Diane didn't expand.

"What do you think of the podcast?" Ruth asked.

"Well, having listened to it, I like my mother a lot less, but I understand her a little bit more. So, it's probably accurate," Diane said finally.

"I should have said earlier, I'm sorry for your loss," Ruth

said awkwardly. She didn't know how to deal with death. Every person she lost had sent her into a tailspin, giving her a secular anxiety that made her wish she had a set of reassuring beliefs about the afterlife.

Diane sighed and took a sip of her water. Her eyes seemed to grow dull, and she didn't acknowledge Ruth.

"How are your kids coping with the loss?" Ruth tried again.

"The older ones are fine. Harper's a bit shaken. My mother left her a huge inheritance, probably just to spite me as she didn't leave me a red cent. When Harper turns eighteen, she'll be able to do whatever she wants. I won't be able to tell her anything."

"And I saw that Reid lost his election," Ruth said.

"Yes, but I don't think you can blame that on my mother, no matter how much he's trying. It's just a fact. The longer Reid talks, the less people like him."

Ruth smiled and laughed obligingly. Diane relaxed and went on.

"You know, when James was born, my mother didn't have much money. But by the time we came along, she did. I grew up in lovely homes, with beautiful dresses, and anything I might like," Diane said. She glanced down, staring at her perfectly manicured hands, as if she was confessing to a priest. "Of course, we didn't keep much when we moved. But I always knew there would be more dresses and dolls in my future, each more beautiful than the ones we left behind.

"Now I think about how she got the money for all those beautiful things and it just spoils everything," she said.

Ruth pictured all the porcelain dolls with rosy cheeks, shining hair, all the frilly dresses as foamy as cotton candy, all those treasures slowly being submerged in filth.

"You're probably not surprised to hear that my mother wasn't the easiest person to live with. In some ways she was a nice mom. She would let us eat ice cream sundaes for dinner in expensive restaurants. She liked seeing us happy. But a good mother would have made us eat vegetables. My mom never worried about what was best for us, what would help us become healthy, well-adjusted people. She just liked to see us smile. And whenever my mom was faced with a choice of what *she* needed versus what *we* needed, she always chose herself."

Ruth knew that it was the truth. She hadn't known Daphne for long, but she knew that Daphne always chose herself. Even when there was no choice necessary, Daphne still chose herself.

"In some ways I understand. No one makes the mother a priority. She did. But I've spent my whole adult life unsure what was normal or how I should parent. And that was when I only thought my mother was a narcissist. Not a murderer. But she *was* my mom. This was a woman who took us on adventures, and always made sure that we had warm coats and bought us a dog even though she hated pets."

Ruth didn't say a word, fascinated by the things Diane was saying. She wished that she could record her but knew that Diane would revert back to her old, prickly self if she saw a microphone. But it amazed her how much more depth there was in a woman she had originally judged as a Bravo knockoff.

Women were so much more than how the world saw them, their secret lives so much more complicated and frustrating than the lives of men, because they had to constantly wrestle with the fact that they had more power than they thought but less power than they deserved.

"I used to see her as this survivor, this person who was born poor, who really made a life for herself. But when she confessed, I felt like we lost the right to be proud of her. But even as we've lost her, we've gained something. My brother James has reached out. But don't mention that on the podcast, he deserves his privacy, even if Rose and I have been robbed of it."

Ruth ignored the slight, too stunned by this revelation.

"James? Really? How is he?"

"He's fine, he seems quite happy actually, even though he's not particularly well-off," Diane said, as if the idea of anyone being happy with a middle-class income was baffling. "I won't tell you anything more as I don't think he'd like it, but I thought you'd like to know he was okay. I think we'll be in regular contact now."

"Well, at least one good thing has come out of all this."

"Yes, not that you deserve any credit for it," Diane said acidly. She shook her head and stood up, the spell broken. Diane stood by the doorway, a clear hint that she wanted Ruth to leave.

"You know, it's probably for the best that she's dead. Now my family can move on," Diane said.

She sounded certain but there was a waver in her voice, a little bubble of hesitation. Because now there were no more chances to fix the relationship, no more chances to get it right. And any more understanding or reflection on who her mother had been would have to come from Diane alone.

*   *   *

379

Daphne had once joked to Ruth that when she died, she wanted a headstone that read "Mother. Fucker." But in the end, she was cremated, and her ashes were scattered on the beach near her old apartment, just beyond the building where Ruth's father died. No one knew if that was what Daphne would have wanted, although Ruth suspected she might have preferred her ashes being scattered on Fifth Avenue.

Ruth didn't attend of course. It was only Daphne's daughters and a couple of her grandchildren, including Harper. And James. After decades apart, he had finally come back to say goodbye. Diane told her later that they had tried to throw the ashes into the waves, but a sudden wind had thrown them back into the family's faces, leaving them sputtering and gagging. It seemed like a fitting tribute to Daphne.

Chapter Thirty-Nine

The day after the funeral, Ruth woke up to an email from Harper, Daphne's youngest granddaughter: The day before she died, Grandma asked me to record a message for her. She said to send it to you after her funeral. There was an audio file attached to the message.

Ruth had spent so many hours listening to the flat cadences of Daphne's voice, every word abruptly snapped off at the end. But it still surprised her to hear a new recording now, a fresh message from a mind and a mouth that were now just ashes on a beach.

"I've asked Harper to record this message so we can have a one-sided conversation. She's actually quite good at this stuff so do me a favor and give her a summer job in a couple years. I think she's got a future in it. But here we are. I know it'll be a lot easier to talk turkey when you don't have a pesky journalist interrupting you."

Ruth sat back on her pillows, frowning at the ceiling. She was still in bed, still in her pajamas, listening to this strange rant. It was so Daphne, to get all her little digs in now, when there was no way to respond to her.

"I've got a lot of things to tell you, so listen up. The first is about my will. I've left half of my estate to Harper. My daughters have squandered enough money and she's the only grandchild I like. But I didn't want to leave her everything and ruin her. So, I'm leaving you the other half. My lawyer will be in touch soon although it may take a little longer to release the funds because of my legal . . . situation. It's a good chunk even though I'd had a lot of fun spending it over the years. You'll be able to keep doing this podcast without wasting your life writing lists for morons on the Internet. Just remember, for women, money is freedom. Don't let anyone try to tell you otherwise."

Ruth paused the recording and slid down her sheets, her chest throbbing and her head spinning. How could this be real? This had all started with her being denied an inheritance from her father and now she was getting an inheritance from the woman who she believed killed him? It was essentially blood money. But she was already making money off Daphne St Clair, why draw the line here? Maybe Daphne felt this was reparation for the damage she'd done to Ruth's life.

The recording continued.

"Finally, I wanted to talk to you about your father," Daphne said.

Ruth froze, clutching the laptop so hard her hands ached. This was it. Her deathbed confession. All the pain would be worth it. Ruth was about to be set free.

"I didn't kill him. I was just yanking your chain," Daphne said with a laugh. Ruth flinched as if Daphne had hit her, her whole body tensing with shock. Daphne had been messing with

her? The cruelty of that decision left her breathless, but Daphne kept talking.

"But I know a lot more about killers than you do. Look at the murder weapon. Someone found his insulin and injected him. So that's someone who knows he has diabetes, knows he takes insulin, and knows where to find it. That's not a casual date or visitor to his apartment; that's someone who knows him. A rich, older man found dead of an insulin overdose doesn't strike me as a crime of passion. If someone gets all het up, they might bash a person with a brick or push him down a flight of stairs, not meddle with his blood sugar. No, this was ice-cold. It was also probably a woman. Women want a job done with as little mess as possible; take out the trash, kill a person, it's all the same really.

"So the answer's pretty obvious, if you think about it. Because if you ask me, the cops were looking at the wrong daughter. But maybe they knew that all along too. Because it must have been a dark day for your half-sister when your father found you. She wouldn't have taken kindly to giving half a fortune away to a girl born out of an affair, a girl her father was now parading around as one of the family. Money, revenge, moral outrage, she had every reason to act before your dad changed his will. I guess she hated him a teeny bit more than she hated you or else she would have whacked you instead. But there you have it, you've got a killer in the family. Most people do."

No. Ruth paused the recording. It couldn't be true. Lucy couldn't have murdered her own father. Ruth shook her head angrily. Daphne was lying ... wasn't she? But the more Ruth sat with it, the more she realized that Lucy had never accepted

383

her entrance into the family, that Ruth's very existence proved that her father had cheated on her beloved mother. If Richard had told her that fateful Sunday that he was leaving half his fortune to Ruth, Lucy would have been furious. This wasn't a story of a seductive black widow, this was a story of greed and revenge, of petty sibling rivalries and dysfunctional families.

Ruth clasped her hands to her eyes, pressing so tight that she could see stars explode across her eyelids. Ruth had been so dazzled by her Daphne theory, the clean way everything fit into place, that she missed the truth, a shabby little creature crouched in the corner.

"I'm sorry, I know you wanted it to be me. You don't have any hard evidence to prove it was her. And that family has a lot of power in this town and likely a lot of cops in their back pocket, so there's nothing you can do about it," Daphne's voice intoned, as if she was sentencing Ruth to a lifetime of regret.

Ruth sighed. She couldn't even lay out her case against Lucy on the podcast, she would almost certainly get slapped with a lawsuit. After all, the world was full of rich assholes willing to sue journalists into bankruptcy and the Montgomerys definitely had a few on the payroll.

"You just have to accept that your sister is the kind of person who was never going to settle for half a fortune when she could have the lot. You were too focused on having a daddy while someone else just wanted the dough. Ruth, you played by the rules and she didn't, and she came out on top. There's a lesson in there for you, but I'm not here to gloat."

The recording stopped but Ruth continued to sit in bed, frozen for a very long time. It had been a momentous message:

the promise of an inheritance and a number of revelations about who killed her father. It was like something out of a Brontë novel, not the kind of thing that happened to a podcast host in 2022.

Ruth had a vision of Lucy Montgomery waking up right now in her luxury penthouse in the Seacrest Building, the home that used to be her father's. She was lying in an all-white bedroom with a view of the glittering blue ocean spread out below her. Lucy would wander around her home drinking a latte, casually treading on the patch of carpet where her father had lain, dying, after she had plunged a needle into his neck. Did she think of him there? Confused and betrayed by his own daughter? Maybe he barely crossed her mind now that she'd gotten everything she ever wanted from him ... which was everything he ever had.

Ruth could see Lucy now, staring vacantly ahead as she pounded on her Peloton bike, the Nineties pop songs and generic encouragements of an unseeing fitness instructor blotting out the violence of her thoughts. Was she thinking about Ruth? Almost certainly. It was terrible luck to be a murderer with a true crime journalist for a sister, especially one with the number-one podcast in the country. It had clearly consumed Lucy's thoughts, made her see Ruth as even more of a threat than before.

Ruth could see her going about her day: showering, getting dressed in a cream designer ensemble, taking an elevator down to her expensive sports car. She would drive to work, listening to the kind of vacant narcissistic pop music that featured on the *Selling Sunset* soundtrack, her cranberry-slicked mouth singing along to every capitalistic refrain. Ruth saw her walking into work at the Sunshine Development headquarters, her five-inch heels clicking on the marble floors, her long blonde ponytail hanging down her back like a noose.

Chapter Forty

An hour later, Ruth received another email from Harper, with three more audio files attached. The message said: She said to wait an hour before I sent this email, so you'd have time for it all to sink in. Ruth swallowed and pressed play.

"Hello again. I know, I know, I'm like a bad rash, I keep coming back. But listen, when you told me about your father, you said to me 'your life is almost over; you could help.' And you're right. Ruth, we had our moments, but I'm pleased with the work you've done, and well, maybe, I see a little bit of myself in you. Life dealt you a raw hand and I'd like to help tip the scales in your favor. So, here's the twist. I'm going to record two audio messages. One confessing to your father's murder and one denying it. You can use whichever one you like, I don't mind. It's simple really, you can go with the truth and that will be fine. It's a great podcast regardless. But you'll still have a target on your back from your sister, her family, and the cops. Or you can use the confession and give the podcast an explosive finale. Ruth Robinson: the journalist who solved her own father's murder? Think of the books, the articles, your own TV show if you fancied it. That would set you up for your life.

But of course, you'd have a secret. And you'd have to accept that your sister would never face justice. So, it's whatever you decide, Ruth. I made a lot of tough decisions in my life; that's part of being an adult. Now it's time for you to become master of your own fate. Thanks again for all the laughs. It's been a hell of a ride."

Ruth stared at the other two audio files, not bothering to click on them. She knew what they contained. The truth and a false confession. Was this a final test from Daphne? Or just a gift? With Daphne St Clair, the answer was always: both.

Slowly, mechanically, Ruth pulled on a tank top and cut-offs and stepped into her sandals. Then she left her apartment and started walking, looking at the world with unseeing eyes as she thought about everything. The cars rushed by her, leaving trails of hot wind in their wake, but Ruth felt nothing but the cracked sidewalk beneath her feet as she walked.

Daphne had left her with an impossible choice.

Ruth could use the false confession. Daphne was dead now; it wouldn't affect her either way. Ruth would be safe from Lucy, who would never know that Ruth believed she was a killer. And it would bring Ruth fame and a career with limitless possibilities. There would be money, plenty of it. For herself. For her mother.

Or Ruth could go with the truth. She would have the chance to do it right, to investigate her half-sister and make a case against the real killer. She might even net an inheritance in the process. After all, the slayer rule would mean Lucy would be denied the inheritance if she was found guilty. Sure, it would be hard, maybe even impossible, but Ruth would know that she had stayed true to herself and done right by her father and even by Daphne. And she would be able to live life in the open, with no secrets to hide, no agendas to protect.

Ruth found herself standing in front of the cemetery where she went to think about Richard. It seemed like a fitting place to make a decision about which story she would tell about his murder. Because that's what all this boiled down to, really: telling stories, making sense of people and the world they lived in.

The lie would set her free. The truth would save her soul. Was it better to have a happy life or a moral one? Ruth realized with a start that these were the very questions Daphne might have asked herself too, if she'd ever paused for a moment of self-reflection.

Ruth sat down on her favorite bench and closed her eyes, feeling the sun on her eyelids. A breeze whispered across her face, and she found herself thinking of Daphne. And Richard. And wishing that she could see them again. Just one more time.

Because that was the other thing Daphne had taught her. Death wasn't the end of the story.

It was only the beginning.

Epilogue: Six months later

"What brings you out tonight?" a tall man, with sun-bleached hair and a peeling nose asked Ruth as they stood at the bar. Ruth glanced back at her table, where her mother, Jenn, and her friend Chelsea sat, bouncing along in their chairs to the generic Latin music playing over the speakers. It made her smile, seeing her mother laughing with her friends. It reminded her that the person was still there, even if there were changes, and she shouldn't let tomorrow's grief ruin today's happiness.

"It's a celebration," Ruth said as the bartender prepared two pitchers of margaritas for her. Ruth glanced back at the table and caught Jenn's eye, finding herself involuntarily smiling. They were just friends, for now. But who knew what might happen in the future?

"Of what?" the man asked. His eyes were bloodshot, and she could tell that he didn't need a reason to drink, that any night might merit a couple pitchers of margaritas.

"I created a podcast and it's just won a Webby, which is this big podcasting award!" Ruth said, trying to keep her voice from racing up the register but hearing it crack with glee. Everything had changed in the last year. People now stopped her on the street to rave about the podcast. Especially after they heard that final episode, the one she released after Daphne's death. For weeks, that episode was all anyone could talk about. It was still being fervently dissected on Reddit.

"Congrats! What's the podcast about?" he said, taking a swig of his beer. Ruth smiled, feeling a squirmy mixture of pride and embarrassment about how much she was bragging.

"Well, it's these interviews with this ninety-year-old woman. I had to piece together the whole story of her life. She grew up in poverty in the Great Depression and she suffered a lot of abuse. Finally, she ended up in New York where she married into money and had children, but the marriages never lasted. It's the story of a woman's life really, her life as a daughter, a wife, and a mother, and the way she struggles for independence along the way."

He nodded but she could already see his eyes scanning above her head, his fingers itching to grab his phone out of—*Good God, were those cargo shorts?*—and even though she didn't like this guy, she resented his lack of interest.

"But see, this woman is also a serial murderer. So, her life story is also about all these people she killed along the way," Ruth said, her voice a little too bright for the subject matter. But it worked, she saw him drop his phone back into his capacious pocket. He took another swig and clinked his glass against her pitcher.

"She's a serial killer? Okay, now that's interesting. I love murder stories. I've seen the Dahmer series three times." He held his hand up to the bartender, ordering another drink for both of them before she could stop him. Then he looked at her and smiled, his face softening. "Piece of advice, you shouldn't lead with the woman thing; people don't care about that. Just talk about the murders. That's how you get their attention."

The End

Acknowledgments

This book has been a labor of love and I am so excited to see it out in the world. So many people supported me through this process and words can't describe how grateful I am for all of them.

A heartfelt thanks to my agent Gaia Banks, who is insightful, supportive and a true visionary. Ten years ago, you took a chance on a twenty-five-year-old student with a YA novel and that changed my life. Thanks also to the rest of the Sheil Land team who worked on this book, including Lauren Coleman and Natalie Barracliffe.

The Italian version of this book would not have been possible without Barbara Barbieri at Andrew Nurnberg Associates and Giuseppe Strazzeri and Fabrizio Cocco at Longanesi. I have always dreamed of having my book translated into a different language. Thank you for making that happen.

To my editor Beth Wickington, thank you for believing in Daphne St Clair and for your unique vision of how this book could be strengthened. This book is infinitely better because of your suggestions and I'm in awe of your ability to see the bigger picture. Thanks also to Isabelle Wilson, Marta Juncosa,

Phoebe Khalid, Rebecca Bader, Sinead White, Ellie Wheeldon, Anna Goldfinch and Helena Newton.

To my friends and early readers, particularly Chelsea Smith and Catherine Kirkpatrick, your encouragement and long friendship means the world to me.

To my family. My mother, my father, my sister, my nephew, and my in-laws. Thank you for being such a vital part of my life. Thanks also to my two grandmothers: Jean Common and Grace Frost, whose stories and remembrances inspired Daphne's early days and some aspects of her personality. I wish you could have read this book. I think you would have liked Daphne.

To my husband Martin. For supporting my dreams and listening to my gripes. Thank you for being my best friend, my confidante, and my partner in life. I love you.

And finally, to my children. You are the reason for everything.